Risk, Return, and the Indigo Autumn

A Novel

By

Tim McGhee

ISBN   978-0-6151-4963-9

Acknowledgements

First, and most importantly, I thank the ladies of my life: my wife Cindy, my daughters Megan and Annie, and my mother-in-law Deanie Samosky. They encourage me in all my endeavors.

I especially thank my good friends and fans from the Parkman family: Ross, Anna, Kate, and fellow writer Karen. Look out…here's another book!

I thank other friends and fans who have supported this four year effort: Betts Abraham, Mary Ellen McDavid, fellow writer Dirk Cline, and any others who kept me going simply by asking how I was doing.

Finally, I thank three people who don't know me: Ned Davis of Ned Davis Research, who provided the economic data from which I fed; Martin Zweig, PhD, one of the best investment advisors in a business in which most professionals cannot even beat the market, and former Vice President Albert Gore, the inventor of the Internet. These gentlemen allowed me to approximate as closely as possible the times and the events and the landscape of the decade of the 1980s, the most intriguing of all the decades I have navigated.

I dedicate this novel to contrarians, and their ability to keep us honest.

One

Noon
Sunday August 16, 1987
Poolside with a beer, Mars Heights condos, Ashton Township, Pennsylvania
Dow Jones Industrial Average: 2,685 - an all-time high

My name is Mason Bricker. It's really Michael Mason Bricker, PhD, Duquesne, writing, but that sounds like the intro to my obituary. So, call me Mason…and welcome to my life. I'm a divorced thirty-one year old sorry-ass stockbroker with a drinking problem, an atrophic career, an old hailstorm-dotted American-made automobile, and a libido that peaks every Monday evening when the pretty prostitute pays a visit. When I'm not contained by the white walls of my leather and tan condo, or stuck at work, you will find me beside this pool, most every evening and twice on Saturdays and Sundays. May through September, I pursue my passions here, which are Iron City beer and observing those around me, looking for the characters, plots, and sub plots for the four novels on which I'm writing. One for every major genre. A romance, with Victoria Principal from *Dallas* playing the love object of the tragic, yet ultimately redeemed protagonist. A western, in which Linda Gray, also from *Dallas,* will ride off into the sunset with the protagonist as soon as he saves his butt by figuring out how to get the land back to the Indians. A work of science fiction, with Carrie Fisher as the princess who…well, it is a neat idea, but I just have to make it a lot different to avoid copyright infringement. Normally, I'm more original, but I do like to think about Carrie Fisher, in a silly, high school pretend way. And, finally, the fourth, a work of fantasy about a stockbroker who garners the respect and admiration of his peers.

I live in Ashton Township, a collection of fifty thousand citizens just a half-hour down the Ohio River from downtown Pittsburgh, the City of Champions. The Steelers and the Pirates haven't won it all since my Olds was manufactured in 1979, but the place is still called the City of Champions. Good or bad, labels stick, and we're damned proud of it. We in AT are also proud to be in many regards like our Steel City brothers and sisters. Drawn together by our collective disdain for the Cleveland Browns and all the evil they represent, our two cities and our ethnic cultures also look like the world, where eastern and western Europe and Asia and Africa peacefully meet one another. All of us together, the descendants of the Italians, the Polish, the Irish, the Germans, the Croats, and any other ethnicity I missed, we work hard at it, and just work hard in general. Anyway, if Chicago didn't have the moniker already, Pittsburgh would be the City with the Broad Shoulders, as the rugged men of the mills and factories toil and sweat, their women take care of them, and their sons and daughters slave for the man downtown. The men and the women and the sons and daughters: that last thought is all you need to describe Pittsburgh, a true city of champions.

There are differences, however. If Pittsburgh is the Other City with the Broad Shoulders, then Ashton Township is the City with the Sculpted Shoulders Honed by Working Out on the Nautilus After a Day at the Air-Conditioned Office. AT is the consummate service economy, a collection of some of the finest yuppies the decade of the eighties has produced. It's a town of doctors, lawyers, stockbrokers, engineers, CPAs, business professionals, professors, teachers, artists, writers and their respective daycare establishments. It's an immaculately well-appointed place, with the beautiful trees and flora and grassy fields of Johnson Park circumscribed by a business district of modern architecture of steel, glass, stone, and brick. Kind of like a diminutive New York City. These buildings provide the arenas of commerce for those who contribute to the tax base that supports the unblemished township, as the revenue rolls in from an average adjusted gross income four times that of the nation and twice that of almost all suburban regions of prosperity such as southern California, western Connecticut, and the way Texas used to be before the oil bust of last year. In other words, Ashton Township is a collection of a lot of people with a hell of a lot of money.

Consider people with money. Not classy people with money, for they know how to handle it. And not necessarily people with money like the TV villain JR Ewing with money. I mean, good people with money. Or, as compelling as it is, otherwise good people with money. As I sit here in the sun drinking that Iron City, brewed just up the Ohio near all that money in Pittsburgh, I re-examine my postulation that people with money is a concept of greed and irrationality and emotion. Greed is the want, the need, the driving force behind a lot of foolish behavior. Irrationality is the result of that foolish behavior. And, emotion, runaway emotion, is the catalyst of both. What a mess it all makes. I know, baby. Wisdom for the pain.

It's like this: there are people with religion, people with love, people with sex. People with money. All are concepts, basically the same concept. The concept of people with sex motors and steers everything a man does. The concept of people with money motors and steers everything the stock market does. So, take us back to sex. Because of this ever-sustaining charging-like-a-bull 1987 stock market, we brokers are very sexy right now, even John Findlay, the oversized asshole I work for. Stock prices are rockin' and rollin' and everyone wants in. Everyone wants something hot. Everyone wants in. People with sex. People with money. People with sex...

The woman over there, the beautiful, familiar older woman over there in a one-piece Land's End black swimsuit, solid black, dark to-her-shoulders hair, Vuarnets over the eyes, tanned silky legs; that beautiful older woman over there, lounging, age apparent only by her two cute teen daughters lying on the other side of the pool; their mother - hot as an August tomorrow - their mother over there, finally, after all these months by the pool, just glanced over here.

Let's say I take a walk. Over there.

"Hi," I say, quickly becoming embarrassed somewhere between the 'huh' and the 'eye.' This man/woman game is nerve-wracking.

"Hi, back," she says to the trees.

"Lovely day," I say, cleansing breath, relaxing. Uninvited, I sit in the chair near her.

"It's hot and hazy, but I'll go along with you," she says with a pack-a-day rasp. Then, silence. She continues to look away.

"So, what do you do?" Do? What an idiot question to ask a woman of such style.

"Not much. I exercise in the morning, do community service in the afternoon, and lay by this pool when I can."

More silence.

"What do you do?" she asks.

"I'm a money manager."

She smiles. "Money manager? Title bloat. That's an awfully high and mighty designation for a simple stockbroker. I've never heard that used with a straight face."

"How do you know I'm a simple stockbroker?"

"Because you just called yourself a 'money manager.'"

"Well, I am what I am, or what I say I am," I say indignantly.

The hot mom laughs at the humor of the moment. "Money manager. So, allow me to ask…"

"Lady, you're allowed to do anything with me." I grin, feeling the initial twinges of…interest.

Another laugh. "That sounded so juvenile, but maybe. You're cute for…what? Late thirties?"

I grimace. "Back it up a few, sister. Just turned thirty-one."

Yet another laugh. "Just kidding about the age." This far in the conversation and she can't possibly know what I look like. I guess she recognizes me. Well, that's a positive development.

I decide to introduce myself. "My name is Mason. Mason Bricker." I extend my hand to air.

"I'm Nicole," she says, keeping her hand to herself. "My friends call me Nikki. When they've had a couple too many, they call me Nikita."

Now, we're getting somewhere. "Well, Nikita, do you want an Iron City? That's all I have."

"I don't swill beer in front of my daughters."

"Do you mind if I have one?"

"You already have one."

"Do you mind if I have another one?"

"Be my guest."

My clouded brain raises my carcass up from the chair. I take the hundred short strides necessary to walk past the pool, through the deck door of my dark cedar condo, and stand before my avocado refrigerator in my kitchen. The bad karma that follows me wherever I go has turned this tony nine hundred square foot cool place to live into a den of mere existence. The three empty Iron City Arns from this morning rest in the stainless steel sink with the rinsed breakfast dishes. A carafe half-empty with coffee sits beside the toaster on the white Formica counter. I can't allow Nikita to see this.

Before I know it, I have returned with two, each in insulated koosies. Two Arns. You never know.

"Something I've thought of, Mason," Nikita says, head still facing away.

"And, what's that?"

"About being a stockbroker," she asks as she shifts her legs. "Can't you find a better way to occupy yourself during the day?"

"No, not really. You see, Nik, I have a meaningless PhD in writing."

Nikita turns to me quickly, finally, raising the sunglasses to her hair. Brown eyes. Wow… "I'm impressed!" she says. "Meaningless? I don't think so. There has to be some redeeming value to that. Do you have a book out?"

I take a sip, relishing the attainment of the upper hand. "I haven't completed several. They're lying on my bedroom floor. Lots and lots of paper. Word. Word Perfect. Handwritten manuscript. Revenue zero. Therefore, I am a money manager, in that way able to pay the mortgage on this sweet crib beside this pool so I can sit beside you. I need a cigarette. You?"

"Yes."

I offer her one of my Virginia Slims from the pack. She takes it and places it between her lips. I light hers, then mine. We draw and blow smoke simultaneously. She turns away.

"Virginia Slims," she deadpans.

"Alright, I lost a bet. My buddy said I couldn't quit."

"Virginia Slims."

"And the rest is history."

A pause. "How long have you lived here in Mars Heights?" she asks.

"Almost six years. Since the divorce."

"I'm sorry."

"As it turns out, babes, I'm not."

"Oh." Nikita shifts her legs again. She is going to have to stop that.

"It's good. Really," I say.

"You're faking it, but you know what they say."

"Fake it to make it."

"Okay, faker-maker, I'm going to put you to work today on this searing Sunday afternoon."

"How's that?" I ask, thinking of the many ways…

"You the stockbrokering money manager are going to tell me about the stock market," she says, reaching to lightly touch my forearm. Oooo… "Everybody I know is in the stock market. It's up seven hundred points this year so far, I'm told. So, you tell me, my new money manager, what is a 'point?'"

I smile. "That's easy. You can wake me up at three in the morning and ask that question and—"

"Is that a come-on?"

"No, that's a lame…no, it's not a…anyway, a point is the unit of measurement of the Dow."

"Unit of measurement?"

"Yeah, like a foot." I glance at her feet. Among the top three pairs I've seen this year.

"So, just what is that thing called the Dow?"

"C'mon, Nik. Make them more difficult than that. The Dow is the Dow Jones Industrial Average, a collection of thirty stocks of companies you've certainly heard of, like IBM, AT & T, General Motors, Exxon, Sears, even McDonald's. The prices of these thirty companies' stocks are added up. That sum is divided by a predetermined number and that gives you an average." I pause. I still have her attention, I guess. But, she keeps looking away. "The Dow is the most widely accepted method of measuring the market and right now it is measuring it at nearly 2,700 points. If the Dow's down thirty points in one day, for instance, it's a bad day. If the Dow's up thirty, it's a good day. And so on."

"Thank you. I've asked, but no one has ever explained that to me." Her fanny squirms in her seat. A slow summer breeze kicks up. Another squirm. That just about does it.

"It's time you know," I say, voice slightly impeded by my waxing desires.

"Now, Mr. PhD Money Guru, help me get it. Tell me, what makes the market tick?"

"People," I say without hesitation. "People like you and me. The same people who fast during Lent and the same people who sleep in on Sundays. People who use coupons at the grocery store, who shop for hardware on Saturdays, who play golf and enjoy it even though they suck at it; people who stare at you too long, who use AutoCAD at the engineering firms up the river in downtown Pittsburgh; people like Lieutenant Colonel Oliver North and other criminals; doctors, lawyers, and CPAs, and their doctors and their lawyers and their CPAs, all these people and more tick the stock market's clock."

"It's that simple?" Nikita asks the trees.

"No. People are the drivers. Money is the fuel."

"I have lots of money."

"I bet you do."

She reaches for the glass beside her chaise. I catch a whiff of the pine. It's a gin and lemonade. Strong. When I have a buzz, drinking plus gorgeous woman makes me think.

"Should I buy stocks right now?" Nik asks, sipping, then holding the cool drink against her cheek. "I've heard it's a good time to buy. What's the best investment now? What's hot?"

"You're hot," I say.

"I know. So, where should I put my money?"

"In the bank."

"That's no fun."

"If you want fun, go to Maui."

"I own a timeshare there. On Lahaina beach. Half mile from Longhi's restaurant. You know what they say at Longhi's, don't you?"

"Yes, but you tell me," I say.

"You're going to get your jollies hearing me say 'whatthefuck,' aren't you?" Nikita says with a smile.

"'Whatthefuck?' I love it."

"Figures. Anyway, my money boy, my daughters have to go to college in a few years. I'm looking at The Seven Sisters. How will we pay for it?"

"Sell the timeshare."

"What's the best thing to do right now?"

Kiss me. "Go to the bank and buy certificates of deposit."

"Don't be a funny man. I'll just find a new money manager, you stockbroker."

"Okay. Since I'm your money manager, I'll get serious. Ready?"

"I'm breathless in anticipation," Nikita sarcastically whispers.

"The bank."

"If you insist. Why the bank?"

"You have to understand what's going on here, Nikita. Bank certificates of deposit are a promise. They're a promise backed by the full faith and credit of the United

States government. You give us your money, the banks say, and we'll use it in our business of lending money, and we promise to give you your money back to you, with interest. Investments like bonds are like that, too. Bonds such as United States Treasury bonds and U. S. savings bonds are like CDs in that they are a promise backed by the full faith and credit of the United States government. Pay it back plus interest."

"This is boring," Nikita says with a whine.

"I'm into boring. Now, on the more exciting wild-ride side, a stock, or equity ownership of a company, is hope. Hope. No promise. Only hope. Hope springs eternal, until it gets bad. When the shit comes down, I guarantee you'll want a promise. If a company were to fail, go out of business, and cash it in, bond holders get what's left over first, then stockholders stand way back in the back of that line. Way back. You gotta understand that, Nik."

"Your point is moot," she moans, obviously tiring of my negative attitude. "I don't see a company like IBM going out of business. That has to make their stock good, right?"

"Maybe," I reply. "You have to think about the overriding aspect of the market: stock prices. It's all emotional, in my humble opinion. IBM is the same company today as it was a year ago, but its stock price is sixty percent higher. Why? Hope. Nothing else has changed in those twelve months but hope. IBM stock buyers hope the company will make more profits and increase its overall value. No one knows. Everyone hopes. They just say they know."

"So, what do you know?"

I know this: I'm having a point/counterpoint with a lovely woman wearing a black swimsuit as a good part of her boobs shows when she leans up from her chair. Only in America. "I know this: business is always about profit, ma'am. A corporation must eventually show growth in profits to justify a corresponding growth in the price of its stock. Profits, also called earnings, are the key to stock prices. Therefore, the key to investing in the stock market is how much in dollars of stock price per share do you pay for a dollar of earnings per share."

"What's that per share stuff?"

"Okay. Let's say a company is worth on the market one billion dollars."

"You think big, don't you, Mr. Market Maven?" Nikita says seductively as she glances at my shorts. I place my towel over my lap. She snickers.

"Why not?" I say, with gravel in my voice. "Let's say that company divides itself into one hundred million equal shares. Well, a little arithmetic gets you a stock market value of ten dollars a share."

"Then, what's earnings per share?"

"Well, the same company makes in profits, or earnings, a hundred million a year. That means the business earns a dollar a share."

"Math was never my best subject."

"Then, think of numbers as dollars, Mrs. I-Own-Part-Of-A-Condo-On-Maui. Dollars for a dollar of earnings; dollars for that very nice swimsuit you are wearing very nicely. Swimsuit, earnings; they're the same because they are the bargains you want when you let go of your money. And, 'let go' is the operative phrase here because there's no guarantee you'll get it back."

"I'm starting to get it, although I don't want admit it," Nikita says with a laugh.

"No wonder you're not married. You bored your ex silly."

"Actually, the other guy did something else to her silly. Besides, she likes younger men, and my youth had become threadbare. In other words, Silly Boy undercut me." Play the sympathy card, Bricker. She'll dig it.

"Do you think I like them young, too? Did you walk over here because you want me to be a surrogate wife and lover to you?" she asks rather pointedly. There goes sympathy.

"Right now, you're a prospective client to me. But, I'll admit, your black swimsuit and a few Arns brought me over here."

"Honesty prevails."

"Honesty is, in my mind, most essential."

"And you are naïve."

"And someday you'll thank me for this. Now, continuing with the dollar of stock for a dollar of earnings, you evaluate your bargains based on the price/earnings ratio, or simply the P/E. Historically, the market average P/E is around twelve to fourteen bucks of stock for a buck of corporate profits. The eight bucks we paid in the middle of the latest recession of 1982, back when we all thought we were all going to die, was cheap. The twenty-four bucks we're paying now at a time when prosperity will live on forever is very expensive. Stock market 'bulls,' with rising prices charging-like-a-bull-in-an-up-market, as opposed to falling prices growling-mean-and-nasty-like-a-bear-in-a-down-market, are hoping, sometimes merely hoping, growth in earnings will justify the growth in prices. Hence, this market is rich and will probably adjust downward, read: drop like a rock, unless earnings rise significantly."

"What's your ex-wife's name?"

"Joan," I answer without missing a beat. "Joan Kissinger. Dr. Joan Kissinger."

"Faculty?"

I grin. "Good one. A dozen years ago, I was her student assistant."

"Did she break your heart?"

"Well…"

"Go ahead. I'll understand."

"Well, understand this. It's emotional."

"Marriage?"

"The market."

Nikita flips her hand to me. "Beer," she commands. I grab the other one and turn the top for her. She takes it and swigs like a man.

"What about your daughters?"

"It's hot. I'll explain that to them later," she says. "Okay, how is today's market emotional?"

"Right now, investors are ecstatic. Stock prices are on average up twenty-five percent since May. May! Three months. In the same three months, bank CDs paid you a miserly one percent. Maybe. It's emotional. The score: up twenty-five percent versus up one percent. Buying decisions are made from emotion and justified logically. What would you do? The analysis: greed kicks in hard."

"Greed is good, Stock Jock. Pigs get fat-"

"And hogs get slaughtered, Nik."

"That's a crock."

"Believe it. The Dow's up almost six hundred points since May. Everyone's rolling in the dough. Therefore, if you don't own stocks, you're not cool. And we all want to be cool. Extrapolate that May to August period to the end of the year and you'll see the Dow tack on another eight hundred points. That's almost another thirty percent by the end of the year. Mind boggling! That's what everyone's looking at. They think it's going to happen and they think they absolutely have to be in there. It's not even hope any more. It's certainty. Blind certainty. That, my lady, is dangerous as hell."

Nikita takes another drink. It's my lucky day. "Obviously, you don't feel you have to be there," she says. "You're blindly certain in the other direction. That makes you a bear."

"True. A bear on this market. This market is scary like a bear."

Flipping her shades back over her eyes, she turns her beautiful face to me. "I believe your mean and nasty outlook is influenced by mean and nasty Joan," she says.

"Maybe, but there are a few objective bones left in my body."

"So, then, what do you think is the key to making money in the stock market?"

"Go against the certainty, the overwhelming emotion. When everyone zigs, you zag. When everyone is a bull, you be a bear. And--"

"Cool," Mrs. One-Piece says. The alcohol has loosened her still more. She's looking at me more. So far, the world has been Nikita and me. I don't care what her daughters think, either. Or, even her husband. I want her, and she needs me.

"Yes, cool, but no," I say. "It's tough to do since we all want to be part of the 'in' crowd, but the emotional consensus is always wrong. And since it's so emotional now, since stock prices today have been run up to levels never seen for little reason, I advise you to seek advice from someone whom you trust. Therefore, banks."

"Oh."

"Banks have worked hard and diligently for your trust. They deserve it, and you would be wise to put your money with a bank. CDs, investment management, wherever, just do it. Trust them. Don't trust us, because banks employ bright, talented people, unlike the hacks of the brokerage business who call themselves 'money managers.'"

"Mason, darling, be proud of who you are. Take it from me, your elder."

"Funny, you don't look like an elder."

Nikita giggles like a high school girl. "So, banks invest in stocks?"

"Banks can help you invest in stocks, and they do it damned well. Still, I don't think you should buy stocks, but that's between you and your bank."

"Then, answer the original question: why not stocks?"

"How many times must I answer the original question? Again, people with money. The people are glazed-eyed and deliriously happy but money is expensive and no one is acting as if there are any problems. We're on a roll to no end, they, the ubiquitous 'they' say, but money is the fuel to keep it rolling. Money is the fuel. People can whip themselves into a mating frenzy, which they usually do at market tops, but if the money isn't right, if, like now, money costs too much money, folks just will not be able to take it where they want it to go."

"Get with it. Your attitude is terrible."

"Just trying to do what's right, Nikita."

"And, you're pissing off a lot of people in the meantime," she says sharply. "C'mon. Get with it."

"The more you piss off, the greater your chances are of being correct."

"The high price of the male ego." She sighs. What a queenie. What a turnoff. No, that's bullshit.

"Anyway, Mrs. Black One-Piece, the state of money, and ultimately the state of the stock market, is measured by how much money costs. The price of money is what is known as interest rates."

"Go ahead, I'm taking notes. Fast and furiously."

"And, you are a smart-ass."

"Whatever," she says, smiling.

"Okay," I say, growing impatient. "Presently, interest rates are rising faster than most people realize. That means, among other things, that businesses and corporations must get expensive money to fund money-making projects, so it will take a helluva project to make the same money as it would if money were less expensive. If interest rates were lower, less money would make more money. The higher the rates, the fewer money-making projects there are."

"It's so confusing. You're overanalyzing the entire situation."

"I don't think so, because fewer projects mean lower, if any, earnings growth, and eventually lower stock prices, not to mention lower employment. Threaten to take your job away and you'll feel mean and nasty like a bear. Then, when everyone's job is in jeopardy, it'll be time to be a bull."

"Huh? Oh, anyway, CDs at the bank. That's as dull as my husband. Are you surprised I have a husband?"

"The ring, madame? And, I would imagine your husband would be riding this stock rocket."

"He is. He's obsessed. But, he's dull."

"You deserve much better."

"Thank you. Now, Mr. Money Manager, how about less pick-up and more stock talk. Let me rephrase my question: what's the problem?"

"At the risk of mixing metaphors like a Mai Tai, there is a huge Wesson oil party on Wall Street while money is becoming more expensive. We're all slathering each other with praise, looking for the good times to roll. But, we're running on empty."

"Just what does all that mean?"

"Let's be careful out there."

"I don't care what you say. I want stocks," Nikita says with emphasis. "All my friends want stocks. All my friends have stocks. My husband has stocks. I want stocks."

"Look, lady," I say toward the woman. "I've developed this interesting yet implausible crush on you, incoherent in that you don't care who I am. However, you are the only woman who could seduce me into selling you stocks, and it ain't happenin'. That's how crazy it is now and consequently that's how risky the market is right now."

"Cut the dramatics," Nikita says. "Where does the market go from here?"

"Down. Even the blue-chips, stocks of the finest companies in the world like IBM, General Electric, AT and T, and Exxon, have been caught up in this buying hysteria and consequently have been run up way too high. The ultimate risk of failure with IBM is almost nil, as we discussed, but since we're in the midst in one hell of an aberration, if you wait a while you'll find that you will pay less for more IBM. No one will want IBM then, so what I'm really saying is you have to be an iconoclast to consistently make money in the stock market. And no one likes an iconoclast. Trust me. This must be your husband walking this way."

And that's where reality bursts my fantasy woman bubble. Diane the Feet is going to love this one.

Two

7:30 AM
Monday, August 17, 1987
Backing my industrial tan 1979 Olds Delta 88 out of my garage.
Dow Jones Industrial Average: 2,685 - an all-time high

My goal each morning of each business day is to beat *The Wall Street Journal* to the door of the Ashton Township offices of Fuller Busher. The investment firm, the stockbrokers of Fuller Busher. So, let me tell you about Fuller Busher. Fuller Busher has been the investment firm to the Northeast ruling class and bourgeois since 1838. Mr. Colin Fuller, the founder, is rumored to, as a boy, had rubbed the buttonwood tree until he had a splinter permanently embedded in his right hand. My good friend Wylie thinks that Mr. Fuller and the buttonwood tree were sharing a moment. Wall Street will confuse you in such a manner.

Under the buttonwood tree on lower Manhattan Island is where the exchange of equities first took place. We should all do business outdoors. Nature and the economy communal. I don't really know the history that well, but that's where the American Stock Exchange was formed…I think. Next came the New York Stock Exchange. The junior circuit took command, just like another junior circuit, the American League. The former had Dow and Jones and Standard and Poor, and the latter had the Yankees. That doesn't make any sense to me, either.

I called Wylie to let him know I am going to be late. To be honest with you, I'm always late. My WSJ is always sitting in my chair when I arrive. So much for goals.

Wylie McInally is an original Pittsburgh Guy; father in the mill, mother in the kitchen, huge Catholic family; scholarship to Carnegie Mellon; financially successful, yet retaining the blue-collar bloodlines. We started with Fuller Busher as brokers the same day in August 1982. I'm pedestrian, but Wylie is the favored stockbroker to the up-and-coming yups and the solid senior citizens of Ashton Township as well as western PA. He hit executive vice president last year with a hideously high production number. Investment firms are the only places where you can become an officer without making your clients a dime. Performance is measured solely by how much money you make for the firm, which is called your gross commissions, or your gross. That's Wylie. A top producer. A so-so stock picker. Needless to say, Wylie has become the seven hundred grand man. That puts three fifty on his W-2, just less than Ronald Wilson Reagan and George Herbert Walker Bush combined. He is by far number one in the Pittsburgh region and among the top five percent in the firm. Why he hangs with the disgruntled, sullen, vexed, pissy me is another mystery of the universe. I have told him he'd be a million if I weren't around. He's in turn told me I'm his only true friend. I'm flattered while at the same time concerned he has some serious problems.

Wylie claims he's the cousin of Pat McInally, Harvard man and Cincinnati Bengals' punter emeritus. Wylie's tall like Pat, has short legs like Pat, but unlike Pat is one of the worst athletes I've ever known. He's the kind of guy who golfs with clients and without trying makes them feel really good about their games. With his BA in history, Wylie and I can together share the angst of the liberal arts major. Combine the CMU *magna cum laude* with his astronomical IQ and his sincerity and Wylie should be on PBS' *Washington Week in Review* instead of in this god-forsaken business.

Mark my words on this one: within ten minutes Wylie will start talking about my college football career, however meteoric as it was. He's obsessed with me because in my only college football game I as a third team wideout for The University of West Virginia caught four passes for one hundred twenty one yards and a touchdown against the hated rival, the University of Pittsburgh, then number one in the nation. Considering that after twelve years of real life I still have those stats permanently etched in my mind, I guess I'm obsessed with me, too.

At least I'm not obsessed with money. Well, that's not exactly true. Not completely. Sometimes I wish I were as prosperous as Ashton Township, with old money mixed in with new money. Nice and new, mixed in with the old, the spawned and those who spawned them, the Baby Boomers with the WWII folks. Other mixes, too. The less fortunate flatlanders of AT on the banks of the Ohio and the upscale denizens of Mount Monroe, the shining city on the hill, or as called by those near the river, Mount Money. Old money and new money, and the unadulterated envy of new money, but still better than no money. However, even as a resident of Mount Money, I can see their point, since there is a right side of Money, where the old money resides, and then there is where I'm from, the wrong side of Money, where the new money lies. In other words, I'm a flatlander with altitude.

After winding several miles through the nooks and turns and trees and the superb houses of the correct side of Money, I am about as correct as I'll be in this lifetime, a visitor to the privileged home of Wylie and Geri, a five thousand square foot, half-million dollar cedar structure on Pine, hanging from the landscaped hillside. Wylie and Geri: thirtysomething, double hyperincomes, no kids. Dinks. New money that feels like old money.

It's afternoon hot already. Geri for some odd reason is in the driveway putting the top down on their red 450SL two-seater. It's really hot. She must have lost paper-rock-scissors because the other McInally ride is a Jag. Wylie doesn't want to leave the Jag in a downtown parking bin and risk it to errant car doors. He therefore hitches a ride with me, because a couple of dingers would probably add to the mystique of my Olds.

Geri is just under six feet, as tall as me. She's blonde, green eyes, a pleasant face, and a lanky model's frame. This morning, she's wearing a white summer dress over her tastefully tanned skin, a very nice pair of white slings, with her shoulder-length hair down. Pretty. Geri resembles actress Shelley Long from NBC's *Cheers* so much that everyone has noticed it. Our boss John Findlay calls Wylie Mayday Malone. Not only is John a dick, he cannot be credited with an original thought.

I drive up to just behind Geri, which is a good place to be. She hasn't seen me yet.

"Hey, Geraldine," I say. She absolutely adores the use of her real name. That's why she turns to me with a smile and flips me off. Nothing like a woman holding the bird. "Where's your man?"

"Choking down a Pop-Tart," she says, hands on hips.

"That's disgusting," I say, "Big day planned today?"

"Office day. I'm showing three homes tomorrow. One's Gene and Nancy's. PPG's promoted her to senior VP. They can trade up now. Most definitely."

I don't know what a Gene and Nancy is, but I know PPG. And, a senior VP at PPG rakes in gobs of dinero. Good score for Geraldine. I'll fake clueless. "Oh. Is that good or bad?"

"Mason, it's good," she says, as if she's disappointed in my lack of awareness about the career successes of others. A stockbroker and a real estate agent. They know everything about everyone. Geri has too often had the if-you-straighten-up-you-could-be-eighties-wealthy talk with me. I have some real money, not including the really big real eighties money I had before the divorce. Joan's lawyer/boyfriend was better, plus a friend of hers said I stalked her. My spineless attorney came up with the bright idea of not refuting her allegations but meeting their demands. Sounds like extortion. In no way did I stalk her, or even want to, and I've never written such a huge, humiliating check in my life. That's not just any huge, humiliating check, but a huge, humiliating check to a woman who is already loaded by virtue of being a trust baby. Well, whatthefuck.

"Oh. Good. I guess I'll take your word for it. You look nice today, Geraldine."

"Thank you," she says. Geri approaches my car. Leaning in, she says with her alto, "Mason, there is a woman I know who would enjoy your company." She pauses.

"Who is it?" I ask, not really wanting to know.

Geri pauses again. "Lia. Lia Frankel."

I twist my face. "Not Lia Frankel. No." A metallurgist for US Steel. Geri sold her house last year. A metallurgist. Kind of attractive, but she's as grim as I am.

"C'mon, Mason. She's nice. She's noticed you. She's interested." Geri places her hand on my forearm.

"She's interested," I say. "Well, you know how I feel about that."

"I know," she says with a scowl. "Groucho Marx. You don't want to be affiliated with an organization that would have you as a member. The same old bullshit," Her smile returns. "We're going to be at Green Boy's today after work. Promise me you'll come by and talk. Just one beer."

I slump, eyes turned to my windshield. "Okay. Just one beer. I'll talk to the Fascist man-hater, then go." Right now, I'll say anything.

"Lia is not a man-hater. She doesn't hate you."

"That's like saying, 'It doesn't suck.'"

Geri kisses her fingers and places them on my cheek. "You'd better be there."

Three

7:50 AM
Monday August 17, 1987
In the Olds, stuck in traffic

Brown, wavy businessman's hair rests atop a slender six-three. With relaxed, angular facial features, Wylie looks like a blue-eyed Jimmy Stewart running the local building and loan. Unassuming and trusting, few would guess this man rules the stockbroker domain of blatant aggression in which we live. Most guys have to have their Zig Ziglar motivational tapes playing in their brains all day, with the latest book from Tony Robbins in the briefcase and Dale Carnegie updates on speed dial. Framed prints of mountain climbers standing on a rock and looking up adorn their office walls. The mountain climber always says something like 'Perseverance' when he should be saying, 'Who stole my goddamn petons?'

Wylie doesn't need all that, even though he's what we brokers call a Big Hitter. It's just that Wylie's odd in that he is that Heavy Stroker while looking like the Dull Plodder, with a voice that goes falsetto when he gets stressed. He kills by just being himself, a concept that has escaped those who ooze pretense. Frankly, it makes a select few very pissed off, just because he does it and they can't figure out why. Especially John Findlay. That, however, doesn't stop John from talking with the home office in Philly and, as the resident manager, taking credit for Wylie's success. It does suck.

I'm proud of Wylie, proud to be his friend or even just to know him. To put a new twist on Smith Barney spokesman John Housman, Wylie makes money the old fashioned way. He's clean while he earns it. He works his ass off. That's the part everyone can't seem to grasp. And, clean? In his five years as a broker he has not had so much as even one terse telephone call. That's really incredible, especially when you realize what has happened. The misery index. Eight hundred dollar gold. A crazy bull market. Prime lending rates of twenty-one percent. A recession resulting in nationwide double-digit unemployment. Investor malaise, then rampant speculation. Takeover fever, with Ivan Boesky and Michael Milken presiding. The farm crisis. Soviet missiles. Oil boom. Oil bust. Wylie steered his clients through it all. Consequently, he has been rewarded with referrals and the ever-growing assets from which his commission base is formed. A good honest broker can put on his check stub a bit over one-half of one percent of his clients' assets per year. That means Wylie tells over *fifty million dollars* what to do. Solely under his control. Under his control, because his clients just love him.

Wylie and I silently sit in traffic. From his fine wardrobe, he has chosen for today a summer weight Joseph A. Bank olive suit, a white shirt, cordovan loafers, and his trademark pink tie. On the other hand, for me dressing in the morning is a lot simpler. I don't own a suit. For office attire, I possess two Corbin factory-outlet navy hopsack blazers, five pairs of Haggar worsted wool charcoal gray slacks, five rep ties, three white buttondowns, three Oxford blue buttondowns, fourteen black socks, ten A-shirts, and ten pairs of boxers. Oh, and one pair of cordovan Bass Weejuns, no tassels. In spite of the heat, I'm wearing a blue shirt today. As always, in mute protest.

Lisa Lisa and The Cult Jam. Head to toe on the radio. Crazy 98. Why can't Geri hook me up with Lisa Lisa? I'd just take Lisa.

We've been silent. I decide to break it in an awkward manner. "So, Wylie…"

"What's on your mind, Bricker?" Is that stress I hear? Perfect…

"Your wife." Bad answer, but I have an honorable motive.

"Excuse me?"

"Your wife. Geri. The woman you should spend more time with."

Wylie pauses. "I don't get what you're driving at."

The black Beemer in front moves several feet. I follow. The traffic is normally not this slow on Oak, even though the switchbacks are at times a pain in the ass. I guess the alternative of plummeting over the hillside like lemmings could be worse. "You don't get it?" I continue. "That's the sad part. You need to spend more time with Geri. You two are in love. You've been married for ten years. I wasn't married that long. My ex has been."

"Well…I…I think I should, but both of us…we have rising careers. This is our chance to—"

"—to take a bubblebath together. Simple pleasures. Romance."

"What the hell would you know about romance?" Wylie's laughing, because he knows he has me. And he does.

"I know it when I see it, and I know you and Geri are truly romantic because I see you. Makes sense to me."

"What day of the week is this?" Wylie asks. Uh-oh.

"Well…"

"It's Monday. So, it follows that tonight will be Monday night. Therefore, that means you will forego an opportunity to be with Lia—"

"The wicked witch of the west."

"She's nice," Wylie says.

"No she's not. She's really a witch. Haven't you noticed? Black everything. She even dyed her hair from a great auburn to…black. Flat black."

"I thought you like black," Wylie says.

"Black's great, but I prefer my black to not come from the bottle."

Wylie smiles. "Well, then, she's still attractive. Like Elmyra. Or Elvyra. Or whatever."

"True…exposed cleavage, but how much did she pay for the makeup and the boobs?" I say. "Too much science."

"True, but at least not a woman you have to give money to."

He has me. "I like Christine. As I've often said, I figure if I want to be screwed in a business deal, it should be with Christine. I never thought I'd ever have to pay fo—"

"Don't say it!"

"Okay. I won't. But, you gotta love the alliteration. Look, Wylie, we've been over this. Most of the time you agree with me. You're letting Lia cloud your reasoning. Don't I make sense to you? You ever really listened to Lia? I'd pay her to leave me alone."

Cars part like I'm Moses. The Delta slips through with the office only five minutes away. I want the logjam back.

"You know…" Wylie says pensively, "it's scary, because sometimes I do agree with you."

"You play the cards to which you are dealt."

"What?"

"It's expressionist. An abstract. A new paradigm. We are thrown into a situation. A hand, dealt before you sit at the table."

"That's not expressionist. That's existential."

"We're both wrong, because tonight I'm going to lay out only five hundred dollars I can afford and have sex two times with a beautiful woman, all the while avoiding the dance, the credit card bills – "

"Now, that doesn't make any sense to me," he says. "Neither does the fact that a college football hero has to hand over—"

"But, the dating…man, I hate that word…the pursuit, the abject aspect of mating. Christine is so pure. But, just in case, I'm condomed."

"Condemned."

"It is pure, Wylie. The oldest profession. Besides, you've never seen her."

A long silence prevails as we weave down the hill to the bottomland. Downtown looms ahead.

"I worry about you, Mason."

"I worry about you, too. I'm envious, truly. So, occasionally, why don't you two leave a thousand on the table and just get naked?"

"Okay, so it's not going to be Lia," Wylie says, ignoring my suggestion. "Jesus, I don't blame you. Geri doesn't even like her. But, you're envious? One of these days, Brick. One of these days, it'll be good for you, too. And, one of these days, you will also make lots of money."

"I don't think so," I whine. "I don't think so on both counts. First, I can't seem to get along with women. I'm either too much of a smart ass or they don't like men who smoke. By the way, I need a cigarette. May I?"

"No. Then, change."

"Too late about that changing part. And, second, I'm in the wrong business to make a lot of money."

"What?" Wylie says, surprised.

"The banks, Wylie. They're positioned to deplete our asset base. Get it while you can, dude, because the banks are moving into the financial services business. Brokerage, insurance, they'll see it all. They're going to capitalize on centuries of goodwill and they're going to roll us. It doesn't hurt that their customers owe them a bunch of clams, either. That'll make them stand up and take notice."

"You're obsessed with banks!" I'm pissing him off. I don't care. "Well, Mason, why don't you just go work for a bank?"

"Some day, my man, we'll all be working for a bank."

Madonna belts it out on Crazy. Open your heart to me. Baby. I hold the lock and you hold the key. Open your heart to me. I'll give you love if you turn the key.

I want to turn that key, but commitment is very scary.

Four

8:15 AM
Monday August 17, 1987
Offices of Fuller Busher, Ashton Township, PA
Dow Jones Industrial Average: 2,685 - an all-time high

The Conference Room. Ugly-ass teak wood paneling is the walls, framing dollar bill green carpeting. Recessed spotlights in the ceiling soften it all, making it tolerable. The teak is adorned with a Monet print and a Manet print, Monet and Manet chosen because they sound like 'money.' Findlay did it. I am serious. So, Claude's here, along with a print depicting fox hunting. Fox hunting as a symbol of money is interesting. I'm sure it has something to do with a way station along Erickson's eight stages of development, as if some people don't quite make it down the prescribed path.

As I survey the conference room, a couple things come to mind: a) ten well-dressed, well-heeled white men sit in still life on cushy padded chairs, with Wylie to my right in the second row. Ten. There must be a billion dollars of investment possibilities in AT alone, and we only have ten men. What an opportunity I squander. And b) as you may expect, there are no blacks, no Hispanics, no Asians, no native Americans, and especially no women brokers here. We're about two generations away from the rest of the world.

A mahogany altar sits underneath two telephones and a speakerphone we call the squawk box. The squawk box is as annoying as its name indicates. The static from the squawk box will soon lead you to why.

"Good morning! Ronnie Miller here with the morning conference call," the squawk box squawks, the definition of cacophony. "Well, it's another Monday, and what a beautiful one it is. Summertime with all its finery and your clients want, no, demand, stocks. Gentlemen, we're going to give it to them."

You can say that again...

"The investing environment cannot be better. There hasn't been this much excitement in the air since 1982, and it's been going great guns since then. Here's what's fueling it all. Crude has dropped through the twenty dollar psychological support level. Gold has been under four hundred forty for six weeks. Inflation is dead. Inflation leads the bear market, and they're both dead, because up we go. And, men, the economy is rolling along nicely, with capacity utilization at a wonderfully high eighty percent. I can't stress that enough. Inflation is dead and the economy is red hot, perfect, I say perfect, for the stock market. Inflation is dead, in spite of the fact that mines are operating at high capacity, too. That means there are millions and millions of tons of commodities out there, and it's all going against supply and demand theory, but that doesn't matter because inflation is dead. It doesn't get any clearer than that."

Clear? Actually, lots of coal and dead inflation *follow* classical economic supply theory, but Corncob has them so hypnotized no one will notice. Even as Fuller's chief investment strategist, Ronnie is the Goober of the business. I've had lunch with the man. One on one. Unusual. Hillbilly accent. All he lacks is the slack-jaw countenance and the stupid hat.

"And, with the Dow Jones Industrial Average sitting at an all-time high of 2,685, there is still some healthy fear out there and no speculation. Bull markets climb a wall of worry, gents, and evidently the investing public thinks there is plenty to worry about. But, we know better, because we're paid to know better."

I can't take it any more. "We're paid to execute transactions, not to be Lester Thurow," I say. Heads turn. Corncob Ronnie draws a breath.

"As for individual stocks, we stockbrokers look good right now. Real good. Merrill Lynch and Primerica are two you should be talking to your clients about. No better way to instill confidence than to recommend your peers."

Say what?

"Christmas is coming up. That's right. Your wives are thinking shopping right now...don't they always?"

Appropriate laughter emits from the mind-numbed among us.

"Your kids will go for Tyco Toys, and so should you. I'm looking for a double out of that one before you open your gifts. And speaking of your better halves, Avon Products is sitting pretty at a price right now where the dividend is yielding five percent. That's on a growth stock, guys. Great income from a growth stock, the best of both worlds. Avon, the world's largest in cosmetics, over half of its sales come from overseas. They've cleaned house by selling the underperforming Foster Medical and buying the upscale Giorgio and Elizabeth Arden. This is not the Avon of the sixties, but they still come calling. Cosmetics and health care—on an upturn. They're among my leaders.

"Back to the market. A weak dollar could give us problems from a liquidity standpoint, and bonds were off a point Friday, pushing interest rates up, but both the bond and the stock markets display very little risk right now. Healthy fear, lots of money, nothin' could be finer. That's it for this morning. I'm short on time, but long on ideas. Read my letter on the wire. Happy selling!"

The squawk box goes dead, as are we.

The resident manager steps up to the plate. My boss, John Findlay. Robert Morris, Pi Kappa Alpha, marketing. Blond, combed-back hair, as if an Aryan guest-starred on *Miami Vice*. Blue eyes, light skin, with a Pittsburgh snarl emitting from his lashing tongue. Handsome bone structure in his face. Six foot and forty and okay husky. Barely okay. He's casual today, wearing a navy Brooks Brothers blazer and tan slacks with a yellow paisley tie over one of his two dozen starched white shirts. That's my John. Hitler's dream man.

"There you have it, men. It truly doesn't get any better than this. I had a prospect call me at home this weekend. Not a client, a prospect. They're out there, and we have to get our share before anyone else gets them. By the way, I order you not to recommend Merrill and Primerica. We are not to refer to any other broker with anybody. Fuller Busher stands alone atop, and we're going to hold them underwater until they stop shaking."

More laughter, frighteningly sincere.

"Speaking of underwater, Mason," John says, smiling and winking at Handsome Rookie Todd O'Reilly. "Just what was the Dow at when you sold—or sold out—in April?"

John hasn't harassed me for a couple of weeks, so I smile, because I knew this was going to happen today. The other brokers think he means it in jest most of the time, but I know better. Anyway, Ronnie has me ready to snap, so here goes.

"It was at 2,450. We've talked about this before, John. You seem to bring it up more in public as the Dow skyrockets. But, of course. Now, get serious. Merrill? Avon? Tyco Toys, for Chrissake? This firm is devoid of ideas so much so that we think we can throw anything out there. Like we're in a fishery." I finish with emphasis. Wylie nudges my leg.

"You got any better ideas?" Nice comeback, Dick.

"Yeah!" Well, not yet, but I can come up with something.

"Tell us. What is it?"

"Ask Corncob," I say. "Where does he get the little risk in the bond market shit? Bond prices have been falling for weeks. That means rising interest rates. That's not good. Besides, why are we even discussing bonds? What pretense! We're fucking salesmen! And now we're fucking the public." I know I've taken it too far, but it's so tempting…

"Watch your language!" blows Ned Studstill, the most senior among us.

"Speaking of salesmen, Mason," Findlay continues, "you bring your PhD in here and you think you're so damned smart, but why can't you produce? You know why you can't produce? For the same reason you're a cancer on my team. You're a loser."

What did I tell you? That is not a shot over the bow. I hear this more often than you'd think. And, with good reason. An acquaintance of mine, a nice-looking blonde, is John's new main squeeze. Purely for sport, the blonde insinuated to John that she and I used to do the 'wild thang' on a regular basis. We didn't, at all. I would have remembered. With John being so possessive and proud, I didn't deny it, just to yank his chain. It's worth all the abuse. Whatthefuck.

"John, we could discuss your disdain for me in private, but since you brought it up…what does anybody know? We just listened to Corncob Ronnie, a politically motivated, ladder-climbing, washed-out adding machine jockey from Arkansas, and we've been led to believe that he is Buddha. What is all this?"

"Keep it to yourself, Bricker," John says calmly, yet tersely.

All the brokers are eerily silent. It's as if the world is The Dick and me. I can't stop. I don't want to stop. "You asked. I'm telling you. Have you charted Ronnie's recommendations? Great now, but who isn't?"

"You, for instance?" counters John.

They laugh. He has me there. Nevertheless, I continue, "Where was Corncob in 1985? In the tank. Where was I? Smokin'. I have the records."

"You're the past, Bricker. The question is, can you do better…now?" Obvious, but unimaginative.

"I've done well. And, I can do better." Oh, no…here's the better idea. I can't believe what I'm thinking.

"I'm not interested in your opinion of the market. I want work!" he says sharply. "And, I'd better be seeing tickets for Avon and Tyco Toys coming across my desk. You got that?"

I pause again. Then I decide to voice this ill-conceived yet ingenious idea. "I'll take you one better, Findlay. We're going to be in a freefall soon, so I'll just short the Dow."

The Dick is silent in what I'm sure is disbelief. I glance to see Wylie rubbing his face.

"That's right," I say. "Short. Short the Dow Jones Industrial Average. You know, John. Short. Sellin' high now. Borrow the stocks I sold to deliver to the buyers. Then, buyin' back low later and returning the stocks to the nice people who loaned them to me. Sell high now. Buy low later. A bet the market will fall, and precipitously. Ass-backwards, but it works. It's worked for me. You know how, but I have the guts to do it. Thirty stocks in the Dow Jones. IBM, General Motors, and their friends. Thirty. All thirty, down and dirty."

More silence. Little motion. Not out of respect, I am certain.

"Your career's half gone," John finally says, "so I'll let you do that just to finish it off and watch you walk. Or crawl."

"Thank you for your support. Now I'll go back to my office so I can short the Dow."

John is smiling. "Desk, Bricker. I'm moving rookie Todd O'Reilly in the office." I'm taken aback.

"You're in your sixth year, just like Wylie. In fact, you should be challenging Wylie. But, you can't get anywhere near one forty. Now, rookie Todd has been here ten months and he's producing circles around you. It's all about the allocation of assets, and now your assets are like your ass. Therefore, you're in the middle of the secretarial pool. Just you and the girls."

I stand defiantly and survey the room. Men, spanning the adulthood ages. Men, clean slates of mind, all of us in summer tan or summer blue suits or blazers and slacks. Ties. White shirts. Cole-Haan shoes. Proper haircuts. Blank faces. Soldiers dressed for battle. With the notable exception of Wylie, they're all George Babbitt. This is what author Sinclair Lewis was warning us about. I, however, am an island.

I take my exit.

What does it all mean?

Who knows?

Yet another question for Diane the Feet.

Five

8:30 PM
Monday August 17, 1987
In my condo, in my bed, not alone
Dow Jones Industrial Average: 2,700 – an all-time high

Christine Smith has been my hired hand since six months after the divorce. August 10, 1982. We shared our fifth anniversary last Monday. I gave her a present, a two-karat diamond pendant. Set me back a couple thousand. That was painful, but worth it. She's done a lot for me. To continue playing her role, she acted as if she were surprised and grateful. I know that indeed is part of the game. And, I'm sure Christine has a fine collection of jewelry provided to her by the others.

For the most part, Christine is a mystery. I do know some things about her. She's told me about her young daughter whom she loves with all her heart and will do anything to support her in all ways. I have Christine's telephone number, even though I've never called her and wouldn't dare. It's not an Ashton Township exchange, and that makes sense. With as much talent as Christine has, she has to be from Pittsburgh. Only a big city can grow a woman who is as walk-into-a-parking-meter gorgeous as she is. Just like Joan. A classic. Just like Joan. I got lucky. Interviewing her first, I knew there could be no other. Full, shoulder length dark brown hair, brown eyes, round face, beautiful smile, year-round tan, nice boobs, great fanny, even Joan's skinny legs. My ex and I did it more than once a week, but I'll settle for this arrangement. I have sex and I don't have to go through those ridiculous rituals associated with women, such as dinner, movie, hormones, trying to read her mind, breaking up, making up, and admitting that I'm wrong. Everyone should have a high-priced whore.

Christine and I are naked on our bed. U2's on Crazy. Album rock. *The Joshua Tree.* With or without you. We're about an hour away from the second round. Five hundred bucks and I get laid twice. Thank God it's Monday.

"Mason," she squeaks out, like Georgette of *The Mary Tyler Moore Show*, "we've been together a long time."

"That's right, Christine. A long time."

"And, I've enjoyed every minute of it," she says as she locks her leg around mine.

"Me, too." I smile, the satiated man.

"I like you, Mason. I really like you, even aside from our business arrangement. You know what I like the most?"

"What's that?"

Christine rolls to prop herself onto her left arm, facing me. "I love the way you've opened up to me. That makes me feel special."

"Thank you, Christine. You're a good listener."

"Why, thank you. It's easy, because you're so interesting."

"I don't know what to say to that, except 'thanks.' I like to think I'm interesting, so, if you say so…" We've been down this lovely lane before. She knows how to stroke me.

"You've told me some interesting things, like how you sent your football coach to prison. Like Vinny. Like your doctoral dissertation."

"My dissertation sucked," I say.

"You've told me," Christine says, smiling.

"I don't know—"

"You don't know how they ever conferred the degree," she says, rubbing my hair. "Six years later and it's time to give yourself a break, honey."

"I wanted to write a—"

"And, they wouldn't let you. I know!" Christine gently squeezes my cheeks. I touch her hand.

"Okay, I know. I can be a real pain-in-the-ass. I guess I have told you everything…over and over."

"Everything except Joan."

I pause, and then pause again, "How did…how…Christine, if I haven't told you about Joan - that is, if there is a Joan - how do you know her name?

She pauses and lies down on her back, head on the pillow, looking up. "It's weird, because over the years, about a half-dozen times, right at that 'moment', you've called me Joan."

"Oh."

"Was Joan your wife?"

"No. I've told you. I've never been married."

"Is Joan an old lover?"

"No," I say innocently. Trying to win back my cool, I declare, "I did once know a Joan who was my professor at West Virginia. Dr. Kissinger. She was also my mentor in grad school at Duquesne."

Silence.

"You wanted her, didn't you?"

All through this conversation, Christine and I have been lying beside each other, looking at the reflection of the silent television on the ceiling. I rise, facing her, propping myself with my right arm. Nice boobs. I pause for a long time, attempting to seem wise but probably looking confused. "Joan and I made love once," I blurt out. "No, twice…okay, a half-dozen times, exactly the number you say I've called you Joan." I don't have the faintest idea why I must continue this charade. Maybe it's because charades define my romantic life.

"She's had an effect on you. That must have been 1981, early '82 at the latest."

"You know a lot about me, don't you."

Christine props herself up on her elbow, facing me. Holy heavenly body… "More than you think," she says. "However, I do know you're good at fooling others. That's why you're a stockbroker. You do tell me you're not a good broker. You could be better than you think. Let me tell you something, Mason. I know people. I read people for a living. So do you. You're a gambler. I am, too. Just like you, a smart gambler. You sincerely know a lot about those around you, but you won't open up to yourself. Just think of what you could do if you opened up to yourself."

She lies on her back. I remain on my arm, gazing around. My ceiling is white. My walls are white. My BA diploma from Duquesne hangs oddly above the bed. In the blue screen emission I can still see the print of Van Gogh's *Terrasse du café le soir* I bought in Paris earlier this year. A cross-stitch sampler given to me by a client who expected more than advice hangs beside a full-length mirror that hangs to the left of my walk-in closet. A picture of Vinny and me taken during the 1975 Pitt game rests by itself on my dresser. Nightstands are on each side of the bed, with four novels by such folks as Vonnegut and Bradbury and pages and pages of my unfinished books scattered below very unexciting curtains, and that rounds out the master bedroom.

It's a sad place.

Neither of us is speaking.

"Darling," Christine says, breaking the ice, "You know I have two other clients. But, you're my favorite."

"Yeah, right," Her favorite. Fat chance. I kind of wish I were, though.

"Tell me about Joan."

"Christine, I did."

"Were you in love with her?"

"Didn't you ask that question five minutes ago?"

"Were you?"

I fail in my attempt to avoid the truth. "Okay. Okay. Goddamn. Yes."

"Ah, ha…did she hurt you?"

"Yes."

Christine draws a deep breath. "You can tell me about it."

I'm irritated. "Why do you insist I tell you about Joan?"

"I'm just trying to help you," she says, curling in closer.

"I'll buy that. Here it is. I was younger than her. I still am. She was beautiful. You resemble Joan, except you're more honest. She was cunning and calculating and she owned my soul because she was beautiful and she was my mentor. I could kick myself. There."

Christine leans up again on her left arm. Yep, what a sight. That hour is going to wind down fast now. She kisses me full on the lips.

"You're not the only guy this has happened to, but it sure feels like it, doesn't it? Oh, Mason, I care for you so much. More than you think. Why, I'd drop the price to a hundred for you." We laugh.

I go from smiles to a scowl. "Christine, don't care for me. I'm damaged goods."

"Think nothing of it, dear. I can't give this job up, anyway. How else can I pay tuition for my daughter at the Catholic school?"

I think of the irony of that, and I sigh. I lie down on my back as Christine places her head on my shoulder.

"I still think Joan was your wife."

"Okay," I say. "Joan was my wife."

"So, you were married."

"Yes."

"I knew that. From Day One."

"I guess we all look alike," I say, sighing again.

"I'm just surprised you took so long to admit it," Christine says with a grin.

"I didn't want anything to come between us," I say, sarcastically.

A short pause. "Well, Mason, you know what that means?"

"What."

"I won," she says with finality. "I won, and I love to win."

10:00 PM
Monday August 17, 1987
In my living room, beside my front door.

Christine and I stand directly beside the door. I believe there's a significant body language message here. Maybe it's too late to make out on my manly brown leather sofa, which is part of my manly brown leather recliner and my manly brown leather love seat, comprising my manly brown leather three-piece living room suite. I like the leather. I like the furniture. I like Christine on it. The furniture contrasts with the white walls, which are further contrasted by art. Van Gogh's *Interieur d'un restaurant* hangs on the wall adjacent to the front door. The wall opposite the door displays that Monet bridge I can never think of the name of. Rust carpeting spreads across the floor. I will complete the decorating as soon as I hang my doctoral diploma beside the windows on the wall adjacent to the other side of the door. Six years ago, I earned it. Today, I retrieved it after getting summarily bounced out of my office. Presently, it rests on the floor. Time flies.

Even here, the sweet aroma from my bedroom lingers. My prostitute is exquisite in a yellow sleeveless dress over her tan…sandals, hair perfect, a little makeup, she looks fresh, like she just got out of the shower. Now there's something we've never tried. Honestly.

"Thank you, Christine. Thanks for everything. Thank you for talking with me, and thank you for making love with me. Twice." I hand her five crisp one hundred dollar bills. She slips them into her white clutch.

"No need to thank me, Mason. I do love you." She kisses my cheek.

"Don't even start that," I say, smiling.

"Goodnight." And she slips out the door.

I walk back to the bedroom and pick up the photo of Vinny and me. *The Pittsburgh Advocate* published it on page 8A after the Pitt game. There we are in our youthful promise. Reaching to touch the place where Christine's lips met my face, I look at my fingers to discover red lipstick. Talk about telling you what you want to hear. Vinny will like this one. I can't wait to tell him that a hooker just told me she loves me, and *after* I handed her the money. He'll absolutely roar!

Six

5:30 PM
Wednesday August 19, 1987
In the industrial tan Olds, leaving the office late.
Dow Jones Industrial Average: 2,665

I always like to look in the rear view at the Horowitz Building as I drive down Hale Street, watching it being sucked into the vortex created as I gleefully vacate downtown. The H, our affectionate name for Horowitz, is a seven-story modern structure built and managed by Fuller Busher. Steel gray tinted windows enveloping the seventy-degree rhombus floor plan of The H reflect the torrid sun today, protecting from the summer radiation our three law tenants, the one accounting tenant, and Ashton National, my bank. Torrid today, in a few months, frigid. Summers and winters are always brutal here in Pittsburgh, but I'd live nowhere else. We may only have a couple of weeks of ideal weather, but I'd still live nowhere else. As we say about one another with our special take on the English language, 'Younse are a hearty bunch.'

'Younse are a hearty bunch?' It may be true, but, man, sometimes I say the strangest things.

I turn onto Oak, headed for Mount Money. My buddy Wylie is with me. Geri is home actually cooking. ETA at his hacienda: a matter of minutes.

"You sure you don't want to join us?" Wylie asks. "Geri has that third filet to put on the grill."

"If The Dick ever found out you let your wife drive the charcoals, he'd write 'queer' all over your walls. Or, as they say in North Carolina, 'quarr.'"

"I don't care. I know I'm all man." Wylie smiles and nods.

"Now, how do you know that?"

"You'd be surprised." Wylie's still smiling. Must have done ten K today.

"I don't even want to hear it. Just as long as it doesn't involve Fenz." I make the left turn to drive up the Oak switchbacks, the final escape route. "I mean, Ally does everything else for you. I'm very jealous."

"Don't talk about Ally like that! She deserves respect! I don't care if she does chase men."

Chase men? Fenz? Yeah. I sigh. "I give her respect. Truly. Our wonderful assistant. She takes care of me, too. She's damned good at what she does. It's just that Ally is cute to a fault and she smiles every time she walks into your office, which is often, more often than she walks up to my new kiosk, even though her desk is so close she shares personal space with me."

"Speaking of personal space, how's Christine?"

"Great. Still lovely. Let's see…three clients, so she's getting by on what I estimate to be a six thousand dollar a month enterprise. Cash. Tax-free. That's a hundred thousand salary to law-abiding citizens like you and me, and that doesn't include her bonuses. Like John says, it's all about the deployment of assets. Plus, since her other two are execs who have early afternoons free, if they wish, she gets to spend a lot of time with her daughter *and* she buys her nice things. An ideal job."

"Mason, you are the definition of cognitive dissonance."

Traffic ahead stops us, a common occurrence while heading for Money in the late afternoon. "Maybe, Wylie, but two things here. First, I like the woman. She's never given me any reason not to."

"I'll say," Wylie says as he turns to me with a smile.

"Second, Mac, I'm in no position to judge anybody. More than enough people think stockbrokers are hookers. Why? Trading unfairly, and illegally, on inside information…how many guys have been taken down on that recently? Worse, how many are doing it and getting by with it? Then, you've got brokers indicted for tax evasion, price manipulation. You know all this. A former director of the Federal Reserve Bank leaks market-sensitive info to a broker. For God's sake, Wylie! And, just when you think it can't get any worse, hundreds, *hundreds,* have been arrested this year alone for buying and selling coke on The Street. Wall Street, that is. Christine's morals and ethics are in question? At least she's honest about it."

"Except with the IRS."

"Good point, but, it makes me think. Have you read Woody Allen's *The Whores of Mensa*?"

"Uh, no, but I bet you the professor are going to tell me about it."

The Olds remains still. "A guy runs a brothel packed with beautiful women from the Ivies, The University of Chicago, Cal, and Stanford, who are hired out to meet with men and provide them with the cerebrally-stimulating conversations they can't get at home. It's like, a young man gets his acceptance letter to Harvard and to celebrate his buddies buy him a babe from Mensa so he can sit in a room and converse with her about the differences between Immanuel Kant and Friedrich Nietzsche and shit like that."

"And, those differences are?" Wylie deadpans.

"Kant was into making concepts intuitive and intuitions intelligible while Nietzsche obsessed on the fact that Socratic rationalism and optimism were the death of the Greek tragedy defined by the fusion of harmony with unbridled passion. In other words, Kant had a very orderly office and Nietzsche never dusted. Kant is an organized, successful mutual fund salesman and Nietzsche is a frustrated, depressed writer. Kant is a Republican while Nietzsche is an anarchist. Kant's sons win science fairs while Nietzsche's beat up science fair winners. Kant is like your wise grandfather while Nietzsche is the crazy, drunken uncle. You're Kant and I'm Nietzsche."

"Very good," Wylie says. "So, you and Christine have this intellectual discourse?"

"Yeah, that, and we screw."

"Mason, take my advice," Wylie says as we begin moving.

"Pull down my pants and slide on the ice."

"We gotta find you a woman."

"Look, Todd Rundgren, you ought to see Christine. She is some woman." Wylie takes a deep breath. "This is not right."

"What's not right about it? Monday, seven thirty on the dot, or sofa, except during the new moon of her lunar cycle."

"Lunar cy– oh, I get it."

"That's right, lunar. If it's not lunar, we do it. Then, we watch TV. Then, we do it again. That keeps my head clear until Sunday evening when I have this Pavlovian response. Then for some reason you and I ignore it on Tuesday and talk about it every Wednesday, like you're the human calendar. Let's change the subject, okay?"

"Okay. Change of subject. How's your West Virginia going to do this year on the gridiron?"

"They open with Penn State, a school that I even after all these years would bomb the stadium. Happy Valley, my ass. I always want to play those fairies. Really bad."

"Who's that new kid at quarterback?"

"Some true freshman named Tony. He's supposed to set Montani on fire," I say as I make the left onto Wylie's Pine. Oak. Pine. Maple. Tulip. Poplar. Bland with conformity. All the heroic people in the history of the world and the best AT can come up with is a grove of trees.

"Let's go!" Wylie says.

"Wylie, they don't play for three weeks. Jesus, I still want to hit one of those guys! Listen to me! How puerile! Nittany Lions! What the hell is a Nittany?"

"It's like a Buckeye."

"It's worse than a Buckeye." I steer the Olds into the driveway of the McInally abode. Right behind the Jag. Nice car. Wylie smiles. He gets a steak, then gets to watch Geri strip. I had a dream about that once. Luckily, it was a Monday morning.

"Thanks for the ride, friend." Wylie's been smiling a lot today. Made a few thousand. I made a few hundred, and that's a great day for me.

"What are you going to do tonight, Brick?"

"I'm going to drive down to a random beer garden, buy twelve Iron Cities, pop one of those Arns before I get home, then hope the mom in the black one-piece is lounging by the pool. It's a wonderful thing, a black one-piece."

We fall silent. Wylie looks out his window, then turns to me. "Someday soon, I'll buy the Arns if you get drunk and tell me once again about your game against Pitt."

He lives vicariously through my one shining moment. So, I fake exasperation. "Okay, Wylie. It's great when you're my captive audience. And, believe it or not, I love to tell the story. It was the one time when I amounted to something."

"Mason, you are something," Wylie says as he pats my shoulder.

"I love you, too, Wylie. And leave your hands in the open around me, okay?"

Wylie scoots his rumpled tan suit out of my car, pulls the yellow tie back down over his blue Oxford, throws a wave over his shoulder, takes several steps and disappears into his kitchen door.

I want beer.

Seven

6:00 PM
Wednesday August 19, 1987
In my Olds, parked in my garage
Dow Jones Industrial Average: I got it where I want it

I wish I had ten bucks for every time I sat in my car staring at my empty garage walls while downing a beer. Empty walls. Hanging tools? You have to be kidding. The only tool I have is my mind, however advantageous and cursed it may be. Anyway, this is a great time to think, which usually in my case means getting angry.

Angry.

In 1975, I was nineteen, living my boyhood dream playing football for the Ridge Runners of The University of West Virginia, an interstate hour south of AT. Never mind I was a walk-on with no athletic scholarship money. It didn't matter that I played sparingly. I wore the silver and navy, complete with a helmet and everything, parlaying hustle and mania for a spot on the kickoff team. An occasional mad dash down the field was somewhat satisfactory, but like anyone else, I wanted more. I got more, just not like I wanted it.

My father had built a fraternity of ex-Marines whose lives he saved on Guadalcanal. After his death, they took care of me. One day in early November, one of them asked for a favor in return. He, a black man, approached me with really incriminating evidence that my head coach received money in the amount of sixty five thousand dollars to bench a quarterback of greater ability, who happened to be black, in favor of a quarterback of lesser skills, who happened to be white. The jack came from a wealthy dude who just so happened to be a racist, funding white supremacy groups to infiltrate organizations such as football, corporations, and the Boy Scouts. The favor was this: bust the bigot.

The captain of the team was my good friend Michael Burton. Michael is now my priest at The Church of the Blessed Sacraments here in Ashton Township. It is ironic that linebacker Michael is Father Michael because linebacker Michael hit you like Amtrak. When Michael played against you, he would have rather seen you dead than see you at all. I knew this revelation would piss him off royally. Since he is black, I felt he had to know before I did anything. Michael was usually the voice of reason, but that day he implored me to take the evidence to the press. I did.

It was the week of the big game with our big rival, top ranked University of Pittsburgh. Nothing happened in the papers for a few days, then came the big surprise. On the morning of the big game, *The Pittsburgh Advocate* blared the story on the front page. In a fit of newspaper impropriety, I was named, for God and everybody to read, as the source.

At the pregame meeting, there were black and white fights. The coach threw me off the team the moment I arrived. Then the blacks threatened to walk. Insanity set in my mind when I somehow convinced the coaches to leave the room to allow us to have an unprecedented pre-game players-only meeting. I then convinced all of them, black and white, to can the coaches and run the game ourselves. Amid all this convincing, my team convinced me to be the head coach. This was not part of my boyhood dream, but what the hell, I thought.

With Vinny as my quarterback, I led the Ridge Runners to an upset victory.

Then, it got weird. After a two-day courtship, Joan the professor and I the student ran off to Vegas to get married. We returned after another two days to discover I had been expelled. I was on the cover of *Sports Illustrated.* Joan resigned. We moved to Pittsburgh. She joined the faculty at Duquesne, where I earned my bachelors and my doctorate. For one fifty K, I collaborated on a screenplay about the events of that week. *Foolish Sages.* The movie was a disaster. Joan and I moved back to Montani to teach at The U. She ran off with the attorney. I shamefully brought my tattered hopes and dreams to Ashton Township, a place chosen by the drunken throw of a dart on a wall map of metro Pittsburgh. In an effort to rejoin the financially elite, just like that son-of-a-bitch lawyer, I put my PhD aside, compromised my values, and became a stockbroker.

And, so it goes...Nikki?

"Yes?" the hot mom in the black one-piece asks as she sits in the passenger seat. "I'm present. So, if I am present, popping up in your mind like the bewitched witch's mother, then the question, my dear Mason, is, just why am I present?"

I'll try honesty. "I have conjured you."

"I know that, but why am I *here?*" Nikki asks, panning her hand around. She is looking at me now as much as she was looking away at the trees beside the pool. Interesting.

"Being in the garage is the place where I reaffirm that my business plan is working, and while I do that I want you to be with me."

Nikki purses her lips. "Bitch of a day, muffin?" She looks really good today, probably because her brown eyes are on.

"Sort of, baby. I was kicked out of my office Monday and transplanted at an open desk beside my assistant. It's turned out okay. The Dick tried to embarrass me, and he did. Now I don't care. More people walk by me now than ever. I'm such the social animal. I'm a magnet. And my production has instantly gone up from a paltry ten a month pace to a still-way-below-acceptable twelve, putting my earnings at what John considers a poverty-level fifty thousand a year. Negative reinforcement does have its advantages."

"I'd say that's a lemon you're trying to turn into lemonade," she sings.

I laugh. "You can't be serious."

"No, I'm not, but you're whining. Is all that money worth the abuse? And, while you're at it, give me a beer."

I oblige, handing her a longneck Arn. "I don't make all that money. The Dick's minimum W-2 for an acceptable broker is eighty thou, grossing two hundred. Not I."

"Then, why?" She sips, and rests the bottle on the seat between her legs. That must be cold.

"Why? I'll make my money another, more honorable way, more honorable than ripping off my clients."

"By shorting."

"Shorting?" I say, surprised. "You know shorting?"

"Yep. Shorting. Selling the market short. I know what shorting is," Nikki says with confidence.

"Really?"

"Mason, dear, this is your fantasy. Therefore, I'm a beautiful older unavailable woman in a black one-piece who knows a lot about the intricacies of the stock market because you taught her one Sunday afternoon. Get with the program."

Nicole is right. This is my fantasy. Anything can happen. "Oh…thank you. Uh…shorting. I still have yet to short the Dow. I just need the money. You can bet I will, though, since I did announce it to the stockbroker community. I've heard the rumors bouncing back from Philly. They all think I'm a joke. Well, I am. So, Nikki, just what is the punch line?"

"Have another beer and call me Nikita," she says.

Under orders, I reach for one of the bottles of Iron City and open it, keeping the top to fiddle with. "As I was saying, Nikita…emotional types are really caught up in this market. It's a buying panic out there because people don't want to be left behind, and not necessarily left behind with regard to money, but…like they don't want to be the last one to get a date to the prom. Thing is, if they own stocks on this their special night, they're all going to look like a bloody Carrie without the telekinesis."

"Disgusting image," she says.

"The naked truth."

"Sounds like you're the Lone Ranger on this one, Mason."

"Not so. I have more skeptical clients who unequivocally agree with me. Primarily, they are by profession engineers. We're on the same wavelength. I've talked to a couple dozen of them for years now. They're the main cog in my broker machine. Servicing engineers is my specialty, largely because no other broker wants them."

"I would think engineers would be outstanding clients," she says. "They have money and they're certainly smart enough to make money."

"And, smart enough to not fall for the hype that is the foundation of this business," I say. "The other guys can't take care of them because the gearheads demand facts and time to consider those facts, two concepts stockbrokers don't understand. So, that's why the engineers love me. I feed them data and leave them alone for a week. Reams of numbers and charts. One fall I took the train to DC to get drunk and pick up for each of my engineers a copy of the annual Congressional Budget Office report on the US economy. Hot off the presses. That was my marketing mailer for the month. Friends for life."

"Friends for life," she says.

"For life," I say. "The engineers are devoted to me because I have a four-letter word in my vocabulary that other brokers don't even know the meaning of. The word is 'sell.' In the brokerage business, it is considered anti-American to sell your stocks."

"Normal people think selling is a slap in the face of capitalism. We should all be buying."

"You're good at this, Nik."

"That's the way you like me."

"I guess you're right again, sweetums. However, I tell the engineers when to buy and also tell them when to sell. It takes them a few days, but they follow my advice. They love to sell. When the sell goes right, which is often enough, it's their validation that their unique combination of analysis and inference is the correct way to think. Example: the summer of 1983 followed a raging bull. Like now, everyone wanted a piece of the action. The few engineers I had then looked at it as an opportunity to take profits and get the hell out. Result? They held cash as the market hit the tank hard while taking the *faux* stock experts with it. Referrals followed. I like my business plan. I mean, whathefuck."

"It must have taken you a while to become so cynical," Nikita says with a smile. "So, tell me more."

"A while. I started my term-used-loosely profession in August 1982, not coincidentally the same month I started with Christine."

"Christine is the Monday night woman, right?"

"Must you interrupt?"

"I must approve of all your women, Mason," Nikita says, like a mom.

"Well, you and Christine are it and it's even more complicated than that, but I will proceed. The Dow Jones Industrial Average was at 819 the day I was licensed. Today, it closed at 2,665. Look at it this way, honey. On a before-tax basis, stocks in the US have increased in value, since the bottom of the Great Depression, an average of nine percent a year, counting dividends. In that time, US Treasury bonds paid about three to four percent a year, maybe. On the other hand, in the five years I've been a broker, if you would have simply bought then gone on a mission with a Mormon to Kamchatka and forgotten about your money, you would have made an easy twenty-five percent a year. That's a double pre-tax in three years, and that's how hard this bull has charged and that's how easy it has been to make money."

"Doesn't say much for my husband."

"You're right. It doesn't say much for your husband."

"Yep," she says, nodding. Nikita picks the bottle from her legs and places it on her lips. I can't take this. It's five days 'til Monday. I wonder if Christine does emergency calls?

"Does he know you're in my car?" I ask.

"Should I tell him?" Nikita asks with an evil grin.

"Yes, you should, punkin, but we know you're not really here. Except...now, back to easy money. My engineers and I manage our money and are way better than that, clocking in at a pre-tax *fifty-six percent a year*. That's a double every two years *after* paying Uncle Sam. When to buy and when to sell. Compare that to my other choking-on-their-Cheerios clients who simply suck at investing, a genre of losers who buy when they should sell and sell when they should hold on, who won't stop trying the same old bullshit even though it keeps going wrong."

"Such as my husband."

"Probably. Trying the same thing over and over expecting a different result: that's the definition of mental illness. Speaking of mental illness, a good deal of my fifty six percent pays for Christine."

"I don't approve of Christine."

"Ahhh...I'll get back to you later on that one."

"How do your engineers feel about shorting the market?"

"I've warmed up a few of my gearheads to the possibility of shorting the Dow. Selling short. Selling high now. Borrowing the stock to deliver the sale. Buying back to return the borrowed stock later, hopefully at a lower price. That's selling short. And, investment firms teach their brokers that selling short is Communism."

"That's strong," Nikita says with emphasis.

"Yet, true. Sometimes, many times, Wall Street is run by maniacal optimists. Like now. Remember hope? And the promise?"

"Hope. Promise. That afternoon by the pool was fun, wasn't it?"

"Yeah. You know, though, Nikita? I can see the engineers. They were taking a break from work today, pouring over the facts and figures and history. Could be a lay-up, the engineers are thinking. Few things could please an engineer more than to make money while everyone else is wrong. Another example: same 1983. Fortune Data was a bubble of a computer company, the flagship recommendation of Fuller Busher. The stock was selling for twenty-two dollars a share based on a house of cards built by the projections of initial profitability a long three years later in 1986. That's three years of the business losing money until Fortune Data made its first buck. That's like a bank giving a mortgage to a college sophomore. Three engineers and I shorted as Fortune Data shareholders lost a fortune, their fortunes unfortunately bottoming out at two bucks. On the other hand, the four of us bought back at four. Another victory for clean living."

"Nice story. A good one."

"So, Nik, sweetie, you ready to take a walk on the wild side?"

"Mason Bricker! What an unimaginative come-on! Your standards are higher."

"No! Not that! Shorting! Are you ready to short?"

"'Are you ready to short?' Sounds like something Lucifer would say."

"That's how the investing public looks at it."

"But, it also sounds like you've been successful at picking the right directions."

"Thank you. But, sweetie pie, strangely, even after my successes, the problem now is not them believing in me. It's that I don't know whether to believe myself. I'm afraid I made my proclamation in *my* fit of emotion. This is worth examining. What does it all mean? Will I be another Philip Nolan? Will I be banished like that man without a country because I'm so goddamned obstinate? Why can't I just go along to get along?"

"I think we know the answer to that question," she deadpans. "But, what's going to happen to the less fortunate optimistic among us?"

"I'll put it this way. My engineers and I see overvaluation that is apparently invisible to others. The last time it took you twenty-four dollars to buy one dollar of Dow Jones earnings was 1972, the beginning of a two-year crater during which the values of the most powerful companies in the world were cut in half. I learned market history from my father's friend the New York City broker. Stan the Money Man shorted for me in the middle of that crevasse that helped define the Nixon Administration, setting me up with some nice money, most of which I gave to Joan after her friend Ms. Perjury said I used to peep in her bedroom window. Extortion, maybe, but they had me because my attorney sucked. When will I ever get over that?"

"Maybe you'll get over it if I'm around more often."

"Now, there's a thought. The beer's getting hot, Nik. I should move this party inside."

"See ya, sugar." Nikita kisses her fingertips of her right hand, then touches them to my lips.

"See ya," I say, red-faced.

Diane the Feet absolutely would not find this one amusing.

As I drop my keys in my pocket and shuffle my Arns to the door, I try to think of a way to be a big producer while being a short expert. A short expert. That's how I like to think of myself. Few investors want to short, so I don't raise many commissions executing the strategy. I'm destined to be on my own bubble by being a cult hero to conspiracy theorists instead of the poster boy for optimism. Shorting does fit my personality better. It's difficult to be an asshole while you're buying.

I turn the doorknob. Nothing happens. Why in the hell did I lock this door? I never lock this door. After digging into my pockets to find my keys again, I'm annoyed. I insert the key. The door swings open and...holy shit!

There's a woman! It looks like a woman. Those distinctive features give her away. I'll call it a woman, since she startled the hell out of me and I don't want a man to be in my kitchen. A woman. Because the glass door to the great room makes her a silhouette, I have not the slightest idea who she could be. My pulse is racing. She is an intruder. Is she armed? Is she real, or is she, too, a fantasy from my warped mind? There's only one way to find out.

"Honey, I'm home."

"Hi, Mason." I still can't see her...but that voice, that vacillating pitch. No. It's not possible.

"Hi, whomever you are."

"Silly," she says as she walks to me. Now she's out of the backlight and the mystery is solved.

"Joan."

"Hello."

Joan looks wonderful, just like the last time I saw her over five years ago. She's wearing a gauze blouse over a white summer sweater with pegged denims, tastefully highlighting all those things about Joan that should be highlighted. It's freaky, because this is exactly what she looked like the day, the instant, I met her. And that's why this whole thing isn't real. Joan's dead and she's come back to haunt me, as if she doesn't do that enough already.

"Joan…" God, it looks just like her. Her face is the same. Her hair's cut a little differently with wispy bangs and a sexy flip under. Her brown eyes are beautiful. A very attractive apparition, but an apparition indeed.

"You look great, Mason."

My ex-wife, the woman who screwed me often then screwed me out of a half-million dollars of my own money, is standing in my condo paying me compliments. After all these years. This is surreal.

"Thank you…Joan," I say, confused but remembering my manners. "Now, tell me this. Are you a spirit?"

"I'm spirited, as always, but I'm a flesh-and-blood woman. As always."

That smile…oh, man. It's all coming back to me, but I'm so pissed off I don't want to hear of it.

"Okay," I say in an imperative fashion, "if you're flesh-and-blood and didn't just appear from heaven, even though you are evil, how in the hell did you get in my house?"

"Mason, you're in the phone book," Joan replies with a giggle, "And, you are so predictable. Darling, you still leave a door key outside just to the right side of the air conditioner, buried two inches in the ground, with a clump of sod over it."

She got me there. "Okay. I concede. You may not be a ghost. Assuming that, why are you here?"

"To see you," she answers, matter-of-fact.

"Why aren't you with Richie or Clyde or whatever his name is? Inquiring minds want to know."

Joan pauses, crossing her arms over her boobs. After the fantasies about Nikita, that doesn't help matters. "My marriage with Tom has ended."

Fuck! I'm furious, but I try to contain myself, not wanting to get into an argument with my ex-wife over the man she ran off with. From me. "Goddamn you!" Well, my intentions were good. "Goddamn you for…being here to tell me how…goddamn it!" I turn away from her and strike the wall with my fist. Damnit, that hurt! I spin back. "Jesus Christ! Why…the…hell…what gives you the right to simply pop back into my life, violate my personal space…just to tell me the…the jerk…you…left me for…and now you're divorced?"

"Separated."

"Legally?"

"Pending."

"Oh! Well, that makes things much better! Now, today, a married woman entered my house against my will. My ex-wife…you know something? You need help."

Another pause. She moves closer, too close. "I just wanted to see you." I know I'm demonstrative, and her calm is the exact opposite.

"How can you do this? How did you do what you did? And, after all you put me through, how can you just do this? Why didn't you simply call?"

Joan relaxes her arms, cocking her body onto one foot. "Because I knew you wouldn't see me."

"You're right," I say softly. I want to cry, but I'm too mad.

"Mason," she says, getting even closer, "I know I've hurt you. I'm sorry. I just wanted to see you again and say I'm sorry."

"You know? I'm tempted to forgive you. In fact, I will, because it's the good Catholic thing to do. You're forgiven. Now, get the hell out of my house."

"I have a better idea."

"You always do. You ran the show, up to and including the moment you left me. That's my own fault. And, now I know why. I couldn't see it then, but I've had time to think about it and now I know."

"Why?"

"I don't want to talk about it."

"You can talk about it with me."

"Fuck you."

She smiles. "Let me make it up to you. I'll begin by taking you to dinner."

I'm screaming acrimony within. "Dinner? How trite, Joan. Just because you own...owned my soul, you think I'm going to go to dinner with you? The gall!"

"We have to eat. So, let me buy you dinner. Okay?" Joan's face is now uncomfortably close.

I'm silent. For another few seconds. Now a half-minute. "All right." I cannot be serious.

"Good. Where would you like to go? Your choice. My treat."

"Let's see...a hundred bucks a dinner over a half mil...honey, it's every night until you're in your fifties. Let's go."

"I'm looking forward to it," she says with a smile and an eyebrow wag. The wag. She's still a master. The madame of disaster.

"Let me tell you something, sweetheart," I say, meaning no endearment, "I'm calling a taxi. The Mountain Wharf downtown has four bottles of a hundred dollar a bottle vintage, and you're buying all of them. I'm getting surf...and turf...and I'm damned hungry. We're taking a cab because I'm getting you drunk and watch your dignity peel away. And I'm going to get drunk so I can laugh while your dignity peels away and also so I won't be able to get naked with you, which is really why you're here. Now, isn't it?"

"Mason, I'm a married woman," she says with a straight face.

I walk to the phone, opening the drawer next to it for the phone book. As I flip through to find the number for the Mountain Wharf, I finally reply, "Like that's always stopped you."

9:00 PM
Wednesday August 19, 1987
At the Mountain Wharf with one sloshed woman. I'm not doing too badly myself.
Dow Jones Industrial Average: who gives a flying rat's ass

To get to The Mountain Wharf, you pass The H on Hale, turn left at Green Boy's, then cross the intersection of Hale and Roberts Street. The restaurant is a half block down Roberts past a bronze-glassed four-story office complex and half-dozen quaint shops and boutiques selling jewelry and hats and such things. The Mountain Wharf welcomes you with two storefront windows sashed with louver blinds, between which is a door, over and around which is no sign. You just have to know where The Wharf is. I was at a sushi place on Rodeo Drive that did that. *The* Rodeo Drive. One has to be a bit lofty to try it on the banks of the Ohio River. But, they apparently pull it off.

The ambiance of The Wharf is upscale indeed, complete with upscale clientele. Yuppies patrol the dark green and white tile floors. The two dozen booths are cherry-stained with white linen cloths. Incandescent lamps hang over each table, extending from the booth walls. To give it a seafarer touch, several mounted game fish hang on the teal walls, mixed among rods, reels, spears, and framed nautical photos. All that's missing is an odorous boat.

I'm still dressed for work. Joan is pegged and gauzed for play. The waiter brings the fourth bottle to our table. He's early twenties young with a handsome chiseled face and frame. Joan's checked him out a couple of times. Still looking for those of us who are subservient.

"The taxi was a great idea, Mashon," she says right before a cackle.

I sigh. "Joan, you haven't called me Mashon for a long time."

"And, you haven't had much to say to your old lady tonight. Maybe the vino...will open up your dark secrets." An air kiss ensues. Yep. She's drunk. Any other time that may push me over the edge, and it just may push me over the edge, but there is that matter of her hasty departure over five years ago.

"There hasn't been any time to talk. We've been too busy shoveling food and guzzling alcohol. So, what do you want to know?" I ask, almost exasperated.

"How's your life," she says after a gulp.

"Great. How's yours?"

"Neat. How's Vinny? I bet he hates me."

"Not any more."

"Why's that?

"He's dead."

Her face drops as she rests the goblet on the table. "Oh, Mason. I'm so sorry."

"Two years ago, he stopped at a tavern to pick up some beer for us. Walked right into an armed robbery. He and another guy were gunned down."

"Oh, no." Joan pauses with appropriate reverence. "How's Jean?"

"She took their two sons and moved back to West Virginia to be with her parents. I don't want to talk about this any more." I belt some wine.

Joan is looking blankly through the air. She contorts her face and whispers, "Vinny. I always felt like he liked me."

"He did," I reply, "up until the day you left me. But, his only regret concerning the end of our marriage was that he was too inexperienced to serve as my lawyer."

"You had a lawyer."

"In flesh, yes."

We're silent. "Okay," Joan blurts out. "I'm dying to know. Do you have a woman?"

She really thinks she can get by with that question. And, she just did. "Yes, I do have a woman." What an opportunity to rub it in. "And, she's better looking than you, too."

Joan leans over her plate with a smirk. "How...is that possible?"

"It happened. I got lucky," I say, taking a sip. "Six months after you left, she was between my sheets. Still is. Younger. Prettier. Smarter. Firmer."

"Bullshit." A faceoff. I'm going to win.

"It's true. She's a better lay than you can even dream of. Your best night is matched by her preoccupied night."

She is silent. Here goes. She's going to nail me with Tom. More pause. "You know, Mason. The most wonderful sex I've had in the decade of the eighties was with you the day I walked. How stupid of me."

"Joan, you're full of shit and I'm too drunk, anyway. So, you can forget it. Besides, no amount of flattery is going to get you me. But, tell me. If that is true, why in the hell did you leave?" Sounds like I bit.

Joan looks up to the ceiling, then to me. "I was bored. I need excitement. You had just gotten your doctorate. We were settling down too much at The U. I was restless."

"You need excitement, so you married an attorney?"

Joan leans back. "Tom stole my heart. He promised me everything."

I smile. "So did I. Obviously, Tom didn't deliver. I did."

We're in the midst of a long quiet period. A smile sneaks on her face. It gets wider and wider still. Suddenly, a drunken laugh. I can't help it. I laugh, too. Joan wipes her eyes with her napkin. Her mascara is running and her face is loose. We've been known to put away a lot of wine in our days, and it most always ended up like this.

I continue, deciding to bring back the venom. "Joan, about Patty. Why did you have her lie about me? I never once stalked her. Never. That lie, your lie, cost me a ton of money. Six figures. Deep into six figures. Tell me why."

She takes a sip. And another. "It was Tom's idea," she finally says.

"Oh, Jesus, Joan. Don't blame it on your lawyer."

"We had to counter our affair. I stood to lose a lot, too."

"You talk about it like you were negotiating a contract. Great metaphor, by the way."

"I'm sorry I did it."

"I'm sorry, too. The divorce was bad enough. Then you had to take away my name. It was high profile, honey. Everyone in The U community found out about it. The only thing I could do was resign my faculty position and leave Montani, leave the entire state. Let me tell you what a mess you got me into. I needed quick income, so had to become a fuckin' stockbroker. No choice. Talk about the loss of dignity."

"I guess you don't want me to spend the night," she says, holding her head high, waiting for me to cave.

The nerve! "You're a bitch." I pause, then I cannot believe what I'm about to do. "You're a bitch, but essential to my plan to take you down is to let you spend the night. It may sound crazy, but I want to see you sleep in my bed while I sleep on my sofa. I want you to wonder what could happen...and what won't happen. Never, Joan. Never again. Now, grab the check and pay for this mess."

10:00 PM
Wednesday August 19, 1987
Back at the condo

Dow Jones Industrial Average: not worth its weight in bat shit

I manage to unlock my front door while carrying Joan. The taxi ride was something else at first. She was never a pathetic drunk, but always funny. I can't remember the things she said. I seldom could. But, she had me laughing. That is until, somewhere halfway up Oak, she softly slumped into my shoulder and placed her hand on my chest. The driver looked at me in the rear-view, nodding his head and smiling, like 'you're getting some tonight, pal.' No, I'm not. But, I'm glad he wasn't looking at my Haggars. Damn that Nicole.

Joan has not awakened through the shuffle. I lay her on the sofa and turn on the end table lamp and the chandelier above the dining room table. She sleeps while I walk into my bedroom to prepare her quarters and fluff her pillows. I return to the sofa and gather her. Walking down the hallway, I debate as to what to do, what to do in the sense of undressing her. Quickly, I decide that if she can't sleep in her clothes, then tough. I'm not subjecting myself to her body, and I also don't want her to think I had my way with a drunken woman, either. I therefore place her on the sheets, cover her, eschew the standard goodnight peck on the cheek, flick off the overhead, and grab athletic shorts and a tee shirt for my PJs.

Ready for sleep, I lie down on the sofa and reach up to turn off the lamp. In the dark with a throbbing head, I decide to be a good host and turn on the bathroom light so she can find her way in the likely event that she has to throw up. It was always ugly whenever Joan yakked, a happening after many a night out on the town.

I return to my sofa. In the dark, I evaluate the night. It amazes me how detached I am.

Eight

4:30 PM
Friday August 21, 1987
Walking back to my condo from the mailbox
Dow Jones Industrial Average: 2,709 – an all-time high

Thank God this screwed up week has been put out of its misery. Still, I take pleasure in the fact that nothing is in the mail for me. No bills, no junk. It all amounts to the beginning of a great weekend. It's stifling hot without rain for about the thirteenth straight day, but the beginning of a great weekend.

For a man who claims he doesn't care, Joan has thrown me for a minor loop. Production became difficult yesterday, the day I got back home from the office to find she had left. Again. It's even worse today. I don't know what I expected, except maybe a phone call or perhaps a note. But, there she wasn't, in all her ebullience. All day Thursday I thought about her, and today, too. I wanted to stop, but Joan stood firm in my obsessive mind.

    I turned up a total of five hundred gross in these two days, pretty sad even for me. The market isn't helping much, either. It's at least not helping Mason. For a couple of months now, I've been on the wrong side of a relentless bull, doing just what my market analyst hero Martin Zweig says to never do: I'm fighting the tape. The 'tape' was originally ticker tape, but now refers to market momentum, the strength stocks have just because the major players are going the same way with a vengeance. My mental makeup is to be a contrarian, and I think I'm right. However, I may be right too soon. And, that's not the first time that's happened.

    The market especially concerns me now because in my fifteen years of conscious investing, I've never seen one like this one. 1987 beats 1982-1983, and it even tops 1972 when valuations got all out of whack and everyone was giddy. Fridays are supposed to be fun, even at work, but I feel like the old man in the wheelchair in *It's a Wonderful Life* while everyone lines up outside George Bailey's house throwing money. I'm missing the party. The Dow is up almost two percent in the past two days, a nice climb in such a short time. I've never cared what other people think, but that tenet of mine is being seriously challenged.

    I think my evening with Joan has weakened me. Sure, I know classes begin Monday and she has to get back to school. But, she departed as abruptly as she arrived. I made the right decision to not be with her. I know that to be true. However, the fog I'm in clues me in that I don't exactly believe that. It would have been nice to hold her and gaze at her and examine her one more time. I blew my chance, but was it really a chance? You bet. A risky chance. There. I think I'm resolved, but actually I've been flip-flopping since the morning I watched her sleep as I dressed for work. Something inside told me she would be there when I returned, and that same voice also told me to forget about it. Life has not been easy since Joan arrived the second time. When I think hard about the woman who lied to me then took my money, life with Joan was at times not easy the first time.

    The week has passed and the Dow remains unshorted. I'm holding one hundred thousand in cash I would want to commit to the project. By the Federal Reserve's Regulation T, that allows me to short safely a quarter million. Against this tape, however, I should be smart and back that down to two hundred. There are thirty Dow stocks spread over that two hundred, so that gives you six thousand dollars of shorts per Dow stock. That's an odd lot of less than forty shares of IBM, for instance. I don't know if it's worth it. I may have to eat my words. Eat my words. I just love it when that happens.

    Entering the condo from my garage, I want the apparition to be back. I'm so messed up right now. Just think how I would have been if we would have screwed. Scary.

    I lay my keys on my circular oak dining room table positioned at one end of the great room. The other end is the living room. Dividing the two is the manly brown leather sofa I slept on in my obstinacy and abstinence. Near the table is an oak corner cupboard in which china is displayed, some of the few things Joan allowed me to keep. Opposite the cupboard is the sliding glass door. I open the door to the sticky air, step onto my patio, and burn a Virginia Slim. The view south from my patio down the valley is exquisite. I can count on it. Never disappointing. Green, autumn colors, bare trees; any season, every day it's there.

Something catches my attention to the right. There's Joan, lying beside the pool. Damn.

Before I say anything, I want to make sure my mind is sane. I race back into my condo and walk briskly down the hallway to my bedroom. There I find her overnight bag on the bed. Jesus Christ! After gathering my thoughts, I walk back to the door. There is but one thing to do.

"Joan," I call from the patio. She raises her head from the pillow on the chaise. My chaise.

"Hi, darling!"

Joan's in a swimsuit. I'm not going over there. She's going to have to come to me. And she does. Slowly. Provocatively. Right here.

It's black, my favorite color. One piece. Joan looks lovely and righteous, like Christine. I don't want to even describe her body, except to say it's just like, and I've said it before, the first day I saw it. She's gotta go. Gone is sixty seconds.

"Hi, Mason," Joan says as she removes her shades. She takes the cigarette and draws. "How was the market today? Great guns, I bet." She does a double-take at the Slim. "This is a woman's cigarette," she says.

"I lost a bet to Vinny. If I couldn't quit, I smoke women's cigarettes. Two weeks later…"

Joan touches my face. "My poor baby."

I'm irritated. "Find your baby's key again?"

"Where you always leave it…baby." Joan's smiling. I generate a scowl. "Don't frown, Mason. Be happy."

"I was happy. Now, I don't know what to feel. This begs the question: why the hell did you come back?"

"Unfinished business," she says as she wraps her left arm into my right. Bain de Soleil leaves a little residue on my blazer. That's the least of my worries.

"What do you mean?"

"Let's go inside." We do just that. I sit on the love seat. Joan sits beside me. No wrap, no towel. I cringe.

Silence, then, "What do you want to do right now?" I ask. You idiot…

"What do you think?" she says, less than coy.

"No."

"Can I talk you into it?"

"Let me think about it. No."

"Look at me. I can't talk you into it?"

Yes, she is, but, "No, Joan. No way."

Joan places her left hand On Me. "I can tell you want to," she says sing-song.

"Maybe, just maybe. But, it ain't gonna happen." I stand in defiance. Big mistake. Not big, just obvious. Joan sits and giggles.

"C'mon, Mason," she says, breathlessly. "Let's do it." She stands and drapes herself around my neck and tries to kiss me. I jerk my head quickly. She remains as I pull back. I see in my periphery her eyes welling with tears. "You fucking son-of-a-bitch!" On that, Joan releases me and scoots down the hallway. The next thing I hear is my bedroom door slamming.

This can't be happening. She's taken over my life. Now, she's laid stake on my house. I'm kind of mad. I march back there and beat on the door. "Joan, goddamnit! Get out of there!"

"No!"

"Get out!"

"Never!"

"Then let me in!"

One minute. Then two. My patience is rewarded as the door softly opens. I pray she's still dressed. She is. Her face is firm and her arms are crossed. She's crying. I'm such a softy. "How can I help you?"

"To be honest with you, you prick, you can't help me. I'm beyond repair."

These are the hormones I pay Christine to avoid. "Oh, cut the melodrama, Kissinger."

"Then, just hold me." Against my better judgement, I do. A foot away from my bed. She feels good, too good. Sobs start. "Mason, remove my swimsuit from my body and fuck me. I order you."

"Let's talk about this," I say, trying the voice of reason route. Of course, if she drops the straps of her swimsuit and…all bets are off.

"I don't have time to talk!" Joan then grabs me by the neck and beats my head against the wall. Oww! I've never experienced anything like this. "You bastard! I don't have time for your bullshit! Do as I say!"

I've never hit a woman, but there's a first time for everything. I shove her back to the other wall. "Joan," I say, calmly, "you've lost it, completely lost it!"

Still leaning against the wall, she sobs, "You're damned straight I've lost it! I've lost it all! Mason, I'm dying."

"Right," I sarcastically say too quickly as she folds her face into her hands, twitching with more sobs.

"Don't you get it? I'm going to be dead!" she wails, face in her hands again.

For some reason, I begin to believe her. I'm afraid for her, and oddly, for me. That's probably because nothing in my life has prepared me for this. I want to be a good man. Joan seems to need me right now, so I'd better do what I can, whatever that is. It's inconsistent with how I've felt the past five years, but now there is no choice.

"Come here." She moves slowly to me, ending up in my arms. I feel her hips. I feel her breasts. God help me.

Joan twitches silently. I draw a blank, simply reacting to her. I truly don't know what to think, except perhaps to find out what the problem is.

"Can you talk to me?"

"No."

Whatever it is, I can't imagine how it must feel. We remain embraced.

"I'm dying."

I know this woman will lie to me for sport, but I squeeze her tighter. She does need me, the bitch.

"I have six months tops."

"Can you tell me what it is?"

"A brain tumor. Inoperable. I have a thing growing inside my head. This head, this head I have always trusted and depended on, this same head that held the brains that made me a highly regarded professor, the same brains that outwitted every man I've known, this head…this head is sick."

I draw a blank. "I'm sorry," is all I think of to say.

"The headaches were unbearable." Joan cries again as I hold her.

"Well, Joan," I clumsily say after a pause, "just hold on to this man, yet another of your outwitted quarry."

We're silent. "I'm sorry for what I did, Mason. But, this is not about you. This is about my failing body."

"Of course," I say, issuing the obvious reply. We snuggle in closer still, standing, avoiding the bed.

"The tumor was discovered several months ago," Joan says into my shoulder. "The doctors considered surgery for the tumor, but that wouldn't work, so I underwent chemo for everything else. I've never been sicker. It was the classic 'medicine worse than the illness.' I was gaunt, pale. This is a wig, by the way." She pauses with a sour smirk. "And the treatments were going to get me only a few extra months. To hell with it, I said. My last session, I pulled the needle out of my arm and walked. I'm not looking back. There's a quality of life issue to consider, and I'm going to leave a beautiful corpse."

I think she's being overly simplistic, but it's difficult to remain objective when she has her boobs drilled into my chest. "That's morbid, Joan, but I do understand how important that is to you."

"You want morbid?" she says, raising her face to smile into mine. "I've always told you that you are to die for."

I wince. That was a good one. "To be honest with you, Dr. Kissinger, you didn't have to do this to fall back into my arms. However, before you get any ideas, please realize I am in control here." I felt an overwhelming need to say that.

"Do you know what the absolute worst thing is?"

I'm waiting.

She drops down onto the edge of my bed, looks straight ahead, and cries. "The…worst…thing…is…my life has been stolen from me. Not the big picture life, but my *life*. Look at me, Mason. Will you look at me? I'm gorgeous! I'm gorgeous and I'm in my prime. And I'll never be able to be intimate with a man again. Never again! Truly intimate, Mason. Not just sex. True intimacy. I see the gawks. Never again. Do you know how that feels? I may as well be dead now! It sucks!" She punctuates by jumping up and clearing my dresser top with her arm. It all slams against the wall and falls to the floor. Joan looks into the mirror for the longest time, then sits, resting her forehead into the heels of her hands.

"Why can't you be just intimate?" Why am I asking this question?

"Because, this is the decade of the eighties. It's dangerous out there. And, I certainly won't have sex with Tom. He's *gay* now. I'm sure you love to hear that one."

I did love to hear that one, and I loved it so much I want to hear it again, but I have to say something appropriate. "You know, Joan, the most handsome attorneys are all gay." We laugh. She bit.

"I just can't do it with just any man," she says, still smiling. "As much as you'd like to think, I am not a one-night stand. I am not some whore. I'm not like that."

"I know." And, I'm so helpless. I'm so helpless because I've finally realized that I have never stopped loving Joan. For Chrissake, Mason! What are you saying? What are you about to say? But, it's obvious. I never have stopped loving her, but my anger forced me to put that love away in some sort of a box. Not to be seen, but never to be lost. Her admission is the climax of a three-day ordeal in which I never dreamed I would be involved. Especially this part, this confession of hers. Especially her misfortune, her hopeless, grave turn of events.

It's time I find the key to that box. I open my dresser drawer to reach for three condoms. Holding them up like a hand of poker, I say, "Joan." She looks at my full house, then looks at me. I think I see a sparkle in her eyes. "This should get us started, sweetmeat."

"No, Mason. You don't have to."

I'm...ready. "Yes," I say, "The day is young."

Joan takes a deep breath, stymied. I try to help.

"Let's put that swimsuit on the floor."

She smiles. "I have an even better idea." Joan stands and moves toward me, sultry face on high power. "Get a pair of scissors and cut it from my body. Slowly."

Wow. My Joan has returned.

Nine

8:30AM
Saturday August 22, 1987
In my bed
Dow Jones Industrial Average: anything pleases me

I feigned hard slumber as she walked out of the shower. As she dressed. As she packed. Rolling over once to make it look even more real, I sleep as she kneels to my side to softly kiss my forehead. Remaining motionless, I hear Joan open the living room door, close it, walk, open her car door, close it, then fire it up and drive away. We certainly did not want to talk to each other.

That was some great sex. This should keep me until Monday. Ex-married couples should sleep with each other more often. In fact, the sex was so good...well...it doesn't get any better than Joan. Granted, complete celibacy is out of the question, but for the foreseeable future Christine will be a disappointment.

I pull myself from my bed and step over the three dead soldiers on the carpet. Looking in the mirror, I decide I don't look too bad naked. Boyish face, brown hair, nice V, legs. Great sex will make you see things your way. I smoke Virginia Slims, I drink Arns, I don't work out, but I eat right. One out of four. Good genes, I guess. Good genes and a healthy diet. Sure, my lifestyle will eventually catch up with me, but I think I'll at least make it to the bottom of the next bear market.

Upon completing the survey of my dominating physical features, I fetch the white lightweight terry robe from my closet. I wrap it around my body, savoring every step I take. Glancing over my shoulder, I proudly wink at the bed. Demolition woman, can I be your man?

I move quietly over the living room floor. Deciding this is not the neighborhood in which one stands on the diving board with arms high and screams something about having great sex, I remain indoors. It's tempting. Very humid, but tempting. To hell with it. I grab a cigarette and a lighter from the top of the television and head…

Something draws me to the coffee table. I turn to see a business envelope. Let's open it. I pick it up and bring it waist-level. No name and no seal. Without hesitating I reach in to find a cashier's check from A & I Bank in Montani. Well, fuck. It's payable to Mason Bricker in the amount of eight hundred thousand dollars. Wow. Damn. Wow. One more look; that's an eight, two zeroes, a comma, three zeroes, a dot, and two more zeroes. It's real.

This is one hell of a taxable event, but I have a few months to worry about that. Live for the moment. I check the pulse of my emotions and find them surprisingly calm. Surprisingly calm, maybe because I just always knew the money would make its way back to me. And with interest. Now I can fulfill my dreams and short the Dow.

I bet Christine never made this much in one night.

10:00 AM
Saturday August 22, 1987
Driving the Olds to the bank, wearing a navy polo, olive shorts, loafers, and no underwear
Dow Jones Industrial Average: when you're not wearing underwear, the mundane things in life just don't matter

I feel paranoid driving downtown with an eight hundred thousand dollar cashier's check resting on the passenger seat. No, I *am* paranoid. I decided in the shower that if anyone approached me to take my check away from me, I will die to protect the check. In fact, I'm having maternal instincts with my check. After having gone through a sixty-six month gestation…hey, that's not a bad metaphor. Other than that, I'm still neutral about the whole money deal.

What about Joan? I just don't know. Last night could have been her final farewell. It is true she's sick, physically as well as emotionally. Somewhere in the passion of the second go her wig shifted. She simply made the adjustment and went back to it. I don't think even Joan would carry out such an elaborate ruse by shaving her head. So, she did need me. I guess I needed her, too. Who's to know? It's weird. Despite the apparent needs, the entire experience was like a consummation of indifference. Of course, I'm making the analysis only hours afterward. But, I can't ignore the non-feeling I'm feeling. Maybe I should monitor this. The woman is dying and I'm acting as if it's no big deal. I mean, I care as a person. I respect what she's going through. Joan is brave. However, as my lover? Maybe she's just not my lover anymore.

What Joan is is technically another man's wife. I'm sure I'll pay for last night. I'll ask Father Michael. It was too good. Gotta back out on that anti-celibacy thing. As penance, I'll fire Christine.

Back to money. Why eight hundred thousand? Quick arithmetic says about nine percent compounded annually will grow over half again in five years. Nine percent was the risk-free rate plus inflation during that time. Sounds like Joan consulted my engineers.

I was already warmed up to the fact that I have – had – only one fifty K in cash with a fifty thousand a year self-imposed earnings plateau and a fifteen hundred dollar a month sex habit eating into my cash. I'll definitely fire Christine. It is irony that Christine will be history after I have the capacity to pay for two Christines. Now, there's something that never occurred to me.

And, now, my life. My increasingly complicated life? Eight hundred grand will simplify my life. My life? Yeah. Right.

I turn into the third row at the drive-thru at Ashton National in The H. These girls are going to drop a brick when they see my check, especially when it comes out of an industrial tan 1979 Oldsmobile Delta 88. How can that car have that check? I'd rather be lucky than good.

The pneumatics tube sucks the check and my deposit ticket through to the girls. I think – share the wealth. I mean, Mason, just how much fuckin' money do you need? Tonight I pound Arns. Sunday I recover. Monday I call Michael. That's the plan. As a priest, he'll know what to do.

"Can I have some identification?" asks the female voice in the speaker.

I step out of the car. With hands extended from my side, I scream, "Christ, Beth! It's me!" I see her laugh.

Beth grabs the mike. "What are you doing tonight?" We laugh again.

"You goldbricker!"

"Call me."

"You're married."

"Then just buy me something." Beth is a teller; blonde, pretty, middle-age, loud, bony, and inappropriate. We've been friendly since the day five years ago when she opened my account. I just love her attitude.

The projectile returns. I get back in the Olds and retrieve it. The document inside makes it official: $800,098 in my checking account. No overdrafts for a long, long time. The Federal Deposit Insurance Company says if AshNat does a header, I get only one-eighth of that wad back. However, I trust Beth and her forty-year-old institution. You have to put your money somewhere.

I do have to give some of this away. Mister Philanthropy. I don't think I am. Twenty bucks in the plate at each mass. Twenty bucks a month to the United Way. That's all for me. It's now time to get better. Keep it in perspective. A hundred to Michael. Five hundred to short the Dow. And I bank another two hundred to use as I bargain with God to save my ass from the consequences of all my future transgressions.

Ten

12:30 PM
Tuesday August 25, 1987
With Ally Fenz at The Café, after shorting the Dow
Dow Jones Industrial Average: 2,751 – an all-time interday high

The Café is charming in that it looks as if the proprietor cleaned out a couple of attics, dusted, then arranged all the stuff into one very small twenty foot by forty foot space. Give it credit for being clean, however, in a haphazard way. Statuettes, vases, boxes, books, knick-knacks; it's everywhere, surrounding unmatched tables with equally unmatched chairs. Art, ranging from landscapes to the nearly incomprehensible, adorns three red walls that lie between the tacky drop ceiling and the classy black-and-white mosaic tile floor. The coffee bar rests against the back wall, with all its necessary espresso and cappuccino equipment. Beside that is an assortment of overpriced pastries that can't possibly be good for you they're so good. A great get-away is The Café.

Fenz and I are by the big window looking onto Hale Street, across which is Green Boy's and The H. She has a lemonade and a muffin; I a double espresso and a short water. There is an aluminum deco table between us. We sit on two metal-tube chairs that look like they escaped from my grandmother's kitchen. Her seat is padded electric blue. Mine is chartreuse.

"Let's do it," she says as she leans in.

I pause. "I was flustered for a few seconds, but I recovered, realizing you are talking about shorting the Dow."

As with every day, Ally Fenz looks great. She is one cute female with a cute dark pixie atop a cute face, a cute summer tan, and a tight little five-four cute body complete with cute perky boobs and cute legs, looking like Mary Ann has been rescued intact from Gilligan's Island. She did the cute female route: Penn Hills High School homecoming queen, Sweetheart of Sig Eps at Pitt, a stint as a hostess in Las Vegas, and now she's settled in with Wylie and me. Ally must be bored to tears. Today, Fenz is wearing a white sleeveless top and a green knee-length sausage-casing skirt. Her brown eyes are filled with eyelashes and reflect her smile. "Just a few seconds?" she asks, her mezzo allure on high beam.

"You're a trap, Fenz. You're a harassment lawsuit waiting to happen."

"Shut up and tell me about shorting the Dow," she says with a grin.

"All right. Here goes. We're betting prices will fall, so we borrow the stocks and sell them now when everyone's joyous and wants to buy them, then we buy them and return them when everyone gets pissed off and wants to sell them, hopefully at lower prices." It's sunny and unbearably hot and I'm excited. I'm sure sweat will soon show through my navy hopsack blazer and drip down onto my charcoal gray Haggars. "Thirty stocks are in the Dow, Ally. I spread most of them among six hundred eighty thousand or so. I put in a half million cash to cover the Fed's Reg T requirement for shorting, giving me some breathing room just in case Corncob hangs in there for a while."

"Excuse me," Ally says, back stiff, boobs out, and eyes wide.

"Yes."

"I know your account. You didn't have all that money. Where did you find all that money?"

"A dead relative."

A pause. "Good. For a minute, I thought you were a dealer."

"No," I say, both elbows on the table. "The short. The short is my drug."

"Why?" she asks.

"Honey, you ask the difficult questions. I'll tell you later after I figure it out myself."

She smiles and leans in again. "I'd have you no other way."

"Oh, Christ, Fenz. Thank you. Now, six eighty K. Okay, you know the Dow Jones Industrial Average consists of thirty stocks of some of the biggest and most important companies on the planet. To get the value of the Dow, you simply add up the prices of the thirty and divide the sum by a predetermined number. You with me?"

Ally nods to the affirmative.

"However, I decided to not short all thirty. There are nine I want to spare the humiliation."

She rests her chin on her fists. "Okay."

"First, metals. U.S. Steel and Bethlehem Steel and Alcoa."

"Metal is Pittsburgh. We don't short metal. We don't short Pittsburgh. Of course."

"I told you you'd be good at this. Next, oil. Chevron, Exxon, and Texaco. It's free enterprise to short, but shorting oil goes against Judeo-Christian virtues. Oil is the blood of our beast."

A pause, then a stare. "I've heard you say some strange things, Mason, but that one just topped them all," Ally deadpans.

"What's so strange about that, anyway?" I continue, "Now, here's where it gets complicated and personal." Two women dressed summer casual at the next table simultaneously glance at us. For an instant, I care. Then, I don't. "No Primerica. I know, I know. They're competitors and their stock will pay the price. However, I have a first cousin whom I worshipped when I was a kid. He's a finance whiz and an executive VP there. Couldn't do it."

"So, you actually do have some loyalties." She's smiling.

"I'm loyal to you, aren't I? Remember when..." I say, thinking back with a grin to her escapade with a married man, a client of mine.

"Don't mention it. Who's next?"

"Woolworth." I realize I have to quell my excitement and keep my voice softer. "Woolworth. I used to shop for Christmas gifts at F. W. Woolworth. These trinkets I got my mother, I thought gold always had some green on it. I was precious."

"That's sweet," Ally says.

"No, Fenz. Not sweet. You have to be a prick to short."

Ally smiles and touches my hand. "In your own way, you're sweet."

My concentration is broken. I actually think it may be possible with Fenz. "Where was I?"

"Woolworth."

"Oh, and Westinghouse. Stan the Money Man. God rest his soul. Stanley Mumphord, the master of the short. Shorts got me through college, then a lot more. Stan always told me to never short Westinghouse. I didn't ask why. Knowing Stan, it was either scotch or sex."

"That explains you."

"Dangerously," I reply as the two thirtysomething ladies in business suits sitting opposite the casual women are now officially interested in our conversation.

"Okay," Ally says, "That's…three…six…nine. Where do we go from here?"

"I sold short with equal amounts of money seventeen stocks. They are, in alpha order, Allied-Signal, American Express—"

"I'm writing this down…go on." Ally scribbles on her paper pad.

"Reach out and touch AT&T, fly-me-to-the-moon Boeing, I'd like to buy the world a Coke, DuPont, a Kodak moment, GE we bring good things to life, Goodyear, International Paper, Mickey D's, 3M, Navistar, goddamn that beer and cigarettes pusher man Philip Morris, Sears for obvious reasons, Bhopal's favorite son Union Carbide, and United Technologies. By the way, forgive my Carbide crack. The disaster was sabotage by an angry Hindu."

"I didn't know that."

"Makes sense to me," I say as I sip the espresso.

Ally stares at her paper. She looks at me. "Short selling. It is un-American, isn't it?"

"It's Fascism, Communism, and anti-Disneyism all rolled into one pathetic, twisted belief system. But, whatthefuck? Somebody's gotta do it."

A pause. "Where's IBM?" she asks.

"This, my dear, is where it gets fun."

"You're so cute when you have fun," Ally says with a slight grin.

"Fenz…" I'm about to say something salacious, but I stop since she's probably heard it all. This morning. Anyway the casual women get up and walk to the coffee bar. A tall, plain college girl in faded red flannel unbuttoned over a t-shirt, ratty jeans, and black high top Chuck Taylors is there to wait on them. Flannel? August? "IBM is one of four stocks I'm going to overweight."

"Why, and what does that mean?" she asks as she takes another sip of her lemonade.

"It means I shorted more than the others because they piss me off."

"That's scientific," Ally comments as she pinches off a bit of her muffin and hands it to me. I eat it.

"IBM. They're so fucking arrogant. They passed me up for a sweet sales job a few years ago. I jumped through all the hoops, but one guy said I had a 'checkered college career.' I'm just not a team player, Fenz."

"News flash. Who's next?"

"Merck. Pharmaceuticals are way overpriced in this country. In Canada, you can get the same medicine for a fraction of the cost in the U. S. They're screwing defenseless sick people."

There's silence at our table. "You're serious, aren't you?" she asks.

"Yes. Next, General Motors. Listen to this. One of my engineers tells me that at DuPont in West Virginia, Ford has them make auto paint. All auto manufacturers brag about their quality programs, but Ford's is the best. They are so good they can have DuPont cook the batch of paint in advance, then test it. If Ford doesn't like it, they don't buy it. Not to worry for DuPont. GM buys it. That's GM. Garbage-Mobile."

"What about your Olds?" Fenz asks quickly.

"Doesn't count. I own it for image."

"What image are you trying to show with a tan Olds?"

"The image that I don't care about image."

"You're impossible." She winks. Whoa. "By the way," Ally continues, "how's Wylie? I haven't talked to him much outside the office."

"I get the feeling Wylie has separated himself from me. Sure, we still ride together, but John's leaned on him pretty hard, you know, Wylie being a leader and all. I am a radical."

"And, you love every minute of it."

"Yeah."

Ally finally takes a bite of her muffin. "You said four."

"Procter and Gamble."

"What happened with them?"

"Those androgynous pixies flying around the moon, the clouds, the rainbow and the lighthouse? It's witchcraft."

"I have no idea what you are talking about," she says, at least once a day.

"No, really, I look warily at companies that own our lives. That's P and G. And, that's it."

Ally examines the notes she has taken. She looks up to me, looks down, then looks up to the original watercolor behind me, then back to me. "It's strange. Very strange. That's why I like it."

"I've corrupted you," I say as a belt down the lukewarm sludge from my tiny French coffee cup.

"I let you."

"Well, babe, after all this, the Fed lets me have one fifty. Wanna go to Europe?"

"Tempting," she says in a very tempting way.

"I can't go on without you. It's the least I can do."

"A labor of love, Mason. A labor of love."

"Shut up, Fenz."

We grow quiet with smiles. I sip espresso, glancing at Ally, then glancing again, only to find her both times looking at me. What the hell is up with that? Then, Fenz' grin turns toward the evil side.

"Seriously, Bricker," she says. "Devil's advocate. What makes you think this will work? You're going against the whole firm. Doesn't that scare you?"

I lean to her. "Thank you for asking that question. Going against the firm is precisely the reason I am not scared. And it is precisely the reason it will work."

"Okay. I'll buy that. I see the crazed looks in the guys' eyes. Still the devil's advocate, though. I've heard all your bullshit before. Put it to me again so I can pick it apart."

A tall blonde wearing a pink dress enters. The sidewalk lunch crowd is thinning, but I'm cranked. "Okay, hon. I'm ready. Okay."

"This I have to hear," Fenz says with a grin. "Again. And, again."

"There are—you're just trying to make a fool of me!" I exclaim.

"No, Mason. I'm just kidding. But, I do want to hear it…again."

"Well, you're stuck, so here goes. There are three components of a market, any market near and dear to you. The shoe market, in your case. Nice yellow pumps, by the way."

"Thank you. Now keep talking." She's still smiling.

"The three components are: sentiment, the people, the buyers, the sellers – monetary, the money, the fuel – and momentum, the surge, the rush. First, sentiment…it's always wrong at extremes—"

"That doesn't make any sense."

"Listen to me. It takes change to move a market. If all you ladies who own pumps decide you want slings, then that's good for the slings market and bad for the pumps market. Stock buyers make a bull a bull. Stock holders just mark time. I know this is sexist—"

"And it is."

"Okay, sexist, but if you already own pumps and you don't need any more pumps, you do nothing for the pumps market. But, you might affect the slings market if you want to change."

The Café is my stage and I'm giving a soliloquy on my favorite subject. "A person is most pleased with something after that person buys it. A lot of people are pleased with the stock market right now because they just bought it. You really like your pumps because they're shiny and new and because you just bought them and your feet and your legs look great in them," I pause, thinking of Ally's feet and legs, "even if you bought so many you probably can't afford to buy any more. Likewise, if everyone is justifying their purchases of their shiny and new stocks by being very happy with them and their statements look great with their shiny and new stocks on them, even though they bought so many they're fully invested and they can't buy any more, where is the future buying going to come from? Answer: it ain't gonna happen."

"More DA." Ally says quickly. I guess she didn't like my analogy. "Then, Mason, what happened in April when you decided to sell everyone out? I've done my research. That was three hundred points ago."

I smile. "Two hundred fifty points ago. Ten percent ago. I was spooked by rising interest rates. The fuel was becoming more expensive so I thought that would slow the market down. I was wrong, because I underestimated the heights to which their own foolishness would carry them. The extreme got even more extreme. But, Fenz, just as my hero Marty Zweig says, it is now time to part company with the crowd, because this party is getting sloppy. It's a toga orgy out there."

"They're all making fun of you," Ally says with a faint frown.

"Fenz!"

"DA! They're all making fun of you!"

"You know I don't care."

"Yes, you do. And that's no DA."

"No!" I say. "Now, back to April, damnit. I made a mistake by selling into a hot market."

"It's still hot."

"It looks hot, but it's taking a lot of energy to sustain it, much less take it anywhere. Today's stock market is like a glistening stainless steel DeLorean spinning on ice. Looks great, but the engine is turning at high RPM and it's going nowhere." The tall blonde takes her to-go cup and leaves.

"So," Ally starts, then stops, then starts again. "So, the crowd's too happy, interest rates are up, and we're all sloppy. How do you know? And, if you know, why doesn't everyone else see it?" She finishes by balling up her muffin wrapper and draining her lemonade.

"Instrument flying," is my simple reply.

"What in the hell are you talking about?"

"The market is like piloting an airplane at night. Investors are in the dark as to what's ahead. Like pilots, you can't see the ground, or the sky, so you have to trust your gauges on your dashboard. In investing, your gauges are called market indicators. You have to trust your indicators to figure out what's really happening out there in the dark and make sure you're not flying upside-down."

"This is getting complicated," Fenz says, slowly shaking her head.

I ignore her. "For instance, here's one. I got it from Marty Zweig. Investment advisors who write newsletters publish publicly their opinions. The information is available on those opinions, so they're easy to count. After counting them over time, history shows that when they go one way, you go the other way. Like now."

"But, they're experts!"

"Individually, they're experts. But, as a group, they all own pumps. And, they're emotional, too. Because they sell their newsletters to the emotional crowd, they in a way reflect the sentiment of the crowd. If the crowd is wrong at extremes, it stands to reason that investment advisors are wrong at extremes. And, the numbers from the past show they are."

"Is that it?" Fenz asks with a hint of impatience.

"No. Marty also says you can also count the number of optimistic, bullish ads run by optimistic, bullish investment advisors in financial journals such as *Barron's*. Just like people. They run ads to sell more newsletters. The happier the crowd, the happier the ads. Therefore, the happier the ads, the gloomier the market forecast is."

"Now, is that it?"

"No. I watch money and valuation." Fenz gives me the blank face, yet I continue. "Take the Dow price to earnings ratio."

"Take it where?"

"Okay. You know, the P/E is how much stock price you have to pay for a dollar's earnings. That's the stock's value. Earnings are like shoes. They're what you want and need. The stock price is like how much it costs to buy a pair of shoes."

"Okay. I understand."

"Take that P/E. Now invert it."

"You've lost me."

I'm unfazed. "Inverting the price/earnings is earnings over price. Instead of dollars per pair of shoes, the inverse is pairs of shoes per dollar, or in your case, a multitude of pairs per hundreds of dollars. That's called the shoes yield. How many shoes per dollar. The shoes yield. The earnings yield. How many earnings per dollar."

"Okay," Ally says. "How many pairs of shoes per hundred dollars."

"Now we're getting there. Think bank certificates of deposit. The interest yield. How much interest per dollar. Now, when the earnings yield of the Dow is significantly less than the interest yield of government guaranteed, risk-free five-year CD at AshNat, the market is way overvalued and stock prices will not go up and will most likely fall."

"Huh? Oh, that's how my CDs are paying now. That's pretty good. And, that's bad for the stock market?"

"It's not bad…well, yes it is. Soon, money will come out of stocks to go for the guarantee because the guarantee is paying so well. That's how it is now. Stock prices are up. Interest rates are up. They're going against each other, multiplying the effect. So, the market is overvalued. Way overvalued. Way, way overvalued."

"Oh, no," Fenz says, clutching her hair. "You've confused me again, Mason. I hate that feeling."

"Look at it this way. Why should you buy slings at Kaufmann's in downtown Pittsburgh when the same slings are less expensive at Shoe Carnival in Moon Township? You're making a lot less money holding stocks with a lot of risk than you can holding a bank CD with no risk. Why take on more risk and not get paid for it? You should get paid more to be riskier. You should buy the same shoes for less money. Likewise, you should buy investments for as little money as possible. In the stock market, these unnatural aberrations are extremes that nature corrects. And, no one fools Mother Nature."

"Mason," Ally says as she stands, "I think I finally get it, but no wonder you don't have any clients. Most of the time, they can't understand a word you say."

"Kiss my ass, Fenz."

"You're a charmer," she says with a smile as I stand.

"Time to go. Let's get back to work," I say.

"I have been working."

Eleven

8:20 AM
Wednesday August 26, 1987
After morning mass at The Church of the Blessed Sacraments
Dow Jones Industrial Average: 2,722 – 1.1 percent off all-time high

"God," I whisper, kneeling behind a pew, "I defer to the Prayer of St. Francis of Assisi. You know the one I'm talking about. 'Grant me the courage to change the things I can, the serenity to accept the things I cannot change, and the wisdom to know the difference.' Or something like that.

"I've given myself a complicated life. There are reasons, I'm sure, but help me untie the knots I create with the scrapes I get myself into. Funny how I've never confessed about Christine. Abject shame will do that to you. Then, I had sex with a married woman, though you have to give me credit for the fact that Joan needed to be with me, and I guess I needed to be with her. Hence, Christine.

"Michael would do well with me if he were paid according to the magnitude of the sins I'm going to talk to him about. I'd blow any vow of poverty he may have. I know You've considered what You could have done with all the money I squandered on a prostitute. For five years. Well, it's time to screw up the courage and change. I'll stop. I promise. Please forgive me for my sins with Christine and Joan and against everything

You. As penance, I won't have sex or touch myself like that until You tell me to. Okay, I'll take it one step further. I won't even kiss, unless it's the monsignor's ring.

"In addition, let me begin to make up for the money I gave for the illicit sex by giving You some money. Two hundred thousand bucks. As promised. Really, it's more than I promised, but I'm not looking for a pat on the back. I've got the check ready for Michael here in my hand. Thank You for Your time and for all You've done for me. And, while You're at it, protect me as I hold a large short position. I did it yesterday morning, but You know that already. I hope I can help mankind in some way after I close out. I ask You, please grant me the wisdom to do so. Again, thanks. And, keep up the good work."

I make the sign of the cross, then look ahead. Michael is coming my way, walking from the modest altar that sits before the Touchdown Jesus hanging from the wall. Blessed Sacraments is an old stone and wood structure about half the size of a basketball court. Seating is tiered and aligned with a long radius for an amphitheatre feel. However, the vaults along the side and the behind the altar are ornate enough to make the church a scaled down version of a cathedral. I'll call it folksy old world.

Michael and I are alone. He's put together as sturdy as his church. It's been years now, but my buddy looks as if he could suit up today and take on the Dallas Cowboys again. Third down linebacker. Abusive hitter. Eye of the tiger. Square jaw of a gladiator. Two Pittsburgh Steelers Super Bowl rings. Local Ashton Township celebrity and priest. My priest. The shoulders as wide as the pews are long, the upside-down delta of his six-two frame, and the huge arms of cut black onyx let you know that this instrument of peace can still kick some butt.

"Mason."

"Padre."

I sit. Michael sits in front of me to my left.

"It's always good to see you here," Michael says as his baritone resonates from the walls. "How's your business? Great guns, I bet."

"Yeah. Look, Michael, I know you're busy," I say nervously, "and I'm in constant need of absolution, but I've already prayed to God about all that and He's going to give me another chance. To show my appreciation, I have something for you."

"Mason, we're all sinners. You want to talk about it?"

"Maybe," I say to my surprise.

"Is this a confession?"

After no time, I cave. "If it isn't, I'm missing a good opportunity."

"Let's call that a 'yes.'" Michael moves back to my pew. I scoot down. Guys just can't be that close to each other. We face at an angle. The priest bows his head. It's going to happen, right here. I oblige with the sign of the cross.

"May God, who has enlightened every heart, help you to know your sins and trust in his mercy."

I begin. "Amen. Bless me Father, for I have sinned. It's been six months since my last confession, but six years since my last true confession. Father, I've been having a weekly tumble with a prostitute since the divorce, and Friday night I topped it off by screwing a married woman. Sorry for the graphic nature of my explanation, but there's no more accurate way to put it."

Michael is silent for the longest time. "Mason," he finally says into my eyes, "the priest in me always knows what to say in these cases. The priest in me knows that those who do what you did are missing something in their hearts, their souls, and they act as they do to salve that wound, that hole. To give yourself a chance, you know that you must do what you can to not only treat the wound, but to heal it."

Michael pauses and places his hand on my shoulder. "In addition, you have been my friend through almost all my adult life. The friend in me also knows what to say, because we have talked of your pain. I think your actions say that you are unduly burdening yourself with Joan. The residual effects of your relationship with Joan are the wounds you need to heal. In my opinion, you couldn't have done anything to make it different, Mason. The issues were hers. Release yourself from Joan."

"I eventually did. She's the married woman."

Michael squinted and actually laughed, albeit quietly. We grow silent again as he thinks of something to say to my absurdity. "I apologize for being inappropriate, Brick...you know, in the grand scheme, and under your circumstances, the best thing you can do is to not make your life shame-based because of that. Even though most call what you did mortal sins, you're no good to anybody that way. Move on."

"I'll try, Father," I say. "Ironically, I think it'll be easier now since I was with her again."

Michael scowls. That remark didn't please him. "You know, to make all sacraments valid, you must confess everything. Have you?"

Probably, no but, "To the best of my knowledge, Father."

"Do you still own a rosary?" the priest asks.

I feel a flutter in my stomach because I know my rosary is in the drawer with my condoms. "Yes, I do."

"Your penance is to pray the Rosary."

"That's all? I should be cleaning out horse stables with my bare hands for what I've done."

"Penance is not punishment," Father Michael says. "It's an opportunity to grow."

"Okay," I say, "The Rosary it is." I bow my head for the Act of Contrition. "O my God, I am heartily sorry for having offended You, and I detest all my sins because I dread the loss of heaven and the pains of hell, but most of all because they offend You, my God, Who are all good and deserving of my love. I firmly resolve, with the help of Your grace, to sin no more and to avoid the near occasions of sin."

"In the name of the Father, and of the Son, and of the Holy Spirit," Father says as he holds his right hand over my head, "I absolve you of all sins. Go in peace with God in your heart."

I make the sign of the cross. Michael moves back to the pew in front of me. He's a big man who needs a lot of room. "What's in the envelope?" he asks as he points to it, smiling. "You have something for us?"

"Yes."

"I was just kidding," he says seriously.

"I'm going to give you this money and I don't want you to put up any fuss. Okay?"

Michael looks at me with a wary eye. "We'll see."

We're motionless except for me handing the envelope to him. He opens the unsealed flap, pulls out the check, examines it, and drops his jaw. "I can't take this," he says directly into my eyes.

"Take it. It's legal and legally binding. A dead relative left me four times that much, so I'm not hurting. It's the least I can do."

Michael looks at the check again. "This is a very generous gift. Extremely generous."

"Here's what I ask," I say as I lean back, "Take one fifty and do whatever you need to do for the parish. Take the other fifty and donate it to neurological research, especially in the treatment of diseases of the brain."

"Why can't you do it yourself?"

"I want to remain anonymous."

He sighs. "I understand that, maybe, and I'll help you out in any way I can, but this is too much to give to the church. I don't know what to do with it."

"Michael, don't you guys have conferences about these things? It has to be a requirement for a priest that to keep his collar he must immediately know ten places to put one hundred fifty thousand dollars. Be true to your scroll, man. Go for it."

Michael sits and thinks. "There are many people in need. You have no idea how far this money will go. I must say, however, I'm both shocked and happy."

"Good," I say. "Remember, anonymous. If my name appears on a plaque or if anybody even finds out about this, I'm comin' after you." I'm almost serious.

Michael smiles his linebacker smile. "I'd like to see that."

"Just give me a few months to stop smoking. Michael, I'm not kidding. I have a reputation to uphold."

He rests his right hand on my shoulder. "This would only further your true reputation."

"I don't think so."

"Mason, as much as you like to think of yourself as bad, and as much as you think you're not a good man, you're wrong."

I pause. I pause again. "It doesn't feel that way to me. I'm just not up to it."

"You're wrong."

"I'll admit. There was a time. But, those days are long, long gone."

"And, they're not forgotten. Not by anyone who was there." Michael lays the palm of his hand on my hair. Wow. A rare double blessing. I bow my head. "Mason Bricker, you are one of God's most faithful servants. In your younger days, you sacrificed for fairness and for the equality of the oppressed. Today, you've done it again. Tomorrow, you will be called. Be prepared to do God's work when you are called. He will need you. I bless you in the name of the Father, and of the Son, and of the Holy Spirit." Michael makes the sign of the cross over me.

"Thank you, Father.'

"You are the man, Mason. Always have been. Always will be."

"I'll try," is all I can manage to get out.

"Now," Michael says, "one more question." He sweeps his left hand toward the walls. "Which one of these fine stained glass windows can I dedicate to you?"

"Got—"

"Kidding!" he says as he laughs a hearty laugh.

"Clergy humor," I say. "You guys are weak."

"I have to get some laughs around here somehow."

"At the expense of your parishioners?"

"Yes," he says, smiling.

"And now, it's time for another episode of 'The Evil Priest.'"

"Get out of here before I wail on ya."

"Later," I say, standing and turning to him. We shake hands.

"Thank you again, Mason."

"Don't mention it." I walk up the aisle. This church has me thinking. The next time I'm married, it's going to be here. Someday I'll have a woman on my arm. Nothing would improve my mood more than a wife.

Maybe I should improve my mood first.

Twelve

4:10 PM
Thursday August 27, 1987
In the office of Dr. Diane Gilson, psychologist
Dow Jones Industrial Average: 2,639 – 4.1 percent off all-time high

"Can I get you coffee?" Diane asks after she walks into the room.

"No, thank you," I reply.

She sits. "So, tell me...how are things?"

Diane's office looks as if the designer was inspired by a sitting room from *Better Homes and Gardens*. Rich blue walls and hardwood oak floors surround my ivory upholstered love seat and the matching sofa to my left. A mahogany coffee table rests on an Oriental rug, making a triangle with the love seat and the sofa. An end table sits in the corner between them. There are two windows with sheers and drapes of ivory, with a pale pink stripe. One window is behind Diane and one is directly across from me. A print of still life, an etching, and a watercolor of flowers are tastefully hung about. Her desk is several feet away from me, spotless and also mahogany. The only things clinical are a black telephone on the far corner of the desk and a bookcase of neatly arranged books. I could live here. For the past two years since Vinny's death, it seems I have.

Diane is average height and weight for a woman in her mid forties. She's pretty with full, curled red hair and green eyes, highlighted today by her nicely cut lime dress. However, nothing about Diane strikes me as attractive. That's because when you're in therapy, the absolute last thing you want to happen is to be attracted to your therapist. It's a hundred bucks an hour here. If I'm hot for Diane, I may as well light five twenties with my Bic for all the good the whole experience would do me. Nothing about her strikes me as attractive. Nothing. Except her feet.

I've taken so long considering her question, I've almost forgotten it. "Fine," I finally say.

"Business must be going great guns," she says with a grin, facing me with her legs crossed. Today she's wearing lime sandals, extending from which are her tanned bare toes.

"Yeah," I say.

"Is it exciting to be part of this market?"

"Oh, yes," I answer.

"I bet your clients are happy."

"As happy as they can be."

Diane pauses and smiles slightly. "Do you want to talk about it?" she asks in her pleasant, precise voice.

"Oh, you know me," I reply quickly.

"That's a resounding 'yes,' I presume," Diane says, still grinning.

"You presume correctly."

"Clock's ticking."

That comment makes me laugh. It's so typical of the reserved-to-witty swings Diane can take at any moment.

"I shorted the market."

She pauses. "I don't know what that means."

"It means I think prices are going to drop, so I sold the market short."

"Sold short." Diane takes a few moments to consider that. "Could that possibly be where the expression 'selling someone short' comes from? Negative on the market? Negative on a person? Am I right?"

"I think. It makes sense."

"How does one sell short in the stock market?"

"It's a reverse buy. You sell first, borrowing stock to complete that transaction. Then you buy back to cover the stock you borrowed, the stock you were short. Hopefully, the price is lower."

"So, if the price falls, you make money."

"That's the plan."

"What's the risk?" Diane asks in a therapist's manner.

"It's like this. When you buy a stock, the ultimate risk is the stock becoming worthless, with a price of zero. The ultimate risk when you sell short is the stock price could go to infinity. Outer space is a lot farther away than the dirt. Twenty to zero is a lot less painful than twenty to two hundred."

"I see," she says. There must be a week in psych school on how to say 'I see.' "I know a lot of people in the market. I'm in the market. But, I've never known anyone who sold short."

"You know the Kennedys?"

"The Kennedys? Like Teddy? JFK?"

"Right. Joseph Kennedy sold short in the stock market crash in 1929. That's how he built the family fortune. Selling short and bootleg scotch."

"I didn't know that," Diane says sincerely.

"Yep," I proudly say, "Selling short is the foundation of modern liberal politics."

Silence. "Have you ever sold short?"

"A few times."

"How did you do?"

"Pretty well."

"When?"

"There was a bad market in 1973, '74 – during Watergate and the Arab oil embargo."

"Mason…you were in high school."

"My broker showed me the way. We made a lot of money."

"You must have really trusted him. That was after your father died."

"He was my father's friend. My father saved his life in the war."

"I see. I remember, too. Watergate, oil embargoes, must have been a bad economy. It was obvious, I guess."

"Not really. Bull markets climb a wall of worry and, despite the beliefs of today's consensus, bear markets fall through floors of optimism. The Dow was at 1,000 in 1972, headed for 500. 1972 was the year of The Nifty Fifty, fifty stocks that were considered 'can't miss.' Locks. One-decision stocks. Buy and hold forever. People were certain, ecstatic, cocky. You're a psychologist. You should know what happened next without reading about it."

She pauses again. "You were in high school."

"That's right."

"Sixteen, seventeen years old."

"Yeah. I'm proud of that."

"Very impressionable," Diane says.

"You're going somewhere with this, aren't you?"

"And, I'm taking you with me. There you were, Mason, in 1973, shorting the market in which most others owned stocks and were watching them lose value."

"Okay."

"Fighting the status quo."

"I wasn't fighting anyone." I squirm. "Stan and I were just trying to make a buck. A legal and ethical buck."

"Think about it," Diane says, shifting her crossed legs and stretching her feet toward me. Well, there goes that no-attraction thing. "Shorting stocks. Against many. Being led by an adult—"

"Stan was my father's friend, Diane. I trusted him."

"No value judgments, Mason. No good or bad or right or wrong. Just going against the grain. Going against the grain with a man who could be called your hero."

"I called him Stan the Money Man we were so close. We were right. It was right. It was the right thing to do."

There is silence. "Two years later, you were fighting again."

My back straightens reflexively. I'm pissed. "That was against wrong! My black teammates were getting screwed."

"Yes, they were. We've talked about that. You were right and courageous. And as we've talked about, at what price?" Diane asks with the calm one would expect from a shrink.

"It was nothing."

"You were expelled," Diane says as a matter of fact.

"So?"

"You were fighting authority."

"It had to be done."

"But, why you? Why did *you* have to do it?"

"Because I was chosen. I know, that sounds grandiose, but it was true. And, why are you being so cryptic? Get to the point like you always do." I'm still pissed off. Even more.

"How's your relationship with your boss?"

"The same."

"How does he feel about shorting? What stocks did you sell short?"

"A few of the Dow Jones Industrial stocks. That's all. And, he doesn't care."

"How do you sell Dow Jones stocks short?"

"You sell the thirty stocks short. Stocks like IBM, GE, GM, AT&T. Simple."

"Those are huge, successful companies, Mason. I don't see them collapsing like you think they will."

"You never know."

"Back to the original question. How does your manager feel about shorting IBM and General Motors?"

"He doesn't care!" Now I'm shaking mad.

"Allow me to rephrase the question: how did you inform your manager of your intentions to short thirty stocks?"

I pause to calm myself. "I just told him."

"I'm going to take a stab at this, so work with me," Diane says. When she gets flippant like that, I've had it. "Judging from what you've told me about your relationship with your boss, I ask: how many people were listening when you told him?"

I feel like I have to circle my wagons, then surrender. "In front of all the other brokers in our Monday morning meeting last week."

There is silence and more silence. "History tells us two things, Mason," Diane says.

"What are those?" I sigh.

"First, you've been right before and you just may be right again. I know a lot about the psychology of a crowd. You're on to something. And I'm selling the stocks I own tomorrow."

"Wise move. What's next."

"You'd throw yourself on a landmine to be right."

That's probably true, but, "It's just money."

"I'm not worried about your money, Mason," Diane says, "I'm concerned about you. You have a standard bearer's mentality. Your history proves that. Now, back to Stan. You were sixteen years old and you saw your hero carry the standard, go against the grain, spit into the hurricane…and win."

"Yes, he did. Stan won a lot."

"Therein lies the problem."

"I know. Someday I'll lose and lose big."

"No," she says.

"No?"

"My concern is you will continue to win, and win so much that one day you'll beat everyone and it will truly be you against the world." Diane punctuates by resting both feet on the floor and crossing her hands just above her knees, the pose of a junior high teacher who just scolded me.

"And what's wrong with that?" I ask in defiance.

"Then, there are those self-destructive tendencies of yours we talk about from time to time, one of which has to be selling stocks short."

"Lots of different ways to make money."

"Mason," Diane says with emphasis, "as strange as it may sound to you, I believe you have a golden touch."

"That's fuckin' ludicrous, Diane. Look at me. Look at where I am right now. Look at what I do for a living."

"You have so much to offer. But, to use your golden touch to benefit others," she says with more emphasis, "sometimes you have to go along to get along."

"If I had to take that coach down again, I'd do it in a heartbeat," I say with more than a simmer.

"I'm not talking about that. I'm talking about the fact that your rebellious noise drowns out who you truly are. Forget 1975. Stop comparing yourself to a once-in-a-lifetime event, no matter how noble it was. Stop trying to look for another huge battle to prove yourself. And start by patching things up with your boss. And you might want to consider buying those stocks back, just wait it out, and don't make any more enemies than you already have."

I'm whipped. "That was strong."

Diane is smiling. "It's my job. What else is going on?"

Jesus Christ. You don't want to know.

Thirteen

8:15 PM
Monday August 31, 1987
Conference room, Fuller Busher
Dow Jones Industrial Average: 2,639 – 4.1 percent off all-time high

I sit quietly as the chatter surrounds me. It's happy talk of summer and party, both of which are amplified by the fact that we are kings of the hill, on top of the world looking down on The Creation that is the source of assets we can easily turn into hard dollar commissions. The problem is that, since the first of the year, these gutteral-huffing, knuckle-dragging Neanderthals think it is indeed as simple as summer and party.

I'm in a very foul mood.

John walks in with his secretary Big Hair Betty, a short, shapely big-hair blonde in a sky blue paisley dress. Big hair. It's everywhere, like Linda Gray's Sue Ellen 'Swellin' Ewing getting drunk and lookin' good on *Dallas*. My ideal woman.

Findlay and Betty conduct their conversation softly, then are interrupted by—
"Good morning! Ronnie Miller here with the Monday morning conference call."
Corncob, ancestor of Neanderthal.
"I know for a fact I was the first one here in the home office to get to work today. Nobody, I mean, nooooobody is as excited about this market as I am. It's my job to do the leg work for you and get you good ideas, but I also look upon myself as the chief cheerleader."
"That's an ugly image," I say, getting a couple of man-giggles and few smiles. Betty walks out.
"Don't think of me as wearing a short skirt—"
Too late…
"—but I am going to get you guys moving today. The Dow's down eighty-three points since last Tuesday. That's a three percent drop, a healthy drop that is nothing but an opportunity to buy at lower prices. In fact, I give you standing orders to buy every pullback, because we are headed for 3,000 in no time flat. You better get in before it gets hotter."
Just what did Corncob smoke this weekend?
"There was so much ballyhoo about the larger-than-expected trade imbalance announced Friday. Now, we know we have a trade imbalance, and we know it's bad for the economy and for the stock market. And, we know why. We're buying too much from overseas and not selling enough from here. The same old saw. Now, that knowledge is already in the prices of stocks. But, this trade number has added onto that wall of worry we like to see. That's nothin' but good. Nothin' but good. I'll tell you why. The biggest part of the unexpectedly high number was a necessary restocking of the petroleum reserves. This restocking doesn't occur that often, but when it does, it's like everyone forgot it happened the last time. In fact, it won't happen again for a while. And, it has nothing to do with the problem. All it is is just another thing for the worry warts to worry about. And that's where you come in. Take advantage of this situation, and do it now. You and your clients will be handsomely rewarded."
I have my notes ready….
"Even with the trade imbalance, both the stock market and the bond market have very little risk. There's enough skepticism to keep us rolling. The money situation is getting better, as the stabilizing bond market will indicate. And, the market still has energy.
"Read my wire for more information on my two best stocks for this week: C. R. Bard, in the medical equipment sector, and Wyse Technology, our best small cap computer systems recommendation. Follow the generals, the stocks of the big companies. They're going to lead the soldiers, the small stocks like Bard and Wyse, to valor. Go get 'em!"
To valor? Yecch.
Hey, I just woke up to notice…this morning everyone is wearing either a tan suit or an olive suit. I guess I didn't get the uniform-of-the-day memo.
"I know, guys," olive John says, "Ronnie's just good ol' Ronnie. But, the man does his homework. He's been on it. Results are hard to argue with, right, Mason?"
Oh, I've been waiting all weekend for this. "You're like my Ed McMahon, John. Here are some results, my man. I've been doing *my* homework." I stand in a professorial

manner, survey the brokers in the room, stop at Wylie and wink, then pan back over to The Dick. "I keep records and track a lot of things—"

"Looking at your production numbers," says John, "you spend a lot of time doing this."

They laugh. I'm unfazed. "In late 1986, Ronnie pointed to the action in the advance-decline number, the MKDS on your screen. MKDS is a measure of market energy, price momentum. No need to go into how and why. We all know what it is. It screamed, as Ronnie said, screamed buy. He was on it. The Dow has climbed over fifty percent since then.

"What Ronnie hasn't told you is that MKDS flashed 'sell' around 2,400 in June. Granted, that was three hundred points ago, but MKDS reads a much stronger sell now than it did then. By the way, MKDS has been a rather accurate indicator since I started watching it in 1980." That was pompous, but I don't care.

"On the interest rate side, it gets worse." I continue. They're still attentive. Amazing. "For instance, if the ninety-day US Treasury bill rate, a key short term rate, is above the Federal Reserve's discount rate, *the* key short term rate, it's a sell. Otherwise, it's a buy. Ronnie pounded the tom-toms in early '85 when the T-bill dropped. Two weeks ago? It flipped to sell. This is the first you have heard of it, and it didn't come from Ronnie. I will tell you this: the last sell T-bill sell signal was summer '83 after a big bull run and before a twenty percent overall drop. Twenty percent, or your clients losing two thousand bucks on a ten thousand dollar investment. That'll make your phones ring. So, combine that with today's skyrocketing long-term mortgage rates reflecting high rates overall and I surmise that the stock market is in big trouble. Big-ass trouble."

I'm so hot right now I don't even care if they're awake. "You don't trust me? How about Marty Zweig, analyst extraordinaire. His monetary gauge, a collection of those like the T-bill indicator and mortgage rates I talked about, said 'sell' this summer. You want history? It said 'buy' in 1982, mid 1980, and late 1974, all the beginning of big gains. It said 'sell' in mid 1983 and mid 1972, both at the onset of substantial losses.

"Back to Ronnie. The MKDS and the T-bill/discount rate indicators are just two examples of the Corncob and his myopic view of the market. You have to ask yourself why his pollyanna life interferes with his market analysis. He sees 'go' indicators, but ignores them when they say 'stop.' That's dangerous, for your clients and for you. Gentlemen, you have to play both sides of the ball."

Great finish. In a Socratic fashion, I look over my followers. Pink Floyd comes to mind. They're comfortably numb.

"Mason," John says, "thank you. We don't need you anymore."

Without hesitating, I walk through the maze of the blind apostles of Corncob and out the door. My resolve will return, but for some reason I want to cry. I never cared how these jerks felt about me. Why is it important now?

Ally meets me as I approach my desk. "Rough meeting?" she says. Her red dress and her red spikes make me feel a little better.

"I don't get any respect, Fenz."

Ally touches my shoulder. "I'm just happy to hear that it matters to you."

Fourteen

5:00 PM
Monday August 31, 1987
In the Olds, surfing out of downtown with Wylie
Dow Jones Industrial Average 2,662 – 3.2 percent off all-time high

"What got in to you today, man?" Wylie asks in an imploring yet less-than-caring fashion,
I do a U-turn on Hale just so I can turn back and watch The H disappear again.
"What the hell are you doing, Mason?"
"I thought I forgot something, but then I remembered I remembered it. And to answer your first question, I'm tired of bullshit, Wylie. I've had it with Corncob."
"I don't see what your problem is. He's been doing very well."
"If you had taped the stock price pages of *The Wall Street Journal* on the wall and given darts to a rhesus monkey, that primate would also have made money in this, the bull market of 1987. The pickings have been that easy."
"I hear you," Wylie says as he adjusts the air conditioning vent to blow on him. "You're good, too, even though you sold out in April." His hair is unkempt. A bead of sweat runs down his temple.
"That's a compliment?" This conversation is making me so upset I'm sweating, too, just like I'm outside bathing in the mid nineties.
"What I mean to say is Ronnie stayed and you didn't. The significance of that is, had you been following Ronnie, you'd be making money *and* your life would be much simpler."
I'm silent as we approach Oak. Good thing August has drawn to a close. I'm tired of the heat and the humidity. I'm tired of my low gross, seven thousand, most of it from my personal account, and by far the worst in the office this month. That's a thirty thousand dollar salary. Fresh college grads just out of school make that and more. Sucks. Since June, I've been frustrated by being wrong while everyone else is right. Ashton Township is getting on my nerves, as nice a place as it is. I've just had it with the people, the sunshine. I wish it would rain. Then maybe I'd really be happy. No, everyone wants this drought to break. I wish we'd have an ice storm. That seems just as likely as this market hitting the tank. What the hell am I saying?
"You're awfully quiet, Brick. I guess I just got to you."
We begin the ascent on the switchbacks. "I don't buy into it."
"Follow Ronnie. He's the front man. That's why he gets paid the big bucks."
"So did the captain of the *Titanic*." I say. To my left, I can see the skyline of AT through the river haze as Wylie and I drive in a tunnel of green along the steep hillside slope.
"Dude, we have to follow someone. We all can't do what Ronnie does."
"So, dude, you let someone else do your thinking for you?"
"In this regard, yes."

"You're CMU. You went to a 'think' school. Can't you see what I'm talking about? About what I'm saying about interest rates and—"

"Sloppy momentum. I know. I've heard it all from you before."

"And I've been right before. Right on the sell side. 1973. Mid '80. Summer of '83. You've got to play both sides of the ball."

"When you get desperate, you say the same things over and over."

Now I am angry. "I'm desperate?" I boom. "You've turned your career over to a chief cheerleader!"

"And I'm doing pretty well with it, don't you think?" Wylie asks in a not-nice way.

I take a cleansing breath. "Wylie, the best way to lose clients is to lose their money. Return is relative, but no one looks at past performance when the account balance is doing a nose dive. Risk is absolute. It is measured on that day. How much are we down. It doesn't matter that you made them a ton of money in the first eight months of 1987. They'll get those statements and feel like they were had."

Wylie twists his torso toward me quickly. "Not one of my clients is getting 'had,'" he says with ire. "Not one of them and you owe me an apology."

Taking a different route, I turn right onto Maple. "What are you doing?" Wylie asks.

"Taking a different route. And I'm sorry. Not one of your clients is getting 'had.' However, they will feel like it when the market gives back twenty percent. By the way, what's your average mutual fund ticket lately?"

"About fifty thousand," Wylie answers. "Why?"

"Well, twenty percent of fifty is ten. How will those clients feel when they drop ten thousand mere months after investing?"

"What would you know about clients, anyway? You don't have any."

I laugh. "I've heard that so much I'm desensitized. Look, Wylie, twenty percent down is now 2,177. We were there in May. But, it'll be different when we revisit 2,177. That's what I mean by risk being absolute." I turn around on Maple and head back for Pine. "Joni Mitchell. Both sides now. It's the market's illusions I recall. I really don't know the market at all."

"You can say that again."

"Get ready, buddy," I say.

"The end is near. Repent."

I cut right on Pine. The McInally's are three doors down. "Just take Corncob for what he is. For what he truly is. A carnival act."

"And what are you?"

"Risk averse."

"You're risk averse, so you short the Dow? You're fucking crazy."

"I've heard that so much I don't care who says it. Free market philosophy says you have to pay attention to falling bond prices, to everything that happens. It's all telling you something. Talk about risk. Rising interest rates, Wylie. The prime rate is up twice since May. It'll reach up and bite your growth fund clients on the ass." Hallelujah. He's home. I pull into Wylie's driveway. Looking at the dash, I notice the Olds' temp gauge is cranking right up there with mine.

"Ronnie says everything is okay. I'm banking on Ronnie Miller."

"Banking is the operative word, man. That's what your clients will be doing if you go with Corncob like the rest of you robots. King Ronnie appeared while his dogs and sycophants followed."

"That's not original," Wylie says sternly.

"No, it's not."

"Who said it, then?"

"Kathleen Winsor."

"Who the hell is that?"

"How the fuck would I know!"

"You're the goddamned Ph.D.!"

"I write fiction!"

"Need I say more?"

I turn to him with an evil smile. "You a betting man?"

"No...not usually. No, but, what's up?"

"Let's put a hundred on it. I say Dow 2,177 by the end of the year."

"I say Dow 3,000, no, 3,200," Wylie says with an evil smile of his own.

"You got it." We shake hands, our most cordial gesture today.

Fifteen

Noon
Saturday September 5, 1987
In my condo, sitting at my dining room table drinking heavily and writing in the newly-established Short Journal
Dow Jones Industrial Average: 2,561 – off 6.9 percent from all-time high in just eight trading days.

Entry: Saturday September 5. Labor Day weekend.

Note to future readers: I'm on my sixth Arn.

This may read like a book report similar in principle to the ones I assigned dumbass football players in bonehead English during the one semester I taught, but I have to write about Scott Turow's new novel, *Presumed Innocent*. Scott is an attorney who can spin a story like a motherfucker. I started two hours ago and I'm halfway already largely because I can't put it down unless I need an Arn. The intrigue. The protagonist, whom I'll call Mason, is an attorney in the DA office. Mason is an otherwise normal man, but has sprouted a fascinatingly intense obsession for a fellow ADA who just so happens to be a beautiful, long-legged, big-breasted, brunette passion machine, whom I'll call Joan. The floods of Mason's desires are unleashed when Joan lets him into her apartment for wild sex in every place on her body a woman can have sex. Days after this release of geothermal heat, Mason is in really deep trouble because

a) his fascinatingly intense obsession has grown exponentially, and b) Joan has been found murdered in her apartment. A glass with Mason's fingerprints is discovered in Joan's place. Mason is now officially fucked because a) his ass is legally grass, and b) Joan, as it turns out, has had wild sex in every place on her body a woman can have sex with most every man in the DA office. To quote Bugs Bunny, 'What a maroon!' I'll save the rest of the book for sometime when I can appreciate the fact that the real Joan hasn't landed the real me in jail.

People or entities I can do without: Duran Duran, Phil Collins, James Baker, George Bush, Ronald Reagan, Michael J. Fox, Samantha Fox, Prince, Lorenzo Lamas, the liberal media (four of five vote Democratic, so much for objective journalism), that Joan-look-alike Victoria Principal, anything to do with Disney, Nancy Reagan, John Elway, The Dick, and Corncob.

Entities on which I am neutral: Michael Jackson.

People or entities I would walk downtown in a snowstorm just to say hello: Walter Payton, Aretha Franklin, Jimmy Carter, The Bangles, Pat Benatar (oh...my...God), Scott Turow, Madonna, Billy Graham, Jackson Browne, Phil Simms, The Pope, Bono of U2, all of U2, Michael, and Fenz. And Wylie, even though he's avoiding me.

Another note: I just cracked open my seventh.

I will now be a recorder of history, because I've got something to say: it's better to fuckin' burn out than fuckin' fade away. I can see that happening to me. Spontaneous Mason combustion.

Here goes: now, why is it every time a Republican becomes President of the United States he tries to circumvent The Constitution? Nixon wanted to be like Chairman Mao and make decisions unilaterally. Hence, Watergate. That surely got him far, although he has aligned himself as a statesman and we've let him get by with it out of pity. On Reagan's watch, our leaders have arranged a sale of arms to our friends in Iran to give us money so we can fund the Nicaraguan Contra Rebel Freedom Fighters in their quest for what they call human rights, which in this case is what we really call rampant capitalism in our favor. The most foolishly contrived plans are the result of money or sex. I can't see Reagan and Nancy naked and hold my lunch down, so it must be the big green.

Congress didn't like this, but James Baker liked it. I know it's all tied back to him, and he was conveniently moved from chief of staff to Treasury so we the 'unaware' can't figure it out. Of course Baker is behind it. He's like John Adams, trying to become king. He's not even an elected official, but when you consider the two who are his bosses, it doesn't matter. Reagan works seven-hour days, getting home to Nancy so they can watch NBC's Thursday night lineup. Bush is a yes-man, his most creative idea as a public servant to date being the arrangement of a loan from Banco Nacional de Panama, an institution loaded with drug money to which no one just said 'no.' The super soldier Oliver North takes a few or so of those billions and gives it to the Iranics so they can buy hostages—I mean weapons—from us. The money is delivered to the Contras, more Contra money is laundered so Congress will never find out about it, and Pablo Escabar, the witness against the defense, is murdered so everyone else will never find out about it. It sickens the lifelong Republican in me. I would change my party, but everyone really cool seems to be a fuckin' Democrat, and you can guess how I feel about cool people.

So, in my estimation, the only man with enough brains and arrogance to execute this clusterfuck is James Baker. If I die today of alcohol poisoning, let this be a warning: James Baker is really president.

Furthermore, the GOP is lining up George Bush for his coronation in 1988. It's insulting to my intelligence to tell me and others that GHWB had no involvement in the Iran/Contra affair. Christ, it's an affair now, not the gross disregard for James Madison and everything he worked for. Give me a fuckin' break.

This is a Short Journal, so let's get back on the subject. I see trouble. I see August as the beginning of the woes of the bulls, with unforeseen and unimaginable dark clouds looming. The economy is at risk to collapse as it did in the depressions of the thirties and mid-seventies. Don't worry, though. I'll know what to do. Trust me. I won't call the inevitable crash a Black October, a Black Tuesday, a Black Friday, or a Black anything. That's not original. It's going to hurt those who own stocks. And, it's all going to be traced back to the day in August I shorted the Dow and the football season following. Why football? It's metaphorical, goddamnit. Anyway, I won't call it black. Not black. Just indigo. Still bad. Indigo. It will be an Indigo autumn. Looks like another indigo autumn.

Indigo autumn? Damn, you can tell I've been drinking.

Just heard Huey Lewis and The News on Crazy. Add them to my list of people I can do without. Throw in Def Leppard, too. Love me like a bomb, my ass. What is now called rock and what rock really is are two completely different things. I'm putting on my Mason's Choice tape.

I'm back. Led Zeppelin's *Hey, Hey, What Can I Do*. What can I do? A little Led for your head is unparalleled in its healing powers. Let's listen.

I love a woman, bored all day.
I got a woman and she won't be true, no.
I got a woman, stay drunk all the time.
I said, I got a little woman and she won't be true.

Sunday morning when we go down to church.
See the men folk standin' in line.
They say the come to pray to the Lord
With my little girl that looks so fine.
And in the evening when the sun is sinkin' low,
Everybody with the one they love.
I walk the town, keep a searchin' all around.
Lookin' for my streetcorner girl.

This is Joan all the way. My streetcorner girl. Just like Christine.

In the bars with the men who play guitars.
They be drinkin' and rememberin' the time.
My little lover does the midnight shift.
She followed around all of the time.
I guess there's just one thing left for me to do.

Better pack my bags and move on the way.
'Cause I got a worried mind, she was what I thought was mine.
Gonna leave her where the guitars play.

Hey, hey, what can I say.
Hey, hey, what can I do.

     It's difficult to say how many there were before attorney Richard Headrick or whatever his name is. It's also up for grabs as to why she paid me a visit. Joan is a stranger to the truth. She shaved her head. Regardless, here comes Pink Floyd.

So, so you think you can tell
Heaven from hell.
Blue skies from pain.
Can you tell a green field
From a cold steel rail?
A smile from a veil?
Do you think you can tell.

Did they get you to trade
Your heroes for ghosts,
Hot ashes for trees,
Hot air for a cool, cool breeze,
Cold comfort for change.
Did you exchange
A walk-on part in a war,
For a lead role in a cage.

     Wish you were here, buddy. And, here you are.

How I wish,
How I wish you were here.
We're just two lost souls swimmin' in a fish bowl.
Year after year.

     I can't take this any more!

2:00 PM
Saturday September 5, 1987
On the living room floor of my condo

     "Let's swab this nasty cut," Tanned, Athletic Mary says. "Then we get you to a doctor to get it stitched up."
     "No doctors," I say. I'm really woosy. Spins. Like a whirlpool it never ends. Was that Tommy Roe?

"Mason," Ally says in that manner reserved only for me while I'm doing something stupid, "Mary's a nurse. Listen to her."

"Fenz, I know Mary's a nurse. Why can't she just stitch it up? Look, she's even wearing white. Nice shorts, Mary."

"You need antiseptics," Mary the nurse says, ignoring me.

"Come on. Let's get in the car," Ally says.

"I'll drive myself, Fenz. You're a wild ass behind the wheel."

"How many beers have you had?" Fenz asks.

"Se—fi—four. Look, at least let me put all this back together. What if I pick up a girl at the doctor's office? She'll be wearing one of those smocks with the teddy bears and balloons all over it. No offense, Mary, but I want her to see me at my best."

Ally laughs, followed by Mary when she thinks it's okay.

My television amazingly stayed upright on the table during the wreck. The last thing I remember is using my head as a battering ram after jumping and tripping over my sofa in an effort to quickly turn off the sounds. The table is askew, the tape player is knocked back against the wall, and the vase and the purple anemones lay around me. I sit upright, my back resting against the bottom of the love seat while my legs are extended in front of me. Mary has already singed my eyebrow with alcohol and is now applying a butterfly bandage she found in my powder room. Fenz is kneeling at my feet, understanding and pissed off as only she can be.

"These butterflies won't stick. I'm going to check my purse for something else. Stay right there, Mason."

Mary gets up. I start at her blonde ponytail and move down, stopping at her fanny. She exits. That was nice.

I was on the floor crying when I heard the doorbell. "Enter!" I shouted. The girls had that look on their pretty faces, like I was knocked unconscious by an intruder. Nurse Mary immediately went to work. Fenz sat with her hands over her mouth.

"Mason, what the hell happened?" Ally asks.

"I saw him, Fenz."

She sighs. "I know." She places her hand on my bare shin.

"He was there like he always was. Was."

"Honey, you have to give yourself a break."

"Beer. Start of the football season. That was Vinny and me."

"Looks like you tried to play football with your tape deck," Ally says smiling.

"Oh, no, Fenz. Then there would have been a big hole in the wall."

"It would have been funny to walk in here to see your butt sticking out." She laughs and rubs my leg.

"You like my butt, don't you," I say.

"More than I'll ever admit to," she replies, still rubbing my shin.

"Ah, you just feel sorry for me because I have a big cut on my face."

"It's not that big."

I pause. "Fenz," I say, "you're always welcome, but why are you here?"

"I don't know," she says, "Just had a feeling."

I reach for her hand. "Glad you made it."

Mary walks in. "Stop that, you two!" she says with a giggle.

"Oh, okay," I say. "Anyway, what would I do without you, Mary?"

"I don't know, but that's an awfully nice Hawaiian print shirt you just spilled blood all over."

"The juices of life wash out in cold water," I say.

"No tape and gauze available. We're going to the doc in a box," Mary says. "C'mon. Upsy daisy."

I stand shakily. Ally holds my hand. "Mary, you ever have a friend die on you?" I ask.

She considers my question. "No," says Mary. "I can't say I have."

"Ya ain't missin' much."

"I bet not," Mary replies.

"I'll tell ya this," I say. We step out of my door. I fetch the keys from my pocket and lock behind me. Turning, we walk down my path to Ally's bronze Toyota Celica. "I don't remember not knowing Vinny. We lived in other towns, but we got together as often as possible. Pass and catch. An entire friendship took place in the arc created by a football in flight. We connected, in many respects."

"We had a dream, ladies," I say as we entered the car. Ally fires it up and we move down the street. "Vinny and I wanted to play for The U. Together. We got one game. We did so well, that was enough. We took brides, started careers, he became a father, then one day he was dead. Just like that. Vinny was the best friend a man could have. I miss him. I'm too drunk to cry."

"What would Vinny do if he would have seen you on your floor?" Ally asks. She always knows what to say and when.

"Vinny would still be paralyzed with laughter," I say.

Mary laughs. "That is true friendship," she says.

We drive away.

Sixteen

8:15 AM
Tuesday September 8, 1987
Fuller Busher conference room with nine of my best friends
Dow Jones Industrial Average: 2,561 – 6.9 percent off all-time high

The cut above my eye is sutured with expertise. It doesn't look as bad today as it did yesterday, and it didn't look that bad then. Still, it is obvious to all I had an interesting weekend.

"Who did you run into?" Tall, Dark, and Handsome Rookie Todd asks.

"Fenz," I say.

"That woman has too much control over you," Skinny and Cute Jason says.

"You know it," I say. I hate those two fuckers.

It's the day after Labor Day parties I did not attend. A thunderstorm on Friday night and the subsequent cooler weather have given us a break. In response to the weather and the change of seasons, some of the men have broken out lightweight navy chalkstripes and gray worsted wools. It's as if they have it marked in their Day Timers.

Gray pinstripe John strides to the front and turns up the squawk box just as—

"Good morning. This is Ronnie Miller with the Monday morning conference call on Tuesday. Labor Day has come and gone, and what a summer we have had. The week before Memorial Day, the Dow was just below 2,200. We shot up to 2,722 in three short months, actually 2,750 interday. That's a twenty-three percent climb. Even after including the recent pullback to the 2,560 area, we're still up over sixteen percent in this summer of 1987, the real summer of love."

"That's proof positive," I say. "Corncob tokes," The air fills with a round of laughter, even though it was me who said it.

"And today, Tuesday September 8, 1987, even after all the good times, there is very little risk in stocks. The economy is strong, the Dow bounced off a down sixty two day last week to close down sixteen, which just goes to show you that the stock market and the spooky bond market have become uncoupled. The bond market is irrelevant."

"I can't believe I just heard that," I say.

"Do not, I repeat, do not let interest rate fears keep your clients out of stocks. I say again, the bond market is irrelevant. Pullbacks of stock prices such as the one we just experienced are great times to buy. If I were you, I'd get on the phones today and tell your clients just that. Do not fear interest rates. The Fed has hung tough through worse times. Alan Greenspan and his Federal Reserve governors will keep your rates low and get them lower. And, have faith in our research department here at Fuller Busher."

I feel the blood boil in my veins. "I don't know whether to puke or say 'Amen!'" I say, again to no response.

"The Fed has done wonderfully well during times of inflation. But, inflation? Right now? I say 'no.' Commodities prices have broken down. How about wages, since wages are two-thirds of inflation. No problem. Collective bargaining agreements are down. Why, even the auto workers have fallen in line. Job security is number one for the Ford Motor rank and file, not wage hikes. Do you think short-term rates will continue to go up? No. The Fed has held the key short term Fed funds below seven percent. They will force the bond market higher by keeping rates lower."

"Metals prices are up, dickhead!" Boy, that woke up Ashton Township.

"Will the Fed have to come through with borrowed reserves? No. There is still lots of cash in this economy. Everything is going well, my friends. Buy."

"This is the present, Corncob. What happens next?" I ask.

"Quiet, Mason!" comes a shout from the corner.

"My sentiment indicators are positive. There are plenty of bears out there, too many for a down market. Index traders are sixty four percent negative on the market. Mutual funds cash is just under ten percent of assets, plenty of buying fuel. And, the answer to bond weakness? Bond funds are liquidating. They're selling. That's why interest rates are going up. They're forced to sell because the public is getting out of bonds and buying stocks. Anyway, as I said before, stocks and bonds are uncoupled. Do we have to have a strong bond market to have a strong stock market? No. That'll be all for this morning. Read my list of top ten stocks on the wire. Philip Morris, Boeing, and Sears are among them. Finally, congratulations! August was the biggest gross month in

Fuller Busher history. Keep the momentum going. I'm going past the up five hundred. It's Dow 3,400 by the end of the year. Happy selling!"

I don't waste any time. "This is utter bullshit!"

"If you can do it without profanity, Mason, tell us why," John says. "Besides, I don't know why I let you talk. On second hand, I do. I want to give you the chance to look more stupid than you are."

"John, I know that, so here goes. I'm profane? Corncob is profane. Index traders are bearish? Buy programs, John. They're buying stocks and selling index futures to hedge. Index traders are not selling because they're scared. It's a program, linked to buying stocks and executed by a computer, which doesn't know its up from down, but can make your up go down. By the way, watch the programs. The computers can flip it without asking permission from Ronnie Miller. When they start *selling* stocks and *buying* futures to hedge, we're all rotting flesh. Or, at least, you are."

I'm shaking angry. "The bond market is falling because the public is liquidating their bond funds? Give...me...a...goddamn break! Pension funds, banks, and insurance companies hold most of the bonds issued. They control the bonds, and they work on asset allocation. A percentage range in stocks and a percentage range in bonds and never the 'twain shall meet. They don't sell bonds wholesale to buy stocks. Then, there is the matter of huge—I mean huge—money from other countries holding—I mean holding—bonds. And you guys tell me you believe that fucking bond liquidation shit? How big..."

"We don't want to hear your foul mouth any more," says Ned Studstill, pretty damn stern.

"Well, Ned," I say, closer to his face, "unlike everyone else, you and I were around in '73 and '74 and '80 and '83. Doesn't this crock Corncob has his ladle into ring a bell? Huh, Ned?" I pan the room. "When are you guys going to learn to think on your own?"

"That's it, Bricker!" John shouts. "That's all for you. You are a major disruption. That's all for you. You are banned from these meetings, and you will meet with me in my office in fifteen minutes to discuss your future here. You read me?"

"Like a Corncob buy list," I say. I rise from my chair and leave, heading for The Dick's office to get this over with and fast.

8:45 AM
Sitting in front of John Findlay's desk

Findlay's office is a pentagon. One side is a door. Two sides are windows. Framed certificates fill the fourth wall. Tacky abstract art and another freakin' fox hunt hang on the fifth one. Otherwise, it's class. The carpet is rich and green. The wallpaper is only the best, a fine subtle print a couple of tan hues lighter than the floor. His desk is in front of the far window and is neat and orderly, just like his life.

John walks in and calmly shuts the door. He stands to the side of his desk with his hands on his thick hips. I remain sitting. For the first time as a broker, I fear for my career. Nah. In his pinstripe imperial splendor, John begins, "Look, after that outburst, you should be packing. In fact, unless I give Ned a good reason not to, he's calling Philly and going over my head."

"Or through the hole in it," I say.

John stares at me and sighs. "Mason, you're buying yourself a one-way ticket out of this business. The truth is, man, you aren't very well liked in this town. If you leave here, I guarantee you there will be no more opportunities in the investment business because I'm not going to help you, to say the least."

I've gone suicide, so I may as well just throw it out there, "John, do it."

"No, you stay. You actually have a small, but loyal client following of people with a lot of money who the rest of us can't reach. For some reason. Some strange reason. So, here's the deal. You're on quota. Your minimum gross is fifteen a month, which by the way is fifty percent over your average. Good luck. If you're not buying stocks, you'll just have to figure some other way to do that. Since limited partnerships are in the shitter, your only courses of action are either short selling or mutual funds. It looks like funds for you because, as I can tell from your tickets, you are one of the few goddamn stupid enough to short this market."

"Rising interest rates, overly high expectations, it's going to be tough on you guys out there," I say with defiance.

"Well," starts John, "let me tell you this. Jason has been doing newspaper interviews with *Post-Gazette* reporters using Ronnie Miller's advice. My man Jason is the spokesman in Ashton Township and Pittsburgh. Our clients, not your clients, but our clients love what Jason's been saying. My advice is get the fifteen by playing the crowd, Mason. It's your only way."

"No."

John sits beside me as a mentor would. Weird. "Mason, the crowd pays your commissions. Go with the crowd."

"I can do it. I can do fifteen my way."

"No, you can't. I'm going to make an example of you," John says as he turns up the heat. "I'll show Todd and Jason and anyone else who needs to hear the message that no one fucks with me."

I contemplate for a moment. Suck it up and suck up, I guess. "John, the only thing I care about is October's paycheck."

"That's new," he says.

"Whatever you say, John, but a deal is a deal. If I show up on September 30 with fifteen, I buy another month and I get paid. Okay?"

"I promise you." John leans into my face. "I just don't see you going another month. I know your asset base. I know what you've been selling them. And, you haven't shown the ability to prospect for new clients. You live on referrals from engineers who are so damned bright but can't decide which hand to use to wipe their own butts. You can't do it. You're soft. You're the only broker in this office with a big-ass cash account. You're not hungry. You're not hungry and you'd rather lose a career than to do it my way. And, that's the message. I'm not going to fire you. You're going to fire yourself."

John and I stare at one another. I stand. He remains seated. I'm mad enough and man enough to take him right here and right now, but that would be incredibly foolish. Instead, I offer, "John, you have yourself a deal." We shake hands.

"You have until September 30th," John says.

"You want a side bet? A thousand says I do it?"

John extends his hand again. "You're on."

"You're easy money," I throw over my shoulder as I walk through his door, pretty goddamned cocky.

Seventeen

11:15 AM
Wednesday September 9, 1987
Walking away from the parking garage to The H.
Dow Jones Industrial Average: 2,545 – 7.5 percent off all-time high

I had therapy this morning. Oddly, I decided to come clean with Diane. The first half of the session was yet another round of true confessions. I told her all. I told her about the fight with John and my general pugnacity and why I'm on probation. I told her about publicly referring to him as The Dick. I told Diane that I had lied to her about having dates and romantic relationships with women over the years. That gave me room to tell her about Christine and the five hundred a week and how she looks like Joan. I told Diane about my inability to quit smoking even though I had told her I stopped. Lie after lie. While I was at it, I told her about her feet.

Seemingly before all this cleansing of my soul, Diane had made a decision she kept to herself until I had purged.

"Mason, I've been thinking about this for some time," she said, "Now, and especially considering what all you've told me today, I'm going to refer you to a psychiatrist."

"Oh," I said. "That sounds like fun."

"I think it's necessary. I think it's necessary because it is my professional opinion that manic-depression is clouding your thinking and decision-making. Don't worry too much, though. Manic-depression, or more accurately called bipolar disorder, is more common than you think. It's caused by a chemical imbalance in the brain and body. For that reason, it is very treatable, and successfully so."

"Jimi Hendrix said manic-depression is a frustrating mess."

"With the proper treatment, it doesn't have to be," she said.

"So, my mind is impaired but 'it doesn't have to be?'"

"Your mind is not impaired. As I said, don't worry. We'll get through it. You'll still come to me for talk therapy. And the psychiatrist will administer medical therapy."

"Shock therapy?"

"No. Probably lithium carbonate and maybe some MAO inhibitor antidepressants. That's all."

"Lithium?"

"Yes," she said.

"Isn't that for people just this side of a strait jacket?"

She wrote on a small pad of paper. "Here. His name is Hans Pedersen. His address and telephone number are here." Diane handed me the paper. "To get you in as soon as possible, they'll make an appointment out front with Dr. Pedersen before you leave."

"Okay," I replied.

"Again, don't worry," Diane said. "And, I'm not abandoning you. We'll continue to meet, once a week for a while."

"Fair enough," I said.

"Oh, and Mason? About my feet...I've heard worse. A lot worse. It was actually a good way to handle something so natural yet so potentially damaging. What you did was like a safety valve. Good job."

"Score one for the home team," I said.

I stand in the elevator on two. Seven takes me to work. I press one.

The H opens to Hale Street. Except for my condo, my life is contained in this one half-block; The H, Green Boy's bar next door and The Café across the street, which is beside the city library. Ashton Township Public Library. The city library. It is odd that after spending years in the Duquesne stacks, I have never set foot in the city library. Never. Well, it's time. In search of the solace of familiarity, I cross the street, walk past the big patina-colored tulip-shaped fountain in front, and slip through the doors of the three-story brick windowless neo-institutional building.

The feeling is as if I have been here every day. Just like Duquesne. It's all coming back to me. The utilitarian high school décor of pastels and wood elicits good memories. Joan is included in those memories, but they're good anyway. The high ceiling, the hardwood floors stretching underneath, and the length of the space opens up the place, allowing plenty of room to breathe. The wooden front desk, the circulation desk, is to my left where seven foot-tall metal shelves of books extend to the back of this big room. Directly before me, rows of veneer tables, some empty, some with computers, run back beside the shelves of books to another big desk at the end of the room. More rows of more metal shelves of books with more tables among them are to my right. I look straight ahead. Drawing on my experience, I surmise the big desk at the end is the reference section. That's as good a place as any to start.

The reference desk is actually three weathered wooden desks connected to form a 'C', each fronting neatly arranged academic slop of books, paper, more paper and more books. Two women man the area. The one who looks like Boy George in a big blue dress sits to the left before a computer screen. The other one is shorter—okay, short—wearing a white top with her ample butt squeezed into tan slacks. She stands to the left of Boy with her back to me, observing the images on the screen. They seem to be having a light-hearted conversation. I approach.

Ms. Tanslacks laughs. "I haven't been to aerobics for three weeks!" She turns to me with her little pooch of a belly and...holy...holy...holy. This woman's head is gorgeous. The rest of her is round...not that that's bad...round, but...and not like Joan and Christine up-top round...a nice up-top...I'll take them...her round is bottom-based...it doesn't seem to...pleasingly...no, that's trite...she's beautiful...so, why are you...not a runway model...different, but...beautiful visage...just beautiful...hell...why not... really...really...really...Mason, you're babbling...and with reason...she is gorgeous. Who gives a damn? The woman has your attention. Go with it.

"Edie," I hear Boy George say, "how do you wo-oh, I'm sorry, sir."

Edie...Edie! So, that's where...oh, my! Oh, sweet Jesus! Go hard, man. You know her! Not now. At one time. Her hair is the same; thick, shoulder-length, raven...with a brown headband holding it back from her captivating face. Raven. She's a raven-hair beauty with dark soulful eyes; dark soulful eyes filling lovely, full, high cheeks curving down to her jaw. Her skin is smooth and tan, like the froth on an espresso. Lovely, just lovely. I can't say this without repeating myself but I must, this woman – in the face – oh, hell, Mason, quit qualifying it – is the most beautifully gorgeous angel I have ever seen. And I don't even have to waste time asking her name. She's an old college friend. She's Edie Loden. I'm certain she is Edie Loden.

"I'm sorry," Edie says. "You didn't need to hear that."

"Hear what?" I say.

"Good. How may I help you?"

She thought I was being witty, when I'm actually stymied. Say something. Here goes nothing. "I'd like to see...a book." Brilliant, Mason. Just brilliant.

"Well, you're in luck," Edie deadpans with a smile as wonderful as the sounds of the words emitting from her saporous mouth . "May I help you decide what book you want?"

Help me decide what book I want? Now she knows I'm a complete dumbass. "No, Edie. I've decided. I wish to see..." I can't think. Wish to see what? Edie Loden. After all these years. Put on some weight...sure has...but...and she's looking at me. At me! God, she already has this overwhelming power to make me feel addlepated. Again. You know, in a good way. Shut up. I haven't told her what book I want to see! "...to see..." Say anything! "your best reference on the subject of nineteenth century French art." How fucking ostentatious can you possibly get?

"I think I have what you need," she says before she disappears around the corner to her right. I wait in a blissful state of mind. Just as I am fantasizing about sharing coffee with Edie at The Café and making furtive glances at her full lips, she returns with a big roaster pan-sized book.

"This is my favorite," Edie says, holding the book at belly level. "Smith is a new, fresh approach to a classic subject. Wonderful narrative, with great photos of choice masterpieces from the Louvre and the Musee d'Orsay."

I want to go to Paris with Edie. "That's just what I'm looking for, Edie." Now, go, Brick, go! Shock her memory. "By the way, if you don't mind, my name is Mason."

She extends her hand. "My pleasure, Mason. Do you make a habit of introducing yourself to librarians?" I feel her soft touch. Wow. And I've given her enough time to remember me. How many Masons could there have been in her life? I forgot my last name. Oh, hell. I'm losing it.

"Well, no...I think...I think...you're the first."

"It's nice," Edie says. "We don't get to meet enough of our patrons."

I'm in space. Outer space. "Well, I'll just take your selection and...sit right over there," I nod my head right over there. "and—and...look at it."

"That's how it works," she says. I sound so fatuous she at least doesn't think I'm coming on to her.

"So, thank you. I'll bring the book back shortly." You're a nerd, Mason.

"Enjoy," Edie says as Boy George quells laughter.

11:45 AM
Wednesday September 9, 1987
Sitting at this table right over here
Dow Jones Industrial Average: not nearly as high as I am

I recuperate from Edie by revisiting France. I begin with the impressionists: the dark *Soliel Levant* of Claude Monet…Monet's *Highway Bridge at Argentevil,* looking more defined than other impressionist paintings…Van Gogh's *Terrasse du Café le Soir,* the print I have, with the yellow light on the streetside café below the violet starry sky…and the man and the woman in Renior's *La Prominade.*

I switch to nudes, inspired I'm sure by my heightened level of amore…Theodore Chasseriau's *Andromeda Chained to the Rocks by the Nereids.* Weird, but she's pretty and pretty naked. Maybe I'd better move on. Uh-oh. Chasseriau lays out *Tepidarium* right before me. I saw this one just a few months ago at Musee d'Orsay. The work made a huge impression on me, and not because there are twenty-two or so women milling about in a huge hall in various stages of dress, but because of the ladies on each side of the painting. The one on the left is beautiful in a flowing gown, but she looks bored. The other on the right is giving me a comely look…and, Jesus Christ, *she is* Edie Loden! I stealthily glance at Edie, then the comely woman. Edie…woman…Edie…woman. That's it. They could be twins. My favorite painting and my new favorite live action sweetie. What synergy! I am absolutely in love with both of them! What am I saying?

I must buy this print.

12:15 PM
Wednesday September 9, 1987
Walking back to The H

Edie was not present at the desk when I returned the book. Boy George took it. I just adore Edie. As I cross Hale Street, I'm reminded that it's Day 6 of a twenty-one day business month and I'm fourteen away from hitting my fifteen thousand dollar goal. I'm sitting on a lot of free cash with no strategy, but I have renewed confidence that has seized my false bravado. Strange, but true. This hasn't happened for a while. I'm looking forward to the challenge, largely because I sincerely think I can do it, and even have fun trying.

Did I just say that?

Eighteen

11:30 AM
Thursday September 10, 1987

At my desk in the Ashton Township offices of Fuller Busher, outlining strategy in the journal.
Dow Jones Industrial Average: 2,549 − 7.3 percent off all-time high

September 10, 1987 − where it begins: strategy for my new career:

Here's the plan. I need fourteen thousand dollars gross in fourteen days. That of course is a thousand a day. I'm short the Dow, so you know how I feel about buying stocks. Very few understand selling short, and almost all of those who do don't want to short largely because they understand it. Three of the engineers have followed my lead and shorted selected Dow stocks. Not coincidentally, they are the ones who shorted in mid 1983, the last choice opportunity to successfully play the downside. The recent shorting is where this month's thousand gross came from. And, that well is dry. Now is the time to take a different tack.

John challenged me to sell my clients mutual funds. Mutual funds. When asked, here's what I tell my clients about mutual funds. A mutual fund is essentially a pool of hundreds of millions of dollars invested in something, like stocks. The money is divided into shares, shares the investor can buy to get their own little portion of that pool. By purchasing mutual fund shares, the investor buys into the stock market. And, it's a pretty good way to do it. The primary advantage of a mutual fund is reduced risk by getting both diversification (called 'not putting your eggs in one basket') and the professional money management necessary to do well in the market (don't believe this until you read the following paragraph). All this means is an investor with as little as one thousand dollars desiring growth of capital can run with the big dogs by owning a portion of a giant portfolio of stocks that is well diversified with dozens and dozens of different stocks and is managed by some yuppie with an Ivy MBA (remember what I said about the following paragraph).

However, here's another way to look at it. Statistics reveal that, considering the population of Ivy yuppies managing money in mutual funds by actively buying and selling stocks in an attempt to beat the market, only one in five of them actually does it. Shocking…only one in five beats the market! This means if I were to take a million and buy the thirty Dow stocks and simply hold them forever, eschew the buy and sell, and spend all my time watching MTV, I would be among the best money managers.

Why is this true? Could the rarefied air of Wall Street ironically surround an avenue for a leisurely stroll? Do the brokers and money runners have that much control over your minds to make us think their advice is essential? Mutual fund investors must realize the dollars they could save in management fees and transaction costs by leaving the yuppie out of it. Better still are the dollars they could make by picking among the top funds, which are those funds that have left the yuppie out of it. In sum, the funds have the public fooled again with its story that money managers add value to the investment solution. My advice? Read further.

Regardless of the incompetence of the yups, static stock mutual funds offer investors the egalitarian opportunity to make money in the stock market with peace of mind. I've never owned shares of a mutual fund and never cared to, and none of my engineers own shares of a mutual fund because no one can tell us what to do with our money. We're doing okay ourselves, thank you very much. But, as I said, they are better for most anyone who doesn't believe in the deceit of The Street and buys the index.

There are also mutual funds that invest in bonds. Remember what I told Nikita by the pool: stocks are hope (and hype) while bonds are a promise. You buy a bond and you get income in the form of interest while you wait for your bond to mature so you can get your money back. Bonds don't grow in value. There are price fluctuations, though. Rising interest rates depreciate the market value of bonds. Falling interest rates make your bonds worth more in the bond market. However, all these fluctuations do not affect the promise.

Bank certificates of deposit are bonds, issued by the banks so they can borrow money from you to lend to businesses so they can both make even more money. Corporations issue bonds for some of the same reasons, using the bond money to fund their business interests. The U. S. Treasury issues bonds to finance the huge-ass deficit. A bank that loaned you money for your house owns your mortgage, thereby owning your bond. Those are the basics.

This is where I come in.

I think the level of interest rates is comfortable for bondholders, meaning that the price fluctuation risk of bonds is becoming minimal. It's a good time to buy bonds and bond mutual funds. And, I'm going to make my clients an offer they can't refuse:

"Mr./Mrs./Ms./Miss Client," I will say, "the stock market's risky right now, but you have to do something with your money. The time is right to own bonds, thereby keeping your capital safe while getting you hard dollar income that you can reinvest or spend. Your choice. I recommend owning shares of a bond mutual fund to diversify over many different bonds. Even better, I think you should buy shares of a bond mutual fund that invests solely in United States Treasury securities, backed by the full faith and credit of your United States government, and to the republic for which it stands. Right now, you can earn and get paid nine percent annually in the Caretaker United States Treasury Securities mutual fund and never have to worry what the Dow does. Any questions? How much do you want to invest?"

What a spiel! It could work. It has to work. And, here's how. Last count, my clients are sitting on four million here at Fuller Busher. Half of that four mil is ready cash parked in money market savings accounts waiting to be spent on homes, cars, and college. The other half is earmarked for investing. If, conservatively, only half that cash goes with me, and since Caretaker pays me an obscene four cents on every dollar invested, that's worth forty thousand dollars gross. What to do after that? Who in the hell knows?

I'm proud of my plan. There is but one thing to do now: go to the library.

Noon
Thursday September 10, 1987
Crossing Hale Street, carrying my journal
Dow Jones Industrial Average: 2,565 – 6.8 percent off all-time high

Handsome Rookie Todd and Cute Jason and several others of my superficial fellow brokers would look at Edie and think: chubby. Chubby. Chubs, tubby, tubs. Porky, hefty, husky. Or they'd cut to the chase and just call her fat. Now, consider her fellow genderettes and what they'd have to say. It would be awful. In my opinion, women are worse and more cruel with their own brand of catty comments. They should know better, but in the final analysis women can get very bitchy about each other.

I say it's just not like that. Edie is gorgeous. In response to Todd and Jason and the girls, allow me to offer these: splendid. Splendid. Exquisite, dazzling, breathtaking. Enthralling, enchanting, winsome. She's Edie Loden and it doesn't not matter what Todd and Jason and the girls or any of those other shallow, arrogant pricks think. I see beauty. She's my Edie, and she is doing *just fine.*

The weather is warm, the skies are clear, free from the oppression of the blazing sun and high humidity. I'm able to go out of doors and not generate a thin film of sweat on my face. Making a pact to enjoy the break in the heat later, I enter the library and walk straight back. Boy George is there. I don't want to tip my hand and lay off waiting for Edie to appear, so I saunter to the reference desk like any normal man trying desperately not to show that he is obsessed with a librarian.

"May I help you?" asks Boy George.

"Hello. Good afternoon. May I please see the microfilm for the *Washington Post* for the first half of 1974?" That was spontaneous, but I'll go with it.

Without a word, Boy goes around the corner as I wait for Edie. A half-minute later, she has the microfilm and is bringing it to me. Edie still has not appeared.

"Here you are, the entire year," she says, barely smiling.

"Thank you."

Edie is probably at lunch.

2:10 PM
Thursday September 10, 1987
At a library desk writing in my journal, which I have to do so it looks as if I'm doing actual research.
Dow Jones Industrial Average: don't know

Entry
Thursday September 10, 1987
In the library

While I'm here, I might as well write about something worthwhile. Megalomaniacs have always intrigued me, so...the year 1974 was one of the worst years in stock market history. Recession and inflation certainly contributed, but there was more to it. Watergate manifested a crisis of confidence our nation had not experienced since the Great Depression. Actually, we're still paranoid, and Reagan is not helping, but what would you expect?

The thing is this: discount the ill-fated, unnecessary break-in; forget the firings and the cover up of the burglary and the dirty tricks played in a ridiculous attempt to discredit the Democrats. Just as the letter to the editor of this fine newspaper read on this my eighteenth birthday in 1974, what's truly bad was the fiasco with the tapes.

When the investigators discovered the tapes, they knew they had the smoking gun. Yet, like a teenage boy caught with beer in his old man's car, the subterfuge of Nixon was comical. He continuously evoked executive privilege even as his support base was dwindling. He had the audacity to erase eighteen minutes without apologies, like no one would notice. He offered only edited transcripts in lieu of the tapes, like everyone would say that's okay. All these were attempts to hide the fact that Tricky Dick was recorded in a conversation concerning an attempt to impede an FBI investigation of his shenanigans. That's when everyone jumped off his train and prepared for impeachment.

Nixon delivered his resignation speech in a tone that was much less contrite than it should have been, sounding more like he was on the stump campaigning for the office he was about to leave. An unusual man he was My point is this: maybe Nixon's detractors would have been more cooperative had he not been so childish and insulting about the tapes at a time when everyone in the free world knew we had him. What an idiot.

The last year of Richard Nixon was my first year of college. It was Vinny and me ready to take on the NCAA. How innocent I was that freshman year. A year later I met Joan. And Edie Loden.

I love this story. I write it now to carry it to perpetuity. Future readers: it doesn't get more romantic and tragic than this. In that fall semester of my sophomore year, Edie the art student and I the English student shared a class called Physics for Liberal Arts Majors. I was pretty good at it. Sometimes she needed some help, so before class I would explain things like Newton's first law. Edie was as stunning then as she is now, but I was so Joan-deaf I really didn't notice.

The day of the Pitt game, the day it all came down, I marched with the team to the stadium. Edie was in the crowd. She found me and pulled me to her. Surprised, I followed. Clutching my arm, she said something like this: 'Mason! Mason! I'm in a group at the synagogue and we've been trying to get that son-of-a-bitch for years. You did it! You did it, Mason! Oh, I love you!' That's when I first paid real attention to Edie Loden. Really paid real attention. It was the day after my inaugural romantic encounter with Joan, but I was a red-blooded American male and Edie was absolutely captivating. Absolutely. Like now. I kept her name in my mental Rolodex.

After the game, Joan and I consummated our love. In celebration, I was to meet her and her sister Pamela at a jazz club. I saw Edie in the parking lot of that club. She was supposed to see her boyfriend there. We talked and one thing led to another and we ended up in each other's arms kissing passionately. Setting a date for that Monday night, we parted for our respective significant others.

The next day I was on my way to Vegas with Joan to get married. Needless to say, Monday night never happened. And I didn't see Edie Loden again until yesterday.

Yesterday. Obviously, Michael's right. I have this black hole of a void in my soul, created in part by my choice to ignore women for years. I'm smart enough to realize that I'm allowing Edie a chance to fill that void because she is in a way familiar. The fact that she ties back to that magical time in my life makes it easier to let her in now, you know, trying to recover for the losses of Vinny *and* Joan. Over my months and years with Christine, I would at times wonder why I was putting myself through that ordeal. Why didn't I just find a real woman? Now that I have, why this woman? Why Edie?

Mason, why ask so many questions? Well, try this one: why not Edie?

I've waited a couple of hours. No Edie. Just missed her. I'll take the microfilm back. Boy George is busy, so I'll lay it on the desk near her.

What can I study tomorrow?

Nineteen

12:30 PM
Friday September 11, 1987
Alone with an espresso and my short journal at The Café
Dow Jones Industrial Average: 2,600 – 5.5 percent off all-time high

Entry: Lunch, Friday September 11, 1987

At yesterday's close, my short equity hit around five hundred twenty five thousand, up a little over five percent. This corresponds with a juxtaposed nearly six percent fall in the Dow. Market experts are calling it a 'healthy correction.' I don't really know what it is, but I wouldn't call anything about this market 'healthy.' Sears and General Motors and IBM are sliding down. They're among my leaders, Corncob. Merck is hanging tough against me. Time is on my side, though. This party will be over.

I called ten clients this morning with my Idea of the Month. Six, representing a total of two hundred thousand in capital and eight thousand gross, gave me an unequivocal 'no,' with reasons ranging from the collapse of the dollar versus the Deutche mark to the desire to invest in provisions, ammunition, and gold in preparation for the impending petroleum war, jump starting the next energy crisis. To continue, two with a potential of sixteen hundred gross said they would think about it, which is a 'no' in lingerie. On the other two, however, I hit paydirt.

Becky is good-looking and blonde, a stressed-out thirty-five-year-old recently divorced mother of two sons, ages nine and seven. Working as a financial analyst for Allegheny Power, she is indeed an informed investor. Becky wants to take forty grand of her rather large settlement and place it in an income fund from which she can draw money for daycare expenses. To get three hundred dollars a month in raw cash, I recommended Caretaker. She said 'yes.' Then we had a conversation that went something like this:

Becky: The bastard got the bimbo, and I got his money. A lot of his money. Paybacks are a bitch.

Mason: (somewhat frightened by her) I know the feeling.

B: Oh, do you?

M: I've been there with you.

B: Men don't know. Look, you got the sale. Cut the crap.

M: Trust me. I've been there with you.

B: (a pause) You really have been.

M: Yep.

B: (another pause) Well…

M: That's okay.

B: (long pause) Are you bitter?

M: I was. For too long. It ran its course. Now, if you want advice beyond investment strategy, I will tell you that your bitterness will probably do the same thing.

B: Maybe some day…but I have a good excuse. It's kind of fun right now. (with a Swellin' Ewing grin) Bitterness can be intoxicating.

M: (thinking, 'holy shit') Go for it.

B: I think I will.

M: If you want some ideas on how to invest the rest of the money, just call.

B: I think I will. And (with another Swellin' Ewing grin) I'm counting on you to keep me posted on how Caretaker is doing.

M: (as a red flag the size of Rhode Island pops up) Whenever you need to know something, you have my number.

Please, God, don't let Becky call.

The next client was much more pleasant. Bernhard Williams is the quintessential older gentleman, fit for his age in a navy hopsack blazer, worsted wool Haggars, a blue oxford button-down, and Bass Weejuns. He's been mine for a while. On my good days, Mr. Williams is a man I aspire to be. He's wealthy, handsome, and bright. He also knows a lot about bonds, but feels he could use people with a proven track record watching over them. Mr. Williams approached me with Caretaker, wanting to invest thirty thousand dollars for his granddaughter and reinvest the income for her future.

In these times of money-as-far-as-the-eye-can-see, I like talking to contemporaries of Mr. Williams. He told me he was sixteen in 1931, two years away from college when his father lost a lot of money deposited in a failing bank. That was before the FDIC, an institution that is now a birthright. Mr. Williams became a man in the Great Depression, then he supported his family while an intelligence officer in France during the war. He sees today's takeover kings Ivan Boesky and Michael Milken as the pillagers they are; men who are playing a zero-sum game with people's lives by buying entire companies and splitting them apart for fun and profit. These two obdurate jerks ignore the fact that there are intrinsic values associated with a going concern, like pride, stable jobs, growth, and did I mention pride? How about family? How about children who are raised knowing that when their moms and dads go downtown or to the mill and do good work, they won't have to watch their moms and dads scrape for the dregs in the unemployment line. They don't have to watch communities being broken up, see school desks empty, and wonder if the concept of 'the college of your choice' is entirely bullshit. Guys like Ivan and Michael and T. Boone Pickens, too, are simply in the free market buying undervalued companies, they say, but what they're really doing is raiding the soul of America. If they'd take their megabillions and provide services or even make products, sell them, and ship them out, we'd all be better off.

Why am I a Republican?

Why? Because I don't want to be a Democrat. My war hero dad said never be a Democrat. Actually, he said never talk to Democrats. That's impossible in places like western Pennsylvania and West Virginia. I'd have to move to Indiana. Maybe I'll become an independent and not talk to anyone. Wait, I do that anyway.

The two casual ladies are back...in canvas flats. Out of season already. What am I going to do with Edie? She has to figure into my life some how. Well, she already does. It happened so fast. I didn't care about anyone. I had a prostitute. Now, I don't know. She's familiar, yet a stranger. There's something there. I just don't know. So, let's go do some research.

1:30 PM
Friday Septmeber 11, 1987
Standing at the reference desk

"Welcome," Edie says. Round black slacks. Pink top. Short sleeves. It doesn't matter what she wears. Edie could show up in a burlap sack and still be beautiful. She'd fill it out, and she'd be beautiful.

"Glad to be here," I say, barely. It's the first time since I saw her the second first time. I've had too long to think about this. My heart is in my throat, like I'm a wallflower at a high school dance and the homecoming queen is talking to me.

"How may I help you?" she says with an electric smile.

Now my heart is thumping in my throat. She has to know something's up. My neck must be undulating. "May I please see *The New York Times* for November 1979?" *The New York Times?* Can you possibly be less interesting than that, Bricker?

"Comin' right up," she says.

"Thank you," I say. 'Comin' right up.' I just love her attitude. Not your typical librarian. Before I can think any more, she returns.

"Here you go."

"Perfect," I say. Perfect.

"Mason, is it?"

"Yes." C'mon. Think, Edie, think.

"I heard you were here yesterday."

Mr. Obvious. "Yes, I was. *Washington Post,* 1974."

"Three more visits," Edie says with a grin, "and you'll be eligible for our volume discount."

I laugh. I'm busted. "Thank you for offering it to me."

"What are you doing, if I may ask?"

"Research. And ask away."

"Interesting."

"I'm researching recent history for my job. The histories of the periods during bad stock markets. I'm a money manager." Sooner or later, I knew I'd say that.

"I bet that's neat."

"Ah, it's like any other job," I say humbly.

"I read that the market's good right now. Why are you studying bad markets?" she asks.

"You have to see them coming before they get here," I reply.

Edie smiles. "Wise. Tell me, what's it like to help people with their money? I bet it's fulfilling."

"I like it," I say. "It's satisfying when you ease their tensions, but people with money can do crazy things. Besides, I'd like your job."

Edie dry spits. "You gotta be kidding."

"No. To be around all this all the time…on second thought, I'd be so engrossed in the old newspapers I wouldn't do your job very well."

"I guess French art would also capture your attention," she says, smiling.

"Yeah. Business and pleasure," I reply, smiling myself.

Edie crosses her arms under her boobs. Mmm…"So, you don't think you can do this job."

"No. Too many distractions," I say, distracted.

"I don't do it very well," she pouts.

"You're doing great, Edie."

"Well…thank you, Mason. Enjoy your research."

Dismissed, I say, "Thank you. I will."

As I walk, I think: my initial reaction of stress and fear; the pounding heart, the erratic breathing? Dead nuts indicators: Edie's the right woman for me. Now, how can I make that happen?

3:00 PM
Friday September 11, 1987
In the library with my journal

Entry: Looking academic with *The New York Times* and Jimmy Carter; I, the accidental essayist.

Let's compare Jimmy Carter, a failed president, with Ronald Reagan, the Great Communicator, leader, and emancipator of the spirit. President Carter showed compassion when he welcomed the Shah into the U.S. for cancer treatment. Then…hostages. In my opinion, the *Washington Post* and *The New York Times,* the journalistic scourge of government, got the rap started: hostages defined his presidency. Too bad.

Carter was, and still is, an intellectual. He was the type of president who ignored his aides' research and summaries and digested his own material voraciously cover to cover. In contrast, Reagan moves his lips when he reads.

The tough part is all this studying didn't allow Carter much time for the requisite congressional politics, which is the way he preferred it. In comparison, Reagan doesn't have much time for congressional politics, either, since he's too busy saving his ass. Besides, Reagan, according to a recent article in *The New Republic,* is in his pajamas by eight every evening.

Carter was different; refreshingly so, I think, even though things did not go his way. Case in point: the energy crisis hit. He responded by asking for sacrifice. Americans are the wrong constituents to hear that. Another: he wisely pulled aid from Nicaragua, but gave the Soviets the chance to move in with their big red, yet bogus wallets. Then, stagflation ruled, his voluntary wage and price controls were a joke, the hostage rescue was a total failure. Snake bit. Everything he did pissed off everyone. As predicted, Jimmy Carter would have been the subject of a recall vote had the Framers of The Constitution allowed such a thing.

What the editorial pages of this fine newspaper fail to say is that Jimmy Carter did all the politically wrong things for all the right reasons. He is an honorable man, unlike President Arms-To-Iran. Life isn't fair and the period of 1977 though 1980 is an example of what amounts to a truism. Example: Reagan is credited for whipping inflation, but the Yoda in that campaign was former Federal Reserve chairman Paul Volcker, the man in control of the banks. Mr. Volcker masterfully squeezed money so tight and raised interest rates so high inflation all but disappeared. It hurt. There was your sacrifice. But, inflation is gone. The irony is that, even though this all happened on Reagan's watch, Paul Volcker was a Carter appointee.

Many people lack the scope necessary to realize Jimmy Carter's legacy. Someday, we'll have to reconcile that. With Rawhide Reagan, that day could come at any moment.

And, that's the way it is.

3:30 PM
Friday September 11, 1987
At the reference desk

Edie is standing, facing the shelves against the back wall. I like it. It's called 'booty.' "Thank you, Edie."

She turns. "You're welcome," she says with those eyes. "What's up for Monday?"

"Probably disco."

"Really?" she asks with a contorted face.

"I'm kidding." I'm having an anxiety attack. Gotta get out of here. "Back to work."

"See ya, Mason," Edie says before she addresses the guy next to me.

3:45 PM
Friday September 11, 1987
Sitting at my desk
Dow Jones Industrial Average: 2,608 – 5.2 percent off all-time high

Looking at the green screen, I'm trying to go over my short position. No concentration is within miles. My knees are weak. I know exactly what's going on here with me and Edie. The right woman. It's been twelve years since the other right woman showed up. Incredibly, I remember the feeling. Fear, awe, and hopelessness. It all wigs me out, especially since Christine is but seven numbers away. God, help me go this one alone. It's better that way. See, You've convinced me of that. Now, make me carry out my end of the deal. And, while You're at it, put in a good word for me with Edie.

Twenty

1:30 PM
Sunday September 13, 1987
Getting out of the Olds in The H garage. Fenz is with me
Dow Jones Industrial Average: 2,608 – 5.2 percent off all-time high

"On one hand, I want to help you out any way I can, Mason. But, on the other hand, I can't believe I let you drag me downtown on a Sunday. And, what's that cool poster in your back seat?" Ally finally finishes as we walk toward the stairwell.

"I appreciate your help, Fenz, but you gotta realize, I spent the best part of yesterday thinking about this whole thing with Edie and I've come to the point where I can go no further until I get you involved. And, I'll tell you later about the cool poster."

Fenz and I descend the four flights leading to Hale Street. She is looking righteous, dressed weather-appropriately in a pink polo, tan shorts, and sandals. There is a part of me that hopes Edie sees her jump into my arms. It's possible. The only place Fenz would jump into my arms is in public.

"I've never seen you like this over a woman. I've never seen you like this over anything except shorting the Dow." We cross an empty Hale Street and head for the big fountain.

"I feel funny. It's been since my marriage…I just feel funny. How do I look?"

"Great, Mason. As always."

"Thanks. She's never seen me in anything but a coat and tie. I hope this goes over okay. Maybe I should have worn a belt with the Levis."

"You never do. You look great casual. Blue eyes, sexy and handsome, Mason." Ally touches my hand.

"This is not the time to bullshit me, Fenz."

"I'm not. Way to go with the pink polo, by the way."

"Don't remind me. We look like Donny and Marie Osmond, for Chrissake!"

"It's funny, and don't worry. And, I am glad you brought me. Really." Ally touches my shoulder.

"It has to be done." We stop beside the fountain. I'm beginning to develop feelings for the fountain. "I have to warn you," I say directly to Fenz, "She's really pretty."

"It sounds like she is."

"She's beautiful, with big booty. I like her."

"I really have never seen you like this. I was beginning to think it wasn't possible."

"Me, too. Let's go in."

Fenz and I walk up the steps to the door and enter. From a distance I see Edie facing to the left. She's wearing a gray pullover and what I think is a tan skirt. Five days into our relationship and I've yet to see her legs, or the feet attached to them. So much to discover.

"Stop right here," I whisper as I usher Fenz to the circulation desk.

"Where is she?" Fenz says softly.

"Follow me." I lead Ally right to a section where there are racks of paperbacks we can hide behind. The few patrons in the library today are all within fifty feet of us.

"I feel stupid," Fenz says.

"Okay, stop. Stand over there. Wait! She's looking!"

"Mason, she's not a Russian spy."

"There. Behind that big desk back there."

Fenz looks intently for several moments. "Oh, wow," she says.

"Isn't she something?"

"Yes."

I sigh. "See what I mean."

"Her hair shimmers. It's really tough to get long hair to sh—"

"Not her, damnit. She looks like Boy George. The other one."

"I'm going to get a closer look," Fenz says suddenly as she walks toward the reference section.

"Don't! Aw!!" I hiss, too loudly. It was a big mistake to come down here. But, there's Ally strolling to the desk, then cutting left toward fiction. My mind goes blank.

After milling about for an eternity, Fenz returns up the aisle from the left. She's carrying a book.

"Oh, Mason," Fenz says, standing close to me behind the racks. "Ohhhh. You're right. She's gorgeous."

I beam with pride. "What did I tell you?"

"I'd give anything for her looks."

"I'd give anything to be near her looks. Tell me, though," I say softly. "is there anything wrong...like...you know..."

"I think I know what you mean. You men are all alike. What's happened to the 'beautiful, with booty?'" Fenz says directly to me, hands on hips.

"Big booty," I say.

"God, Bricker, she's absolutely gorgeous! And, you knew her in college?"

"Yes."

"And, she doesn't recognize you?"

"To the best of my knowledge, no."

"Go tell her you knew her, right now," Fenz says, nudging me.

"I can't."

"Why?"

"I'm not very good at that." A couple of people stir in our direction. I am getting too loud again.

"Not good at what?"

"Wooing. Playing the 'game.' I'm afraid I'll say gormless things, like 'nice butt.'"

"Wha—gorm—I'm going back up there, then."

"No!" I grab Ally by her right arm.

"Mason, she is flat-out gorgeous, like a movie actress. God, she's beautiful. And you let her get away in college? How did that happen?"

"Joan."

"Well, Joan must have been Superwoman."

"At times."

"Go ask Edie out on a date."

"No."

"Now."

"No."

"Why not?"

"Probably because I haven't been on a date since I've known you. Since long before then." I bow my head and draw circles in the floor with my foot.

"You mean—"

"I didn't say that."

"How—"

"Don't ask."

A pause. Heads jump quickly to look at us. A pause. Fenz touches my hand. "Go, Mason. Go ask her out."

"Fenz, can't you see how difficult this is for me?"

"Yes, I can. Go."

"I can't."

"You're a good-looking guy." Ally gets close. "Really good-looking." She closes in more. "Extremely—"

I'm uncomfortable. "Okay. Thank you. I'll go!"

"Now, do you know what you're doing?" Ally asks as a teacher would.

"No."

"Let me help you. It's this simple. If you were to ask her out on a date, where would you want to take her?"

I look hard into Fenz' eyes. "I've thought about this so often. I have. Here it is. What do you think? The Café, to get a cup of coffee."

Ally glances around. "Ooo-kay…that's a start." She seems disappointed. "Now, go ask her."

"You don't approve, do you?"

"If that's what you want…it doesn't matter what I think."

"Of course, it matters what you think. That's why you're here."

"I know, honey," Fenz says, grabbing my elbow. I check the reference desk. I don't think Edie has seen us.

"I can't. As pathetic as it sounds, I can't."

"Just go ask her."

"No."

"Yes."

"No."

"Chicken."

I pause for a few moments, then capitulate. "All right. I will. Now, when I'm done, I'll walk out first, then a minute later you follow. Don't—"

"Mason, you sound like a high school girl."

"Fenz, right now, I feel like a high school girl."

"Well, become a man and ask your woman to…" she sighs, handing me her book, "…join you for a cup of coffee."

"Wish me luck."

I stride with confidence through people at desks. They have no idea I have a monster crush on their librarian. Finally, I complete the voyage from circulation to reference. Edie is there awaiting me. Or…so I wish. She is wearing the skirt…with black hose over her thick but shapely legs, and black flats on her tiny feet. I feel a stirring. That's all I need right now, but this time I'm looking at it positively. That indeed is all I need right now.

"Hi. Hello," I say. Edie's eyes stop my heart, then defib it.

"Hi. Are you having a good day?" she asks.

"Oh, yes. I'm ready to…research."

"How may I help you?"

I think of all the ways I can answer that question, like, 'jump over the desk, crawl into my chest and wet kiss me.' Yeah, that's my favorite. "Do you have, uh, the microfilm for *US News and World Report* for 1984?"

"Nixon and ten years after?" she asks with a grin.

"Yeah." I try to look like I'm pondering. "Question: will we ever trust the GOP again?"

"Not if I have anything to do with it," Edie quickly retorts. Uh, oh. Get…out…Mason.

"Really, there was a time…" I say.

"Hoover?" Edie asks again. Damn, the woman is good.

"Well, a time in the academic sense. Actually, there was that bad stock market in 1984 I want to revisit." I'm *thisclose* to stammering uncontrollably.

"Fair enough. I'll be back."

Ask her out. It's just a cup of coffee. It's not anything advanced, like dinner. Just…oh, shit, she looks good. Five years of Christine. I don't deserve Edie. Yes, I do. Here goes. I'm about to revisit breakfast. She's back with the microfilm. Time to bail.

"You know, my pager just went off. I think they need me at the office." I don't even have a fuckin' pager, but if she asks, it's in my pocket and it's on vibrate.

"You work Sundays, too?" she asks.

"Yes."

"Stinks, doesn't it. You've told me you're a money manager. Where do you work?"

"An investment firm. Fuller Busher, over in the Horowitz Building."

"Oh. That's neat."

"Yes. Well, I'm going to get a cup of coffee next door." That is one lame attempt, Mason. Get the hell out.

"I thought you said you were going to the office?" Edie asks, tilting her head. Oh, what a heart-breaker…

"Ye…Ye…Yeah. After coffee."

"Well, good luck getting that coffee next door." The corners of her mouth are turned up slightly.

"Thank you."

"The Café is closed on Sundays."

Hell. "I knew that. Thanks for reminding me."

"Come back for the magazines," she says pleasantly.

Oh, my. "I will. Thank you."

"Anytime. It's what I do."

"Bye. Better run." On that, I turn and walk with what I'm sure is a noticeable wobble back to the front and out the door. Damn, the alarm just went off. How did I get Fenz' book? So much for a low profile. I step up to the circulation desk. "Sorry, I forgot." The librarian issues a disgusted look. I just remembered. I still don't have a goddamned library card.

Making it down the steps, I see Fenz beside the fountain. I'm sure she went first because she couldn't bear watching me.

"Well?" she asks.

"I am such a loser," is all I can think to say. It's very accurate. "I really suck at this, Fenz."

"Yes, you do."

"Thanks. I think I'll just stick my head in this fountain and breathe."

Fenz looks at me with a combination of compassion and disappointment. More disappointment, really. "What's your problem?"

"I don't know. I absolutely do not know. I look in the mirror. Objectively look in the mirror. I'm not too bad. Why am I acting like this?"

We pause and stand. "I've been thinking, Mason," Ally says. "If I have to put it into one word, it would be inexperience. So, let's get it back."

"Let's get it back to The H before Edie comes out here and sees me at my absolute worst." We walk down the steps to cross the street. A string of five cars is approaching, so we wait.

"Okay. Try it again, Mason. We're going to get it back. Let me ask you, if it's not too much to ask, how did you first ask Joan out?"

"Fenz!"

"C'mon! Let's get it back!"

"Thursday I told her I loved her—"

"Okay! Now we're getting somewhere."

"Friday, we kissed. Saturday, we screwed. Sunday, we were married."

Fenz looks straight ahead across the street. "You know, that's so weird I can see it happening. Now, what happened with you two before then?"

The cars pass. Fenz and I cross Hale. "I worked for her. I wasn't about to ask her out. That would have been inappropriate."

"What! Inappropriate? Jesus!"

"I was nineteen. That's how I felt."

"What about Friday and Saturday?"

"I told you...I was nineteen."

We're headed for The H. I know the front door is locked, so we have to wind up the parking garage ramps to get to the guard's access to the building.

"Okay. Forget Joan. The one before her," Ally says.

"Alice. We were freshmen. We never dated. She seduced me and we had sex for two weeks. Then we became friends."

"I would have liked to have known you when you were in college," says Fenz. I look at her. She's not smiling.

"I would have liked to have known you. Maybe you would have talked me out of marrying Joan."

"It was destiny. Anyway, I was eleven and looked like a boy. The one before Alice."

I can't imagine Fenz without boobs. "I was a senior in high school. She was a college grad. Ursula. She worked in her uncle's diner. I used to hang around and drink coffee. Ursula and I read and walked through the mountains."

"Edie. Ursula. Didn't you know any Janes?"

"Frankly, no."

Ally rolls her eyes. "Anyway, Ursula. How did you ask her?"

"I never did. She asked me." We turn onto the second circle.

"All the time?"

"Every time."

"Even the first time?"

"Especially the first time."

"I always thought you were unique, Mason, but this takes the cake."

"I'm rather proud of it. Women chase me, except for the past five years. Or, maybe I just wasn't paying attention."

"Something has got to change before you get Edie to chase you. In fact, Edie won't chase you. You can't just wait for her to ask you to take a walk in the mountains or buy you a cup of coffee."

I pause, then I pause again. "I need your help, Fenz."

"You need a date."

"I just told you how difficult it is to even speak around Edie."

Fenz stops and grabs my hand. "Not Edie," she says.

I look at her. "This…is scary."

"You need a date. A practice date. In fact, I have someone in mind."

"I knew it." I continue walking. Fenz follows. "A freakin' set-up. So predictable."

"Screw you," Fenz says in the figurative sense. "Actually, she's a friend of Geri's, and I think she's okay."

"Her name isn't Lia, is it?"

"No, but you know her. Or, at least, know of her."

I halt. "Okay. Lay it on me."

"Margot Montgomery."

"I know her and know of her and I say no to her." Waving my hands through the air, I continue. "How could you even suggest Margot Montgomery? She's not my type!"

"You don't have a type, Mason!" Fenz exclaims as she storms away.

"Edie's my type!" I say, still standing.

Fenz stops and turns, about three car lengths away. "And Edie will keep ignoring you unless you get on the stick. It's my way or the highway, the highway to loneliness. Loneliness, dude. That's the mud you're stuck in right now." She turns around and begins to walk briskly around the third curve. I stand too long, then run to catch up with her. Uphill. Damn, these cigarettes are tough on a man.

Finally there, I say, "Okay, Fenz. You're right."

Ally turns to me. "You're damned straight I'm right. I'm your friend. I want what's best for you. That's probably Edie. And I think the way to Edie is through Margot Montgomery."

"Okay. You're right. But, let me ask you. You ever talked with Margot? Listened to her? Fenz, she can't string a noun and a verb together without the aid of a teleprompter."

"How did she become the number one news anchor in the Pittsburgh area, then?" Fenz asks with her hands on her hips.

"She has the mind of an anchor. A boat anchor."

"Oh, fuck you, Mason," Fenz says, hands still on hips. "Not all of us can be a PhD. You asshole." She bolts up the ramp again.

"Ally! Al—oh, damnit! Ally. I'm sorry," I say immediately and wisely and while wheezing after my second run in a minute's time. "I'm sorry. I deserved that."

Ally stops. There is silence. A car winds around the turn. Fenz and I move to the side to let him pass. "Apology accepted, you asshole." She doesn't look happy.

"Fenz, I'm going to do as you say."

"Margot is not a woman—"

"She's in drag? Does the TV station know this?" I joke.

"Mason!" Fenz says, like my mother used to. "Margot is a rung on the ladder to Edie."

"Well put. I like your practice date idea," I say, feeling a need to suck up. "Besides, I'm not looking for intellectual stimulation."

"However," Fenz says, moving closer as only she can, "what if you find stimulation in that special way?"

"I'm saving myself for Edie," I say quickly.

We pause. Fenz and I resume walking. "How long have you been saving yourself?"

"Since Saturday August 22, 1987, just after 12:30 in the morning."

"I didn't know you were having sex," Fenz says in all earnestness.

"You don't tell me when you have sex. And, I don't want to know."

"I don't want to know about you, either. Except maybe when you have sex with Edie," Fenz says with a nudge and a smile.

"Oh, you'll know then," I say.

"It'll be as obvious as the silly grin on your face," she says with the smile.

"Positive imagery," I say. "For it to happen, I must first imagine it."

"How often do you imagine it?"

"When her back is to me."

Fenz and I are silent as we walk to the fourth curve. Rounding it, I can see the Olds.

"Mason."

"Yes, Fenz."

"I believe in love at first sight."

I pause and take a breath. "I do, too."

"Go ahead and say it," she says, stopping and standing.

I stop. "Say what?"

"You know what."

"No."

"Say it for me."

"No."

Fenz grabs my hand again. This is where I usually do whatever she says. "Say it."

I pause for a long time. Two cars go by, one up, one down. The occupants of those cars must think I'm getting ready to propose. If they only knew...

"I'm in love with Edie Loden," I say. "Yep, I am."

"I knew it!" Ally says with glee. "How does it feel to say it?"

"A sense of fright. A sense of relief." We're still holding hands.

"That's the way it should be. It's been so long since you've been in love that you've forgotten how frightening and wonderful it is."

"I love Edie," I bravely say.

"I just love love!" Fenz squeals right before she hugs me.

"Yeah, I guess," I say, bewildered by why women do that.

"Good. Now, here's some advice. When you're out with her, don't tell her right away. You might scare her off." Fenz smiles.

I pause. We drop hands. "You want scary? There's my car. I have something to show you." We walk to the Olds in silence. After reaching in my pocket to find my keys, I unlock the industrial tan door of my longmobile. The bag I'm looking for is in the back seat on the driver's side. I push the poster aside as I reach back there to grab the bag. My stomach churns because I'm about to show Fenz the most obsessive thing I've done in my life to date.

"Here," I say as I pull a five by seven picture frame out of the bag. I hand it to her. Fenz examines it.

"What is it?"

"That's from *Tepidarium*, my favorite work of art. I bought the poster at an art show at the William Penn Hotel in downtown Pittsburgh. I cut this out, had it enlarged, and took it to Flowers Frames to frame it. Over here," I say as I motion over an area to the left of the frame and above, "are twenty-two or so women in various states of nudity. My interests do not lie with them. This woman in the frame sits to the right in the painting. Look at her."

Ally contemplates as she looks at the picture. "No," she finally says. "No. I mean, yes, she does look like Edie, but you...this is weird."

"The dark hair, same length. The rich, brown eyes. The look, like she owns the world. Fenz, I saw this painting in Paris earlier this year. I looked at it and looked at it for an hour. You believe in love at first sight. How about love before first sight?"

Fenz looks at the frame again, quiet for the longest time. She then looks up to me. "Mason," she says, "I know you're not sick. I know that. You've always treated me right, and people around you, except for John. But, this confirms what I've thought all along. You're a brick shy. You're a shingle short. And, you know something? That's all right with me. I understand why you feel like you do about Edie. I understand you love Edie and I even understand why...you see her in this painting. And, to show you how crazy I am, I understand why you would frame part of a painting you saw in Paris because it looks like a woman you met...again...five days ago...a woman who now owns your heart. And even crazier, I approve. I'm with you." Fenz moves her head up to kiss my cheek.

I know I'm blushing. "You know, Fenz? I guess we're both fucked up."

"I guess so, you freak."

"You can just see this woman's attitude. That's what really gets me about Edie. It's her attitude. And her face. Really, her beautiful face. And her fanny. I appreciate her ass. But, mostly her attitude. It's her attitude. Always has been. She's upbeat. She's witty."

"She's everything you need in a woman, Mason. God knows you need more of that. So, you have to be upbeat and witty."

"That's going to be one helluva transformation."

"Not so bad. So, how are you going to get started?" Ally asks with a smile and a wink.

"Stop smoking," I say.

"Damn. You're serious."

"It's like kissing an ashtray."

"You know it, sweetie. Now, what else are you going to do?"

"Call Margot Montgomery."

Fenz pumps her fist. "That's my boy! My boy!"

"Vinny used to say that," I say before I realize it. "He used to say it just like you said it. 'That's my boy! My boy!'"

Fenz grins big. "We're both right."

"Vinny was as pretty as you. Damn, what a head-turner. I was invisible when I was with him." I'm smiling as I recall those days.

Ally touches my hand, "I would have liked to have known him."

"Yeah," I say, "You showed up a few months after. God's watching out for Mason, Fenz." I grin as I give her a good-ol'-boy punch on the arm. I take another cleansing breath. "Thank you for everything. Come on, I'll take you home. You deserve that."

As I open the car door for her, I notice a tear on Ally's cheek. "You bastard," she says, "Anyway, next time, can we do this on a Wednesday?"

Twenty-One

1:10 PM
Wednesday September 16, 1987
Standing in front of the reference desk, holding my journal, silently chewing nicotine gum.
Dow Jones Industrial Average: 2,541 – 7.6 percent off the all-time high

"Where you been?" Edie asks me.

That face...those eyes...finally I reply, "Working."

"Since Sunday? Don't they let you out occasionally in the money management business?"

Resplendent simplicity. Light blue long sleeve oxford blouse. Drive-me-crazy black slacks. Her closet most likely contains racks and racks of black slacks. I'd like to find out. "It's controlled by a lottery." Upbeat and witty. Just as Fenz says.

Edie flashes the deadly smile, "They draw lots and stone the winner?"

"No, Shirley Jackson, they don't," I say with a grin of my own.

"You're good," Edie says, not releasing the smile or my heart that's attached to it.

"Yeah. Th-thanks." There goes witty.

"Now, how can I help you?"

"WSJs. Early 1981. Around April."

"Reagan?"

"In a sense. David Stockman."

"Be right back." Edie leaves, right in front of the business end of her black slacks. I...absolutely...have to stop thinking about sex with her. All normal guys think about sex all the time. Edie seems to be a woman who doesn't go for normal guys. But, if that were the case, she'd be in my arms right now.

She returns. "Here. Please don't tell me you're a fan of David Stockman."

"Not necessarily. There was a bad stock market around that time. That, plus I just find people committed to their principles interesting."

"Like Stalin and Mussolini?"

Get out while you can, Mason. "Like Jimmy Carter."

"This should be good." Edie's smile had disappeared right at about the first Stockman.

I trudge on. "They are as moral as any good person. True, they are on the opposite ends of the political spectrum, but they did stick to what they believed. Both were at times wrong and both at times had some good arguments. However, as a result of their guts, both Carter and Stockman were vilified more than most others by the people who were most threatened by them simply because both of them tried to do what they thought was right. And, they were right. Both of them."

Edie props herself up on the top of the desk with her straight right arm and holds her left hand on her hip. A powerful statement is that pose. A day goes by.

"Okay," she says, same pose, same stare. "I'll let you off the hook." An ever-so-slight grin returns.

I'll try witty again. "Why let me off the hook?" Not...quite.

"Because," she pauses, same pose, same stare, "you're good."

"We could have some great arguments," I say. "That one was just the beginning."

"Go do your research," Edie says. "And let this be known: I could have kicked your ass if I wanted to." The grin grows.

I laugh. "Thank you, Edie." I turn and walk. And she still doesn't recognize me.

3:00 PM
Wednesday September 16, 1987
Sitting at a library desk, writing in my journal
Dow Jones Industrial Average: somewhere around 2,500, I guess.

September 16, 1987. In the library. The pseudo-research continues...

You know, all Stockman needed was forty-four billion dollars in spending reductions and the proposed budget, Reagan's first budget coming off a campaign of fiscal responsibility, would have been balanced. That was all. So, he jumped over dollars to find pennies and pulled a frontal assault on what he called the welfare state by going after such perverse programs as Job Corps, Head Start, and the women's, infants' and children's food program. What a pinhead!

I believe in smaller government, too. David Stockman and I agree on ridding the nation of tobacco subsidies, farm programs, and other programs that encourage solar energy in Vermont and luxury hotels in ghettos. David Stockman and I are proponents of the free market. And, David Stockman and I agree on the importance of a strong military to defend the borders. However, that's where we part. The United States government should be a compassionate government. In addition to armies and navies, the United States has a duty bound by God to care for the poor, the sick, and for those who made this nation great, the older folks. Stockman wanted to leave them in the wake of the rising tide that was supposed to float all boats. It doesn't work that way, Dave.

He wanted forty-four billion? Well, follow the money. The defense budget. The quarter trillion dollar defense budget. I know, I just said defend the borders, but you don't need to buy gilded generals to do it. As Lee Iacocca wrote in his autobiography a couple of years ago, any good businessman can wring ten percent out of anything. It wouldn't have taken much effort to find forty-four billion in the Pentagon hallways. There's your balanced budget, the nation's safe, and no one was inconvenienced.

David Stockman never found that forty-four, mostly because he was looking in all the wrong places. In fact, today's deficit is much worse as Reagan turned out to be too nice and bemused to lead his own revolution. As well, you have to consider the fact that the Revolution had some credence. There were many money-shovelers, such as Senator Jesse Helms of North Carolina and Congressman Jim Wright of Texas, money-shovelers who had to be exposed and rooted out. Problem is, those guys are just two examples of two white men leading millions of other white men in the protection of their white man personal interests. The senator and the speaker are not the statesmen they claim to be. They're simply vendors and peddlers.

Next problem? Let us convince Reagan that the Soviet Union will fall under its own weight, without the threat of gazillion dollar defense systems in space. The Soviets are so broke they can't even afford to be desperate. Result: so much money will be saved we'll be writing tax rebate checks well into the 1990s.

3:30 PM
Wednesday September 16, 1987
Crossing Hale Street with a journal filled with opinions and musings that I would die to protect from anyone ever reading.
Dow Jones Industrial Average: I'll find out soon enough.

Edie wasn't available for more political sparring when I returned the microfilm. That's just another activity in which we can partake when she finally realizes that she should do again what she did twelve years ago.

Oh, well, it's time to get back to work.

Since Monday, the only Caretaker ticket I landed was a young attorney who was on the big end of a big lawsuit that went his way in a big way. He put in fifty thousand, one-tenth of his winnings, with the other nine-tenths going in stocks. He also wanted some stock ideas from me. When I gave them to him, he of course didn't like them. I wished him luck and sent him to Wylie. Mr. McInally prefers to not be seen in the office with me, but he still honors our agreement of paying me a dime on every commission dollar I send to him. Not gross, but hard cash in my pocket. I know. I'm profiting from recommendations of stocks as investments, but at least I'm not padding my commissions. In a convoluted way, I have to stick to my principles.

The Caretaker sale upped my score to fifty six hundred, with ten days remaining. I'm slightly ahead of my thousand a day, hence the afternoon in the library with Edie. I'll do that fifteen, and I won't stroke out from stress trying.

3:50 PM
Wednesday September 16, 1987
At my desk, writing my new investment newsletter for my engineers, actually doing anything I can to avoid talking to prospects and clients.
Dow Jones Industrial Average: 2,522 – 8.4 percent off all-time high

The Instrument Pilot
Volume 1, Issue 1.

The Inaugural Issue – Already a collector's item

Greetings, loyal clients! Here's the latest by way of The Instrument Pilot:
The good news is the market's instrument flying indicators are in the worst shape since December 1983, the start of a seven-month slide that saw the Dow give back fifteen percent and fare much worse for the stocks of smaller companies. Corncob says the market is following the script for higher prices, except for the action in the bond market. Ronnie's logic is like saying your house is beautiful except for that pesky collapsing foundation. In fact, the monetary signals are very bearish. The aforementioned bond market is in a waterfall decline and has been for a couple months now. Short term rates, rates that define the liquidity necessary to drive stocks to rising levels, are rising themselves. In other words, the price of money we need is going up, up, and up. Not good. Furthermore, sentiment is poor because everyone is too slap-happy in spite of the stall and the seven percent decline. There is a consensus that we'll simply turn it around like a red Mercedes 450SL on a wide street. That'll be hard to do because too many speculators are buying stocks now. Remember what I've told you: speculation is the epitome of emotional investing, most always wrong at market turns. Consider that with the added risk of choppy, frothy, disappearing momentum; a loss of momentum at a time when the market needs that extra oomph to fulfill the expectations of all those ecstatic people. The strength required to overcome all the problems is just not there.
If I were a guest on public broadcasting's *Wall $treet Week* this Friday night, *Wall $treet Week*, the paragon of cheesy metaphors, here's the cheesy metaphor I would use: this Mercedes of happy investors is going nowhere but reverse unless someone releases the parking brake of higher interest rates, I don't care how much gas you give it.

We're in the right place with our shorts. Believe me, we are. And, I ask all of you who aren't with us to get with it. Just kidding about the 'get with it' part.

My advice to those who don't want to short: protect your capital; visit your friendly banker. He or she will take very good care of you.

4:10 PM
Wednesday September 16, 1987
At my desk, telephone in hand, fingers on the buttons
Dow Jones Industrial Average: 2,527 - 8.2 percent off all-time high

1-744-2032
One ring. "Good afternoon. WCRZ. Channel 5."

"This is Mason Bricker calling for Margot Montgomery. May I please speak with her?"

"Okay…" the woman behind the switchboard is surely consulting a list. "Yes, sir," she finally says.

Silence. My cravings are so bad I could smoke a Virginia Slim while having wild sex. "Mason!" says a polished female television voice.

"Hello, Margot?"

"I've been expecting your call. Geri told me to expect your call. I'm swamped. Very busy. Gotta go on in an hour. How does tomorrow sound? Mountain Wharf? Seven? Looking forward to it. The station has let me off."

"O—okay."

"See you there. I'm looking forward to it. I already said that, didn't I? Gotta run. Don't be late. Bye now."

The line goes dead. And the streak remains. I still haven't asked a woman out.

Twenty-Two

12:30 PM
Friday September 18, 1987
At The Café with Fenz, acting disgruntled, sullen, vexed, and pissy
Dow Jones Industrial Average: 2,516 – 8.6 percent off all-time high

"We're down three percent in three days, Fenz. That's not good."

"It's good for you," Ally says, taking a sip of her café au lait.

"That's the bad thing about being on the short side," I say, running my finger around the rim of my espresso. "For me to be successful, there must be pain. I don't like that part. Well, I like being right, but—"

"I know."

"In three days we're down hard. Haven't seen anything like that for a long time. Maybe fall 1985. Then, we bounced. I owned stocks then."

"I know. That's when I started with you guys. Like you said, it was 'we're all going to die,' then 'rock and roll!' Talk about mood swings," Fenz says, tearing off a bite of a scone and handing it to me. "Eat this. You don't eat enough."

"I'm too nervous to eat. And this heating oil I call coffee is making me sick." A guy in a dark three-piece suit walks up to the counter to get a cup of joe. Then, he's out. Doesn't he know vests are yesterday?

"What's wrong?" Fenz asks.

I pause. I sigh. "I've made sixteen Caretaker pitches in the past two days. Six were in person. Net result? One measly ten thousand dollar ticket. Four hundred gross."

"That's not too bad, Mason. You'll do it. I predict. You'd better do it. You're the only one keeping me sane over there."

"Thanks. You'll be okay, though. I counted at least six men who gawked at you and your gold spandex business suit on the way over here. We didn't walk the width of a football field and you got 'em dropping." Fenz smiles at me, then shoves a big piece of scone in her mouth. She takes four chews and opens wide to show me her food just like I used to do to my little sister. "That was disgusting, but, my dear, you can get by with it because your skirt is doing that up-under-the-butt thing that's hot right now among you young women." Ally takes two more chews and shows me her food again.

"Okay, you've just mentioned my butt and twice you complimented me on my shoes." She's grinning.

"It's those spikes you have for heels. Very attractive, especially when I consider how much they would hurt if you forgot to take them off. By the way, never give up sex and smoking simultaneously."

"Bricker…" Fenz says, leaning in and touching my right hand. "I've never seen you this horny. What did Margot do to you last night?" She smiles.

I contemplate my answer as I gulp the espresso. Wincing, I decide to tell the truth. "Margot…is not attractive."

"Bullshit! Men love her. That's what the ratings say."

"Fenz, you're attractive. Edie is the most attractive woman I've seen in the decade of the eighties," I say, conveniently forgetting about Christine. Hell with it, Edie has her in a photo finish. "Margot can't hold your slingbacks, Ally, especially after you have a conversation with her."

"So," Fenz says, placing her chin in her hands, elbows on the table, "I guess you had a bad evening."

The three-piece walks back in to fetch a stack of papers he apparently left behind. "On the surface, you could probably call it your standard date. But, deep down, she's scary."

"All women are scary, to you."

"No. Let me explain…"

*   *   *

Margot is at the bar of The Mountain Wharf, to the right of the entrance. She's dressed TV, like a flag in a royal blue dress and red stilettos, making her blonde-and-

blue-eyes radiate. I don't want her to look this good. As I approach, she extends her hand, saying through a fake smile, "I said to not be late."

"Sorry. I was working," I say, lying in my defense.

"I'm running on TV time, you know." *The fake smile does not disappear. I try a different direction.* "You look great, Margot."

"I've looked better. Our table's ready."

*   *   *

"So, you were late," Fenz says.

"You're missing the point..."

*   *   *

We're sitting at a booth. The incandescent light over our table does nothing for Margot's incredibly average face, but there is the matter of her long legs and the narrow feet at the end of them. It's salad time and the conversation has offered little. I figure the best thing to get her talking is to talk with her about her favorite subject. "How does it feel to be on camera?"

Margot strokes her beer. Stop that. Finally, she replies, "I try to make the news good news."

"Oh," *I say sincerely,* "That's good. How do you do that?"

"I do it good."

What?

"I know it's supposed to be well," *Margot says,* "That was just a figure of speech. Geri says you were a professor or something."

How did we get here? "Well, yes, I was."

She gives me a sly grin. "I bet you hit on the coeds, didn't you."

"No," *I say succinctly.*

"C'mon," *Margot urges with a nudge to my arm.* "Tell me the truth. You at least wanted to. I had a great-looking psych prof who did it with at least four of my sorority sisters."

"When did he find time to teach?" *I ask, hoping to get beyond this ridiculous subject.*

"He was scum."

"What am I?" *I ask before I realize it has jumped out of my mouth.*

"Good, so far."

*   *   *

"That didn't set very well with you," Fenz observes.

"I was a restrained gentleman. It got worse..."

*   *   *

The first bottle of wine is drained. The next one arrives as the salad plates are being cleared. 'Lull' is the word I use to describe the evening so far. However, my bargain with God is seriously challenged as I'm again thinking of the long legs and the narrow feet.

"So, you're a broker," she says.

"On my bad days," I say in an attempt to inject a little fun into this otherwise humorless date. It bombed hard.

"My broker has me investing in these market things called selling naked puts that he says are a lock to win. He says I'll make money as the market goes up or even just stays up."

Buying puts, or put contracts, is a complicated way to 'invest' that market players use to play for the likelihood of lower stock prices. In the opposite sense, selling naked puts, or reverse puts, is an even more complicated way to play for the likelihood of higher prices. They're called 'naked' because, similar to selling short, the player is naked, completely uncovered against the chance of infinite losses if she is wrong. Therefore, as a player selling naked puts, Margot is just another speculator. The clues are a) 'these market things called selling naked puts,' meaning the investment is something she doesn't understand or can't even identify, and b) 'a lock to win,' or more accurately stated as broker bullshit. Stockbrokers can make a lot of gross from their clients' speculative investments because speculators move and trade and create executions in an execution-based compensation system. Why does one speculate? Greed. Lack of scope. Impatience. Combine all these with a very persuasive broker and you've got the punch line: Q: How do you get to a hundred grand in the stock market? A: Start with a million.

"Margot, it sounds to me that if the market goes down, you're rotting flesh. I can't think of a better way to say it."

"He says that won't happen."

Yet another instrument flying indicator in my favor.

*   *   *

"Damn, Mason," Fenz says wide-eyed, "That's frightening."

"Look, the lure of easy money…speculation has done investors well this year, so well that everyone evidently has forgotten about the incredible risk you assume. If they understood what could happen…well, this bull market has them so snookered they'd probably still do it."

"I think Todd and Jason have some clients who do naked puts," Fenz says, tapping her empty cup.

"A perverted way to play the upside. If I could think of a way to save their clients and make those two look like the fools they are…it's not healthy how I feel about them. Anything involving Todd and/or Jason brings back my kickoff team instincts. I gotta get off them. Back to Margot…"

*   *   *

Margot is most of the way through her pasta alfredo. Very little of this evening has been fun. I've gone beyond the legs; she does not impress me. She can barely successfully execute a valid declarative sentence. She has the imagination of her half-

*empty plate. However, there is still the matter of my libido. I'm struggling with my
libido. My body says I should have been with Christine four times since confession.*

"That stockbroker I told you about?" *Margot says out of the clear blue.* "He's my
boyfriend."

This is interesting. "Your boyfriend. So, Margot, does he mind that we're out
together?"

"Oh, he doesn't know. But, we're on a break, anyway."

Jeez Louise, another one of those dating rules that's beyond me. "What's a
break?"

"You know, a break," *she says as she sips wine,* "Just a break, not a break-up."

This girl hasn't left the greek life. "What are the rules of engagement of a
break?"

"We were engaged, but we decided it wasn't good for our careers."

Or future gene pools. "Good move," *I say, biting on a big slice of filet. God,
lodge this steak in my trachea before I have sex with this woman.*

*   *   *

"Mason, you should have just taken her in your arms and gotten it over with,"
Fenz says with a grin, leaning back.

"Do...not...say that," I say. "The next time I will be making love. And, it looks
like it'll be Edie since she's the only woman I love. So, there."

"With your hormones raging," Fenz says, keeping the grin, "I admire your
convictions. I've heard your descriptions of last night, but I've heard the talk going
around about the news princess. She wants you."

"And, others. But, she's shallow, Fenz..."

*   *   *

This is good cheesecake. Margot has a slice, too. It's like we're going steady.

"What religion are you, Mason?"

Where does she get all this? "Catholic."

"Me, too!" *she wails as if I had announced my sister is an Alpha Chi.*

"Match made in heaven," *I say. The sarcasm is like the tree in the forest.*

"What do you think about abortion?" *she asks.*

*I pause, looking like I'm giving the question due consideration. In reality, I can't
believe she asked. And, I can't believe I'm going to answer.* "Like many, I don't want
any abortions. Not at all. However, I believe the Roe v. Wade decision. I think abortion
should be a decision between a woman and her physician, and only between a woman
and her physician. Everyone else should stay the hell out."

"I've never looked at it that way," *Margot says with a blank stare. After a few
beats, she refocuses.* "Do you want another bottle of wine?"

*   *   *

"I guess you're right," Fenz says as she stands.

"Fenz, if this was a successful trial date, I'm becoming a priest." I stand and walk to the door. Ally follows. "Or, maybe it was a success in that it reminded me that there are but a few good women available and I can therefore scratch Margot off my list."

"Mason, don't let Margot get you down." We stand on the sidewalk, ready to cross the street and back to the office. "Go see Edie," Fenz says.

"I'm going to have to be in a better frame of mind before I see Edie," I say.

"Go."

"I need to prospect for more Caretaker." The stream of cars becomes more endless.

"When has business ever stood in your way of doing anything fun? Go see Edie," Fenz says, "Get her to get you in that better state of mind. Then get back to work."

I pause. "Okay."

"Good. She'll make the weekend better. I'm sorry about Margot. I feel responsible."

"Margot confirmed my beliefs."

"How's that?"

"Never date a blonde," I say as I bend down to kiss Ally on the cheek. "Thank you. I'm going to take your advice. Later."

Ally grabs the sleeve of my coat. "Don't give me that dumb blonde stuff," she says to my surprise.

"Why should you care?"

"Mary is a blonde, damnit." She does care.

"Fenz, it's not the dumb thing. There are plenty of smart blondes. Mary. Candice Bergen. That bouncy girl who plays Lucy Ewing. It's just that male America looks at blondes as the ideal—"

"So, you zag," Fenz says with a smile. "Is that it? That's what I'm worth to you. A zag." She punches my arm. "I'm insulted."

"Shut up. Besides, it's not her hair, Ally. It's the eyes. It's Edie's eyes. It's your eyes. It's Meg Tilly's eyes."

"Meg Tilly?"

"*The Big Chill*. Meg Tilly. What a frame. It's brown eyes, Fenz. Brown eyes are deep. I like deep."

"Okay," Ally says. "How can I not like that? I'm going to run. Go see Edie," Fenz grabs my hand, then walks and heads across Hale.

Follow the directions. Go see Edie.

1:30 PM
Friday September 18, 1987
At the reference desk
Dow Jones Industrial Average: along with sex and cigarettes, just one more thing to worry about.

I've counted five people Edie and Boy George are waiting on. No conversation today. I don't even feel like research. I don't even know why I'm here.

It's taken a minute for Edie to turn her attention to me. Now, I know why I'm here. My optimistic side wants me to believe she hurried.

"Good afternoon," Edie says, smiling, hands folded on the desk. She's wearing a cream blouse, a navy skirt and ivory hose very well. Her beauty takes my breath away.

"Hello, Edie," I say, smiling back. I think of Margot and feel guilty for cheating on Edie.

"Can I help?" she asks, the message being, 'please hurry.'

"May I please have *The New Republics* from earlier this year?" I ask spontaneously.

Her face beams into an 'I'm impressed!' look. I'm just a bit irritated that Edie obviously thinks that simply because I'm a stockbroker I must be a Reagan Republican and therefore can't possibly read the best liberal journal available.
But…whatthefuck…she can get by with it. "I'll take care of it," she says.

I purposely avert my eyes from her butt as she walks. It's been almost a month, God. Give me a sign to keep hanging on, or I'll call Christine.

Edie returns with several magazines. "Here are a few good ones I liked. There's even a piece on the stock market."

She's interested… "Oh. What did you think?"

"I don't know. I don't understand it." Edie rubs the cover of one magazine with her left thumb.

"It's easy," I say. "When you have the time, I'd like to explain it to you." Christ, Mason, how about that for a couple of yuppies' first date? Yuck!

"One part of one I found interesting. The writer talked about the false hope of the Reagan administration being reflected in the markets and about how dangerous that can be."

"What did I tell you? It's easy. You're a natural. Investors have to be careful out there. You see what others miss."

"Go away," Edie says with a grin and a blush.

Make a graceful and timely exit, Brick. "I appreciate it, Edie." I turn slightly and say, "What a crowd. Are you being paid piece work today?"

"I wish," she responds. Then, she winks.

That's it. That's what I'm looking for. No Christine. Thank you, Jesus.

2:30 PM
Friday September 18, 1987
In the library
Dow Jones Industrial Average: nothing can be further from my mind

Entry: in the library

I borrowed a few sheets of legal paper and a pen from an older woman next to me because I didn't bring the journal. I'll just staple this in. There is something I need to write now and I must write it in Edie's presence. I know it's only been nine days, and I know I am feeling the emptiness of five years of sexual squalor, but this is where I am. I accept that.

Regardless of how disconcerting my thoughts are, these are indeed my thoughts. In the past nine days, I have done nothing to cause her concern. My words have been appropriate. My actions, however bumbling they are at times, are not a threat. The total duration of my conversations with her is measured in minutes. I haven't been here every day, and when I'm here I have successfully sold her on my intentions to research for my job. After all this, Edie may be flattered, but she can't seriously think something's up.

That last sentence comes from a man in denial.

Okay. What if she can read my mind? Well, let her read this.

I awoke yesterday morning dreaming that I was making love with Edie. The feeling was more intense than ever. Dreams are a way of dealing with unresolved conflicts and issues, but that one launched me into a spin the magnitude of which I cannot recall experiencing. Unresolved, indeed. Unfortunately. My hope is that one of these days, there will be resolution. Therefore, my duty is to straighten my life out so that when the opportunity arises, I'll be deserving.

I will be deserving. Christine is history. I haven't had a cigarette for a solid week. Okay, six days. I haven't prayed the Rosary, but I held it this morning. Okay, I moved it. I mean, I brushed it with my hand. Anyway, Edie's good for me. I will be deserving.

Having said that and believing it, I can now let my mind run with Edie. To me, Edie is not about sex. Sex with Edie is a bonus. The real Edie will simply love me as I love her. I know it will happen. Sex will be good, but for now I see us walking through Johnson Park in the autumn. In a matter of weeks, there will be plenty of leaves for us to crunch under foot, a sound that will keep the rhythm of our souls in tandem. Our love will be a beautiful dance, a mix of romance and whimsy. Edie will hold my heart as she shares with me her wonderful wit. Her voice will be so melodic I will be compelled to give her all the time I have. And more. I, too, will capture her attention as she has mine, making her laugh and giggle with me. The experience will be more pleasurable than anything I have imagined. It will be better than sex as I know it. With Edie, however, I may change my tune on that one, but for now give me the leaves and the walk.

Selling short, clients, and Caretaker are merely things that occupy my life until it is time to meet Edie. I've thought a lot about it. The day is cool. I'm in a herringbone wool blazer, a white pinpoint, Levis, and beat-up loafers. There will be no reference desk between us today. Edie is waiting for me beside the fountain. She's elegant in a black long sleeve cotton blouse, faded denims, a black leather coat, and black flats. As always, what she wears is secondary. It's her face. It was twelve years ago. It was last Wednesday. And, everyday I see her face is like the first day I saw her face. The incredible eyes will look at me in reflection of the undying love I have for her. Then she'll lay the wink on me, the same one she gave me just an hour ago, the one that says, 'You are the only man in my life, so let's have some fun with this, okay?' Okay. In the matter of several dozen steps, we will be seated at The Café. Hers will be a cappuccino. Mine will be a double espresso, just to prove to her I can handle European coffee and live to tell about it. In fact, I'll use that line, and, even though it's not very funny, she'll think it is. From there, our laughter will know no end. We'll rock and guffaw and hold on to our splitting sides, and touch occasionally. More than occasionally. We'll talk about everything. Politics, movies, books, music. The past. The present. The future, perhaps? We'll hold hands. We'll caress fingers. Then, we'll close the place down. I have a couple bottles of wine at my condo, just for us. We'll curl up in the floor with Sinatra in the air and toast to the library that brought us together. Then it will occur to her: she'll finally figure out who I am and from whence I come. Before I can respond, Edie will softly kiss my lips. She'll offer another toast, this time to the past, and urge me to forget about what happened because what really matters is what we have now. What we have now is nothing short of nirvana.

My writing hasn't made me cry in years. I have to pull myself together before I take the stacks of *The New Republic* back.

3:30 PM
Friday September 18, 1987
Standing before the reference desk
What Dow Jones Industrial Average?

Some teacher from the parochial high school must have assigned a big project due Monday. There are a dozen students in oxford blue shirts and navy slacks standing before Edie, getting a jump on it before their weekend. I have no chance to capture her attention, so I merely lay the magazines on the desk and turn to walk.

"Thank you, Mason," I hear.

I turn back to see Edie looking at me. Holy Mary, Mother of God…the eyes. "Happy Friday, Edie."

"Two more hours," she says.

Is that a message? Is it?

I can't. I don't have the courage. I simply can't.

Twenty-Three

11:00 AM
Friday September 25, 1987
At my desk, alone among my colleagues
Dow Jones Industrial Average: 2,575 – 6.4 percent off all-time high

It's not happening today, and for good reason. Business sucks ass. After John laid down the gauntlet, I started off like a bat out of hell. Then, I hit the wall. That's a shopworn simile and two unimaginative metaphors in less than twenty words, but there is no better way to describe the action. Action. There has been lots of action. For the week: fifty-six calls, seventeen of which were face-to-face meetings, all of which had a total potential of one-and-a-quarter million invested and fifty thousand dollars gross. Never have I prospected so hard. Why, I haven't seen Edie for a week. I tried. I made it over there a couple of times. We just didn't hook up. No wonder everything is so frustrating.

Thing is, after all that sacrifice, there have been very few results: forty-four 'nos,' ten temptresses saying 'I'll think about it,' with only four actually leaving money, twenty seven thousand to be exact, for a fribbling thousand eighty gross. With today and three other days remaining, I need a little under eight thou to walk out of this unscathed. Presently, I'm fried, so I've decided to write off the rest of this Friday and call my gross bogey twenty seven hundred per day, amounting to just under two hundred grand invested total. I know that's a lot of numbers, but letters don't pay the mortgage.

Pick up the sword again on Monday. All I have to do is talk two hundred thousand into an investment I personally wouldn't get near. Just super. Besides, procrastination leads to resourcefulness, and rationalization makes the world go around. Quoting from Jeff Goldblum's character in the movie *The Big Chill,* 'Rationalization is more important than sex. Have you ever gone a week without a rationalization?'

Lunch time.

11:30 AM
Friday September 25, 1987
Sitting in Green Boy's with a delicious, saturated fat-laden double cheeseburger, and a couple of Arns on deck.
Dow Jones Industrial Average: give it a rest

My favorite bar is situated directly across Hale Street from the library and The Café and next door to The H. Location, location, location. I could spend the rest of my career here, all four days of it. Things reek so badly I may. And, why not? Green Boy's is more inviting than The H. This is a fine establishment of advanced partying. It's a friendly tavern of comfortable ambiance. You enter to natural light pouring in from the windows. The ornate oaken bar, the racks of booze surrounding the mirror, and the chrome beer taps all shine as if they are at the gates of heaven. Then, you stay.

GB's is the consummate neighborhood watering hole, owned by and operated by and named for Sean McKown, AT's 1984 Businessman of the Year and our most famous Notre Dame alum. Too many bars in the eighties are not like Green Boy's. They are tethered to franchised institutionalization with no local flavor. In response to all that mediocrity, Mr. Green Boy has decorated Green Boy's walls with artifacts and photos, like a bat Pittsburgh's Willie Stargill cracked a homer with in the 1979 league championship series; like an autographed shot of two local boys done good, Beaver Falls' Joe Namath talking with Monongahela's Joe Montana; like a picture of Michael roaming the field in his Steelers' uniform; like photos of AT's championship softball teams, along with several World War II vintage pictures of steel mills, and a comparison of the Pittsburgh skylines now and fifty years ago. The tavern is a museum of the good times in western Pennsylvania. And clean? You could proudly get drunk with your mother here.

I'm sitting at a four-man table near one of the windows surrounded by a sparse pre-noon crowd. Lunch has been uneventful with exception to the dripping of a drop of grease on my white shirt. Thankfully, the spot can be covered by my jacket. Despite the fact that it's mid eighties hot and sunny, I will indeed leave the blazer on. I know. It's inconsistent that my life is a train wreck, yet I have pockets of fastidiousness. Diane the Feet has told me that's a symptom of obsessive-compulsive disorder. Just great. My mental affliction lineup sheet is becoming so crowded it is little wonder I can't face it. I canceled my last appointment with her and haven't called the good Dr. Pedersen for my Randall McMurphy analysis. Chief, get out while you can.

1:00 PM
Friday September 25, 1987
Still in Green Boy's, third Arn, writing in the Edie/short journal
Dow Jones Industrial Average: no sweat; it'll still be there when I return on Monday

Entry: evaluating my strategy

For those of you who fifty years from now are reading this entry while visiting my memorial library: when I refer to anything about the market as 'good,' I mean it is good for mankind and Corncob and I'll call those things 'Corncob.' When I refer to anything about this market as 'bad,' I mean it is good for me and I'll call those things 'Mason.' Recall the basic truth: you have to be a prick to short.

Below are recent comments I've picked up from Corncob's wire, along with my replies.

Corncob:	There is lots of cash available to buy stocks. Money markets funds are at record levels.
Mason:	Investors like money market funds because there are no fees, there is no risk, you can get your money tomorrow, and you get paid high rates of interest while you wait. Brokers hate money market funds because they get to watch dollars walk in and out the door while they get no commissions. That makes money markets the best way to save for homes, cars, college, and vacations. That's milk money, not stock money. Only a fool like me would put that kind of milk money in the stock market.
Corncob:	There is a movement to invest in economically sensitive stocks, like steel, autos, tires, chemicals, plastics, paper, and aluminum. Basic industries. This is a signal of future economic strength beyond the horizon, and the future's so bright, I the Cobster have to wear shades.
Mason:	You can take off the Ray-Bans, Corncob. There has been enough overreaction to the rapture of Reaganomics to make it too dangerous for me.
Corncob:	The valuation of the Dow Jones Industrial Average with respect to 1987 projected earnings is at average levels. It won't take much of a push to get the Dow up to and beyond 3,000.
Mason:	You can fool all the investors some of the time, but one day they will grow wise to the fact that you are one hell of a one-trick pony. To you, saying 'sell' anytime is as disgusting as yelling 'Walt Disney is a child pornographer!' during the Pledge of Allegiance. Besides, I'm looking at this market differently. I trust my numbers and the sources of my numbers, sources that have not failed me. Buy or sell, the sources have not failed me. Stan the Money Man said to always keep my eyes on the instrument panel, no matter what is going on, advice I've been heeding since I was in the coalfields returning kicks for my high school football

team. Ronnie, if my numbers read like your numbers, I'd be with you. Trouble is, you are dangerously dialed into one frequency, and that, my man, makes you an unparalleled snake-oil salesman.

Corncob:	Business executives polled are looking for fourth quarter sales results to be the best in three years. That justifies high stock price/earnings valuations.
Mason:	That statement appeals only to those who are trying to avoid the pain associated with thinking since you recently said valuations are at average levels.
Corncob:	As a show of confidence in the bull market, General Motors executives last week made an additional one billion dollar contribution to the employees' pension fund.
Mason:	An executive decision to make an additional contribution to the pension fund? Why, those angels of mercy!

Bottom line: if the Dow falls to average valuation, as I think it will, I get all my Christine money back. If Corncob's right, and he's been right before, I lose my ass.
I like those odds.

I'm tired of writing about the market, so I put the journal aside. In the future, I'll keep my comments succinct, avoiding prolonged discussion until after I have sex again. However, I'm so much fun to be around, it could be a while.

Wylie walks through the door. He sees me almost immediately and begins to move toward me. The times have been tough on our friendship. He hasn't bummed a ride with me since the argument. Why he wants to talk now, I don't know. I thought he'd have an aversion to the stench of career death.

"Hi, Mason."

"Dude. Have a seat." I couldn't care less, but have a seat.

He sits to my left. Wylie is wearing his favorite battle uniform, a charcoal gray chalkstripe, a bright red power tie with a tiny print of paisley, a starched white, and black spit-shine Allen-Edmonds with tassels. Direct from the successful stockbroker stamping plant. He's not particularly handsome, but take it from me and my under six-foot vantage point: when you're tall, it doesn't really matter.

"Drinking lunch today?" he asks in a light yet superior way.

"Yes," I answer sincerely.

"How's it going with John?" he asks too quickly.

"Fine. Thanks for asking."

A pause. "Can I help you in any way?"

"Nope. Thanks for asking." For all I'm concerned, this conversation can end right here.

Another pause. "Mason, you want me to slide—"

"Absolutely not, Wylie. I'm not a welfare case. I'm just a stockbroker who just can't pull it off and unless I come up with the money I will be out of the business sundown Wednesday. And, I'm cool with that."

"Look," Wylie says as he scoots in closer, "I have a prospect John knows nothing about who asked me to invest two hundred thousand in Caretaker for her. She could just as easily be yours and that would do it."

"Wylie," I say as I turn to his face and lean in, "the trouble with us stockbrokers is that we think there are two types of people: stockbrokers and those who want to be stockbrokers. We stockbrokers think we are so fucking fascinating that everyone is planning their days around the possibility of having a conversation with a stockbroker. We think that if someone doesn't have a stockbroker working for them, then the question must be asked, is that person a contributing citizen of this great nation of ours. My point: there is intelligent and meaningful life beyond Wall Street."

Wylie straightens his back. "Whoa! I'm just asking, man!"

"Well, there are a lot of questions we should be 'just asking.'"

There is a pause in my fireworks. Wylie moves back to me and places his hand on my shoulder. "Mason, you're a great stockbroker—"

"Oh, no, man—" There goes the tough guy façade...

"Listen to me. You are. You're smart, you're a great investor, and you genuinely care for your clients. I don't want to see you go. Hang in there and do what it takes to get to the next month. That's all *I'm* asking."

"Wylie, thank you, but I don't want to be a 'great' stockbroker because being a 'great' stockbroker is not about investing. It's about feel-good, warm fuzzies as well as second homes, third cars, and retooled wives. It's about power and influence. Wall Street is the Hollywood Walk of Fame now, and it has little to do with how much money is made for clients, but rather with the appearance of possibilities. You, my friend, are the Heard on the Street poster boy, and I'm not. I'm not wired to do what it takes. It's for you. You're a natural, and your success says you are. And, Mac, if this is the end, it is not the end. One of my clients is the department head at Pitt. She tells me she has an instructor's position available for me whenever I'm ready. Whatthefuck, it's an attractive option. Besides, coeds in the 1980s are very pretty."

"I don't want to see you go," he says with a long face.

"Either way, I'm not going anywhere. Besides, I'll need a broker."

Wylie smiles faintly. "You'd have to tell me what to do. I have no idea what the hell is going on with you and your money."

"I'll be easy to service. Just let me know what Corncob is up to. That will be my comic relief amid the drab of academia."

"You still have four days, man."

"Three. I'm off the clock now. You want a beer?"

Wylie stands. "Raincheck. The evangelist is coming in at three."

"Evangelists. They're all wealthy. Now, take Billy Graham. There's a salesman for you. Trust and credibility selling a concept. Fiery success with religion, the ultimate intangible. We sales guys could learn lots from Billy Graham. Too bad Jim Bakker and Jimmy Swaggart taint the profession."

Wylie smiles. "You're at the throes of a rant, and I love it when you rant, so I'd better go before I stay all afternoon."

"See ya, man," I say as we shake a hearty handshake. He departs from my left. I'm glad he's back, even though it was from the high ground.

"He resurfaces," I immediately hear from my right. Out of my periphery, I see Edie. My heart jumps. Will I ever get used to her? The hopeless romantic in me says I hope not.

"Yes," I reply. "I'm still here; in another context, but still here. So are you, I see." Pulse, ninety and rising.

"Business?" she asks. Edie. Back in black. A hundred if you do a slow spin for me.

"Very busy-ness," I say, still thinking about the slow spin.

"We miss you in reference. I guess our paths haven't crossed lately." A pause. "Too bad. You've become one of our favorite patrons, if not the most persistent." What a smile.

"Huh. Persistent patron." I smile back.

Her smile grows wider. "You gotta love the alliteration."

Trying to think of something to say, I decide to ask, "What's for lunch, if I may?" referring to the white paper bag she's holding. Yet another weak attempt...

"Tuna on rye. Half a sandwich, and that's it. I'm on a diet."

I want to watch Edie eat. "You don't need to diet." Pulse one ten.

"Thank you, but are you joking? My clothes are getting tight," she says with a pout face. Clothes? Tight? That's one of the things I love about you.

"Well, you're welcome to stay." Finally, I ask her out.

"Thank you, again, but I have a girlfriend holding a place in the lunchroom." She's still standing. Sit. She nods to the Arn. "Wish I could drink my lunch."

"I'm taking a half-day. I deserve this beer. After I drain it, I'll be over to partake of your services."

"A suggestion...try Bill Clinton today. We just subscribed to the *Arkansas Democrat-Gazette,* you know."

"That's intriguing, but why did you pick up an obscure newspaper?" I'm oblivious to the post-lunch crowd. Edie will do that to you.

"My call. I have a friend moving up with the Democratic National Committee. She says Clinton is a rising star. He's on the short list for the convention's keynote address next year. Powerful speaker, I understand."

"Why not? Besides, the GOP's easy pickings right now."

"Ever consider climbing over the wall?" she asks suddenly and with confidence.

For your gaze, I'd pole vault the wall. "You can read my mind. In fact, I'll run down to the court house and change, then I'll be over to read about Bill."

"Drive to Pittsburgh just to become a Democrat? You're either committed or you should be committed. Or," she says as she winks, "you're just placating me."

"You said it yourself. I am a persistently placating patron. Now there's your alliteration."

Edie gives me a toothy grin. "Become a Democrat. I'll believe it when I see it."

"Iran-Contra."

She sighs. "Don't blame you."

"I mean, how freaking arrogant do you have to be to try to pull that one off?"

A pause. "You're serious, aren't you?" she says, crossing her arms...under her boobs.

"Yes, Edie. I'm serious."

"I'm impressed."

I'm impressed. "Well, I wasn't going to study Democrats. I'm re-reading John Updike's Harry Angstrom novels. *Rabbit Is Rich* is next for me." If I ever get a library card...

"What's Harry Angstrom up to now, I wonder?"

"I don't know, but I'll write a review for you." I look pensively at the corner of the ceiling. Before I know it... "Write. What I'd give to write like John Updike."

As if I purposefully gave her an opening, Edie reaches her hand out to tap the cover of my journal. "What's in that book you carry around? Is that a journal?"

"Yep." Oh, boy...

"Can I read it?"

No...way. "I...don't know about that."

She smiles. Eyes. "Well, I'd better go, anyway. Nice talking with you, Mason." Stay a little bit longer...please, please stay. "Same here, Edie."

Edie takes one step, and turns back sharply! "Just read me an excerpt and I'll leave you alone," she says quickly.

Pulse...one twenty. "I don't think so."

"Just a couple of sentences? Pretty please?" She rests the bag on the table and clasps her hands under her chin as if to beg.

"You're going to make me do it, aren't you?"

"'Coerce' is the word I'm thinking of," Edie says, grinning.

This woman owns my soul. "Okay, I have one."

"Goody!" She sits across from me, leaning forward, hands on the table.

I open my journal and begin to flip through the pages, not really knowing what to find, but knowing that I'd better find something fast while she's my captive audience. Reagan and the Soviets...too boring. Instrument flying...yuk. Here...here's the written rant from the day I cracked my head on the wall. I like this one...

"Here you go. This a piece about Iran-Contra, mostly about James Baker—"

"What a slimeball," she spits.

"I simply love your attitude, Edie." Our eyes meet. And hang.

"I feel as if I've known you," she says, the words I've been longing to hear. I savor them, then it occurs to me: what do I do now? Try this...try what?

"That was silly of me," Edie says, "but, it just feels that way."

Still, no words...

"Do you believe in reincarnation?" she asks.

"Yes, I do," I say. Her beautiful face is alive with...questions?

Edie slaps the palms of her hands together. "That's what it is," she says. "I knew you in another life. See if this fits...I was a Navy nurse in the south Pacific."

"And, I was an F4F Marine fighter pilot," I say. Why not?

"Yeah! That's it!" she exclaims. "I died of malaria in Hawaii in '43."

"I was killed in the second wave at Midway," I say, thinking that if this is a joke, I'm definitely playing along.

"Man, this has been bugging me since I first met you," she says.

"Me, too." She's completely serious about this. A weird woman...I'm yours forever.

"Okay, read to me," she says quickly, as if she has the attention span of a teen girl.

"Okay," I say as I scramble to find the journal. "Okay. James Baker. Here goes…" And, I read. "Now, on Reagan's watch, our leaders have arranged a sale of arms to our friends in Iran to give us money so we can fund the Nicaraguan Contra Rebel Freedom Fighters in their quest for human rights, which in this case we call rampant capitalism in our favor. Congress didn't like this, but James Baker liked it. I know it's all tied back to him –"

"Stop," Edie says calmly.

What? I hate to be interrupted.

"Mason, I have to go." I look up to discover her face is pale.

"Is there any way I can help you?" I ask, helplessly.

"No, I'm sick, just suddenly, and I don't want to get sick in a bar, so I'm going to go across the street and get sick where I work. At least I know the bathrooms are clean. Here," Edie says as she hands me her bag. "Yuck. I don't want to even touch containers of food. Oh, I have to go. Oh, this is not going to be pleasant. Oh, I'm sorry, Mason. Read to me again soon."

"Can I walk with you?"

"Gone. Bye." Edie scoots to the door and out quickly.

I'm stunned.

Twenty-Four

4:30 PM
Monday September 28, 1987
Sitting at my desk, oblivious to all, writing in the Edie/short/general life journal
Dow Jones Industrial Average: 2,590 – 5.6 percent off all-time high

Entry: The End Game

Today was all Caretaker, as the days have been in the past week. All Caretaker, and no bites. Zips. Zeds. Air balls. The count: dials – fifty-five, not available – thirty-seven, contacts – eighteen, dollars invested – brother, can you spare a dime?

By end of day Wednesday, all the think-about-its from the past will have heard from me. I'm going to rattle their cages. They get one more chance to do it my way.

Today, I called my career women…ages twentysomething to fortysomething, post-floppy bow-ties, independently-thinking…with smart money. Men won't listen to me talk about a conservative investment, not with this stock market looking ripe for their caddy-give-me-my-driver egos. Besides, if I'm going to hear a 'no,' I'd rather it be in the form of one of those 'Oh, it sounds good, but…I can't. I shouldn't. No.' You know the ones, a touch of pout, a dash of whine, a couple of tons of empowerment. There's a broker adage: don't pitch the bitch…meaning of course, don't prospect women. Not only does that phrase reek, it's founded on outmoded country club logic. This is 1987 and there is indeed plenty of money out there being run by babes, and they're going to do it well and do it *their* way. It's a huge market that most brokers are ignoring. Women are frustrating, like engineers. You have to give them time. Time to think and time to feel. Think and feel: two words foreign to a broker's vocabulary.

This is it for me, the last opportunity to stay in the business. And, it hinges on the ladies. They've had their chances to ignore me. And, after today, they're obviously still ignoring me. My women and romance and my other women and investments. There are parallels.

I need a) four thousand gross a day over the next two days, and b) Edie.

4:30 PM
Tuesday September 29, 1987
Sitting at my desk, oblivious to all, writing in the Edie/short/general life journal
Dow Jones Industrial Average: 2,596 − 5.6 percent off all-time high

Entry: Well, at least the stock market is cooperating with me.

The instrument panel remains the same: interest rates are rising, speculators just know we're going to turn the corner any day now, and it's taken a lot of heavy lifting to get the Dow up just one hundred points in the past two weeks. I mean, a lot of heavy lifting. Straining, blue-veiners. Plus the older folks are becoming wary. It smells like 1929, most say. Unbridled luxuriance; a runaway stock market and wrist watches that cost as much as a vintage Ford Mustang Shelby. I must admit, amid my prospecting failures and the resulting loss of confidence, I've thought several times about cashing out my shorts. But, especially after talking to the seniors, my gut tells me to stay. Like stud poker, stay to see the next card.

Dials: forty-three. Not availables: twenty-eight. Results of the pitches to the bitches: oh-for- fifteen. Then, only a half-hour ago, I had a conversation with Wylie that went something like this:

M: It's hopeless, man.
W: It's not impossible, Mason.
M: The odds are against landing a two hundred thousand dollar ticket on any given Wednesday. Or, any given Sunday. Speaking of that, you've heard the NFL is going to play with strike-breaking replacement players next weekend. That's a bookie's nightmare.
W: I wouldn't know.
M: Of course. You're straight-laced Mr. Producer.
W: And, look at you. Your ass is on the line, and what do you do? Produce!
M: (sarcastically) And, your point?
W: (seriously) There's a lesson to be learned here, Mason.
M: (in serious disbelief) Excuse me?
W: Had you followed my business model, you wouldn't be in the position you're in now.
M: Fuck you and your business model.
W: Great comeback.

M: Well, how's this for a comeback. I was going to talk with you about being my stockbroker after Wednesday, but since you're limited to Corncob's investment *du joir*, you don't have the scope to even take orders from me, you condescending driveler.

I walked back to my desk to clean out a couple of drawers.

How's Edie doing, I wonder? Is she still sick? Did I make her sick? Was she really sick? I went to the library that following Saturday, finding the courage to ask Boy George about her. Boy said she did indeed get sick and also was taking a couple of vacation days early this week. I can't believe Boy told me that. I could be a stalker. There are legal documents that say I am.

I…have…a great idea. The thing about me with Edie right now is I won't get off dead center. No commitment. Now is the time to stick my neck out. I have to do something to prove my love. A couple days off means she'll be back tomorrow. And, when Edie returns, she'll be greeted by flowers.

I know…I know…any half-aware Cro-Magnon can dial a florist and send roses. But, I have to do something. So, the deal is I won't send roses. An Ashton FTD florist with the unlikely name of DiFlorio's specializes in creative arrangements with flowers of the season, preparing bouquets in lieu of jamming long stems in a box and attaching a typed note. How do I know this? I give, or gave, flowers to Christine every July 22, her birthday and, interestingly enough, the feast of Mary Magdalene. Anyway, Christine really liked them. What woman wouldn't? And, Edie is some woman. At least she was when I woke up beside her this morning. In your dreams, Mason.

5:00 PM
Tuesday September 29, 1987
At DiFlorio's on Roberts Street
Dow Jones Industrial Average: Ah, who cares. I'm incredibly ambivalent to be a guy with a big-ass short position

I love Ashton Township. It's such the neighborhood. Five minutes from my desk and I'm entering DiFlorio's door. However, just as the bell to signal my arrival stops ringing, I lose my nerve. It's as if Edie is with me as I order flowers for her. Looking back to Roberts to head for the exit, I scan the arrangements in the two storefront windows. No funeral wreaths. That's a good omen. I wink at the winged-foot Hermes FTD symbol, and turn back to continue my mission.

The place has what could be a thirty-by-thirty foot floor space, jammed-packed with flowers and plants. From the door, there are two aisles extending at opposite forty-fives, narrow with vases, baskets, and statuettes cascading on each side, rising from the knees to above the heads of the customers. The aisles bend right on the one to my left and left on the one to my right, leading to the desk visible down the middle aisle. If I go left or right, I risk taking too long to get to the desk and therefore giving me plenty of opportunity to lose my nerve again. In eight steps down the middle, I have arrived.

A man my height wearing faded Levis with a 30 W-34 L tag beside the right belt loop and a red checked shirt, a man who from the rear could be described as gay, stands with his back to me working on a basket of flowers. I am ignorant of what exactly those flowers are. I am likely ignorant of a lot of things because when this man turns to me, I can't help but think that his thin frame is riddled with AIDS. But, my brother's gay and he doesn't have AIDS, so why should this guy have AIDS. Anyway, maybe, with his blue eyes and his long-limbed body, looking like a skinny, shorter version of Wylie, just maybe he's a transvestite on weekends. Maybe he doesn't wait for weekends. It sounds like I'm really more ignorant than I think I am.

"Yes, sir," the gay guy says.

"Yes," I reply. "I…need…to order some…flowers."

"I can help you." He's smiling.

"I'm sure you can," I say, afraid my latent homophobia is surfacing.

There is a pause. "Are your flowers going to be for…a woman, perhaps?"

"Oh, yes. A woman. A woman…can I be honest with you?" I can't believe I said that.

The man folds his hands on the desk. "Why not? I hear it all in this business. Flowers have a way of opening the souls of us men." He grins.

"Then…I'm sure that's true." Uncomfortably, I continue. "The woman…well, this is my initial foray of…letting her know how I feel about her." I stop.

"How do you feel about her?" the gay guy asks as only a gay guy can.

"Uh…shit…sorry…damn it, I'm in love with her and she doesn't know it and she's probably not in love with me because we haven't even touched except for a handshake when we met again and I think about her all the time…" My hand waving stops long enough to allow me to bow my head. There has been no eye contact. "And, this isn't going to work but I have to try it or I'll be sorry later…oh, Christ – "

"Allow me to give you some advice," the gay guy interrupts. "Guys like me have all kinds of advice for the lovelorn." Now he knows I'm a homophobe and he's toying with me.

"Uh…please. Please continue," I say.

"She knows you're in love with her."

I can't think of a response, so I just look at him. I don't even know him and I'm spilling my guts to him on the most important thing that is going on in my life right now. It's like one of those air travel instances where you and the completely unknown person next to you exchange secrets.

"Go ahead," I say.

He leans in. "She knows you're in love with her because women are a helluva lot smarter than you straight guys."

"Then I'm doing the right thing," I quickly say.

"Yes."

"You're just trying to sell me flowers," I return, suspicious.

"No," he says, softly yet firmly. "You're already sold. You just need someone to hold your hand. So to speak." A grin ensues.

I laugh. "That was good. Please make up a forty dollar bouquet of flowers in season, wonderfully well, just like DiFlorio's always does."

"Forty bucks," he says, winking. "Hey, big spender."

I laugh again. "That's all I have to offer."

"What shall the card say?"

"I…don't know," I say pensively. "Here," I reach for a blank card. "Let me write it out."

"Cool," the gay guy says, "Most guys try to make it as easy and as thoughtless as possible. 'With love, Dumas.'"

"Well…" I start thinking…'To Edie, You have the microfilm to my heart.' How stupid. I think again. 'Come view French art with me.' Ibid. I don't know…more thinking. 'Can I buy you a cup of coffee?' Ah, that's my trump card for later. Maybe, I should try, 'To Edie Loden…You bring back memories of jazz.' That is it! I grab a pen from beside the mint dispenser and write my message on the card. After signing it, 'Your old pal, Mason Bricker,' I place the card in the small envelope, handing it to my new friend. He rings the sale up on the cash register.

"How do you wish to settle?"

"I have a charge account here. Mason Bricker."

The gay guy flips through a file, finding and pulling a long ledger card. "Lucky girl. It's not July 22 and she still gets flowers."

"Thanks," I say, laughing. That is truly funny.

10:30 AM
Wednesday September 30, 1987
The Ashton Township offices of Fuller Busher, sitting at my desk, the end of the end game, and writing in the journal about it.
Dow Jones Industrial Average: 2,604 – 5.3 percent off all-time high, the only thing going my way.

Entry: a career self-eulogy.

Now I *am* a major disruption. As all watch this old stockbroker fade away, work progresses in the office, albeit with a cloud hanging over the place. A veritable pall. My associates are glancing my way, morning greetings were even bestowed on me, yet no one except Fenz is really talking with me. And I don't cast an aura of Mr. Sunshine, anyway. Having never been fired from gainful employment, I don't know what to expect. It doesn't feel like it did when I was expelled, since that event came after unusual circumstances and major victories. Today just feels like an old-fashion I-didn't-do-my-job-so-my-ass-is-on-the-street. Until that happens, I'm the proverbial elephant in a room, and everyone would rather I just go so they can get on with it.

I can't work today. Sure, the phone is attached to my face, but I'm feigning conversations. The only response emitting from the receiver is 'If you would like to make a call, hang up and try again, or hang up and dial the operator.' So, my demise is imminent.

Five years surround me, both on my desk and in my mind. Actually, my desk looks as if it is ready to be cleared, dusted, then ignited with kerosene to welcome a new stockbroker at the throes of his new career. Or, it possibly could be one of those places common to offices around the nation, there to accumulate junk. It is nearly devoid of things personal, except for the Edie cut-out print and one framed photograph of me nailing two Pitt players, blocking while Vinny runs with the ball behind me. Funny how, after all these years, that photo remains worthy of its place in my professional life, beside my screen, there for all to see and for me to never take my eyes off of. Edie. Vinny. Sometimes I think that one day is all I have.

Five years in the making. Five years in the unraveling. Biggest month: September 1982, I, the neophyte. The big bull just started rumbling. I was committed to it, having learned from Stan the Money Man in October 1974 when something like that last happened. I was sure. I was confident. I was self-assured. No…really, I was arrogant. Whatever, it was translated to my prospects and new clients that I was a man who knew what I was talking about, and they followed me. That effort landed, excluding my small wad, a million in the market, one million dollars of new money invested in stocks from fifty of my new friends. I worked my ass off, and it paid off. That month, with investments ranging from a thousand to a hundred thousand, I grossed twenty-four five, leading the office after only two months in the business and averaging twenty a month for my first twelve months. A rising star.

A shooting star. The Dow stalled at 1,300 in August 1983, corrected for fifteen percent a few months later, and didn't see 1,300 again until mid-spring 1985. That's a year-and-a-half of futile efforts at production as, to mix metaphors, burned clients were frozen solid. Except for my engineers and their referrals making money hand-over-fist, one-third of my clients walked in frustration, another third became dormant in procrastination, and the lucky ones switched to relatively safe bond mutual funds, allowing me one-time commissions only. Ugly it was.

And ugly it still is. Even though I made enough that first year to be a titular investment officer, my narrow clientele of traders, however successful they are, earned me the ten level I am stuck at. Not bad, though. I got to work at eight, spent the time on the phones with the gearheads, kept up with the news, took two-hour lunches, and left between five and five-thirty. For this, I was paid in the more-than-reasonable upper forties range, the easiest upper forties a man could hope for. I pulled that in, drank Arns, smoked Virginia Slims, wrote on my four books, and screwed Christine. In short, I had fun in my decadence.

It's over. College teachers early in their careers pull in considerably less than fifty, so they have to be independently wealthy to supplement their meager earnings. With three-quarters million in total cash equity before taxes, I'm far from destitute. However, I'll still have to make some serious jack in the stock market to fund my lifestyle without bleeding capital. That and stay away from money-sucking coeds.

Come to think of it, I'm not too sorry I'm out of this business. The easy commissions have been made. After the impending crash, there will be a jailbreak, mass exodus, school's out, lights out bear market of 1987 as the bookend of the year's bull. Stock holders will all lose a third to a half, disappearing in a fog of apathy and bewilderment. That's the foundation from which banks were built.

Then, there is Edie. In an hour, she'll remember the truth about us. This afternoon, I'll confront her to put a face behind the flowers. After that, who knows? I'll take my chances. Whatthefuck.

Who…am I kidding? What seemed like such a great idea is now a big mistake making my gut twist. But, I have to stay. I can stay. My forty days and forty nights of no sex proves I have the power to overcome my body. Christine was so close and so available. After Joan returned the money, I had enough to get Christine to move in for the month. Except for her daughter. If she even has a daughter. If Joan really has a tumor. If Edie was really sick. If Fenz really likes me and is not faking it. If they're all

faking it, I'll collapse. Then, I'll really be pissed. I have to get out of this flower deal.
End of entry.

    As life gently swirls around me, I hurriedly pick up the phone and dial DiFlorio's
from memory. One ring, and…

"DiFlorio's."

"Hello. Hi. This is Mason Bricker."

"Yes, sir."

Fenz walks up and lays a paper on my desk. I ignore her. "Yes, sir. Yes," I
manage to get out. "Yes. I ordered flowers yesterday and I have a problem."

A pause on the other end of the line. "How may I help you?"

"I've chickened out," I say as my voice quivers slightly. "I've become unnerved.
I can't send the flowers to the lady. I just can't take it. Have they left yet?"

"We have a no refund policy, sir," is all the dick can come up with.

"Charge me double. I don't care. I just need the flowers back." I'm near panic.

Another pause. "Let me check." I hear the sounds of a phone being laid down.
What a mistake I have made…

"The library, right?"

"Yes!" There is hope.

"Sir, the flowers left a half-hour ago to be delivered."

I suck a breath. "So, when do you think they'll be delivered?"

"Sir, I have no way of knowing."

"Just a guess," I say, perturbed.

Still another pause. "Soon."

"Gotta go." I hang up, grab my coat, and dash for the door. "Fenz!"

"What?" Ally says without looking up from her desk.

"I'll be back!" Todd's in his office on the phone. Jason's at the receptionist's
desk. John is walking out of the conference room. I see only white shirts and ties as I
bolt past them headed for the elevator. In four strides, I jump through the institutional
gray hallway and lunge for the down button. A week later, the door slides open to the
elevator car on my right. I jump in and punch '1.'

It's taken me this long to realize that the odds of successfully intercepting the
delivery of Edie's flowers are remote. Yet, I am not deterred as the door opens to the
lobby. Nobody is in my way as I smartly run past AshNat, through the double doors and
cut a left, winding around the shade of the maples in the atrium, accelerating in as much
of a sprint as the Virginia Slims residue will allow.

As if pulled from the pages of a romance novel, the DiFlorio's van is double-
parked on Hale in front of the library, and a man is exiting on the street side with a
bouquet. I dart in front of a silver Jeep CJ, making the driver lay on his brakes. He flips
me off. I blow him a kiss because I am now officially off the hook, and very excited
about it.

"Excuse me," I say after a hack. "I'm the guy who ordered those flowers."

"Congratulations," the portly young nicely-dressed Italian-American man says
through a mouth surrounded by short hair.

"Now, I want them back," I say with emphasis on every word.

Stubble Boy looks at me incredulously. "You're nuts," he says.

"Yes, that's true. But, I still want the flowers back." A woman in a red Chevy truck toots her horn to get us out of the way.

"You may want them back, but I have to deliver them or my ass is dead. *Capisc?*"

"Look, do me a favor. Give me the flowers back, please?" I hate to beg, but...

"Look...no," he says, leaning in.

"Okay, I can prove I sent them. Read the card. It says, 'To Edie Loden, you bring back memories of jazz,'" I recite.

He reads the card. "Lucky guess. I still can't give them back, dude."

"A hundred says you can."

"You're right. A hundred says I can."

"Fifty more says you will."

"You got yourself a deal, weirdo."

The man hands me the bouquet. I give him three fifties from my pocket. That's after taxes on two fifty, or six hundred gross, or fifteen thousand dollars of a client's money invested in Caretaker. He smiles and heads for his truck. I smile at the flowers in relief, which of course is short lived. Edie has exited the door and begins walking this way. I don't think she has seen me. Without thinking, I quickly douse the flowers, vase and all, into the fountain, pushing and holding them underwater so they will sink right away. The cuff of my shirt sleeve absorbs water like a bath towel.

Mercifully, Edie stops to dig through her purse. That gives me the opportunity to retrieve the card I so foolishly dunked in the water along with the flowers. As I stand there holding the soaked card, Edie looks up and sees me. "Mason!" she calls.

"Edie," I reply, still holding the wet card. Just as she begins the seven steps to me, I jut the card in my left front pocket of my slacks. Immediately, I feel the sop, and water shows through.

She's here. Edie looks down at the wet spot. "You must be excited to see me," she deadpans.

"I dropped some money in there." I'll say...

"You get good luck only if it stays."

"I was making change," I say quickly.

She laughs. "Are you coming to see us to—" Edie looks down at the fountain pool. "Flowers," she says.

"Yeah, flowers. The delivery guy you just saw drive away? He dropped them and had to go get some more."

"Oh...I hope he comes back. There's some lucky girl in the library who will be surprised with flowers."

"Eventually, we all get what we need," I say, trying desperately to change the subject.

"It's not getting what you want, it's wanting what you got," Edie says with a grin, hands on hips.

"Cool. I wish I would have said that." Now is the time, Mason. Go, man! "I'm going to Montani this afternoon." You have to be quicker on the uptake, Brick.

"Good luck to you. Or, more appropriately, icky."

"You don't like Montani?"

"Uh, no."

"I did a tour there. Made it out unscathed," I say, shocked that this is not going as planned.

"Been there. A month one night. That's enough."

I'm speechless. A man, my height, male-model handsome, looking like that asshole Todd, walks up to us, grabs Edie's hand and kisses her on the cheek. "Hi, dahlin'" he says.

"Well, hello," Edie replies with a peck of her own, on the son-of-a-bitch's lips. I'm motionless.

"Greg, this is Mason, one of our most loyal patrons."

Greg extends his hand. I reflexively grasp it. "Hi, Mason," he says, firmly and pleasantly.

"Greg," is all I can manage.

He looks at my wet leg. The flowers in the fountain must have also caught the corner of his eye because he slowly turns to them. "That's weird," he says to Edie.

"Yes," Edie says. "A mystery. Mason, we'll leave you to figure this out because I'm on the lunch clock. Sorry to be so rude. See you soon."

"Nice to meet you," Greg says.

"My pleasure," I say. They walk.

I finally exhale.

Twenty-Five

6:00 AM
Thursday October 1, 1987
Sitting on my manly brown leather love seat in my living room, donning a sweat shirt and gym shorts, finally praying the Rosary
Dow Jones Industrial Average: 2,596 – 5.6 percent off all-time high

Rosary in hand, I whisper…

"The fifth sorrowful mystery: The Crucifixion. Jesus is nailed to the cross and dies after three hours of agony. Our Father, who art in heaven; hallowed be Thy name. Thy kingdom come, Thy will be done on earth as it is in heaven. Give us this day our daily bread and forgive us our trespasses as we forgive those who trespass against us. And lead us not into temptation, but deliver us from evil. Amen. Hail Mary, full of grace, the Lord is with thee. Blessed art thou among women and blessed is the fruit of thy womb Jesus. Holy Mary, Mother of God, pray for us sinners now and at the hour of our death. Amen."

The only good thing about yesterday is the fact that I wasn't sloppy drunk. Sure, I'm jealous of Greg in a major way. The guy is probably waking up beside Edie as I speak and pray. But, I came around before I had a chance to get torqued.

What was I thinking? Now that I step back and review the
entire…situation…how could I construct such a sham in my mind? It was all in my
mind. My first clue that I am messed up should have originated from the fact that there
were absolutely no clues except the one by which I thought she looked like Edie Loden, a
woman I barely knew for a short time during the Ford administration.

"Hail Mary, full of grace, the Lord is with thee. Blessed art thou among women,
and blessed is the fruit of thy womb Jesus. Holy Mary, Mother of God, pray for us
sinners now and at the hour of our death. Amen."

Two…or is that one?

Okay, I was led astray by the coincidence, the fact that this woman, last name
unknown, is an Edie. That served only to get my imagination rolling, and it's highly
dangerous when that happens. Edie Loden working at the library, the art major…why,
why did I think that? I know why. I continue to have issues with the past. Diane is
helping me work on them, if I ever go back to see her and her feet.

I'm sure Edie Loden, wherever she is now, remembers me. I mean, two days
after I saved college football from the evils of bigotry, I stood her up to get married. That
alone would at least earn me a place in the catacombs of her long-term memory. So, why
did I think either Edie might have forgotten that one? Head trauma? I'm the one with
head trauma.

"Hail Mary, full of grace, the Lord is with thee. Blessed art thou among women
and blessed is the fruit of thy womb Jesus. Holy Mary, Mother of God, pray for us
sinners now and at the hour of our death. Amen."

Three…or two? I'll call it three.

Another question: is my attraction to the pleasantly plump woman…sooner or
later I knew I'd say that…anyway, is it real, or is it based on the house of cards I built
with my Edie Loden fantasy? You know something? Whatever it is, it is. Library Edie
is indeed pretty, but still, after my last two women being among those generally accepted
as world-class knockouts, it is odd I would think so. And, even after yesterday, I still
think so. I enjoy looking at her. There, another good thing about the ordeal…my range
with women has broadened. Forgive the pun.

Fenz says Library Edie has a movie actress' face, and she most definitely does. I
really do like her big booty, no matter how big others may think it is. Or, did I like the
fact that Edie Loden was attached to that big booty? It's all so complicated now, not like
it was when I was just her secret admirer. What am I going to do about Library Edie? I
have to see her. I can't just stop going to the library. That would tip my hand. Those
last few sentences are the best proof I have that I'm neurotic. Calling Dr. Pedersen…

"Hail Mary, full of grace, the Lord is with thee. Blessed art thou among women
and blessed is the fruit of thy womb Jesus. Holy Mary, Mother of God, pray for us
sinners now and at the hour of our death. Amen."

Four.

I feel stupid. I feel jilted. I feel jaded. I'm angry, and I'm hurt. I had convinced
myself that Edie, whichever Edie, and I were going to be together, and Gay Greg shows
up. Greg has to be gay. Guys that handsome cannot be straight. It wouldn't be fair to
the rest of us flawed mortals. So, Greg's gay and Greg and Edie have a gay guy/girl
relationship, which is a lot like a just-us-girls relationship. On the other hand – oh, my

God! What if Edie's a lesbian? Not to worry. I'm a lesbian. We'd have a lot to talk about.

Edie is so nice to listen to. She's truly witty and funny and bright...I'm really going to miss her. The love we could have shared is...it chokes me up.

"Hail Mary, full of grace, the Lord is with thee. Blessed art thou among women and blessed is the fruit of thy womb Jesus. Holy Mary, Mother of God, pray for us sinners now and at the hour of our death. Amen."

Five.

I'm going to have to find another woman.

"Hail Mary, full of grace, the Lord is with thee. Blessed art thou among women and blessed is the fruit of thy womb Jesus. Holy Mary, Mother of God, pray for us sinners now and at the hour of our death. Amen."

Six.

Finally, I do penance. It's rather perverted that it comes down to praying the Rosary or...you know...ah, maybe it's supposed to be that way. I am one continuous impure thought. My thoughts are so impure right now I am running down the list of women I have interfaced with in the past weeks and granting each of them one of my best impure thoughts. All, even Margot and Diane and Lia and the two casual ladies in the canvas flats. All of them at the same time. If I'm going to have impure thoughts, they're going to get into one big naked knot and I'm going to do it right.

"Hail Mary, full of grace, the Lord is with thee. Blessed art thou among women and blessed is the fruit of thy womb Jesus. Holy Mary, Mother of God, pray for us sinners now and at the hour of our death. Amen."

Seven.

What sorrowful mystery am I on right now?

"Hail Mary, full of grace, the Lord is with thee. Blessed art thou among women and blessed is the fruit of the womb Jesus. Holy Mary, Mother of God, pray for us sinners now and at the hour of our death. Amen."

Eight.

One thing's for sure: I'm a sorry mystery. I'm about as far away from being married as I have been since the sixth grade when I founded my school's pre-adolescent I Hate Girls Club. Who would be my bride today? The news anchor? No. She's only a solution to my more short-term impure thoughts problem. The metallurgist? Oh, yes, if I wanted to share the rest of my life with a Gothic anachronism. Looks like it's Fenz. I'm really glad she slept with me last night. I would have called Margot. Definitely. Okay. Ally Fenz Bricker. It would work. It felt good to hold her. Our time was not conjugal, however. The new moon of her lunar cycle. Anyway, it is said the worst thing friends can do is screw...uh...my apologies, Madonna...no, not that Madonna. Anyway, friends, no? Now, there's a basic principle I don't believe. It was great to see her there when I woke up a couple hours ago. Peaceful. We both knew we shouldn't. She'd laugh as I held a pillow over me. 'What's wrong, Mason?' It was funny. Ha, ha. Hence, the early morning Rosary.

"Hail Mary, full of grace, the Lord is with thee. Blessed art thou among women and blessed is the fruit of thy womb Jesus. Holy Mary, Mother of God, pray for us sinners now and at the hour of our death. Amen."

Nine.

Why did Fenz sleep with me? To keep me from doing anything mindless, I guess. Maybe that's all it was to her. However, the worst thing one can do to a friendship is to take it to the romance level. Sex, okay. Love, not recommended. I risk pushing Ally away at a time when I need a friend. It all depends on how I handle this rebound thing.

Maybe, just maybe, I should have moved earlier with Edie. Moved. Another one of those dating words. Sounds like a military offensive. Edie knew about my ardor for her. I was indeed easy to read. Yet, she kissed Greg as I was the witness. Still more confusing…what was the deal with the Navy nurse? Where was she taking that? It was weird. The last thing I need right now is a weird woman. Unfortunately, all I attract are weird women. Fenz has to change that for me. Ally can pull me out. Strange…she was all for Edie, but she's always touching me. Hell, she slept with me. What am I supposed to do?

"Hail Mary, full of grace, the Lord is with thee. Blessed art thou among women and blessed is the fruit of thy womb Jesus. Holy Mary, Mother of God, pray for us sinners now and at the hour of our death. Amen."

Alright…ten.

I hear the padding of feet in the hallway. As I reach to the end table to switch on the light, Fenz appears from around the corner. She rubs her wincing eyes with her fists. Now I wish she hadn't stayed, for an inch of white panties is showing from under the front of my black and gold Steelers t-shirt. That does not do me any favors. It's the best thing I've seen in 1987. Mother Mary, patron saint of women everywhere, protect me from your gender mates. And, while you're at it, protect me from myself.

Fenz takes the three steps to my love seat and rests her cute fanny on it. The Steelers shirt does nothing to cover her underwear. They're French cut. C'mon, Mary…

"What are you doing, Mason?" Fenz asks, head on my shoulder. Always touching…

"Praying the Rosary," I say.

"What's that?" she whispers. "I've heard of that. Let me see." I show her my rosary, green plastic beads like a necklace to which is attached a white plastic crucifix. It's cheap, but my mom gave it to me. It has survived all these years of neglect. "What time?" Fenz grabs my wrist to look at my watch. "Honey, why pray so early in the morning?"

"Because, you barbaric heathen," I say, looking out my window into the darkness, "it is time to pray. The Rosary is my penance from my most recent confession."

"You Catholics have way too many rules."

"I agree, but I'm comfortable with it."

Fenz places her hand on my chest. I'm ignoring this from now on. "Confession. What did you do wrong now?"

"Never mind," I say succinctly.

Now Fenz raises her head and softly kisses my cheek. "You're a good man, Mason Bricker."

"Thanks," I say, patting her bare knee.

"You don't deserve what happened yesterday," she says as she leans back.

"Fenz, it's not a matter of deserving. It just happened, probably for the best."

"A simple case of mistaken identity."

"Okay," I say. Then, I have the idea I should have had weeks ago. "Hey! I have The U yearbook for 1976. I saved it because there was a quarter page, only a quarter fuckin' page mention of our revolt, the dolts. Anyway, let's see if Edie Loden is in there."

"Why didn't you do this weeks ago?" Fenz asks directly into my eyes. "C'mon. Let's get it."

We rise from the love seat and walk down the hall to my bedroom. I flick on the overhead light to find my queen bed and the floor below it strewn with gold blankets and green comforters. The green sheets are a mess everywhere. Green, gold – I know, but I'm a guy. A straight guy. The last thing I'm able to do is coordinate colors.

"Up here, Fenz," I say, looking at the shelf above my hanging clothes in the closet. I reach across the floor to grab the desk chair. Sitting it partly in the closet, I step up to the seat of the chair so my head is in the shelf.

"Nice legs, Mason," I hear Fenz say.

"You're killing me, Fenz." I search through a stack of books to find *The Ridge Runner – 1976*. "Okay," I say before stepping down. "Here it is." Without looking at it, I tuck the yearbook under my arm and head back to the living room, trying to limit my time near a bed with Fenz.

Ally leads me to the love seat. I turn on a light, we plop our butts there, place the yearbook between us, and open it.

"I don't want to get into this yearbook with you," I say. "I—"

"Where's that quarter page?"

"I don't know and I don't want to talk about it."

"Ah, c'mon, Bricker! Show—"

"Take it home with you if you want to see it. I'm here just to find Edie Loden." I leaf through a couple of times, then, "Here they are, senior portraits. Look for her," I say as I slowly turn the pages. It's difficult, since some genius of a yearbook editor had the bright idea to not alphabetize, what he considered to be his *coup de grace* against the institution.

"Lots of bad haircuts here with you guys," Ally says with a giggle.

"I plead the mid seventies. That and it was West Virginia. Holy hell, here she is! Edie Loden."

Together we examine the portrait of Edie Loden. "This Edie's eyes are narrower than the other Edie," says Fenz. "Her lips aren't as full. And, her forehead is bigger. Christ, she looks nothing like the other Edie."

She's right. How could I have been so far off? "Yeah, Ally," I sigh. "I guess I see." Fenz touches my hand. I squeeze her fingers.

"It's okay," she says.

I sigh again. "I don't want to admit this, Fenz, but it is true. I have 1975 problems. There's a 1975 tint to most everything I see or do, especially women. Anyway, this Edie thing is just symptomatic of the issues I need to deal with. Did I ever mention Diane the Feet?"

"Yeah, the head doctor, but you never talked about her feet. What's up with her feet?"

"Long story."

"I know about you and feet."

"Diane's helping me through all this."

"When's the last time you saw her?" Fenz asks.

"The day I met Edie."

"There's something to that," she says, hand to chin, tongue in cheek.

"I'm crazy."

Ally places her hand around my upper arm. "You're being too rough on yourself. It's okay. You're okay. Trust me."

In silence, I contemplate a second confession, this time to the modern day saint beside me. Saint Fenz. "Fenz, I'm not okay. I have this penance because Joan was in town and she's still married and we ended up in the sack."

"So, that's the 12:30 AM woman. I thought I felt some heat back there," she says quickly and with humor.

"I guess you're not surprised."

"No. Not after what you've told me about you two, no."

"But, it's serious, Ally. She's still married." I pause for a while in an attempt to gain perspective. Fenz squeezes my arm. "You know? We were married. She hurt me. Five years, I don't see her or even hear from her. All of a sudden, sex. Furthermore, she's sick. Joan has an inoperable brain tumor that's going to take her down. I held off until I heard that. Then, I felt sorry for her. It was good for me, too."

"Damn. This is too much."

"I'm complicated."

"Mason," Ally says with another soft touch to my hands, "it sounds like she needed to be with someone, and it's a good thing she was with you."

"That's the pretense," I say.

"Don't worry about it, baby, you know, the married woman part. You're in the clear. You just prayed the Rosary, just like whoever told you to."

"Michael."

Fenz takes a deep breath. "What a waste of man."

"Yeah, but he's a stand-up priest."

"Anyway, that's the best you can do right now."

I shake my head softly and look at her face. "Not really. Strict Catholics think my impure thoughts are sins."

"Impure thoughts!" Fenz laughs. "Who calls them impure thoughts?"

"Strict Catholics."

"Well, that really sucks if you can't have an impure thought every now and then," Fenz says with a smile.

"Yeah," I say seriously.

"But," Fenz says, still smiling, "you may still be okay if you didn't have any impure thoughts since you prayed the Rosary."

"I had impure thoughts while I prayed the Rosary."

"About who? Edie?"

"About you," I answer.

Fenz squeals and leaps onto my lap, laying her head on my shoulder. "About me? That's so sweet!"

"Anytime," I say.

"What's wrong, Mason?"

"Nothing. Fenz, thank you for staying over. You are truly my friend. I know you have to get ready for your cruise and all."

"I have all morning to do that. My plane doesn't leave until four."

"A cruise. You and Mary, free and unencumbered by commitments, on a big meat barge." We giggle, and we haven't moved. Fenz remains on my lap, her head on my shoulder. I like Ally.

"Mason," Fenz says. "it was fun to be with you last night. You were hilarious, absolutely hilarious. The drunken insulting Frenchman you did had them all splitting. I know you were just trying to deal with everything, but I was rolling."

"*Sacre bleu!* It's my way of dealing with the shock," I say with a smile. "Shock on both fronts."

"What are you going to do today?"

"Do the unemployed stuff. Hang out. Go to the library."

Fenz raises her head and looks at me. "The library! Good move!"

"Yeah, that, and John asked me to come by the office after hours to get my things."

"I'm going to miss you," Fenz says.

"Fenz, you and I…we're great. Sure, it started because of work, but we've gone way beyond that."

"All the way to impure thoughts," she says with a grin.

"All…the…way."

"May I shower here?"

"You're a tease, Fenz."

"It's a hobby. But, to return the favor, you can pick me up at the airport next Wednesday. Mary has to take another flight to a conference or something."

"Anything for you."

"I'll hold you to that."

"Good one, Ally."

Twenty-Six

3:00 PM
Thursday October 1, 1987
Walking to the reference desk at Ashton Township Public Library
Dow Jones Industrial Average: I fold

I approach her. She stands, awaiting me.

"There he is," Edie says with the ever-present smiling face atop her black sweater and slacks.

"Edie. How are you?"

"Wonderful."

"I'd say you are," I say, in an off-handed reference to Handsome Greg.

Oblivious to my implied snide, Edie leans in. "Did you ever find out about those flowers?"

"No," I answer. "I don't know where it went from there."

"Hey, Molly," she says to Boy George sitting at a computer to her left. "Mason saw the flowers."

"Did you see the guy drop them?" Molly asks. She tugs up on the top of her gray smock.

"No, but I heard him swear." That one gets me a round of laughter.

"You're funny," Edie says.

"Thanks," I reply.

I don't know why I'm here. I never needed to be here, even when she was Edie Loden. So, why am I here now? Edie would never take me over Greg. Why? Why look at my mug when you can have his sculpted face staring into yours? Why do I care what she thinks, anyway? Whenever I stand before a guy like Greg, I feel so conspicuous in my ugliness. Still, Edie's not who she used to be. Worse still, I'm not who I used to be, even though I have the blazer and the Haggars on right now to make one think otherwise. But, you know…this entire game has changed and I'm obviously not ready to accept that. That's the real problem.

"I've asked around," Edie says. "No lady here got flowers."

"No lady got flowers and no man got the thank you he was expecting," I say

"How do you know it was a man?" Edie asks slyly.

"Good question," I say quickly, "But, I'm a money manager. I work with odds."

She giggles. "Good answer. By the way, I'm sorry I ran out on you at Green Boy's."

"Are you okay?" I ask, feigning caring.

"I was the next day."

"Okay." No inflection. Flat.

"Are you okay?" she asks, sensing I couldn't give a damn.

"Fine as wine. How 'bout the *NYT* in mid-1962…please?"

"Interesting," Edie says. Her face has a hint of concern. "Another bad stock market?"

"Yes."

"I know you, Mason, Marine pilot." On that, she grins, turns, and walks, an experience that is different today than it was yesterday.

She has to realize that I've gone from cuddly puppy to growling beagle, still cute but pissed. That's another 'why.' Why should she care? Edie probably doesn't know she was playing the gumdrop fairy in my game of Candy Land. Come to think of it, I should care. I should care about the fact that I am not reality-based.

"Here," she says as she returns with a spool of microfilm. "I brought you the entire year."

"Thank you."

"You know?" Edie asks me out of the blue.

I allow time to pass. She doesn't fill it. "Know what?"

"I became a teen in 1962. I was the 'it' girl." She's smiling again.

Quick arithmetic says she's another older woman. "I bet. What day?"

"October 19."

"Wow, Edie," I say, my mood improving, "We're looking right down the barrel at that one."

"Don't remind me," she says with a pouting lip. "Birthdays are getting rougher year by year."

"Why?" I ask, thinking this woman looks good for thirty-eight, despite the fact that I don't want to think about her.

"Advancing in age."

"Aren't we all?" I say.

"Feels like just me," Edie says.

Part of me wants to hold her and part of me wants to tell her she deserves it. "Funny...you seem to be a woman looking for any reason to celebrate."

"Advancing...in...age," she repeats, staring softly.

"Edie," I say quickly.

"What?"

I fall silent, feeling the crush coming back, but this time laced with hurt. There's nothing to say, so I say nothing.

"What, Mason?" Edie asks, imploring me to tell her how I feel, the truth about how I feel.

"Celebrate." I pick up my microfilm and walk. There is indeed no looking back.

3:30 PM
Thursday October 1, 1987
Sitting at a microfilm screen, writing on paper with a pen, both of which I borrowed from another older lady sitting next to me.
Dow Jones Industrial Average: there is not an instrument fine enough to measure how little I care about the Dow Jones Industrial Average.

I've asked the question before: why not Edie? Well...
Edie is seven years older than me. Joan is eight years older. Bad Karma.
Again – what's the deal with the Navy nurse?
Edie is beautiful, but she's chubby with that rather large butt, no matter how you look at it. She's probably lost weight to get down to where she is and...that's mean spirited...sorry...but I bet Fenz looks better in underwear.
Edie's career...she's bright, so how long can she go on serving old newspapers? Her work life is fetch and file. That brings me to...
How can anyone be so goddamned happy all the time? What a pain in the ass.
Edie's so superficial. Look at her boyfriend.
She's rude. She interrupted me while I read. She was sick? Oh, sure...
Works in a library...hates Republicans...good friend with the DNC...low paying job...that means Rich Old-Money Liberal...the annoying left-wing equivalent of the even more annoying Religious Right.
Why not Fenz?

5:00 PM
Thursday October 1, 1987

Standing before my old desk at the Ashton Township offices of Fuller Busher, packing my gym bag.
Dow Jones Industrial Average: a capitalist tool serving as a symbol of the oppression of the proletariat.

John recently had the office redone. In a fit of conformity, he patterned the space after the conference room; the same money green wallpaper appointed with the same ugly-ass teak, along with Monet and Manet...sounding like still more money. Money, the dip-stick of success. Possessions, the first derivative of money, the public display of wealth and therefore the assumption of class. And happiness. Money can't buy happiness, so those with little money say. Then again, those with money and possessions are outwardly happy but usually in debt up to their leveraged asses. So, it's all in the show. Coming my way is one example to support that theory.

"Hi," says Wylie as he walks to me. White shirt. Red power tie. Navy slacks. No coat. Pleasant grin.

"Yeah," I respond.

A pregnant pause. Two will get you three that the next thing out of his mouth will be a cliché fitting of the situation.

"I don't know what to say."

"Wylie, there's nothing to say. We've talked about this. I'm okay."

"Well..." he says, trailing off. "I know. Basically."

"Really."

Another pause. "Have you talked with the professor from Pitt?"

"No," I say, "but I'd better."

"How 'bout the engineers?"

"I warned them of the possibilities. Don't worry, though. You won't have to meet their demands. One of them is becoming a broker. He started at Shearson in downtown Pittsburgh last week."

"Oh. That's interesting."

"Yes, it is," I say. "He's very analytical, but so are his buddies. So are a lot of people, surprising to those in this business. Regardless, my man will pick up where I left off with them."

Wylie tilts his head back. "Why don't you be his client?"

"I don't know. Should I?" I snap.

There is silence. "Is that really what you want to do? Be a college teacher?" he asks with superiority.

"I know what I don't want to do."

"Step into my office," Wylie says. I walk the twelve paces with him over the tan carpet. Because Wylie is such a big hitter, John paid for his personal decorator, a self-proclaimed, yet unimaginative bisexual woman from Sewickley. Great view up the Ohio she worked with, but the place looks like a dump truck from The Sharper Image catalog store backed through the door and unloaded a sample pile of overpriced, tacky, yupped-out goods. Things like art deco lamps and a Greenwich Meridian Time clock. Lots of black and chrome and cherry and mahogany...a sharper image indeed.

"You could have been much more," Wylie says to me as he stands at his desk.

Incredulously, I stare at him. "I can't believe you said that. But, then again, I can."

"You know what I mean."

"I don't care about that, but I'll tell you this," I say, moderately perturbed. "I'm covering my shorts."

"No," Wylie says, taken aback.

"Yes."

He pauses. "Does that make you a Ronnie Miller convert?" He smiles.

"When Satan laces up his ice skates. Wylie, I won't be here to watch them, and I can't ask you to, so I'm out."

He nods. "That's understandable."

"Buy all twenty one tomorrow at the opening. Market orders. Check my account info."

"Got'cha, Dr. Bricker."

"Dr. Bricker? Is this the major sucking up you give all your clients," I ask, half in jest, "or is it reserved just for me?"

Wylie grins. "I make it feel like it's just for you," he says, like he's confiding in me his secret of success.

I pause and snicker. "As I've said, this doesn't mean I think the bull will roll again. At least, not yet. There will be more pain, Wylie."

"And as I've said, I'm going with Ronnie." Wylie takes his hands out of his pockets and crosses his arms.

"Good luck," I say. "Enough with the market, anyway. I have a more interesting topic to discuss."

"Oh, yeah?"

"Romance."

"You?" he screeches.

"Yes."

"And she doesn't invoice?" He's smiling again.

"Fuck you," I deadpan.

"Oh, my!" Wylie exclaims like a girl. "Anyone I know? Margot?"

"When Satan slaps the hockey puck."

"Okay then, smart ass, who is she?"

"Fenz."

Wylie is silent. "Uh, Mason..." he finally says.

"I'm attracted to Fenz, Wylie. I..."

"Who isn't?"

"Wylie, she's special to me."

Wylie takes a deep breath then sits at his big cherry desk on his black leather and chrome chair. "You're in trouble, my man."

"Why? It's not the company anymore. No harassment. What's the problem?"

"Ally gets around," he says with a furrowed brow.

"So? That's better than any other offer I have now." I take a seat in the black leather chair in the corner beside the interior window.

"Be careful. She loves them and leaves them. Oh, Mason, so many good women out there and you're making it so complicated."

134

"Ally's a good woman."

"Ally has a rep. She screws anything that walks."

Now I'm a trifle agitated. "Look, Mac…how do you know –"

He sighs. "Heard on the street."

"Why haven't I heard it on the street, then?" I say with some saliva.

"You're out of touch with the street," Wylie says calmly.

"And, that's the way I prefer it, and Ally does not screw around." I stand quickly.

"Be careful, Mason. You ever seen her with the same man twice?"

"Yes…I think."

"Just be careful," Wylie says, slowly wagging his finger at me. "She'll rip your heart out."

"I've had it ripped out before and I've survived."

"You call ignoring an entire gender and hiring a prostitute surviving?"

"Well, yes." I take a deep breath. I'd better change the subject before I kick his skinny ass. "Say, have you been keeping up with the NFL? They have strikebreakers this weekend. Replacement ball, they're calling it."

Wylie looks as if he's about to emit a 'Ha-rumph.' "What's the use?"

"Football. Replacement ball, Wylie. The dreams of hundreds of marginal players come true."

"Sounds like you should do it, Mr. Touchdown-against-Pitt," he says with a smile.

"Too old, too small, too slow, too many Arns, and too many Virginia Slims. Other than that, I'm a lock."

We pause. "Smith Barney's hiring. So's Merrill."

From flattery to parenting. "Where the hell did that come from?" I say.

"Reality," he says.

"Well, reality sucks. Anyway, brokers always hire at the top. It's a good bearish indicator. So, you be careful, Wylie."

"I will." We pause and look each other in the eyes. "As a friend, friend. Keep in touch." Wylie stands and extends his arm. I stand and comply. We shake hands. Our relationship of polarity motors on. "Well," he continues, "if you don't want to watch the market, you should think mutual funds."

"I knew you'd start working on me," I say with a smile.

"Good advice from your broker." He stuffs his hands back into his pants pockets.

"I don't mean to be too confrontational, but I'd rather sleep with you then buy one of your mutual funds." Whoa. Air pocket.

"You're bull-headed, Bricker," Wylie says with a smolder in his eyes. "That's why you're out of here."

I return the glare. "Why do you insist on being such a prick?"

"Just looking out for you, my man."

"Do you sincerely believe you're 'just looking out for me?' How pompous!"

Wylie's hands go from his pockets to his hips in the classic power stance. "You're a ticking time bomb, Mason. And, this thing with Ally is just one symptom. Then, there's the minor matter of the self-destruction of your career. A ticking time bomb."

"And, you're an—"

"Children," says the familiar voice behind me. I turn to discover John. White shirt. Red power tie. Navy slacks. No coat. Pleasant grin.

"Hey," says Wylie.

"John," I say. A tense pause hangs among us.

John takes a shallow breath. "Thanks for waiting."

"That's okay. It doesn't take long to pack a gym bag, anyway." I look at Wylie. "See ya," I say. Wylie nods to me. I walk past John to my ex-desk. He follows. We arrive.

Pause. "You may not believe this, but—"

"You're right, John. I don't believe it."

"I mean it, though."

I'm silent and uncomfortably looking around.

"What are you going to do?" John asks.

After I realize he's sincerely trying to be nice, I stop my defensiveness in its tracks. I take a breath. And another. "First, I'm going to pay you the thousand I – "

"No way," John says quickly.

"Yes."

"Can't."

"John, I simply lost the bet. I pay all my obligations."

"I can't take your money."

"You of all people know it won't hurt me. Is a personal check okay?"

There is a long pause. "Okay," he says, "What's your favorite charity?"

"Mental Health Association," I say quickly, trying to come up with the best way to help myself.

"I get the deduction," he says, smiling.

"But, of course."

"You got it." We shake hands. Now, *I'm* smiling.

"In the mail," I say. We laugh. So, I take this opportunity to announce, "Also, John, I'm covering my shorts."

"What?" he says, shocked.

"I'm going to cover. I can't keep my eyes on them, so I'm going to cover."

"I'm surprised, Mason. Aren't your shorts what this was all about?"

"Not by any stretch of the imagination," I say definitively. "So, Wylie's buying back at the opening. God knows he needs the commissions."

John grins, then sighs, "You could have been there with him, Mason."

"Bullshit."

"Could have."

"On this, I go." I grab my gym bag filled with two framed photos and three books of charts and graphs. John extends his hand. I clasp it. Again. Lots of handshaking in the world of investments. "It's all yours, Findlay. Carry on." Walking several paces to the receptionist's desk, I turn left to exit to the elevator doors. Seconds after pressing the down button, a car arrives. I step in, leaving behind five years of mild sweat and leisurely toil. I'll be back, though. I shall return.

Fuller Busher has a half million of my money.

Twenty-Seven

12:30 PM
Friday October 2, 1987
At my dining room table, writing in the real life journal, Arn in hand, one on deck, and one in the hole.
Dow Jones Industrial Average: How about the Love Jones Industrial Average? Now there's a concept. A Love Jones is far from industrial and never average.

Entry: It's the reverse osmosis of storytelling: writing a novel based on a movie. Sounds like something I'd do. 'I got a book deal out of my movie!' Now, I'm not just talking about any movie. I'm talking about *Foolish Sages,* named by *Sports Illustrated* as one of the Top Three Worst Sports Movies of The Decade of the Seventies. As a genre, sports movies leave much to be desired, so if you're the worst among the worst, you'd better keep your day job. I don't have a day job any more. Anyway, it follows that if *Foolish Sages: The Movie* was that bad, writing *Foolish Sages: The Novel* will be excruciating. A real challenge it is, primarily because the author and the screenwriter are one in the same. On the upside, I may be a lousy writer, but I'm a damned good re-writer, and that's wonderful because this movie needs some bitchin' re-writing. Every man deserves a second chance. I just have to make my second chance work. That means one thing will definitely change: the story. *Foolish Sages,* as Disney did it, was about a young man overcoming all the odds ever known to win at everything, every time, while exhibiting high we're-talking-Eagle-Scout morals. So, to make this possible in a really swell feel-good way, the truth had to be altered somewhat. Omit the fact that the hero and the best buddy kept the bong hot. Never mind that the hero's late father had been in collusion with neo-Nazis. And, forget that the hero shagged the teacher. With all that left out and more, it is little wonder *Foolish Sages* sucked. Suggestion to my readers: skip the football and go right for the sex. In fact, I'll make the whole book sex, just to show Disney. Talk about fiction.
Time for soaps. I wonder if *Ryan's Hope* is still on ABC? Was it 12:30 or 1:00? Joan and I used to watch it. I would be Jack, she would be Jillian. What a super way to spend summer afternoons. Kind of a strange thing for a married couple to do, but it was neat.

11:30 PM
Saturday October 3, 1987
Writing in the real life journal, Arn number five in the freezer, five minutes away.
Dow Jones Industrial Average: the muse for a future novel.

Three days and all I've done is write and drink. Write, drink, and sit on seven hundred fifty thousand dollars of cold cash. Who's to complain? Well, the IRS for one, if I don't file my quarterly estimate as the code dictates. I owe them about two fifty. Now, they could get surly.

Fuck them if they can't take a joke.

Tonight I'm getting a beer buzz thinking of the time *I* was 'the one that got away.' Jennifer Pierce was the fisher of men who lost a big one to the ocean known as Joan Kissinger, her American Lit instructor. As mixed metaphors go, that sentence was sad. I digress. The story of Jennifer Pierce is a nice subplot to the college romance of *Foolish Sages: The Novel.* Jennifer Pierce was my height and pretty, with long brown hair, almond-shaped brown eyes, legs all the way up to her ass, a runway model's boobs, and by now you're wondering why I walked. Well, Jennifer Pierce was a sorority girl, an intellectual zero, with whom a relationship was like a *stalag.* She took prisoners. How do I know? I spent several hours under her incarceration. I met her family. Glazed-eyed. Glazed-eyed and smiling uncontrollably. Dr. Pierce, Mrs. Pierce, Jennifer Pierce, and her li'l sis, what was her name? I'll call her Moon Unit. Moon Unit Pierce. The Pierces heard the filtered version of me through the daughter Jennifer Pierce. They loved me, especially Moon Unit Pierce. They loved me up until the moment I stiffed Jennifer Pierce in favor of marrying Joan, but only after Jennifer Pierce showed up at my room the night before Pitt wearing only an Aigner raincoat and proceeded to snuggle my lights out, if you know what I mean. Those lights went out only hours after I had told Joan I loved her. Joan never knew my secret about Jennifer Pierce. Or Edie Loden. November 8, 1975. It was Jennifer Pierce for breakfast, the fight against racism later that morning, a major college football victory that afternoon, then Joan, then Edie Loden, then Joan again, a world-changing day of victories and women only Jesse Jackson could appreciate. What if I would have married Jennifer Pierce? Nah. Three kids and one Junior Leaguer would have been way too much this heretic, this rebel without a pause could have taken.

3:10 PM
Sunday October 4, 1987
In the weight room at the Downtown YMCA, looking for a priest.
Dow Jones Industrial Average: up, up, and away

I used to work out. When I played football, college football, I was a work out demon. I ran wind sprints until both you and I puked. Weights? I ate them. Push-ups, sit-ups, crunches. I did it all with the fervor of a nineteen year old gone mad. It paid off: kickoff team, touchdown against Pitt, five eleven, one eighty-five, thirty waist, forty-four chest, fast and nasty. I was a bell ringer. When I hit you, you hurt.

Then...Joan. Interesting it is that my last day of football was the first day we made love. No more sprints. No more lifting. Just wine, beer, food, and sex. Straight from denial and discipline to hedonism, in record time. Then...the end of that; the end of my *la dolce vita.*

Fortunately, I'm genetically predisposed to have a good bod. It has been twelve years since I seriously exercised, but I look fine in the khaki slacks and brown wool blazer I wear today. The numbers also do not lie: five eleven, one eighty-five, thirty-two waist, forty-four chest. Still able to motor, but I'm a pacifist. Make love, not war. Well, for me the former has been almost two months, but I trust God will take care of me. He'll find me a girlfriend.

Gee, I wish Fenz would hurry home.

As I walk through the maze of steel bars and iron plates and mirrors and muscle and well-oiled, bulging, curvy men's and/or women's spandex, I finally make it to Michael. In his red tee shirt cut sleeveless, standard black gym shorts, and white Reeboks, he is put together like a brick tower of prayer. Women see him in his collar and cry. They're not fair, those canons of The Church. Not fair at all.

Michael arises from the bench and looks at me in a detached manner. He's got three fifteen on the rack and I just counted ten easy ones. What a guy!

"What the heck are you doing here?" he asks, awakened by me, sporting a friendly smile.

"I'm thinking about starting to consider the possibility of moving in the direction of working out, perhaps," I say.

He laughs. "A man of commitment."

"You know it."

Michael rubs a white towel over his neck. A blonde babe checks him out. "How are you?" he asks.

"Fine. And you?"

"Rushed and pushed to the limit."

"Oh."

"Do you need me?"

"Not really," I say, lying.

"Then, I gotta run. Important priest stuff."

"Okay."

"Say," Michael says as he punches my shoulder. Why does everyone do that to me? "What are you doing in the mornings of this week?"

"Writing insipid tripe and loving every minute of it. You have better ideas?"

"Why don't you come to mass tomorrow morning? Wear your painting clothes."

"Painting?"

"Painting. God calls. See ya!"

Painting. Maybe it's a good career move.

Twenty-Eight

1:10 PM
Monday October 5, 1987
Sitting at a research table in the AT Public Library, dressed for what used to be work
Dow Jones Industrial Average: whatever

Last night I finally counted the chips. On August 25, I put a half million at risk. On October 2, I took that money off the table. Plus more. In a thirty-eight day period during which the Dow fell about six percent, I made fifty five thousand dollars before taxes, over one year's work at Fuller Busher. Pay Uncle Sam and the Commonwealth their dues and that leaves me with around thirty-three. That's a little less than seven percent in those thirty-eight days, or, if you believe in the deceit of annualized return, a whopping sixty six percent per year.

To review: Thirty-eight days. I'm up seven percent. The experts are down six percent. Not bad for an investment firm washout.

Two newspapers sit to my left: Friday's *The Wall Street Journal* and the business section from Sunday's *The New York Times*. They read from opposite ends of the market opinion spectrum. The white Reagan men of the *WSJ* look for more trillions to be made after this bull market commercial break. The more-diverse anybody-but-Reagan men and a few women of the *NYT* are awaiting the dark days of our reckoning. My response? Most guys my age are piling up investments, debt, and salaries while becoming more and more politically conservative. When they zig...

Edie is standing at her desk helping an older gentleman. I bet he likes that. On this chilly early autumn day, she has chosen a white sweater to wear with dark gray slacks. Today is the second time I've seen her since Gay Greg Day. I don't know why I'm mad, but I am. Just because I extend my love doesn't mean I deserve it back. And, maybe she would have returned the favor had I personally said something to her about it. I seriously doubt I would ever do that, though, knowing the way my feelings were scary to me. Or, are scary to me. So...there is no one to be angry with except Mason. It's just more fun to be pissed at Edie.

However, I am here. Why am I here? Am I really a stalker? There's a frightening thought. I'd better leave, but I can't. Okay...Wednesday, Thursday, and today. Don't sit around waiting for an invitation to the regional perverts' convention, Brick. You're gone.

I lift myself from my chair with each newspaper under my arm. A half dozen paces lead me to the reference desk. The man has left. Edie is on the computer. After a couple seconds, she turns her attention to me.

"Did you find anything interesting today?" Edie asks.

"Same old stuff," I say, laying the papers on the desk. "Do you golf, Edie?" I ask before I knew I was going to.

She looks at me, confused. I don't know why I asked that question, either. "Uh...never have. No."

"Golf's a game of the little things. Grip, head down, relax." I still don't know why I asked that question. "The way to save strokes is to use fewer when you're closer to the pin. Yet, the big man concentrates on the drive from the tee, because that's the show. You drive for show, and putt for dough. So, what's more important, the tee, which is the show, or the pin, the dough?"

Edie stares at me for a standing eight count. "Mason," she says.

"Yes?"

"You went way over my head with that one."

I'm defeated. "Sorry. It didn't make any sense. I take one hundred percent responsibility for making myself understood."

Edie looks at me again for a moment or two. "Okay," she says.

"I'd better go," I say.

"How's work?" she asks.

My stomach tumbles. "Okay." Another patron walks to the desk. Edie turns to her. That's the signal to grab my driver and my balls and get the hell out.

8:20 PM
Monday October 5, 1987
In the condo, in bed, in a stupor.
Dow Jones Industrial Average: wherever it is, I'm sure I'm wrong.

'Make certain brain is engaged before operating mouth,' is my credo. Yeah, right.

Four things here: a) I wasted all the intellectual equity I had built up with Edie on one lame analogy that had no direction and meant nothing even if it did, b) after the flowers and the pager, I don't think I had any intellectual equity with Edie anyway, so the golf thing puts me way in the red, c) why should I care; like, why am I subjecting myself to these mental gymnastics about a woman who couldn't pick me out of her romantic lineup even if I were wearing her favorite colors, and d) why should I care, as in, why should I care because I don't care, obvious by the fact that I scooted out of there in mid-conversation. Jeez Louise.

Fenz is coming home Wednesday. Thank God. Now, there's a woman who appreciates me. I'll give her that night to unwind, then Thursday I'll make my suggestion: let's do it, get it on, turn on the hot blood, make love. Listen to INXS, Fenz: I need you tonight, because I'm not sleeping, there's something about you, girl, that makes me sweat.

10:00 AM
Tuesday October 6, 1987
In a room in the Rectory, standing on a drop cloth, dipping my roller in paint called Mint Verde.
Dow Jones Industrial Average: I don't know. I just don't know.

It doesn't take an hour of staring into this bucket to figure out that Mint Verde is a hideous color. Is it paint, or dessert? I'm just a volunteer. I do as I'm told, which, considering my judgment of late, should be my mantra.

I'm not a bad painter. I splatter on the floor only during those times that I don't feel a need for a safety net, which is a direct parallel to the high wire act I call my life. Fortunately, the drop cloth has always been there for me.

Yesterday's room still looks good today, so I guess I'm doing something right. Leave it to Michael. He's taken me back to my essence, which of course is playing in goo and pasting it on a wall. We should all return to kindergarten occasionally.

Wylie says Fenz is all about sex. Well, I'll bowl her over with romance. That tactic probably doesn't occur to the men in her life, who think with their peckers. Anything but sex. That'll confuse her. Then she'll be mine.

All that money and little to no discretionary spending. Over the past five years, my only luxuries were Christine and the vacations in France and Maui and the manly brown leather furniture. And Virginia Slims. And endless Arns. Maybe it's about time to spend a lot more on myself, you know, treat *numero uno* to the finer things, whatever they are. For instance, a new car. A 1988 Saab 9000 turbo, steel blue. Convertible. Like, more travel, like back to Paris. This all sounds so right. Out of eight hundred fifty, I gave away two hundred. That's way more than the Protestant tithe of ten percent. I'm better than a Baptist. I'm miles ahead of a Methodist. I'm luckier than a Lutheran. But, watch it, dude. I'm sounding as pious as the PTL. Jerry Falwell to the world: a) how much money do you have, and b) when are you going to send it in?

The telephone message from the department head at Pitt said all positions are filled for spring 1988, but she can take me as a part timer to handle a couple of night classes. Wonder what kind of women sign up for an evening of freshman composition? With regard to the fact that my other best employment prospects are on the fuzzy end of this roller, I'm sure I'll find out.

Dr. Bricker, is it 'farther' or 'further?'

It's farther, as in, 'I've never been farther in outer space than I am now.' Or…it's further, like, 'Can I get any further out of my mind?'

Twenty-Nine

Noon
Wednesday, October 7, 1987
Listening to creaking footsteps down the hallway just outside Michael's study as the second coat of Mint Verde is wet.
Dow Jones Industrial Average: it's become interesting again – down 92 yesterday to 2,549, a huge one-day 3.7 percent drop.

"Here," Michael says as he enters the study. He's in his priest's uniform. Black is not a slimming color on Michael. His shoulders look as if they are going to burst through the walls.
"What?" I ask, glancing back down to the bucket. "Oh. Jeez, Michael. I'm sorry." I've been thinking of a million things while painting. I see he has two beers. "Thank you." I reach for the Arn. We raise our bottles in a toast to nothing apparent. He sips, then I sip.
"Isn't it a little early for a beer?" I ask.
"Not today," he replies.
"Works for me." I turn it up.
Silence ensues. Michael bends down to sit on the drop cloth on the floor. I follow. We face each other, legs crossed, beers in left hands. A desk, a table, and two bookcases are among us, moved in toward the center of the room, all covered by drop cloths.
"You're really into this," he says.
"Why do you say that?" I ask.

"You're relatively quiet. The painting must have you spellbound." He's smiling.

"Spellbound. A priest referring to the occult. Your secret is mine."

"Thanks," Michael says, still smiling.

"Yeah. I have been wondering, though: why do they call it Mint Verde? *Verdi* is Latin for 'green,' right?"

"Close," he says, "*Viridis* is the root."

"Okay. So, you have 'mint', which implies green, and 'verdi,' which also implies green. It's redundant, like 'vestal virgin.'" I sip again.

"How long did it take you to come up with that?" Michael grins as he takes a big swig. I'm talking big swig. I bet it was a tough morning for clergy.

"Couple days," I say.

"You're slipping." A pause. Michael turns his gaze to a corner of the room, then back to me. "It must be difficult, Brick," he says, obviously referring to my no-job status.

"Could be," I reply.

"Wanna talk?"

"No. Oh, yes, you and I should talk like always, but not 'talk,' like I have something I need to 'talk' about. I'm okay with it. I don't have anything I need to 'talk' about." Another pause. "Strange to you, maybe, because there have been many things happening to me in the last couple of months, but nothing I can't handle. Not that there is anything to handle, you know, but, if there were, I could handle them, or it, even."

Silence. Michael looks into my eyes. I look at his. I decide to continue with something else. "I've made a major breakthrough with the novel. We're back to the real story. All the way. I found out I, even I, was sugarcoating it, just like Disney. I can't believe I was doing that, after all my bitching. I was trying to keep it less controversial, but hell, Michael, it *was* controversial. Major. I'm writing about a major controversy."

A long pause. Michael takes a sip. Damn. "Mason – "

"Michael, are you okay? You're knockin' that Arn down."

"I'm stressed," he says. "I'm also worried about you. Have you talked with your friend from Pitt?"

That question leaves me a little pissed, but it's Michael, and I'll give him the latitude. "No. No, I haven't, but I'm going to. Honestly. I left her a message on her answering machine. She left me a message back that she had no full-time positions available, but she may need evening classes help. I haven't gone beyond that."

"Evening classes. That's pretty good news. Now, remember, you also have CMU, Duquesne, California State, Grove City, Robert Morris, many places around here you can teach. Don't forget about them."

"You really want to see me do this, don't you?"

Michael grins. "I think you're a natural."

"Thanks."

"You're welcome."

"Yeah, a natural. Why didn't I do that all along?"

"God provides in his own way," Michael says as only he can and get by with it.

"Yeah. That's it. Considering Joan and how we got started and then how we ended, God did the right thing. Otherwise, I would have probably blown my teaching career chasing coeds."

"You may have. But, I think you're ready now."

"Michael, I was so vulnerable, I think the woman from the…escort service…kept me out of a bad relationship," I say with a wink.

Michael scowls and slowly shakes his head. "Either that was an attempt at dark humor or you have completely surrendered your mind to rationalization."

"You know what the guy in *The Big* – "

"I saw the movie. So, just let me say, don't feel so all alone." There's a twinge of pain on his face.

"I do feel alone."

"Well," he says. "bounce that off me when you can."

I don't know when that will be. "Got'cha."

"By the way, how's Wylie?" Michael asks.

I hesitate. "He's funny, Padre. Not funny ha-ha, but funny strange. You know what they say about brokers. They have to eat a lot of fish to feed their shark. In fact, they are sharks. Sharks have to move to live. Eat and move. I don't miss that part of it."

"I can see why he'd be so stressed," Michael says.

"But," I say, "he always comes out of it."

"Yeah."

"Ally Fenz is coming home today. I'm going to pick her up at the airport."

Michael went with my complete lack of segue. "Where's she been?"

"On a cruise."

He raises his eyebrows. "Must be nice."

"This is the moment for a 'there goes the vow of celibacy' punch line if I ever saw one," I say.

"Give me a break or I'll break your neck," Michael says in jest.

I laugh. "Anyway, I'm looking forward to seeing her."

Michael sips again. I'm going to have to wheel him out of here. He cocks his head slightly. "Does she know about…"

"Oh, I think she knows that there is a potential for me to…possibly…not come on to her…but, be sweet. Yes, sweet. I've talked with her about other women, though."

"Does she know about the…escort?" Michael asks with a squint. "Have there been other women, if you don't mind me asking?"

"No. And, only Joan. And, no, I don't mind you asking. Anyway, Ally and I have this special friendship that I think could easily be turned into love. I mean, we love already, but we're not lovers."

"And, now you want to become her lover."

"Well, yes."

"That's nice to hear from you."

"It could be the most constructive thing I've done in years."

"Then there was your gift to us." Michael smiles and nods.

"Yeah," I swig, hoping to not talk about that. "I told you not to mention that to anyone, especially me."

A pause. "Speaking of money," Michael says. "the market took a real tumble yesterday, didn't it? Down almost a hundred points?"

"Ninetysomething," I reply. "I haven't given stocks much thought lately, but I took notice of that. We had a few craters like that earlier this year, but the market continued up, in a big way. The danger here is that clients – listen to me, will ya – anyway, *investors* think that we'll be okay again. The truth is, things are very different now."

"That different? Since the first of the year?"

"Yep. Interest rates are way up. The dollar is weak overseas and despite that we have these Godzillas of a trade deficit and a budget deficit, neither of which seem to have a solution. We need a strong dollar to keep Japan and everybody invested here to prop up this flimsy economy we have built into a marsh in our own swampland, but a strong dollar makes it worse since it makes selling overseas difficult, which leads to the trade deficit and the budget deficit."

Michael laughs. "If this is how you write, I'm buying an autographed copy."

"Thanks, man. I'm countin' on ya." I pause appropriately, but I feel a need to continue my dissertation. It's been a long time. A week. Have I ever gone a week without boring someone with my take on money? "Now, that's what we know and what we know is, by the free market theory, already in the prices of stocks and bonds."

"You sound like a teacher," Michael says.

I roll my eyes in mock disgust. "Okay! I'll be a teacher, damnit! Now, be a student and just listen to me! What we don't know is how the market will react to something called program trading…get this… computerized program trading. I mean, investment programs in which *computers* make the decisions…and execute them. All by themselves."

"Computers. Making the decisions, then doing it. No humans."

"Humans write the software, install it, then hit the switch. After that, it's all computers."

"Really?" Michael says in disbelief.

"Yep. Computers. Buying and selling stocks. And, not just any computer, but computers with big ass bucks. Really scary."

"No lie." Michael sips. I join him.

"It's like this." I hesitate.

"Go ahead," Michael says with a grin.

"Okay," I return the grin. "You have the market of stocks, which has redeeming value to our society. Then you have the market of stock derivatives, the primary purpose of which is to basically lay a wager on the direction of the market of stocks."

"Derivatives."

"Yeah. They are investment…instruments, for lack of a better word…instruments that are another way to take advantage of stock price movements because they, the instruments, are derived from the stocks themselves. Stocks can exist without derivatives, but…well, you know what a derivative of anything is."

"Do we need another six-pack for this?" he asks as he punches my arm.

I sigh and laugh. "You're an old finance major, Burt, but for six I'll tell you anything you want to hear."

Michael snickers. "Lay a wager. I don't want to hear this, but I want to hear this. Sounds frightening."

"I'll give you the Cliff Notes. The computers use stocks as well as derivatives, in this case called futures contracts, to run the investment programs. That's possible because the market of futures is a proxy for the market of stocks, but the relationship between the two is not perfect. There are slight differences between them, differences called spreads."

"Spreads," says Michael. "There's your wager. Sounds like sports bookmaking."

"Something like that," I say, smiling. "And similar to sports bookmaking, futures/stocks spreads are created by human imperfection. That means we can't keep the two markets completely in phase because of our inherent humanity. A computer can pick up on these ever-so-slight spreads as well as their changes, as only a computer can. The computer, not a person, but the computer, then hits the buy or sell button based on which way is the better way to take advantage of the situation. Believe it or not, and this is the truly ironic and provocative part, when you combine futures and stocks like this, the result is about as risk-free as one can get on Wall Street. And, that's really dangerous."

A long pause. "Why's it risk-free? And, why is risk-free dangerous?" Michael asks.

"Since the futures act like the stocks, you buy a future and sell a stock, or the other way around, and you don't pick a direction. It's arbitrage. In arbitrage, you play the spread. The spread is easy money. The choice of the direction is the risk."

"Damn," he says.

"So, if you have a big enough computer, able to figure all this out and then to be able to almost instantaneously buy a helluva lot of stocks and sell corresponding futures, or sell a helluva lot of stocks and buy corresponding futures, and if you have the big-time jack to make this interesting, you yourself can make a lot of big-time jack."

"How much big-time jack is enough to make this interesting?"

"Multimillions. Multi multi. Who knows, but for sure it is out of our range."

"You still haven't answered the question, Mason. If it's risk-free, then why is it dangerous?"

"It's risk-free for those with the computer, but as you the priest may guess, someone pays. If enough big shots do it, enough big shots making instantaneous buying and selling decisions with big bucks, those big shots can control the market and rock it pretty damned fast. They can exacerbate the euphoria, or panic, already present. It happened this year on the way up. It'll happen anytime now on the way down. And, Michael, they can do it and they don't care. They don't care about the things we care about, like earnings or company value or anything. All they care about is what the computer says. And all the computer cares about is what the damn spread is. That's why it's dangerous. Our market of pension plans and savings for the future can be wiped out by futures, futures and stocks positioned by computers working with differential and integral calculus, with their cold electronics and the icy gaze of the screen. It's powerful."

Michael looks at me hard. "Cold electronics? Icy gaze of the screen? You've been writing too much," he says with a smile.

"Okay, that one was overdone," I say, "But, I'm right about what could happen. This futures game fu- scr-…puts a lot of honest investors at much more risk then they bargained for."

"So, you see a lot of risk right now."

"Yes, definitely."

"Where's your money?"

"Fuller Busher, in a government-guaranteed money market account earning about six percent interest. Plus, some of it is at AshNat."

"Isn't Beth just great?"

"She makes banking fun."

Michael pauses. "No stocks?"

"Not one."

Michael pauses again. "The computer people have scared you off that much."

"That, and interest rates are sky high and we have deficits and I could go on and on."

Michael pauses again. "I hope you're wrong."

"Here's to being wrong," I say, clinking my bottle to his.

Thirty

9:00 AM
Thursday October 8, 1987
At the reference desk, Ashton Township Public Library
Dow Jones Industrial Average: huh…rather intriguing…in a Dow Jones sort of way.

"Good morning, Mason," Edie says with cheer.

"Good morning," I politely return.

"Well, look who was beating the door down early," she says with more cheer.

"My library fix." I must be *so* vulnerable. The tight black skirt and black stockings she's wearing today are incredibly hot. Or, maybe I'm just incredibly fervid. Saturday August 22, 12:30 in the morning? Safe bet on that fervid thing.

"How's the Dow?"

"Rather…intriguing." I attempt to remain grounded by being urbane, acting and dressing like a real, live money manager.

"I've heard."

"Intriguing. And, dangerous," I add.

"How's that?"

"Big drop the other day."

"So," she says, "what does all the history you've been studying tell you?"

"Watch your backside…uh…" Back. Watch your back, I meant to say.

She tries to keep a straight face. "Can it be that bad?"

"Yeah. If you own stocks, your butt could...really be in...a sling." Damn. Help me! Aghhh!

"Don't worry. On this salary, I can't own stocks. You won't see me losing my ass," Edie says with a wink. Now, she's having her fun at my expense.

"I don't own stocks, either," I say. "It's just your booty – my duty – to look out for my clients." Ohh...no.

She squints and drops her chin. Her face falls into the palms of her hands. "Okay," she says, looking up and grinning. "What is it today?"

I'm sure I'm visibly shaken. "Let me look at your..." For God's sake, don't say it! "Uhh...*The Wall Street*...well, look at the time, will ya?" I say as I glance at the wrist without the watch. "I have to pick up a friend at the airport."

Edie places her hands on the desk and leans in toward me. "Is it your friend you were here with on that Sunday?"

My gut does a free fall. "Well...yes...Ally...Fenz...we're just friends...we don't...I mean, we aren't...you know...really, I really better go."

"Come back," she says with a finger-wagging wave.

10:00 AM
Thursday October 8, 1987
At the downtown levee on south bank of the Ohio River
Dow Jones Industrial Average: the least of my worries.

I don't know what to say. I truly don't know what to say. Never has a woman, or a man, intimidated me so. Why can I not make any sense around Edie? Tomorrow is our one-month celebration and the PhD in me has yet to surface. If I told her I have a doctorate, she wouldn't believe it anyway, so that aspect of my life is not important. So, it's one month and I've spent most of that time thinking she was someone else. What a complete imbecile I am. Maybe I should get away from these chilly waters on this chilly morning before I voluntarily become barge fodder.

I've really lost my whattthefuck swagger.

Fenz better come through for me. This siege I've put myself under is backing up to my brain and it's beginning to cloud my reasoning. If she would just do me and get it over with, then maybe I can go to the library in peace. If she'd do me on a regular basis, then maybe I could just stay away from the library altogether. Edie is not the woman for me. As Jim Morrison might have said at one time, 'This is the end, my beautiful chubby friend. The end.'

Noon
Thursday October 8, 1987
Gate C-22; Greater Pittsburgh International Airport; Coraopolis, Pennsylvania
Dow Jones Industrial Average: I can't help but keep track on the Olds' radio – 2,550, down a point at the 11:00 hour.

It's autumn and Thursday and the only place people in an airport have to go to is work, so business attire dominates Concourse C. That is, until Fenz appears from the tunnel. Oh, yeah. I've seldom seen a woman more…luscious…than her as she wears the denim jumpsuit very well. Period. The tan. The curves. End of sentence. Wow.

"Hi," Ally emits, a surprisingly solemn greeting. She approaches me, drops her carry-on, and lands a peck on my cheek.

"Tough cruise," I say sarcastically.

"No," Ally says, as if I need an explanation, "Great cruise. It's just sad to be back to the grind."

"Ah, reality sucks."

Fenz drops her head and dips it toward my shoulder, "Yeah. It sucks so bad." She then jerks back up and grins. "Well, guess what I did!"

I'm taken aback by her sudden change of moods. "You got married?" I ask reflexively, scorned before I even had a chance.

"Do I *look* crazy?" Fenz walks. I follow.

"No. Good girl."

"Then, guess what I did?"

"You met a sugar daddy," I say, knowing I could qualify.

"No!" Fenz exclaims, leaning in to me.

"Honey, I'm out of answers."

She pauses and smiles. "I talked to the purser. What a hunk, by the way. I talked to him about becoming a cruise hostess."

Completely surprised, not at all expecting Fenz to leave me, I say, "I'll be damned."

"I did it in Vegas. I'd still be good at it. I'm still in practice. All the girls at Fuller Busher are such airheads, I'm the hostess there."

"You'd be good at it. You are good at it. You make people feel good."

"Thanks, Mason. I appreciate your comments. I appreciate everything about you. Everything." She steps in. A pause ensues. "Will you write a recommendation letter for me?" Fenz clasps her hands under her chin. "Pretty please?"

"You're really serious about this, aren't you?" I say. "And, after that major ass-kissing, I'll write the letter."

"Oh, how can I ever thank you! I really want to do this."

"It's exciting," I say with a touch of sullenness, realizing I did indeed expect a more permanent relationship.

"Oh, yes, it is exciting," Ally says as she wraps her arm in mine. "Now, I don't want to dominate the conversation with the man who so kindly picked me up, so what's new with you?"

"Oh, the same ol' stuff." There is a break in the talk as I am released from Ally's spell. This is not turning out the way I expected. For the first time since she arrived, I notice the hurried crowd. How disappointing it all is.

"How ya making it?"

"Pretty well…well, not really."

"Mason, sweetie, don't worry. It's only been a week."

"Eight days, actually. I'm still better off. I think."

"You know it. I'm leaving, too! Yea!"

"Yea!" Yeah. Whoopie.

"Have you seen Edie?"

"A couple times. Saw her just this morning."

Fenz delivers a soft punch to my shoulder. "Sounds like *you're baaack!*"

"I don't think so."

"Dude, one of these days, you're going to sweep her off her feet."

"Who cares?" We cut right to the escalator leading down to the baggage claim area.

"What do you mean?" she asks.

"I don't want to sweep her off her feet, but if I did, I'm saying all the wrong things, and then when I try to say the right things, I get even more wrong and more wrong until I morph into the Incredible Hulk of risibility. This is stupid. I'm calling this mission off."

"Oh, I've seen you in action," Fenz says with her hands on hips. "But, it's probably not as bad as you say it is."

"Yes, it's that bad. I quit."

"What am I going to do with you?"

"Oh, I can think of some really juicy things, but really, there is nothing to do. I give up."

Fenz smiles. "Don't give up."

"I'm lost." Expressionless faces on the up escalator cross with us. There is a long lull in our conversation, atypical of Fenz and me.

"So, you're lost," she finally says.

"Damn straight." We exit at the bottom and walk straight ahead. The crowd grows.

She pauses. And again. "Remember what you said about Paris?"

"Paris?"

"Paris."

"France?"

"Paris!"

"Okay, what did I say about Paris?"

"You told me that after a couple days in the French Alps, you got off the TGV at the station in Paris one afternoon, then you went to the subway and headed for…what was it?"

"*The Arc de Triomph.*"

"Right. So, you got off near…"

"*Champs d'Elysses.*"

"Mason." Fenz stops. I follow suit.

"What."

"You're turning me on with all that French," she says with a touch of sultry.

I laugh. "Christ, Fenz, you *are* a tease. They're just French words spoken by an Irish Catholic…from West Virginia!"

"Maybe. But, back to France…it wasn't the…how did you say…"

I moan. "*Champs d'Elysses.*"

"Ohhh. Keep talking." Ally takes my hand to hers and looks directly into my eyes.

"What the hell is this? You keep talking. So…your point is?"

"You were lost."

"And?" I shrug.

"You're bright, rich, nice, good-looking...everything I want in a guy."

"Except I don't have a job."

She grins. "Despite that, what I mean is you're everything I want in a guy."

This could be it, but I want to toe-dip this one. "But, you want the purser. What did Mary do while you went after the purser?"

"The captain."

"Oh."

"Anyway, you're everything I want in a guy."

Time to pop the question. "But, you *don't* want me."

"Because you're in love with Edie."

"That was the other Edie."

"No, you're in love with this Edie," she says as she drops my hand. "Library Edie."

"I don't know about love. You could say I'm in love with you."

"I doubt it," Fenz says, crossing her arms. "You just described being in love with me like you're talking to someone about flying indicators or something."

"Ah...I guess it's just lust, then. So be it."

"Probably just lust." She smiles, arms still crossed.

"Probably. And, that's not too shabby." My best shot...

She looks at me, still smiling, then nodding. "Now, back to Edie."...fell short.

"Okay, whatever you say."

"You love Paris."

I sigh. "I've had it with your circumlocution."

"What? Oh, I don't care what that means. The point is, you love Paris."

"Okay...that's the point. What point?"

"You love Paris, and you got lost in Paris."

"Okay..."

She slices deeply into my personal space. "I believe a man is most lost right when he falls in love."

"What?"

"You're lost around Edie," she says.

"Yeah, but that's because I'm a moron."

"You're lost in Paris. Paris is Edie. You love Paris."

A long pause. Really long. "I can see that. I believe you." An epiphany! "I do believe you! Damnit, I'm *not* a moron!"

"I knew you'd come around."

Foot traffic hovers around us, but my world is Ally and me. A strange sense of relief overcomes me. "How do you know so much?"

"You can't talk straight around Edie. From what I saw, you never could."

"Yeah, I guess. How am I going to learn to talk around her?"

"By admitting you're in love with her."

"Again?"

"Not Edie Loden, the fantasy Edie. But, Edie, the real Edie. You're in love with the real Edie. Library Edie. So, when will you find out your lover's last name?"

"Whenever I can form the sentence that asks her."

Fenz laughs. "Go for it, honey."

"I can't." A strange sense of fright overwhelms me.

"C'mon. Take your chances."

"That's like drawing three cards looking for a straight. Chances aren't too hot."

"It's like the leap of faith you always talk about."

"I can't believe you actually listen to me."

"You told me that in the stock market, you get all the information you can, but it's never everything, so you have to take the leap of faith to make the decision."

Another long pause. And, there's that familiar feeling. "Oh, Christ, not again. I'm frightened, Fenz."

"I know. Love's scary."

Yes. Again. Ohhh, boy. "When were you in love?"

Fenz grins. "The purser."

"What does a purser do?"

"I'm not telling."

Long pause. "This sucks."

"No. No sucks. Take the leap of faith, Mason."

I finally feel like smiling. "Okay, short stuff...you win. For the second time in a month, I've fallen in love. With the same, yet different woman. I'm in love with Edie Whatshername."

"That's my boy!" she exclaims, throwing herself into my arms.

Thirty-One

2:30 PM
Sunday October 11, 1987
In the reference section, Ashton Township Public Library
Dow Jones Industrial Average: 2,482 – 9.8 percent off all-time high

With the love of my life sitting over there behind her desk basically doing nothing but looking really good, I read the Sunday *New York Times* and contemplate. Edie would be impressed with my mind. I am thinking. I am thinking about what NYT contributor Anise Wallace writes. Most interesting is how the Japanese, with their rampaging but rice paper-thin economy, dominate the US stock market and how potentially damaging that is for Wylie's mutual fund investors in places like Aliquippa and Monaca. I'm thinking how Wylie, the trusted advisor, has talked these people from these industrial towns in western Pennsylvania into putting their faith and their life savings into this same US stock market that is controlled by investment bankers backed by dangerously, astronomically high real estate prices in a land (or lack of land) a half a world away.

Scary? Here's scary: the Japanese get their money from loans against the dangerously, astronomically high real estate market. Then, they use that money to buy almost exclusively the stocks of US name-brand companies, the identities of which are recognized worldwide; like Coca-Cola's red can, McDonalds' golden arches, IBM's name, and the silhouette of the Boeing 747. Now, why is that scary? If the flimsy real-estate prices give it up, the Japanese will need quick cash to cover their leveraged portfolios. Where will they get that quick cash? Likely, from the same name-brand companies they have been eating up. The frothy market will not be able to withstand the massive selling. The subsequent collapse of prices in Coca-Cola, McDonalds, IBM, and Boeing will begat the rampant selling of stocks of other companies. Investors' capital, from the wealthy and middle class alike, will wither.

I am a ton of fun, aren't I?

3:00 PM
Sunday October 11, 1987
Standing alone at the reference desk
Dow Jones Industrial Average: much higher than it will be in the future

Edie walks to me. "How ya making it?" she asks. My heart melts at the sight of her. She's dressed to kill me in a black skirt just above her knees. A beige mock turtle brings out her brown eyes like never before. Yep, I got it bad.

"Fine. Oh, so fine," I answer.

"'Oh, so fine?'" she says with a grin. "You have to know something I don't."

"I've just had a lot of things go my way." My Levis stir.

"So, you're on a hot streak."

"You could say that."

"So am I." Edie crinkles her nose at me. I laugh to myself at myself.

"Then, let's both bask in the glow of good fortune."

"Before we tan at the sight of our own rays," she says with a grin, "I have a question."

"Shoot."

"How can a money manager have things going his way when the market had a record drop like last week?"

"Good question. And, the answer is, my clients and I are out. We're protected. We're holding cash. Cash is king."

"Nice move."

"Kind of."

"Kind of?" She tilts her head slightly to the side. Whoa.

"My clients are safe, but others who are in the market right now are losing money."

"You can't help what others do. Adults make their own decisions, no matter how stupid they are."

"Well, yes, but for me to be right, there must be pain elsewhere."

Edie smiles. "You're nice to say that, but it's only money."

"Now, there's a different perspective for the eighties." I smile back.

A pause. "You know something?" she says, reaching to tap the desk in front of me.

"Know what?"

"I don't think we've been formally introduced."

"Really? Yeah, really."

"I don't know your last name."

"Oh. It's Bricker. Mason Bricker." I think I've told her before, but I'll tell her again if it means she might sit on my lap.

"Nice to meet you, Mason Bricker. I'm Edie Marie."

I love you, Edie Marie. Edie Marie, will you…"Well, Edie Marie, it's my pleasure. Actually, it's been my pleasure since the beginning, even before knowing your…well, you get my drift."

"Yes, I do." She gives me that familiar grin, the one she has always issued during my bumbles.

"How's the library today?"

"So far, quiet. It's a beautiful crisp fall day. People have better things to do."

"Is that good or bad for you?"

"Bad, in that the afternoon drags," she sighs. "Good in that it is as American as burgers on the grill to do as little work as possible, and I intend to continue that tradition."

"Interesting. So many people now subscribe to the 'work hard, play hard' mantra."

"Well, I'm half of that."

"I like your point-of-view."

"Think about it. Almost all inventions in the US, the world's Innovation Central, were created to reduce the amount of work so we can seek pleasure."

"We're a nation of screw-offs, masked by…masked by the accomplishment of tasks."

She lightly slaps my hand. "You're not your typical yuppie."

"I hope to hell not."

"I can tell. I can read you like a book, Mason Bricker, but that only makes sense."

"How's that?" I ask with a wary squint. She's figured me out. "How are you able to read me?"

"I work in a library."

"You got me there," I laugh aloud.

"Let's have a seat." Edie walks from behind her desk to a table nearby. I check out her big round nice butt before she places it in a chair, then I sit beside her. "Now, what spooks you the anti-yuppie so much about this stock market?"

"Well," I say, preparing my professional persona. "the market is propelled mostly by foreign investors."

"How xenophobic of you," she says like a rich liberal would.

"It's not a fear or an ideology, Edie. It's a practical matter. The Reagan administration has reeled our nation into a crisis of confidence, a crisis of confidence here and overseas."

"You really aren't a yuppie, are you."

"Nope," I say proudly. "Look at it this way. Take Japan."

"Okay."

"The Japanese in 1981 held eleven billion dollars in US stocks. Now? One hundred eighty billion."

"Those commissions paid for a lot of Beemers."

"You are a live wire."

"Twenty-four seven, sweetie."

Oh, you little heart squeezer, you. I grin. "The danger of all that is, if something pisses all that Japanese money off, they'll walk, meaning 'sell', and they'll most likely take West Germany and the rest of Europe with them, countries which own a boatload over here, too."

"What will upset them?"

"You're a Democrat. You know, the same stuff that upsets you. Namely, the twin deficits. The fact that our government continues to borrow at an alarming rate, and the fact that we are buying much more from them than we are selling to them, well, that's not good."

"Don't worry," Edie says with a smile. "I predict we'll be out of this mess in '88. But, talking about a crisis of confidence, how about Reagan's failure to pull Robert Bork through this week. I love it!"

"That's because Bork was so brutally honest, an ultra-conservative judge with no apologies. Doesn't say much for the appeal of Reaganism right now, does it."

"We've been waiting for cracks in this dike for years now. I think Iran-Contra only scratches the surface."

"Bork. Iran-Contra. Double-edge deficits. Foreign investors are wondering when it's all going to fall. And, I repeat, they'll run if they have to."

"Wow."

An exceptionally beautiful woman saying a simple 'Wow.' Wow. I recover. "And, Japan will lead the way, where, in my ironic opinion, it could be worse."

"You're just the torchbearer for optimism, aren't you."

I smile at that one. "I was reading *The New York Times* this morning. A columnist by the name of Anise Wallace writes just what I said, primarily because I plagiarized it from her."

Edie giggles. "You're something," she says.

This…is a fun conversation. "Another one: an investment banker with an American investment bank in Tokyo wrote also in the NYT that US stock prices are tied to the Japanese real estate market, a market in which land prices are up four-fold in three years."

"Hot property."

"Three years! Do you know that if you buy office real estate in Japan today, you can't expect better than a one hundred year payback period. One hundred years! And, Japanese stock prices are way out of whack, with valuations screaming ridiculously high. This is the model economy? It's an economy ready to face the music, and they'll take us down with them. That's the risk."

"Doom-and-gloom, aren't you?"

"I'm a blast at a party."

"I bet you are. And, I understand you. You just want to save money. I admire that."

"The best way to make money is to not lose too much." I want to say more, but something makes me hesitate. We look into each other's eyes. I think I see admiration…

"So, you think foreign investors are looking over here and wondering?" she asks.

"Exactly. Prices for many things are way out of sync. And, if they the foreigners see something they don't like, they'll scoot. And, Japan will lead the way, where, as I said, it's a helluva lot worse than here."

"So, then, everyone is vulnerable. Worldwide."

"That's what I think."

"Do you think there will be a Great Depression again?"

"I don't know about that, but there will be a lot of depressed Republicans walking around in a year."

Edie laughs. "C'mon now. I bet you voted for Reagan."

"Reagan '84, but Carter '80."

"That's schizo."

"Voted in '80 with my mind and in '84 with my—"

"Wallet."

I nod to the affirmative. "Essentially. I'm a money manager. It was a union vote."

"I can't fault you for it, Mr. Money Manager," she says with a grin. "But, you seem to have seen the error of your ways."

"You liberals get cocky when you're right."

"We're never right, but we're always correct."

"Arguing with you is futile."

A man slowly steps up to the reference desk. Damn it. "Guess I'd better go," Edie says. "I would ask you to come back, but you always do anyway."

"Just as long as I'm not a bother."

"In no way are you a bother."

'In no way are you a bother.' Those are some sweet tunes right there.

Thirty-Two

10:00 PM
Monday October 12, 1987
Watching Monday Night Football in the condo – Denver 14, LA Raiders 3
Dow Jones Industrial Average: 2,471 – just over 10 percent off all-time high

If you're a true football fan, you will be able to find some entertainment from replacement ball. Granted, the athletes aren't as gifted, but they seem to want it more, since only three weeks ago they were bartenders, bouncers, teachers, construction workers, insurance agents, and maybe there were a stockbroker or two. A chance to play in the NFL after several healthy doses of real life can really stoke your heart. Not knowing when your gig is up implores you to sell it out every weekend, and that makes for great pure sport. Being an ex-player who had a lot more desire than body, I know how the replacement players feel. And, I could use a shot of their juice right now.

The cordless phone beside me is ringing. Can't be Wylie; he's not going to go out of his way to talk to me. Fenz is probably with a man. Must be Michael. The replacement Steelers called and he wants me to paint more while he's on football sabbatical. I pick up the phone and punch the button.

"Hello."

"Hi, sweeties!"

"No, it's not...no."

"Yes, it is!"

"Oh, God, a blast from the past! Christine!" I say before I know it. "I was just thinking about you!" Not really, but, boy, I could have.

"How does it feel?" she says with a giggle. "I haven't felt it for a while."

I'm feeling it. "I haven't felt it for a while either, but my face is split with a grin." I laugh.

"Is it too late to come over to see you?"

"Well, it's never too late." Oh, hell. I almost forgot! "But, there has been a positive development in my life you should know about."

"And, what's that?"

"I'm in love," I say proudly.

There is a pause. I'm wondering what she thinks about that. "Oh, Mason, that's so nice! I'm so happy for you! I mean it! No one deserves it more than you. I just love new love! I love it all, from the very beginning. Tell me, what did she say the first time you told her you love her?"

"I haven't told her yet."

"What the hell are you waiting for? You'd better hurry! Someone else will steal her away! What's she like? Tell me. Oh, this is so wonderful!"

This is sweet. "She's gorgeous. She's bright. She's nice. She's funny."

"Oh, that's so wonderful. You're making me cry!" she says with a moan.

I'm so excited to have pleased Christine, as strange as this conversation is. "Maybe you can meet her someday."

"Uh...maybe I shouldn't."

That would be foolhardy. "Yeah, I guess not."

There is an uncomfortable pause. "Well," we say simultaneously. We laugh.

"Go ahead," I say.

"I have an idea," she says immediately.

"Okay."

Another pause. "Is there any way to make money in this stock market?"

"My opinion?"

"That's why I called."

"Then, no."

"Why?"

"Everyone's looking for the good times, but prices are falling and they will continue to fall until everyone thinks they're all going to die. Then, prices will go up and it will then be time to make money in the stock market."

Christine is silent long enough for me to notice Denver has scored again in this rout. I hate to have said that, though. I think I burst her bubble.

"We've talked about that," she finally says.

"You mean you actually listened to me?"

"Of course."

"Then, you know to stay out of the market."

"Mason, my other two clients – I don't have a third yet, was still holding out for you," she sings. "Anyway, they think, well, they say something like, 'Buy every pullback, Chrissy, because this market's going to five thousand.' Whatever a pullback is. Sounds like a football player."

"Both of them say that?"

"Well, one says forty eight hundred. I guess that's four thousand eight hundred, and they're smart men, business leaders in the western PA, but what's important was their eyes when they said it."

"Greedy eyes, I bet."

"Crazy eyes," she says.

"Cocky eyes."

Christine giggles. "Well, not the kind I'm used to dealing with, but…you understand."

I laugh hard. Then, it hits me. She's started me thinking, and it's usually dangerous when that happens. But, now, I think it's okay to put my mind to work. I have been slowly convincing myself that the time is right, as right as it was in August. Maybe even more so. I've said it to others: Wylie, Fenz, Michael, Edie, and now I'm compelled by Christine and her 'street smarts.' Her instincts have always impressed me. She senses what most others have no chance of seeing. Plus, she has those execs to play off of.

Huh…

Shorting is a possibility, but there is another way to make money in a down market more approachable for small-time investors like she probably is. Go for it, Mason. "Okay. Now, I have an idea."

"You do?"

"Yes."

"You mean you can make money in a falling market?" she asks excitedly.

"Yes."

"How?"

"It's complicated."

"I want to learn more about this."

"Before that, I must ask you: how much can you stand to lose?"

"Mason, I want to win!" she exclaims.

"Christine, what I'm thinking about, it's the all-or-nothing round, meaning you could lose it all at the drop of a hat."

"Well…"

"Think of it as the amount of money you can use to light cigars with."

"Uhhh…twenty thousand dollars," she says quickly and with surprising confidence.

Twenty thousand dollars? She's crazy! Christine is a girl who has always had surprises, but this one beats them all. I'll roll with it. "Okay. Now, you can part with twenty thousand dollars like it blew off a cliff into the ocean below?"

"Yes."

"Are you sure?"

"Mason, I've never sold your gifts," she says, "but I sold the others through the years."

Ah, ha! "And, that's where—"

"But, I've never sold yours."

"That's okay if you did."

"I mean it. Never."

"And, that's where the twenty big ones came from."

"Yes. I never sold yours, though."

"It's okay. Now, give me a chance to sleep on it and we'll meet—"

"How about in the morning after I drop Eva off at school?" she asks.

She is excited about this. "Where do you want to meet?"

"The Café, near your office. Give me enough time to get up there from here in Pittsburgh. Ten o'clock, let's say?"

"Ten o'clock," I say.

"Gotta run. Mom's calling me. Bye."

And, my life finally becomes more thrilling.

1:00 AM
Tuesday October 13, 1987
Writing in the journal, nursing my fourth Arn.
Dow Jones Industrial Average: 2,471 – a little over 10 percent off the all-time high…beautiful, just beautiful.

I'm writing this to get it straight in my head because it is rather complex. My new investment strategy will be recorded here in the event I don't survive. Otherwise, no one would believe someone actually did what I'm about to do.

Here's the plan. Christine has twenty thousand she can walk away from. Obviously, no one wants to lose money, but I know Christine and I know she knows the potential and the pitfalls of risk. We've talked about that. Look, she's in a risky business herself. Just like Tom Cruise and the movie. Anyway, her bundle came from the gifts of her triumvirate. The triumvirate? Why, of course she sold mine. I'm not a fool. But, it doesn't matter. It is by the sale of those gifts that she can lose it all and that it won't hurt her and Eva. Therefore, I harbor no guilt for what is about to happen, even if my hooker friend and I are ready to…speculate.

I realize I have in my standard investment diatribe often talked junk about speculators. They deserve it. I do look upon them as buffoons and their actions as contrary indicators. Eat words if I have to, but I think it's different for me because I'm speculating against the rage, as in "stocks are *all the rage!*" That means, in my humble opinion, there's a better chance of making speculative money betting on the downside than there is taking your chances with everyone else on higher stock prices. Why? Sentiment remains too optimistic, especially when you consider the bombs that went off in the market in the past two weeks. Then there are the indicators confirming the intuition, namely the seniors and their justified fears of a crash. There is more confirmation from the women, the gender that thinks inferentially and is not impressed at all with this market. The older folks have seen it all and the ladies have heard it all. And, if you listen closely, you will find that the men who rule the business world and profit from the stock market are making decisions based on testosterone. They will be trumped. And dumped, to put it mildly.

You want more? As well, money is tight. Interest rates continue to rise. That'll choke off troubled stocks like these, especially at a time during which the men are still wild-eyed and the insanity of the programs and of using futures for portfolio insurance over the past couple of weeks have been taking this fighter jet of a market on an occasional dive. If I continue to write like this, I'm going to talk myself into going big. Big, as in standing at the roulette wheel and placing the entire stack of chips on black odd, black being my favorite color of Edie's garments and odd being…well, me.

Be careful, Mason. You're motivated by testosterone, too.

That's correct.

So, both the greedy bastard in me and the arrogant academic in me will reach into my bag, pull out my driver, tee up the Titlest, and grip it and rip it. I know what I want to do (make a lot of money), why it will work (because the instrument flying indicators say it will), who I want to do it with (Christine), and how it will happen. How will it happen? Well, let me tell you.

Christine and I are going to play options. Now, many a Monday night over the past five years she gave me plenty of options, but we're not talking about those. We're talking about contracts, the subject of which I have touched on during the Margot fiasco others called a date; contracts that give the holder of that contract the right, or the option, to buy or sell a stock of a company at a stated price. We're talking about the same contracts that expire on a stated date, and the same contracts that have market value because they trade in their own special market. That's what we're talking about. We're also talking about risk. We're talking about hot and heavy, balls to the wall, go hard or go home. That's the options market. It should be driven only by those who can handle them. Bonds are a Buick LeSabre. Stocks are a Porche 928. Selling stocks short is a Lamborghini. And the options market is a rocket sled on the Bonneville salt-flats, providing an exhilarating ride, but if you crack up, you get atomized. On the aptly-named expiration date.

There are two types of options: calls, and those about which I have discussed, puts. Calls allow you to 'call' for a stock, meaning you buy it. Puts allow you to 'put' a stock, meaning you sell it. You buy calls if you think the stock's market value will rise. You buy puts if you think the market value of the stock will drop. Those are the basics.

Let's use IBM put options, or simply called 'IBM puts,' to discuss the boring mechanics. You can skip the next paragraph if you wish.

However, if your curiosity has kept you with me, I will tell you that some IBM puts expire in December, for example, at 4:30 PM on the third Friday of the month. So, we can buy a contract to sell one hundred shares of IBM at a stated price. Trouble is, the contract disappears in several weeks. Call that, if you will, a little dicey. If you the reader can stand to continue, here are more details, like nomenclature. Option contracts are named by a) the underlying stock (IBM), b) the expiration month (December), c) the strike price, or the price at which you can sell the underlying stock (150) and d) the type of contract (put). One IBM December 150 put gives you the right to sell one hundred shares of IBM at 150 by 4:30 PM on the third Friday of December, in this case, December 18, 1987.

Now, everyone read. We're getting to the important stuff. Wake up and pay attention.

Options contracts have their own markets and market values. Today, IBM December 150 puts closed on the Chicago Board of Options Exchange (CBOE) at 5, or five hundred dollars per contract. IBM the stock closed on the New York Stock Exchange (NYSE) at 155, or fifteen thousand five hundred per one hundred shares. That means that for a mere five hundred you can control over thirty times that much stock. Do you feel the power of leverage?

Now, feel the weight. Consider this: the five hundred you pay is backed by nothing. It is a time premium, or what you pay for the right to buy it, wait it out and see what happens. It is merely a bet that by December 18, the price of IBM will fall below 150, giving your contract real value. In fact, IBM better fall below 145 by December 18 for you to make any money since you spent five hundred dollars of time premium for that IBM December 150 put. Furthermore, any price higher than 145 on December 18 means that you will lose money. Worse still, any price above 150 on December 18 means that you will lose all your money. There's your risk. Considering the time premium of the option being vapor, that risk is very real, and indeed absolute.

Very few options players (read: riverboat gamblers) exercise their rights the option contracts afford them, much less hold them on the expiration date. They trade in and out of the options upon moves of the market price of the underlying stock. Let's go back to the IBM December 150 put selling for 5. IBM the stock is at 155. If during next week or so the stock falls to 140, which could happen in this bursting balloon of a market, the put is worth in real terms 10 (150 minus 140) plus some time value, let's say 3. The put's market value is therefore 13. You paid five hundred dollars plus commission for the put, and you can now sell it for thirteen hundred dollars less commission. The stock drops a little over ten percent and the option gains one hundred sixty percent. That's the leverage, and that's the appeal. And, the broker's appeal is that he probably scored a little over one hundred dollars gross through your transactions. Wylie will love Christine and me. Especially Christine.

Forget IBM at 140. As I said, if IBM doesn't see 145 before December 18, we lose. If IBM stays above 150, we lose everything.

My strategy is to buy puts on the twenty-one Dow Jones Industrials Average stocks I shorted in August, establishing my private passively managed Collapsing Dow index fund. That's cumbersome to control, but it will provide a level of diversification and therefore take a bite of risk out of the speculation.

Yeah, right.

I intend to invest Christine's twenty thousand, a huge-ass position in options for any individual investor. But, wait…it gets better. My investment will be thirty times that, amounting to six hundred thousand dollars, or Joan's repayment to me less what I gave to Michael, an unheard of play for any entity. To put six hundred thousand dollars in any speculative investment that could get sucked into a black hole any day now…that's crazy. But, that's me. My rationale is a sound one: I was living well with only one hundred fifty thousand before Joan graced me with her presence. If I lose, nothing ventured and so on. If I win, maybe I could buy my own real condo in Kaanapali and become Maui's own Jimmy Buffett. There's booze in the blender.

There's booze in my arteries headed for my brain if I'm serious about dropping six hundred K in an investment that will cease to exist by Christmas. However, as they say at Longhi's restaurant near my new home on Maui…

Thirty-Three

10:00 AM
Tuesday October 13, 1987
At The Café, trying out my new cellular bag phone
Dow Jones Industrial Average: 2,491 – 9.5 percent off all-time high

"Ally Fenz, please," I say into the receiver of my new cellular bag phone. Men and their toys. The line is silent. I think of Ally at my condo the night after I was fired, and I think of Christine planting the puts idea in my dormant brain, then I think of Edie and my general lack of lucidity. Women really like to mess with my head.

"This is Ally," Fenz' voice says into my ear.

"Fenz," The noise on the line is scratchy.

"There's a bad connection. Are you home? Where are you?"

"The Café."

"There's no phone at The Café," she says in an accusatory fashion.

"I'm trying out my new bag phone, or whatever the hell you call it. It's cellular."

"Why do you need a cellular telephone? You don't even have a job."

I laugh at my plight. "Cut it out and tell me where the Dow is right now."

"Uh…let's see…2,491, up twenty." Fenz sounds exasperated. This market drop surely has John on the warpath.

"How's the action?"

"Lots of volume. I can barely hear you."

"I'll speak slowly. Now, could you please check Wylie's schedule?"

"Why don't you call him yourself?" Oooo…that was ugly.

"Because he reacts better to you than to me," I reply calmly.

"Okay! Let me check." I should let her get on with her day before she runs over here to kick my ass. "His only opening today is 10:30 this morning. Tomorrow is better."

"This can't wait until tomorrow. Will you please ask him to meet me here? At 10:30?"

"At The Café? Why don't you just come o—oh, yeah."

"Oh, yeah?"

There is a pause. "Sorry I'm such a bitch, honey. I really miss the Love Boat. I'll make sure Wylie's there. Promise."

162

"Great. It's important. Very."

"Can you tell me?" More static.

"If you're here, too."

"Give me a clue."

"I'm going to invest big."

"I thought you…ah, you're going to short again."

"Not exactly. See ya at 10:30. Gotta go. This bag is draining power." I hang up, which involves pressing a button and stowing the receiver in the pouch, but not before getting it and my arm tangled in the strap. These things have to get smaller.

10:05 AM

Tuesday October 13, 1987

At The Café, watching Christine walk in. No one is here to witness this. Their loss. Dow Jones Industrial Average: All we are is dust in the wind.

Talking about testing my mettle. I'm thinking…can I still love Edie and get laid by Christine? No one would know. Think about it though…I have that bargain with God. And, my only prayer with the puts is to keep God on my side. On the other hand, Edie really doesn't care. Greg probably did the deed last night, anyway. So, why not?

I'm back to that bargain with God. With the puts, I'm going to need God. Don't want to anger God. In this case, that's a bad career move.

"Hi," Christine says, sitting her bottom in the electric blue padded chair beside me. By the way, that is some bottom she has artfully inserted into her model-tight denims.

"Hi. Glad you could make it." I absolutely would not miss the five hundred, and in my state of libido, it would only take a minute. How efficient.

"I'm so excited!" she whispers like a high school girl.

"Don't get ahead of the game." Her white long sleeve sweater has been sprayed on. I glance down to see a black pump dangling from the foot at the end of the crossed leg.

"I can't help it!" she says.

I reflexively reach to touch her hand. "Let me explain this to you."

"Okay."

"Now, there are stocks, which is the traditional way to invest. And, there are derivatives of stocks, or non-traditional ways like the way we're going to do it."

"Okay. Non-traditional. We're going to do it non-traditional," she says, calmer. I had forgotten how beautiful her face is.

"So…there are stocks, and there are contracts to buy or—"

"Options, like puts and calls."

"Yeah," I say, a lot more surprised than I sound.

"One of my fellas explained it to me."

"He does it?"

"Yes."

This I want to hear. "How does he do?"

"He's doing calls, but he doesn't say much else."

"Then, he must be losing his ass."

"I don't know," she says with a blank look.

"Yes, you do. Why didn't you tell me this before?"

"Mason, I don't talk details about the fellas with the other fellas. That's bad business."

Chastised by a hooker. "I can see that."

"So," Christine says, now steering the conversation, "we're going to buy…"

"Puts."

"You still think the market's going to fall?"

"Oh, yes."

She changes legs and dangles the other pump. Highly effective marketing. "I agree," she says.

Damnit! This deal could be derailed before it starts down the tracks. "Oh, fuck!" I exclaim before I know it.

"What?"

"I just remembered…you've got to sign a suitability agreement. Damn it to hell, I wish I would have thought of that earlier!"

"What's that?" Christine sits up sharply.

"It's an agreement by which you state that you want to do this, you know, buy options," I explain, "and that you think you're suitable, and that you won't sue Fuller Busher if it goes sour."

"Let's sign it," she says as she pounds a fist on the aluminum table top.

"You have to state income, Christine, and prove it with your W-2 and 1099s." This sucks. I really wanted to do this with her.

"I see what you're driving at, but I have a job. A good job," she says with pride. "A legit job. Well, kind of legit."

"What?"

"One of my fellas has me on his payroll. I'm an administrative assistant." Christine lays her million dollar smile on me.

"He gets by with that? I mean, you are?"

"Executive VP. Big company. Huge company."

"Oh, wow." I'm thinking US Steel or PPG. "Not—"

"I'm not saying. Remember…the fellas?"

"Yeah, the fellas…okay, I have to ask, for the sake of the suitability agreement—"

"Fifty thousand a year," she says.

"Jeez Louise! That's one hell of an administrative assistant."

"I'm good at what I do."

"I know."

"The other job with the other one?" she adds.

"Other one? Wow! This is some good stuff!"

"He could only swing thirty."

Ho! Good for her! "Christine, darling, you were really slumming it with me."

"Because," she says, reaching for my cheeks. "you are soooo very cute."

"It's a gift," I say with a hot face.

"So, let's get that agreement out."

Oh, no! "Hell! Not so fast. I have to get a grip." Fortunately, there's no one else here to witness my outbursts.

"What's wrong this time?"

"Wylie has a lot of high profile clients at big, huge Pittsburgh companies. I don't trust him to remain confidential with you."

"I thought you were…"

"I'm taking some time off. Stress."

Christine touches my cheeks again. "I'm sorry this job is stressing you out so much. Should we forget this?"

"No! This is fun!"

"Are you sure?"

"Yes! It's fun! I have to do it." I smile my best six hundred thousand dollar smile. "Okay now, to avoid all this signing sap, here's what we're going to do."

"Okay."

"I'll do the investing. You go light twenty thousand with me—"

"Oh, no, no, no," she says with her arms crossed. "Christine always pays her way."

"And, Christine will most certainly do that if we lose. But, if we win, I'll pay you four percent of my winnings, which is twenty into my six hundred plus a little extra because you think I'm cute."

There is a pause. "And, I do," she says with a grin.

"Thank you."

"You've got yourself a deal." Christine extends her hand. We clasp, just like we did after the interview five years ago.

Silence grows as we savor the moment. It is almost as good as the other moments we have shared. "About this new girl," Christine says out of the blue. "Just go for it, Mason. You are a catch."

My throat knots up. I ignore her. "Wylie will be here in a few. You want to stay and listen?"

"Maybe I shouldn't."

"Maybe you're right. Don't worry, though. I'll take care of you."

"You always have." On that, she rises, leans over to kiss me, turns, and walks. Forget Donald Trump. Christine is an expert in the art of the deal.

10:40 AM
Tuesday October 13, 1987
Still at The Café
Dow Jones Industrial Average: the trough from which we pigs feast.

As Wylie and Fenz stroll through the door, I'm pondering: they're not going to like this. They both think I'm a Tazmanian devil anyway, so what's it going to be like after they hear I'm going to lay more than a half-million on the table for one round of blackjack?

It's my money. Why do I feel like I have to talk these two into it, anyway? Maybe it's because I always seek approval, however inconsistent it is with my rebel attitudes. My father and my mother were dead by the time I was eighteen. I was on my own. Then came Joan. That was awfully Oedipal of her.

Wylie's tall in a charcoal gray suit with the red and navy rep tie. Fenz is attractive in a dark violet suit and a white blouse. The difference is interesting. I've read that short girls like height in their men.

"What's up?" Wylie asks.

"Step into my office," I reply, leading them to the metal tube table. They take a seat.

"What kind of craziness are you into now, Mason?" Wylie asks.

"Might as well say it. I'm going big on puts."

"What's big, Self-Destructo Man?" Wylie asks without missing a beat.

"Six hundred thousand dollars," I say.

Fenz and Wylie are both stunned silent.

"I know, I know," I say, anticipating resistance. "But, I can afford it. I ran into some money."

"The settlement of an estate," Fenz says. "He's a wealthy man. A wealthy, fuckin' stupid man."

"You know about this?" Wylie asks.

"Not the puts part," Fenz says.

"Why, Mason?" Wylie asks with a hint of frustration. "You have a death wish?"

"I'm committed, guys. I'm committed because I'm playing the correct side of the market. That's what my street-savvy advisor is saying now."

"Zweig?" Wylie spits.

"Marty, and…I'll call her Xaviera Hollander."

"And, what's this you're doing now?" Fenz says. "Playing?"

"Guys, especially Wylie, dig this. Twenty one Dow Jones companies. Six hundred thousand dollars. Approximately thirty thousand per. I estimate twenty thousand of commissions at least before it is all over. At least. And I'm not even going to ask for a discount. We're pals, Wylie."

"I can't take this back to the office," Wylie says. "John will shit a cow."

"You and John draw up the document that absolves Fuller Busher of all responsibility and I'll sign it. Just get it done today or I'll go to Merrill Lynch. I've already asked. They'll do it."

"Done," Wylie says immediately. I always knew he was quick to roll over.

"Wylie!" Fenz exclaims.

"I'll meet you here for lunch with the papers," Wylie says, ignoring her.

"I am not a part of this!" Fenz shouts.

"It's okay, Ally," Wylie says. "I'll watch it."

"Not like I will," I say.

"I'd better run for those papers. See ya!" Wylie says as he scoots off through the door.

"You idiot!" Fenz yells. "Whatever possessed you to…just think of the good you could do with that money!"

"I'm going big," I say, Mr. Haughty. "then I'm going to Maui. Or…is it Paris? Oh, I can't decide."

Ally is completely frustrated with me. I don't give a damn. "Aaghh! You're crazy. No, you've always been crazy. But, this time, you have completely lost your mind!"

"Once a day, Fenz," I say as I sip from my tiny European coffee cup.

"Once a day?"

"Once a day you tell me I'm crazy. Why should I start listening now?"

Fenz grabs her hair. "Part of me wants to see you lose it all. Damn it! The poor, the needy. Goddamnit, Mason! Me!"

"I know. But, it's my money."

"Not for long." She spins and she's out of here. What a parting shot.

Thirty-Four

9:40 PM
Tuesday October 13, 1987
In my manly brown leather recliner, watching ABC network television, fourth Arn in hand
Dow Jones Industrial Average: 2,508 – 8.8 percent off all-time high

I've come to the point in my celibacy at which I am blindly obsessed with sex. I mean, here I am doing something as simple as spacing out with the self-absorbed baby boomers on *thirtysomething* and wood is drawn every time Hope and Ellyn are on the screen together. Besides, this good-looking carpenter is flirting with them and has them drooling. That could be me. I could be a good-looking carpenter, too, if I knew anything about carpentry and was good-looking.

There is one advantage to my more recent rampant preoccupation: my will against nicotine has been tempered. I really haven't experienced the cravings I should, probably because at this stage my body can accept only one craving at a time. And, this all says a lot about my fortitude in general. If I can resist Christine this morning and not…you know…in the privacy of my own home this afternoon, then a cigarette doesn't have a chance.

There's the phone. As I pick it up, I think…good thing. Gary and Melissa are together on the tube, sailing through the electrical-charge of mutual fantasy. I can't take that right now.

"Hello," I say.

"Mason," the female voice in the telephone sings.

"Hi, Christine." I can't take that right now, either.

"How did it go today?"

"It went well."

"Sorry I had to run, but it was for the best."

"I understand."

A pause. "Are we in?" she asks.

"You bet. You are now an official speculator."

"It feels good. Really good."

"Rule number one," I say. "When speculating, the worst thing you can do is get excited."

"I'll remember that."

"Be sure you remember that."

Back to the television. Michael is having this weird dream about being put on trial by his friends for crimes against the social justice values he sold out to his advertising firm. I never had that problem. Yeah. Right.

"How did we close?" she asks.

I laugh. "Close? Close? Where did you pick up language like that, young lady?"

"My fella from US—whoops! My fella I'm an administrative assistant for plays options and he takes a call from his broker after four o'clock where he asks just that question."

"That makes sense." US Steel. I knew it!

"So, how did we close?"

"I usually don't count my money when I'm sitting at the table, but today the market's up, so therefore we're down."

"When are we going to be up?"

"Christine!"

"I would say I want to win, but you said to not get excited."

"That is correct." Maybe this partnership deal is a mistake.

A pause…"Talk to your lover today?" she asks.

"For a minute. She was busy."

"Where does she work?"

"Public library."

"Ooo…the quiet ones are always the best."

"We've only talked, but I can tell from our conversations that she is not a quiet one."

"Yeah, the spirited ones are even better."

"One can only hope."

"Well…gotta run," Christine says. "Eva needs me to help her study."

"That's sweet."

"Bye…for now."

"For now," I answer.

I press the button to hang up the portable, then glance at the TV. If you were to put Ellyn's legs and her curly black hair on Hope's bod and face, I would need a long cold hands-free shower.

The phone rings again.

"Hello."

"I would do Michael Steadman on your floor right now!"

"Good evening, Fenz," I say.

"Oh, my. Oh, my," she moans.

"Sweetums, I'm trying to save myself for Edie, and you're not helping."

We pause. "I need my purser."

"I am sorry."

"I am, too."

"When's your birthday?" I ask. "October 29, is it?"

"Oh, thank you!" she squeals. "You always remember!"

"You're my best friend, Ally, so, happy birthday. I'll give you a three-day cruise, on the purser's boat."

"Noooo…"

"Yes."

"Okay!"

"Now, stop worrying, do what you gotta do, and don't describe it to me. It's getting tough for me out there, too."

"Mason?" Fenz says meekly.

"Yes?"

"I'm sorry I yelled at you today. That was selfish of me."

"It's okay."

"Just think…you might win."

"Odds will eventually be in my favor, but I have so much time premium bought into these things, it has to happen quickly."

"But, if you lose?"

"Book the cruise now, Fenz. I can't have both of us running around like…this."

"Yea!"

"Now, go! I have to do some sit-ups or something."

"Poor baby!"

"It's okay."

"Love ya, Mason."

"Love ya, Fenz."

I push the button and lay the phone down on the sofa. On *thirtysomething*, they're all sitting around at the housewarming party singing…wouldn't you know it…Joni Mitchell. You know, there were plenty of Republicans and other redneck warmongers in the sixties. Or, even worse, the silent majority. Why is it every baby-boomer is now depicted as an old protester? I'll tell you why. The media and entertainment are bastions—damnit, why is the phone is ringing off the hook tonight?

"Hello," I say sternly.

"Mason," the female voice whispers.

"Who—"

"Come over."

"Who the hell—"

"Come over now."

"Well—"

"It's Geri!" she says.

"Geri!"

"Please!"

"Be right over, Geri."

10:15 PM
Tuesday October 13, 1987
At Wylie's and Geri's front door
Dow Jones Industrial Average: I should be frightened.

The McInally home is a shadow against the waxing half moon in the western sky. Blackened trees lurk ominously in the still, cool air. Geri never calls me and would never invite me over to her home while she's alone, even if she did call me. I don't like how this feels.

She must have heard me arrive near the door because the front light just flicked on. The door swings open slowly. There is no Geri.

"Geri—"

"Get in," she whispers.

"What?"

I finally get a good look at her. She's still in her gray tweed suit and white blouse with too much boob, but something is amiss. In the yellowish light of her tastefully appointed home, I can see she looks awful with puffy eyes jutting from her ashen face.

"He's in the powder room," she says.

"What's up?"

"He has a gun."

BAMM!

"Oh, shit!"

"Wylie!" Geri screams.

A hole the size of a basketball has exploded near the ceiling from the adjacent wall. The white mist of a plaster cloud hovers over us. I find Geri on the floor, under me. I jump up and run to the door of the powder room. Geri remains. I absolutely do not want to look in this room, but as the man I feel it is my duty.

Preparing to flinch or throw up, I slowly peer around the corner. There's Wylie, sitting on the floor, huddled with the john. There is no bloody mess. He's technically alive, albeit catatonic, a motionless figure in his navy suit, white shirt, and red tie. The pistol dangles between his knees. A shard of wallboard falls from the hole in the wall above the mirror.

'Are you insane?' is what I want to shout, but that's obvious. I decide to get the gun away from him. Calmly.

Kneeling, I say, "Give me the gun, Wylie."

No reaction at all.

"Nice and easy, man."

He drops one hand from the trigger, continuing to hold the pistol with the other.

"C'mon," I say, encouragingly. "The gun, my man."

Wylie slowly, without looking at me, hands the dangling gun to me. I set it beside the baseboard to my right.

"That's a good man." My stomach is queasy. My heart is racing.

"Now that that's over," Geri says from behind me.

"Get her away," Wylie says.

"You stupid motherfucker!" Geri says.

"I don't want to see her!" Wylie shouts in return.

"You foolish motherfucker." Geri says in a more civil tone.

"Stop your incessant bitching." Wylie yells.

"Both of you, what the hell is going on?" I shout.

"You fucking bastard," Geri says.

Wylie drops his face into his hands. "Leave...me...alone!"

"Why?" Geri says, "So you can kill yourself?"

"Might as well. They're going to kill me anyway."

"Whoa!" I say. "Right there! Who are 'they,' Wylie?"

There is a long pause. "The Mob," he says.

"Why would they do that?" I ask.

"Gambling. My husband has run up a huge gambling debt." Geri turns and pounds her fist onto the hallway wall.

"Well, just pay it!" I say. "You can pay it! You guys make a half-million dollars a year! Pay it and be done."

"It's not that simple," Wylie says sullenly.

"Yes, it is," I say. "They just want their money."

"My fucking husband has fucked up everything, every fucking thing we have fucking worked for! The fucker!" She's out of control.

"Pay…them," I implore.

"We can't," Geri says.

"Why?" I ask.

"We don't have enough cash," she says.

"How—"

"We don't have fifty thousand dollars in cash. We don't have five thousand in cash."

Goddamn! Fifty…thousand…dollars! Holy…"Can't you guys just liquidate a mutual fund or something?" I say, trying to keep my head while those about me…situations like these are definitely what Kipling was talking about.

"I have until tomorrow," Wylie says.

"They're going to kill you, Wylie. Then they're going to kill me, you stupid motherfucker." Geri is *completely* out of control.

"I…don't…want…to…hear her shit any more!" Wylie shouts as he dives his face into his hands. "Get her away!"

"Oh, you'll hear my shit!" Geri shouts as she stomps off.

"Take it easy," I say in a measured tone. Wylie sits, one hand around the toilet and the other over his face.

There's a break in the action. I'm thinking: the perfect couple. Perfect lives. A perfect home I stand in, decorated immaculately by the woman from Sewickley. The taste, the class…in an interesting way, it all really pisses me off. I'll tell you why. First, they don't have the cash, meaning it takes all they have, plus possibly more, to keep the nimiety afloat. Second, Barney Lunchbucket working on Neville Island, and other Barneys from other mills and plants, love to see the upper crust fall apart like this. This is the stuff from which the nighttime soaps are made. Barney and his wife Betty watch *Dallas* to see J. R. shot, Cliff Barnes lose, and Swellin' Sue Ellen get wasted. Never mind that Barney's and Betty's families have their share of drunken revengeful chumps. It's just so cool to watch the rich fail at life. Now, Wylie in his idiocy – well, it's really an illness when you ring up five figures – anyway, in his illness has given Barney and Betty more ammunition. Thing is, it has been the healthy *and* wealthy Wylie who has interestingly guided Barney and Betty and their own incomes and their own net worth through the roller coaster markets. They will have a comfortable future, largely because of him. However, on the rumor of Wylie's problems, they will surely side with their beer buddies and tear him down even more, all the while avoiding introspection on why they don't have the guts and determination it takes to be wealthy, thereby giving their lifestyle validation. That's what really angers me about this entire deal, that and the fact that Geri has taken this time to pack a suitcase and is now walking toward us with purpose.

"I'm going to Mama's," Geri says. She's carrying that suitcase and wearing the same clothes. "You work this out, you dumbass."

"Go, you bitch!" Wylie says.

And, she does.

He moves to stand up from the powder room floor. I hold him back, figuring we've had enough excitement for one night. "Let her go," I say. "She'll be back."

"You don't know what a fucking bitch she is."

"Yeah, any woman who would set me up with Margot Montgomery..." I say, deciding it was the time to interject some humor. Then I decide it's time for the obvious question. "How?"

"Saturday, I was five short—"

"Thousand?"

"Thousand. I was determined to get it back. I started doubling down. Pitt covered against Notre Dame. I took the Irish—"

"Wylie, never bet a Pitt game. You can't pull yourself from the emotion."

"Yeah. Sunday, the Eagles killed me."

"Wait," I say.

"What?"

"You bet replacement ball?"

"Uh...yeah."

I'm speechless, except for the reflex response of, "You know that was pretty foolish."

"Then, Monday night," he says, ignoring me. "It was almost a push, but some replacement dickhead ran out of bounds on the last play...I've got the money, just not tomorrow."

There is a pause in the conversation. Wylie is a blank. "I haven't slept much since Saturday," he says.

Damnit. "You can't be rational with sleep deprivation. Let's get some rest."

"How can I rest? Mason, they know where I live. They know where you live." The muscles in his face collapse.

"I know."

"What am I going to do? I don't take pain very well."

"We'll think of something."

"I don't want to die." He begins to cry. Oh, hell. It looks like I've just cleared my schedule.

"Wylie, you're not safe out there."

"No shit," he says between sobs.

"You're not going to die. They want your money, not your head. The safe I'm talking about is...I'm talking about...not safe from you."

"Me?"

"Just minutes ago, you blew a hole in your wall."

"Yeah, but that was—"

"Was what?"

We pause again. "I'm okay, Brick. Trust me."

"Frankly, you're not. And, no, I don't trust you." I extend my hand to help him up. He grasps it and uses me as leverage to rise to his feet. "C'mon," I continue. "I'm going to take you someplace where you're safe."

"I told you—"

"No. Not Mars Heights." Here goes..."We're going to Drucker."

During the entire long pause, he looks at me incredulously. "No!" he finally yells. "I'm not crazy!"

"No, you're not." Yes, he is. "But, you're not safe, either."

"No way am I going to a fuckin' psych hospital!"

It's time for more true confessions. "Mac, would it make you feel better if I told you I was there once?"

"You?" His mouth is agape.

"It was just after the divorce and I had just moved here. It was all too much for me to handle, so I went in for a tune-up."

"Really?"

"Yeah. It's okay. I'm a rather well-adjusted guy, don't you think?"

"Sometimes," he says with a rather serious look.

I smile. "I was in a bind and couldn't find my way out." Nothing happens, but when you're mental, it takes a while to come to your senses. I think Wylie is seriously weighing his options. I also think he doesn't have any other, but he's going to have to arrive at that conclusion himself. "It was one of the best decisions I've ever made, if not the best," I conclude.

"Won't they drug me up?"

"Not necessarily. No. They're going to give you something to sleep, though. You need some shut-eye."

"They're going to lock me up, aren't they?"

"No one can get in. That's the important part right now. And., they'll let you out when they think you're safe."

"Really?"

"Yep," I say. "Actually, I left on my own, making the decision on my own." It was unwise to say that, but a man like Wylie needs to have a way out.

"You left? Just like that?"

"Well, my doctor didn't protest in a big way, so I decided to go. But, I was like you. I hadn't slept for days."

"You've never told me this."

"Well, no, I haven't."

"And, you walked?"

"Well, yeah. They call it against medical advice, or AMA. That means the insurance company won't pay for the visit, but you yourself have enough money to cover it if you choose to leave." Again, I may not be firing on all cylinders by saying this, but at this point, I just have to get him in. One needs strange psychology when confronting the mentally ill. Having been confronted on a few occasions, I certainly know.

"Yeah. That'll give me a chance to move some assets arou—" He stops and teeters a bit. "What the hell am I going to do about the bookies? Oh, shit!"

"I'll take care of it."

"No!" he protests vehemently. "I can't allow that!"

"Do you have a better idea?" I ask.

"Where will you get the money?"

"I have enough at AshNat."

There is a long pause. Wylie looks away into his living room.

"I'll pay you back," he says.

"Damned straight you will."

"You are my only true friend." He reaches out to embrace me and begins to cry again. God help him. And, while you're at it...

Thirty-Five

9:00 AM
Wednesday October 14, 1987
At the condo, one foot practically out the door
Dow Jones Industrial Average: 2,508 – 8.8 percent off all-time high

The most significant thing Wylie said last night was, 'I never could do it on the field, so I tried to do it with my wallet.' I knew this was significant because, as we traveled to Drucker and waited to check in, he said it a dozen times. I also knew it was significant because I recognized the all-too-familiar message. I knew his admission was a brave first step, having been there. He got right to the point.

Wylie is a frustrated jock. A frustrated jock is something most of us men become when our athletic talents are surpassed by those of others and it's time to hang 'em up. My day came the afternoon of the Pitt game. Wylie's occurred sometime in high school. The state of being a frustrated jock can be viewed as a rite of passage. It also makes you a pain in the ass. Frustrated jocks look back to the days, all too often with a wistful lament that can manifest in something as harmless as glory fantasies or as mind-bending as the expensive thrills of gambling. For me, it was the movie, and it continues with the vain attempt at the novel. And, the state of being a frustrated jock probably has something to do with becoming the Han Solo of options.

The fact that I threw most of my net worth into the turbulent air of puts on the day Wylie had his meltdown is not lost on me. It sounds like I'm laying the wager, too, but it's not the same. Well...yes, it is. Bookmaking and the options market are merely games with no substance, meaning nothing actually grows from either except the wealth of those who run the action. Whether it's a bookie named Hit Man or a stockbroker named Fuller Busher, the house gets rich. Betting against the house...that means Wylie and I have overwhelming odds to beat. There is one difference, however. Wylie's game lasts three hours and he has absolutely no control over the outcome. If I play it right, I do. So, I'll give myself a week, then I split. Now, that's control.

Sort of.

I called Hit Man last night after leaving Wylie. When I offered to pay in my friend's stead, The Hitter wasn't exactly happy, but the prospect of getting fifty thousand merely by showing up eventually appealed to his business instincts. He agreed to have one of his 'assistants' (read: goon) meet me at the downtown levee at ten this morning. I am to bring five hundred unmarked one hundred dollar bills in a supermarket bag. I asked for a receipt. He said the orthopedic bill Wylie will not receive will be my receipt. Ooo-kay.

As I walk through my kitchen to my garage, inserting my arms in my gray herringbone blazer along the way, the doorbell rings. "Goddamnit," I spit as I reverse and move to the front door. For an instant I think it is unwise to twist the knob without asking who is on the other side. I do it anyway. The door opens to reveal...

"Christine?"

"Hi."

It's a chilly morning, so she's dressed in a pink cowl-neck angora sweater with those model-ass jeans...and pumps. Her hair is up. Her brown eyes are sparkling like never before. Whoa.

"Come in," I say. "Is...is everything okay?" The signals from my brain have quickly made the shift from Wylie's problems to sex. Back to sex. Damn this celibacy.

"Oh, yes." She steps through the door. "I just thought us option players could hang out together and watch the market," she says. "CNN does the market all day."

Christine in my condo through mid-afternoon...yet another test from Above. "That sounds great, but I gotta tell you...I...uh... have some business to take care of first."

"Don't let me stop you. I'll just be here when you get back." She sets her purse on my coffee table and looks to my television. "We open in a half-hour. How do you turn this thing on?"

"Here." I fetch the remote from the sofa and hand it to her. "Let me put some coffee on for you."

As I walk through the dining area back to the kitchen, the telephone rings. In two steps, I have it answered.

"Hello."

"Mason?"

"Yes?"

"It's Pamela. Pamela Kissinger."

"Hi, Pamela," I reply, as if Joan's sister calls me everyday.

"Do you have a minute?" she asks.

I recall Pamela from the months before the divorce, the last time I saw her. She was all lips, eyelashes, and dark curly hair... "Of course." Christine flicks on the TV and begins flipping the channels.

"Mason...this is difficult." Uh-oh. "I'm calling to tell you that...last night in her sleep...Joan passed away."

I go on automatic. "Oh, Pamela, I am so sorry."

"Thank you. She was not only my sister, but my best friend," she says with a choke.

"I know. I know." Cruise control.

"Joan was a good woman. I realize you two didn't get along—"

"We did the last time I saw her," I say before I know it.

"Yes, she told me about it."

"All about it?"

"All about it."

"Everything?"

"I assume," she says before a little chuckle.

Why does that not surprise me? "Kiss and tell. That's our Joan."

There is a pause. I hear a sniffle. "I thank you for what you did," she says. "You gave her good memories at a time when she needed them."

"Your sister was a beautiful woman, Pamela. In many ways."

"I don't know what I'm going to do without her." Her voice breaks again.

"I know."

"Mason," she says. Silence lingers. She draws a breath. "Mason, the funeral mass will be held here in Chicago on Friday. I'd like you to attend."

Ohhh...I don't think so. "Pamela...I'd like to be there, too, but you wouldn't believe the...I want to be out there with you, but I have a friend I have to take care of who has bookies after him because he has a huge gambling debt, which I have to pay while he's drugged up in a mental hospital. His wife has run out on him and I'm his only hope."

"Holy hell. I've had patients do that. He's in the best place for him."

"I hope."

"You sound like a good friend."

"Well...I'm sorry I can't be there. Maybe we can make it another time. I want to see you." Want to see you?

"I'll be in Pittsburgh the weekend after next. Can I call you?"

No. "Absolutely."

"That makes me feel better."

"You are in my thoughts and prayers, Pamela."

"Thank you. Good luck with your friend."

"Thanks."

"Bye."

I hang up, still on autopilot.

"Sorry I listened in on your conversation, but I really only heard the part about gambling," Christine says.

"Yeah, he's in deep shit," I say, jolted back into the reality of the day.

"Who's the bookie? I might know him."

"Some guy named Hit Man."

"I do know him."

"Yeah?"

"Yeah, back when I was starting to network. I haven't seen him since then, but he'll remember me."

"I can see that."

"How much?" she asks.

"Fifty grand."

Christine nods a few times, looking away. "I can help," she says confidently.

"How?"

She saunters to the front of my body. Hanging her arms around my neck and thrusting her pelvis into Me, she plants her lips on mine "How, he asks?" she says just after releasing the suction. "Well, just by being…me."

The hang, the kiss, the arousal. I feel as if Joan had done it. "You are definitely you, but this is a job for guys." I'm trying to buy some cool. It's not working. Lots of amps from a lot of sources are going through my circuits now.

"That is so chauvinistic." Joan kisses me again.

9:30 AM
Wednesday October 14, 1987
Walking through the doors into Ashton National Bank.
Dow Jones Industrial Average: Two touchdown favorites

AshNat indeed looks like a bank with its quiet gray marble cavern of a lobby and the pretty tellers all in a row. There are presently no customers here, only bankers and lawyers going to their offices upstairs. Several paces after we enter, Christine stops. So do I. All eyes are on us. I must be particularly handsome today.

"Is this where your friend's money is?" she asks.

"Yeah, but we're using my money."

"Why?"

"Your buddy Hit Man wants his fifty today. It'll take my buddy a week to raise that cash. I'll have it in ten minutes."

"That's good. Hit Man can get nasty."

"Just fuckin' great, Christine. Let's go."

"You go ahead," she says. "I'll be over here."

"After all, you are a walking distraction." I smile. By reflex, I touch her hand.

Beth is standing near the vault. My favorite blonde is wearing a black dress that, if you accessorize, would knock them out at a party. I walk to her.

"Beth," I say.

"Are you here to be my officer and a gentleman and carry me away from all this?" she asks.

"Are you still married?" I ask with a grin.

"Is that still a problem?"

"It depends, but here's why I'm here…I need fifty thousand from checking."

"No problem."

"Oh, yeah?"

"If it's from your account, no problem," she says.

"In cash?"

"If it's over ten thousand dollars, I'll have to report it to the IRS, but otherwise, it's no problem."

"That's cool."

"How do you want it?"

"Hundreds."

"Be right back," Beth says as she wiggles away.

The Internal Revenue Service. I had forgotten about them. I hope I don't have to swear an affidavit or anything. Hit Man wouldn't like that. I glance at Christine. She looks so good CPAs and attorneys are running into the elevator doors. How is Hit Man going to trust me—well, dumbass, that's why you're taking Christine. Now, I get it. Sometimes, Mason…and here's Beth, complete with money and documents. What a lady.

"I forgot to ask," she says just as she returns.

"Yeah?"

"Why do you want it?"

"I'm buying a car. Porche."

"I thought so. Then, sign here, and here, by the Xs." I do so without reading why. Beth takes the papers and deftly hands me the stacks of one hundred dollar bills. The bands around each stack indicate there are fifty in each of the ten.

"Here you go, sweet thing. Happy motoring."

"Thank you, Beth."

"Who's your friend?" she asks.

"Friend?"

"The woman you so conveniently left at the door. Your friend."

"Oh yeah…she's my cousin."

The nose goes up. "Sure. Good luck anyway."

"Bye, now," I say. I turn and walk. It's amazing how easy that was.

10:00 AM
Wednesday October 14, 1987
In the Olds with Christine at the downtown levee
Dow Jones Industrial Average: it's out of my hands

The Ohio is up, due to the nighttime drenching autumn rains the Three Rivers valleys have had over the past week. Leaden skies reflect a dull light from the greenish tan river. A passing tugboat and its barges have created wakes that lap the sides of the levee, with water splashing up on the concrete moorings, creating puddles on the deck. Looks like a scene from the standard mafia movie. I don't have a good feeling about this at all.

Christine and I sit and wait. We've been here several minutes and I for one am damned happy to be first. I'm still surprised Hit Man agreed to this meeting venue.

"He's got it staked out well, I bet," Christine says, breaking the silence.

"Don't say 'bet,'" I say.

"Yeah, you're right."

A pause. "Christine, I have a question."

"Okay."

"Why here? Aren't we all rather exposed? All of us?"

"It's simple. The Ashton police commissioner still owes him money. The cop took Denver and the points in last year's Super Bowl. Stupid to go against the Giants at the height of their game, but here we are. We're safe. Trust me."

I crane my head to her. "How do you know all this?"

"I keep up. And, here they are."

I turn back to look through the windshield to see a late-model eggshell Jeep Wagoneer ease up to within a couple dozen yards from us. The doors open. Two really big men emerge. One is blond and slicked-back. The other is dark-haired and shaggy. They both are wearing windbreakers, jeans, and new sneakers. Each takes several steps toward the Olds and stops. I look at Christine.

"Showtime," she says.

Grabbing the bag of cash, knot squarely in gut, I open my door and get out. Christine does the same. Call it a mission of mercy or whatever: I'm in way over my head.

"Let me see it," the blond Goon One says as he walks to me. I open the bag and hand it to him.

"You'd better not be short," Goon Two says.

"Count the stacks. Hundreds, just like Hit Man wanted," I say.

"Natalie?" says Goon Two.

"Hi, Hank," Christine says.

"Natalie?" I whisper in surprise.

"Lookin' fine, baby," he says.

"You, too."

"What are you doing with this pencilneck?" he asks. That would be me.

"He's a business partner," she says.

"Oh, yeah?" Hank says. "What kind of business?"

"Real estate."

There is a pause in the scintillating conversation. Goon One has apparently completed the inspection of the stacks. He just stands there looking like…a goon. "Nat, how about you and me get together again?" Hank asks.

"It's been a long time, Hank. But, I'm married now."

"Married?" I whisper. Life swirls around clueless me.

"Who's the lucky guy?" Hank asks.

"Ex-Steeler. Linebacker," she replies.

"When did he play?" Hank doubts she is telling the truth. Me? I just don't know.

"The year Mark Malone was drafted," she says.

"Okay," says Goon One. "It's all here."

"Yo, dork," Hank says to me. "Keys."

"Keys?"

"I didn't stutter."

I hand him my car keys, actually, all my keys. Hank walks to the driver's side, opens the door, and inserts the key in the ignition. He unlocks the column. Goon One jogs to the rear of the car and begins pushing. Hank pushes, too, steering it to the right. They both turn loose and jump back. My beloved industrial tan 1979 Oldsmobile Delta 88 drifts into the Ohio River. I'm silent and astonished as the front sinks like a rock and the rear bubbles down slowly, finally slipping under the water's surface.

Damn.

The goons hop into the Jeep and drive away.

10:25 AM

Wednesday October 14, 1987
Striding with alacrity down Hale Street, halfway to The Café
Dow Jones Industrial Average: hopefully awaiting the same fate as my Olds

A linebacker's wife named Natalie legs it quickly beside me as my automobile swims with the fishes.

"For God's sake, are you married?" I ask, finally saying something.

"No."

"Are you sure?"

"Of course, I'm sure," Christine says, walking with purpose in pumps.

"Good. I've spent the past several years trying to avoid screwing a married woman…well, one…and I'd hate to begin the rest of my life by pissing off an ex-NFL linebacker."

"Don't worry," she says.

I pause. "Okay, I won't worry…Natalie?"

"Only to Hank." As if that should be sufficient explanation.

"Natalie."

"Natalie Johnson. Or…Claudia Brown."

I've just about had enough. "Banana-nana fo-fanna, Christine…which name is yours?"

"Claudia. For real."

"Claudia. For real," I say, mocking her.

"Yes."

"Here's a test, what's on your driver's permit?"

"Claudia Brown."

"What does the exec at US Steel call you?"

"Claudia Brown."

"How about your tax return?"

"Claudia Brown."

"What's your middle name?"

"Claudia. My first name is Elizabeth."

"Jesus Christ," I say, slightly exasperated.

Christine/Claudia places her arm in mine. "I'm sorry, Mason. It's time you know the truth. I didn't mean any harm. It's just that in my line of work, you can't be too careful."

"So, now, after five years, you trust me."

"It's not trust, baby. It's just being careful."

Her touch impels me to acquiesce. Women… "Well…I understand. I think." I pause, and pause again. No need to get upset. Christine/Claudia and I go way back. "So, from now on," I say, "I call you…"

"Elizabeth Claudia Brown. Claudia for short."

"Not Christine."

"The Christine days are over."

That was a knife to the back. "Apparently, they never were."

"It's just a name." Claudia Brown wraps her arms around my waist. "I still think you're a tree-top lover."

I throw my hands to the heavens. At least Joan was Joan. "You know just what to say to a guy," I whine. "Okay, okay. You win. And, even though you lied about your name…for five years…we still have a deal."

"You're an honorable man, Mason. You honor all your promises."

"Okay, Claudia…Claudia…will I ever get used to that?"

"Don't worry. By the way, sorry about your car."

"Oh, my car…yeah. Thanks."

"I knew he was going to do that. I should have warned you. He likes to do that sometimes. It's his way of getting the last laugh."

My calm masks my anger. "Why didn't you—"

"Because when Hank sinks your car, he and Hit Man are done with you. Don't bother reporting it to the police, though."

"Why?"

"The police commissioner, Mason! Pay attention. It wouldn't do you any good."

"Yeah, you're right."

"The police commissioner sold out to Hit Man. Hit Man runs his operation, telling the police commissioner where and where not to patrol. It's all very balanced."

"I'm glad you explained that to me…Claudia."

"There!" she exclaims, kissing me on the cheek. "You're getting used to it."

11:00 AM
Wednesday October 14, 1987
Just outside The Café door
Dow Jones Industrial Average: up, if my luck doesn't change

Hale is the main drag through Ashton Township, running from the levee to Mount Money. It's about a mile to The Café, straight down the pike. Claudia and I didn't stop, except for intersections.

She sighs. She walked the entire mile in pumps. Her feet have to be throbbing. "I do need a cup—"

The presence of Edie startles me. "There she is," I whisper reflexively.

"Who—oh, my!" Claudia says.

I see through the window that Edie is sitting at a table on the blue-padded chair, facing the left-side wall. She is professional chic in a gray suit with slacks, and a black sweater. The profile of her beautiful face…I must be honest…Edie couldn't begin to squeeze into Claudia's clothes, but Claudia doesn't have that 'look'…and doesn't own my soul.

"My treat, another time?" I ask Claudia without looking her way.

"Yes, I'll take you up on that. Mason, she's some woman!"

"You know it."

"Bye, for now. Call me later?"

"Bye."

Claudia turns and walks away, I guess.

So many things have hit me in the stomach this morning, but presently that region of my body is inhabited by many tiny butterflies. I take a deep breath and step to Edie. She turns her head and looks up to me. Her eyes…

"Hello," Edie says, more blankly than I would have wished.

"Hi, Edie," I say, as my voice almost cracks like an adolescent boy.

She waves for me to sit. I do. "I haven't talked to you for a couple days," she says, not looking at me now, raising the coffee cup to her lips.

"Sorry. I've been busy."

"I can see that."

A little jealousy never hurt a relationship. "She's an investment partner—uh, client. Claudia. Claudia Brown."

She looks at me, like 'yeah, right.' "I was considering calling your office this morning, but since you money managers don't work in jeans, I assume you and your client have a day off today?"

I'm really happy she didn't try to call my office. "Oh…yes, day off."

Edie takes her purse from her lap and makes the motions to leave. "I'll go somewhere else with my investments question."

A mild panic nearly overcomes me. "Oh, well…I'm back on the clock." A little upset, darling?

"Okay, here it is," she says, gazing at the window. "The library needs a new bookmobile. The old one blew a timing chain or something, which then stripped the engine, I think. It was a rust trap, anyway. Anyway, we're dead busted broke and every self-respecting library has a bookmobile. And, this is the bad part…" Edie turns to me to deliver the bad part. "The director has put me in charge of raising the money for a new one."

"What's so bad about that?" I ask immediately.

"Do I look like I know anything about raising money, Mason?" she asks with more than a hint of panic.

"Then, I'll help. I'll help you with the money, and I'll help you realize that you know more than you think you know."

Her eyes beam, not lovingly, but as if I had just eliminated a nuisance, like unstopping her kitchen sink. "Would you?"

She apparently didn't hear my compliment. "Absolutely," I return.

"I knew it."

"What?"

"If I invoked enough pity, you'd be there for me." Edie grins slightly.

Thank God. My witty Edie is back. Pissed Edie was scary. "Anytime," I say. "Now, first question."

"I'm listening." She's all ears…and boobs, and while you're at it, do sit on my lap.

"How much do you need?" I ask.

"The director says fifty thousand dollars," she answers quickly.

"Nice bookmobile." Damn, that number haunts me. This is going to be tough.

"Actually, it's new, from Cleveland."

Feigning horror, I say. "You mean, you're relying on Browns' fans?"

"No, Bricker. Browns' fans can't read."

I laugh, not knowing what to say next. "I can help you," somehow comes out.

"How?"

"I'll get a list of potential donors for you, and I'll even coach you on how to ask for money."

Edie smiles and blushes slightly. "You're sweet."

And, I love you…"So, let's get this off on the right foot by walking over to the bank with me for your first donation."

"Ooo-kay," she says. I think she's sincerely excited. I stand up, extending my hand to her. She takes it, stands, and releases my hand. It was nice to touch her. Proximity does not allow me to sneak a peek at her butt, but maybe later, because there is financial transaction afoot. I'm going to end up buying the entire fucking bookmobile for her.

We walk out of The Café and take three steps to the curb, heading across the street for AshNat. I stop. Edie continues, right in front of a Volvo screeching to a halt. They barely miss each other. It was enough to make me suck in a breath so deep I instantly became lightheaded.

"Make it across the street, Edie," I say as I walk to her side, shaken. Taking her hand again, I help both of us the rest of the way.

Edie presses her other hand to her chest just below her throat, gulping for air. "You know, this is an omen," she says, still walking with me. "I don't think you should be doing this."

"Doing what?"

"Making the first contribution. Making any contribution."

"Why not?"

"I feel…" Edie pauses for a while. "I think I'm taking advantage of you." I start to place my hand on her shoulder, but I decide I've touched her too much for one morning. "Ms. Marie," I say. "here's the first rule of asking for money."

"Okay. Tell me," she says.

"Never turn it down."

Edie looks forward and nods her head in approval. Our walk together becomes silent and remains that through the bank door and into the lobby, where back-in-black Beth greets us.

"Hello, again," Beth says to me. "Hello, I'm Beth Nottingham," she says, extending her hand to Edie.

"I'm Edie Marie," Edie says, seemingly a bit overwhelmed. The women are smiling and looking at each other, so much so that this transaction will either be pleasant or erupt into a cat fight.

"How can I help you two?"

"Please cut me a check payable to…" I turn to Edie for instructions. She's doe-eyed and speechless. "…Ashton Township Public Library?" I ask Edie. She's still speechless. "That's right, Beth. Ashton Township Public Library," I say.

"And…the amount?" Beth asks.

Oh…the amount…well…let's start small. "Ten thousand dollars."

"Comin' right up," Beth says.

Edie looks at me in amazement. "Mason! I will not allow you to do this!"

"Remember the first rule?"

"Fu—to hell with the first rule!"

"Always follow the first rule," I say with a smile.

"No!" Wow, she's really angry. "I'm putting a stop to this!"

"Well, Edie, there's more where that came from," I say, the cockster yuppie.

"How much more can I take?" she asks as she turns her back to me. I look down. Impetus has been provided.

"I'm taking another fifteen thousand and investing it for the library."

Edie returns sharply to my face. "Oh, we don't gamble at the library."

"No gamble on your part," I say. "Your fifteen thousand is safe, no matter."

"That's twenty-five thousand dollars!" she says, dropping her jaw.

"And, congratulations! You're halfway there!"

"This is not right," she hisses.

"What's wrong with it?"

"It's…you're…" Edie crosses her arms. "You're just doing this to—"

"Promote literacy. Reading is fundamental. Why, if I never would have learned to read, I'd have never met you, and you wouldn't be…halfway there!"

Teeth clenched, looking at the ceiling, then the floor, then me…Edie probably wants to speak but can't think of a word to say to express her feelings. "I feel…I…thank you. On behalf of the library, I thank you."

My spine stiffens. I smile. "You, my darling, are welcome."

11:45 AM
Wednesday October 14, 1987
Beside the library fountain
Dow Jones Industrial Average: considering the money I dropped this morning, it would surely be nice if it falls a few hundred points.

"Now, I'll take this to the director," Edie says, "then, tell her about the other fifteen thousand, then call 911, because she'll crack her head on her desk as she passes out."

"Okay," I say with a laugh.

Her eyes pierce mine. I swear to God, I'll write another check if she kisses me. "She'll want to meet you. Are you in the book?"

Anything but that. "I'm anonymous."

"Oh, no."

"Oh, yes."

"No."

"Yes."

"No—damnit, why not?"

"I'm…that's all I ask."

"Okay."

"See ya?"

"Yep."

Edie walks up the steps and through the doors. I think we've connected.

Thirty-Six

3:00 PM
Thursday October 15, 1987
Drucker Hospital, in the waiting room, twenty bucks lighter due to exorbitant taxi fare
Dow Jones Industrial Average: 2,385 at around 2:30 PM – 13.3 percent off all-time high

This isn't too bad. Just as I remember it. Not too bad. At least it's not Jack Nicholson's *Cuckoo's Nest* too bad. The waiting room, or 'family and friends greeting room,' as it is euphemistically referred to, is a wide corridor on the ground floor of this two-story structure. The corridor cuts to the left to the patients' quarters on one end, with the hospital door from the lobby on the other end. The door is of the heavy steel security variety that unlocks remotely by a nurse at the nurses' station nearby, and only by a nurse at the nurses' station nearby, and only when the nurse is satisfied that the person on the surveillance screen should be in and/or not be out. And, just in case, a wire-reinforced glass pane is mounted at head level so the nurses can get a first hand visual if that is necessary. Rather totalitarian is the door.

In spite of the door, the folks of the family and friends greeting room necessarily did not need a huge guy carrying five-point restraints to patrol the hallway. The place is too nice for him, and everything is under control. Once you're buzzed through the door, you are greeted by a yellow wall to the left and one-way windows running the length to the right. On the wall hang four obsessively and compulsively spaced floral still-life prints. The windows look out peacefully onto a rock and water garden. Lush plants, track lighting, and soft sofas and chairs add to the calm, because calm is the objective here. You can imagine the family and friends of us the mentally ill are anything but.

Wylie has turned the corner from the patients' quarters and is walking toward me. He's dressed casual in a maroon Brooks Brothers buttondown, tan Land's End chinos, and loafers with no socks. He'd look great if not for his slumping posture and haggard face, like he had just recently awakened from a long sleep.

"Hey, man," I say pleasantly, standing to shake his hand.

He gives me the perfunctory clasp, obviously wanting to get right to it, whatever it is. "You got to get me out of here," he says softly, leaning in to me. "Give me a ride home."

What a greeting from someone whose carcass I just pulled out of the muck. "You're welcome."

"Look, thanks...the doctor told me this morning. Again, thanks, but this place is making me crazy. Group is crazy. It's twice a day, with all those crazy people smoking and telling their pathetic life stories."

"This place is saving your ass, and, by the way, Mr. Fifty-Thousand, you are crazy," I remind him, but on second thought maybe I shouldn't have led with the c-word.

"*You* saved my ass," he says, ignoring my diagnosis. "I figured out a way to repay you next week by—"

"You *will* repay me, but right now that's not the problem."

"Right. The problem is you helping me get the hell out of here."

I place my hands under the gray blazer on the hips of my Levis, a classic power stance. "The problem is you have a gambling problem."

"The problem is you won't get off my ass over a little…gaming."

"Gaming. Gaming? The problem is you lost your ass," I say, analyzing appropriately, "and I had to save your ass and you never should have put either one of our asses in jeopardy like you did."

"Look, I'm sorry. But—"

"No, Wylie, you're not sorry."

"Look, Mason, I appreciate all the help you gave me. I couldn't have done it without you."

"Couldn't have done it without me? You make it sound as if I just helped you paint your goddamned house or something."

"Mason, I can take it from here."

My voice is feeling the tension. "Yesterday, your bookies took fifty thousand of my money, then they pushed my car with my keys, my bag phone, and other personal belongings off the levee into the Ohio. Granted, the Olds was not a Jag, but it was the only car I had."

He's obviously stunned, and should be. "I'll pay for your car."

"Don't you get the message here? They don't fuck around!"

"I said I'll pay for your car, damnit!"

"I'm afraid my car is the least of your worries, my man."

"Look, don't worry about the car and the money. I'm good for it."

I take a blow, trying to settle down. The meeting with Hit Man's associates gave me a shot of adrenaline that did not subside yesterday, or today. Holding six hundred thousand dollars of puts doesn't help matters either. Even though I'm winning, that comes with a big 'so far.' I've been here before, with huge bets (there's that word again) on the market direction while running the edge on empty. I look Wylie in the eyes. They're still tired. Choosing this time to resume speaking, I say, "I know you want to check out of this hotel, but considering everything, maybe you'd better stay a while."

"No!" he exclaims.

I'll take another deep breath and try it again. "The dichotomy, the irony is astounding. You run a solid, tight business and your clients love you, but you go fifty thousand in the hole participating in an illegal activity with a dude named Hit Man."

"How about you and Christine, Mr. Law-Abiding Citizen?"

"I don't owe her a dime, Mac, and she's never threatened to hurt me. Besides, she helped you get out of the jam."

"How's that?"

"She provided the necessary T and A."

"And…I'm out! And, I want out of here."

"You can go AMA anytime you wish, but if you do, I'm not helping you any more."

"I don't need your help. I paid them what I owed them!"

"*I* paid them what you owed them! And, I suspect it's not over because, noting the location of my Olds, they're punitive."

Wylie slowly rocks back, finally looking as if he gets it. He stares at me during a long pause. "Then, what should I do?" he asks.

"Stay here. Let it fade. Give yourself a chance to heal, and then figure out where to go next."

"I have healed."

He doesn't get it after all. "Considering the fact that less then two days ago you had taken yourself hostage in your powder room and were perfectly content with splattering your brains on the wall, have you really healed?" I ask, rather pointedly.

"That was just a moment of weakness."

"No shit." I extend my hand to him. He grabs it. "Wylie, there is nothing else I can do. Feel free to give me a call sometime." I turn and walk to the door.

4:30 PM
Thursday October 15, 1987
At The Café, writing in the new, dry journal
Dow Jones Industrial Average: 2,355 – off 14.4 percent from all-time high

Thursday October 15, 1987
Journal entry: market commentary from the wannabe guru.

I just got off the new, dry, replacement bag phone with Fenz. The Dow closed down fifty-seven, still reeling after the down ninety-six day yesterday. That's over six percent in two days. Good for me, bad for most others. It's as if the group-think has finally realized how top-heavy this overbought, overly wrought market is. There is now talk in the news of how low dividend yields are compared to US Treasury bond yields, a condition that is still bad, and is interestingly, thanks to lower stock prices, actually better than it was two months ago. Now, the wacky valuation is one thing, but the psychology is becoming even more jittery. Wednesday's opening was greeted by a worse-than-expected trade deficit, causing bond yields to vault past ten percent for the first time in since 1984. As well, a key House committee proposed tax penalties on corporate takeovers. Takeovers have provided the stock market fuel and verve throughout the bull run. Eliminating this rich white man's game may cause the white men to really freak out. Right now, this white man would like to see that.

Last night saw Tokyo and London get hammered even harder than New York the previous day. That overseas selling begat today's selling in the US of A. That's bad, or good if you're me. Momentum is decidedly in my favor. Here's why: there are investment programs called 'portfolio insurance' that use the crazy futures market to 'insure' stock portfolios against losses of, say, over five percent. Trouble is, when portfolio insurance is used by too many in a big way (like now) in an already overreacting market (like this one), futures are driven to discounts and thereby kick in index arbitrage programs which propagate more selling and create the need for more portfolio insurance and where does it all end? Insurance programs, arbitrage programs…it is obvious that this market is programmed to be one giant slide down the waterfall.

Don't say I didn't warn you.

I still don't know the value of my gains. Fenz had to leave early today. Adding up the prices on the puts of twenty-one companies is too time-consuming for a woman headed for the spa. I'll just have an espresso and sleep on it.

Claudia called the bag phone early after closing, probably the same time her US Steel guy heard from his broker. I'd like to know if he's still going for the upside. I'd say he is. Men like that are stubborn and headstrong. I, however, am not stubborn and…well, that's bullshit.

Anyway, Claudia called and pressed me hard for the end-of-day winnings. I didn't want to disappoint her, but I don't work that way. I try to avoid counting my money while sitting at the table, doing what I must to heed the lyrical advice of Kenny Rogers. Granted, it does sound a little desperate to hinge my fortune on a graying, aging, fading, hairy country singer, but I look for any edge I can get. Maybe it's because if the future looks right, it doesn't matter how much you have on the table. Maybe it's superstition. Maybe it's an OCD ritual. It's probably because I'm too lazy to add up all the numbers. Still, Claudia will just have to deal.

Until tomorrow, my dear diary…

6:00 PM
Thursday October 15, 1987
At Green Boy's, sitting at the bar behind my second Arn.
Dow Jones Industrial Average: it's difficult to remain objective when you're right.

I'm here for the evening. Not able to drive since I will soon be legally impaired and I don't own a car that has not suffered severe water damage, a nice taxi will take me home. Yesterday with Hank and the goon was an experience. Thank God for the key beside my air conditioner. I still don't know what I'm going to do about my mail. Who cares? It's just bills and junk. The summer after my freshman year, Vinny and I lived off the previous tenant's utility rebate checks, but I don't envision getting that lucky again.

Lucky…lucky…with regard to the market, I want to examine this, but I must feel blessed that I'm not the mother in Texas with her baby daughter Jessica stuck down the well. The rescue efforts are all over CNN tonight, and…that must be just terrible for her. I am lucky. I grab the journal and my pen from my new satchel. Here goes:

Thursday October 15, 1987
Spontaneous entry.

Love – Christine is history and Claudia remains a distant possibility, but both are a cash drain, anyway. Edie has my heart and seems more interested since I opened the wallet for the library. However, no commitment. Neutral.

Money – I've never seen a market move this quickly in my favor. No one ever calls it so precisely. This is the closest I've ever been to being Marty Zweig. The options gods are smiling on me, but Thor may strike tomorrow. Lucky. For now.

Health – Breaths come easier. My heart's slower. My blood pressure is down, according to the measurement made by Michael's secretary. But, there has to be long term damage from abuse. Neutral.

Mental Health – I need talk therapy, so Diane the Feet is probably wondering where I am. I need meds, but Dr. Pedersen will have to keep his prescription pad dry because there is no way in hell I'm going to see him. And, I'm out of the brokerage business. Neutral.

Faith and Ethics – I pray. I don't miss mass. I regularly participate in the sacrament of reconciliation. I'm prepared for the afterlife. I just have to find some way to cure this foul fuck mouth I have and curb my overwhelming passions for women. Neutral.

Career – It's October and only one college has called, maybe because I've only called only one college. My novels suck. I suck. And, I'm out of the brokerage business. Lucky.

Intangibles – My dad was a neo-Nazi. My wife left me for a gay man. I haven't had an orgasm in fifty-four days, the last one being with a woman who recently died. My car is at the bottom of one of the world's major inland waterways. And…you guessed it…I'm out of the brokerage business. Neutral

Sum of the Parts – I'm a survivor.

Later…

"Hello, Mason." It's Edie, to my left.

"Well, hello," I say, barely breathing. "You know how to startle a guy." I close the journal.

"How are you?" she asks. Edie's in a fine high-neck violet dress that basically accentuates the boobs when you think the effect would be other—Jesus, Mason, you're discursive! To yourself! Get a grip!

"Fine. You?"

"Just great," she says.

We pause. Her eyes are burning a hole in me, and it's not with loving intent. "Beer?" I ask.

"No, but let me help you with yours." She reaches for my draft glass, picks it up, and splashes the contents in my face. Wow. I'm soaked. I look at her. Once again, she has rendered me unable to speak.

"I called your office today," she spits.

"Uh, oh."

"And, guess what?"

"I can explain."

"No need to. Either you work there, or…you don't work there!"

The bartender hands me a towel and moves as far away as he can while remaining on the job. Other patrons are forming a wider radius around us. I have to say something, even if it's wrong. "There's a reason—"

"Like, making promises you can't keep?"

"Now, wait a minute!"

"I called you because the director wanted to meet you," she says. Edie has not taken her flashing eyes off me. "I showed her the ten thousand dollar check and told her about the other money and how you were investing it. Then I called. Then, your sham came tumbling down."

"You have to let me explain." It must be difficult to be taken seriously while dripping with Iron City.

"No need. Your actions speak for themselves."

"Actions? Like the ten thousand? That's a cashier's check! It's cleared funds!"

"Oh, yeah. Well, if you don't…what I mean to say," she says, shifting her feet. "…is thank you…but I'm not so sure I like the idea of where the money came from."

"What the hell—"

"You lied to me about your job. So, why not just continue the parade of lies and give me money that you possibly are not…not…to hell with you, Mason Bricker!"

"Edie, let's not—"

"You already have."

"Listen. The library's already making money on the fifteen. I'll show you." A drunken gentleman in a gray chalk-stripe suit brings his beer and sits to my right. He's probably a lawyer offering mediation.

"The goddamn market is falling!" she screams, "How can that be possible?"

"It is. I'm trading contracts called puts on—"

"Contracts? What is this, a casino?"

"No, it's viable investing that works."

"You lied to me, and now you're running a casino? With the library's money?"

"It's not tha—"

Edie grabs the drunk's mug and throws his beer in my face. "You have problems."

Before I can see, she's out of here. The front of my blue oxford shirt is positively pluvial. Green Boy's is silent. Everyone is staring at me. I have no choice. I remain sitting at the bar.

"Trouble in paradise," I say to the bartender. "Could you please refill us?"

Thirty-Seven

3:00 PM
Friday October 16, 1987
Drucker Hospital family and friends greeting room
Dow Jones Industrial Average: still moving in my favor

I was home this afternoon watching the lady on CNN flip back and forth between stories about baby Jessica and the how the market is getting hammered today. Wylie called. 'I need to see you,' he said excitedly. 'Now.' Even though I had planned to visit tonight, I dropped everything and called for a taxi. I knew it would happen. When your mental illness becomes apparent to you, sometimes like a submarine blasting through the ocean's surface, you can be even more egocentric and self-absorbed than you already are. Therefore, here I am. He most likely has had one of the many of the stark realizations he'll experience as his treatment progresses. Who knows? His doctor? Maybe. Psychiatrists prescribe meds, dealing in probabilities and statistical outcomes. So, in an irony of all ironies, Wylie's shrink plays the odds.

Here he is, wearing the same clothes he wore yesterday.

"Hi," he says as he approaches.

"What is it?" I ask.

"Thanks for coming."

"Okay, but—"

"I had to see you."

"All right. What is it?"

"I have to hear it, Mason."

"Hear what?"

"The story…I have to hear the story."

Oh, Jesus…the story, the story of my mystical Saturday almost twelve years ago, relevant in part because Wylie wants to hear it on a regular basis. "Have a seat," I say. Wylie sits on the sofa, butt on the edge, like a teen boy in company with his favorite sports hero. I sit in a nearby upholstered chair. Here goes.

"We played our guts out at Penn State and lost when their last-ditch long-range field goal caught a gust of wind and went through for the winning points. We were so heartbroken that it carried over into the next game against lowly North Carolina State. They beat the hell out of us in our own house. Suddenly, man, our undefeated season was history and we were in a shambles with number one Pittsburgh coming to town."

"Oh, man, you must have felt doomed."

"Well, yes."

"Sorry to interrupt. Go on." He leans more toward me.

"Interrupt anytime. You've heard the story so much you could tell it," I say with a smile.

"But, not like you. Go on."

I continue. "The evening after the NC State loss, my father's friend came to see me with the evidence against the coach. It was ugly. I knew we'd hit bottom."

"You had evidence against the coach and then on game day you became the coach. Head coach."

"You could say that." The more story I let him tell, the more quickly we'll get to the end so I can go home.

"You're a leader, Mason. A born leader."

"Well…thanks." It's not true, but, you know…

"On to the game. They were tough, Pitt was, weren't they?"

"Oh, yeah," I say. "They had rung up fifty on four teams and had seven shutouts in nine games. Brutal."

"But, the Ridge Runners?"

"We were sixty very talented individuals who had that Saturday morning to become a team. When we walked out there, I didn't know whether or not that had happened."

"What was your first clue?"

I laugh and softly shake my head. "Mac, the same clue it was the last time I told you the story. Vinny."

"Okay. Go on."

"Vinny began the week in the same position he had been in all year, third team quarterback who hadn't played a down all season. On Monday, the second team guy trashed his knee in the shower, of all places. Then, that Thursday, the starter had to have an emergency appendectomy. All of a sudden, Vinny's the man."

"Wow! What did he do when he found out?"

"Puke," I say, smiling, remembering the moment.

"Man, I would have, too."

"He recovered. By kickoff, he was so calm and composed it was frightening. A sophomore. A skinny sophomore, the skinniest guy on the team. I was the third team wideout, the third receiver off the bench. No way I would play. Gunner, that's what I called Vinny, Gunner, right before he went on the field that first time, turned to me and said, 'Brick, you get out there and you and I are going downtown.' The possibility was so remote, but it felt good to hear him say it." My voice is tight. I swallow hard.

"I bet it did."

"Yep, especially after the second play. Vinny launched a long ball, hit the receiver perfectly, and it was seven-oh West Virginia early against the number one team in the nation."

"All right."

"Then they started beating the shit out of us. I stunk as a coach, Wylie. I was absolutely fetid. Everything I tried didn't work. So, I revamped the offense by putting an extra receiver out there and it stopped the blood bath."

"See, you were a good coach."

"Yeah, but the third receiver had his bell rung and had to be carted off. The fourth guy wrecked a knee and barely made it to the sidelines. Enter number five, the coach."

"Oh, yeah!"

"I had dreamed of that moment since forever. Suddenly, there I was, in the huddle. All the guys were clapping and smacking my ass because everyone knew no one wanted it more than me. I wasn't big, I wasn't really fast, I didn't..." I feel a sob, but manage to quell it. "I always thought they kept me around because I wanted it so much and I had just enough talent to make it interesting. That, plus I was so stupid I sacrificed my body anytime it was necessary."

"What is it you always say?"

"Whatth—"

"No, the football one."

"Oh...I hit like Amtrak."

"The game needs more guys like you."

Sighing hard, I'm unable to speak.

"Then, what happened?" he asks.

Deep breathing helps. "First play I was out there, Vinny and I went downtown. He put it up, I ran under it, did this juggling circus catch to make it entertaining, and it was a touchdown. Vinny Vacca, fifty-three yards to Mason Bricker, score tied at fourteen."

"Cool."

Vinny. Now I know I'm going to cry. Damnit, not here!

"So, it's halftime..."

"And, I had to give a halftime speech to keep us up." My voice cracks, but I recover. "I couldn't think of anything to say, so I just went on auto. I said, 'Okay, gentlemen, we're thirty minutes into this, and we're still here. We're here to do something we know we can do very well. Keep at it. We're at home, and the breaks fall your way when you're at home. Play hard, hit hard, help out your teammates, and never, never, I say never give up!'"

"That's beautiful. You are a leader."

Wylie may need me now, but if I continue this story, I'm pudding. "We didn't give up and we won the game," I say with finality.

"Yes. Beautiful."

We look into each other's eyes. I reach for his hand. He takes mine. Tears begin streaming down his face. You son-of-a-bitch, don't make me lose it…

"Wylie?" I say.

"Yes?" he chokes out

"Never, never, I say never give up."

"Okay, man, I won't." We stand and lose it in an embrace.

4:15 PM
Friday October 16, 1987
In the backseat of a taxi, headed for Green Boy's
Dow Jones Industrial Average: sucking air through a straw

"Margaret Joan Kissinger, PhD," I say to the Iranian taxi driver, "Margaret Joan Kissinger: daughter, sister, professor, Northwestern alumnus, wife, wife again, woman, sexpot. It is interesting that today, on the day of her Mass of Christian Burial, I resurrect her. I told Wylie the story of the magic again. If I had enough time I'd tell you, Muhib, but my friend coaxed it out of me, and surprisingly that brought Joan back."

Muhib drives on, looking straight ahead and silently at the road. "I was in love with Joan from the very beginning," I continue, "from the day I was introduced to her as her teaching assistant in the English department. Of all the wimpy men and the frumpy women from which there were to choose, the dean assigned me to Raquel Welch. Oh, yeah, I was often heard to say. Joan fell in love with me, too, but didn't spill it until…that magical day. Our love was scandalous: older woman/younger man, teacher/college student, but we didn't care. We were wine, beer, food, and sex, including just enough academics to make it respectable."

The taxi slows down on Hale and nears Green Boy's. "For six years, Joan was impetuous, wild, spontaneous, lustful, unpredictable, everything I love in a woman. Then, she was gone. Christine was her physical legacy, but I sorely missed the daily task of trying to deal with what she was going to do next. I got a taste of it in August, and, until then, I didn't realize how much I missed that."

"Goodbye, my dear Maggie J. Keep the saints in heaven guessing."

Muhib turns to me. "Twenty dollars, sir," he says.

I hand him a fifty. "Thanks. Keep the change. It's cheaper than therapy."

4:45 PM
Friday October 16, 1987
Sitting at Green Boy's bar, nursing the first Arn.

Dow Jones Industrial Average: I saw it on CNN here in the tavern; 2,246 – 18.4 percent off the all-time high, down a record 108 points from yesterday's close.

As I dial the bag phone to check in with my mole, the silent television shows the paper-strewn floor of the Chicago Board of Options Exchange as a symbol of a bad day on Wall Street. Silent TV. The tune on Green Boy's sounds? Bon Jovi's *Living on a Prayer*.

"Ally Fenz, please," I say into the transmitter.

"This is Ally, o wise one."

I smile and laugh. "Cut the major suck up. You'll get your birthday present. I'm over here at Green Boy's watching you market types on television. Where do we stand?"

"You're watching TV?" Fenz asks. "How's baby Jessica doing? I hope she's okay. Her mother must be…"

"They're digging a hole beside the well. They'll get her."

"All we can do is pray," she says. We pause, and pause again. Money seems so trivial now. "Okay, where do we stand?" she continues. "I spent a lot of time adding this up for you. Math was my worst subject in school, you know."

"Your best being looking good."

"You got that right, babe."

"Lay it on me, Fenz."

"You finished the day at…drum roll, please…one million eight hundred thousand five hundred five dollars."

"Well…that's a triple since Tuesday. Damn." Todd and Jason stroll in wearing three hundred dollar suits, averting the glance I lend them. They walk to a table and sit as far away as possible. They look smug, even though Fenz had told me they and their clients are heavily into the upside. They have to be getting killed. If I were Todd or Jason, I'd fear for my life.

"Congratulations, Mason, you're a millionaire," Fenz says.

"Yeah, I guess so, even after paying Uncle Sam and William Penn."

"What are you going to do now?"

"I have to stick. The markets are closed until Monday. Who knows what will happen on Monday? Who knows what will happen this weekend? Reagan has to retaliate for that Iranian gunboat attack. How will we handle that news? I don't know. I'm going to try to not worry about it, because, like it or not, I'm in."

Fenz sighs. "Yes, you are in."

"How's the mood over there?"

"These guys were not going to have a good weekend, so a half-hour ago, Ronnie Miller got on the squawk box and rallied the troops."

"What did the Corncob say?"

"All the selling has been done. Monday will be the start of a good week and the next big rally. Most of the guys headed out smiling."

"Yeah. I see two of them over here. What an idiot Corncob is! And, he's called me stupid, behind my back? All over the firm? Jeez!. Well, on to more important matters…I understand Edie called."

"Yes, I took the call. I'm sorry. I just spewed the line John told us to. Then, she introduced herself and she was…how do you say…"

"Disenchanted."

"What did you do to her, Mason?"

"I gave the library money for one of their fund drives and I guess the director wanted to talk to me. Edie called for me at where I told her I worked. I saw her after that. The scene was ugly." Two lawyers in love enter, staring at the bag phone. I feel so…cutting edge.

"I'm sorry."

"I guess I'm going to have to find another love interest."

"Well, being the millionaire you are…"

"A millionaire for a weekend. I'd better take advantage of it." Men glare at me after I use the M word. Women glance, eyes askance. Chicks are so much more subtle.

"Don't worry. Hey, I gotta run. John needs me."

"Tell The Dick I said hello. And, have a great one."

"Call me," she says.

"You golddigger."

"Oh, get fucked," she says in a friendly fashion.

"Yeah. Today could be the day."

5:15 PM
Friday October 16, 1987
Still at Green Boy's, second Arn.
Dow Jones Industrial Average: the October surprise

The tavern is full; all the tables are taken, the floor is packed. I'm lucky to have gotten here early, and I'm not about to give up my seat. Green Boy's is a traditional yuppie hang out, meaning a lot of affluent attorneys and their stockbrokers are on the prowl. I catch snippets of conversation. Most of the talk is of the market's latest woes, as if they've all just discovered there is risk.

The bag phone rings.

"Mason," I answer.

"Hey, sweetie."

"Claudia."

"Oh, Eva and I are glued to CNN watching baby Jessica, and I heard the market news."

"We're okay."

"What? Oh, I'm sorry. I just can't imagine losing my child…I can't talk about it!"

"I won't talk about it, but she will be okay. So, don't worry about your money. Even after all these years, I still can't get used to how a market collapse can be good news." CNN is interviewing Federal Reserve chairman Alan Greenspan. He looks worried, but he always looks worried.

"But, it is for us, right?" Claudia asks, a little nervous.

"Oh, yeah. Very good."

"Tell me, now!"

"Claudia, dear, you're getting way too excited about this."

"It's just a game to me, baby, and you know how I like to win."

"Okay, just as long as it's just a game."

"So, what's the damn score?" she asks, a trifle agitated.

"You're four percent of me," I say, "and that makes you…less my twenty…a little over fifty thousand, fifty-two, to be more exact." Nearby necks crane in to me, as if EF Hutton just spoke.

"Wow."

"Down two hundred fifty-seven points in three days. Unprecedented drop, and unprecedented timing, if I may say."

"Your timing was always good," she coos.

"I just hope my new love thinks so, too. That is, if she ever speaks to me again."

"Oh, what happened, sweetie?"

"It's a long story. Anyway, don't bet on a market fall of this magnitude happening again." The guy next to me seems relieved. People are a little too interested in my bag phone.

"So, what do we do now?"

"We hold. The markets are closed until Monday. Holding over the weekend makes me nervous, but there's no choice now."

"Why are you so nervous?"

"Anything can happen over a weekend. Foreigners own a ton of stocks, and James Baker's in Europe. He's such a cowboy. Combine this quaking market with the fact that he's liable to say something to piss them off, that's good. Then again, foreigners may go for bargains, that's bad."

"Well, you do what you think is best. You're the smartest man I know," she says.

"We'll see how smart I am on Monday."

"Bye for now, Mason. Pray for Jessica."

I place the telephone hook in the bag. Considering the market and how I aligned myself in it, I think, what possessed me to do such an anserine thing? What Freudian event took place in my early childhood to make me do this? Am I bi-polar manic just like Diane says, or does it originate from the mild sociopath in me? Sure, the weirdness is handy now, but I have spent almost all my time suffering as a contrarian, winning presently, but always doing battle with today's losers. If I keep this up, I will alienate everyone. Maybe I should take Diane's advice and stop exacerbating the situation.

Fuck that.

5:30 PM
Friday October 16, 1987
Still at Green Boy's, just asked for my third Arn
Dow Jones Industrial Average: you gotta know when to hold 'em, and know when to fold 'em.

After everyone has had a few, I evaluate the mood of the bar. Conclusion? The crowd is Nero. Wall Street burns.

"Mason?"

"Yep," I say as I turn to the female voice. Edie has made her way through the crowd to me. Cream fall sweater, and I can't see her bottom. Right now, that's probably good.

"Hi," she says.

"Hi." The bartender starts to place the third on the bar. He holds up when he sees Edie.

"How are you?"

"You're not going to douse me again, are you?"

"I am so sorry," she says, sincerely contrite.

Hearing that, the bartender places the beer in front of me. I take a sip, looking into the bar mirror. It's the first time I've seen Edie and me as a couple. We are good together, damned good, with her definitely as the better half. It's the eyes…they don't stop…they're so beautiful…

"Well, maybe I'd better go," she says.

I turn back to her. She's too pretty to leave me…her eyes own me. "Let's work this out, Edie," I say. "Believe it or not, it's okay. I kind of deserved it. Still, I've pissed off my share of women in my life, but a beer in the face has never happened."

"I am sorry. You're a good sport."

"What can I say? And, remember, I asked for anonymity."

"You still lied to me."

"Or, you could say I never found a convenient time to tell you the truth."

"Well put," she says, not smiling.

I take another sip. "I was fired because a) I was going against the grain and being an asshole while doing it, and b) I wasn't bringing in enough commissions to be an asshole." I'm sure our conversation is interesting to others, especially those who were here yesterday afternoon. But, I don't seem to hear anyone or feel anyone. It's just me and Edie, and I prefer it that way.

"Well…I didn't give you a chance to explain," she says. "I'm sorry."

"That's correct. You didn't give me a chance to explain."

Edie looks directly in my blues. I'm putty. "I plead PMS. I'll be better soon as that's over. Sometimes, I hate being a woman."

"I under—"

"Other times, it's great, especially when the guy…is like you."

My heart flutters. My head buzzes. My stomach twists. I reflexively look away. I turn back. She's still locked in. Now, I'm hot putty. "You don't know how much I've wanted to hear that from you."

"Yes, I do," Edie says, with a sultry look of confidence. It's my biggest laugh since the night after I met Greg, and the largest arousal in my trousers since Joan.

"Guilty," I say.

Edie looks to one of the televisions. "How's Jessica doing?" she asks.

"They're going to get her, and she's going to be okay."

"I agree. She has an entire nation praying for her."

A pause envelops us, and we turn to look at each other directly in the eyes. I hope it's as powerful for her as it is for me.

"I'm not a mother…" she says.

"But, I know what you mean."

"Honey," she says…to me…'Honey'…she called me…'Honey,' "I'm too bloated to have a beer. How about we go over to The Café and I'll buy you a cup of coffee."

And, there it is, Fenz!

6:00 PM
Friday October 16, 1987
Sitting at The Café with Edie. Finally.
Dow Jones Industrial Average: leave it to the experts

The Café is empty. Everyone is at Green Boy's. Regardless, a band is setting up for tonight's live music. I'm happy, still smiling from the look I got at her black skirt on the way over. Booty...maybe today is the day I get to touch it.

"So, let me get this straight...you stood in Green Boy's and threw a beer in your ex-husband's face after the divorce was final?"

"Uh, about a half-hour after it was final."

"Jeez Louise!"

"He was in there with the bitch," Edie says. "I couldn't help myself."

"I bet he doesn't get near you now."

"Yes, he did. That was Greg you met at the fountain."

"Ohhh..." Fuck, Mason, you don't stand a snowball's chance.

"He sweet talked me for a couple of days and I fell for it. Turns out, he wanted money. Hell, no."

Back in the game, buddy. "Some guys..."

"You ever been married, if I may pry?"

"Oh, yeah."

"Oooo...doesn't sound good."

"It was like a good movie with a bad ending."

We sip our espressos. Our eyes meet, then turn away, then meet again. Edie smiles. I'm probably wearing some sort of a goofy grin. "You know, Mason?"

"What?"

"I apologize for the casino remark."

"Ah...think nothing of it. There's some truth to that."

"I was volatile."

"Volatile women are my favorite."

"You're kind."

"Interestingly, the remark made me think. You had really hit on it because what I'm doing is a gamble, much more a gamble than stocks and bonds. The good thing is it's not an arbitrary gamble. The other good thing is it's working."

"I've been keeping up with it in the news. And, I've thought about it, you know, making money as the market falls. Well, to me, that's like Robin Hood," she says, touching my hand. "You're Robin Hood."

"The original socialist." That was pretty good...it's difficult to be witty when you're reeling.

"You steal from the rich stock market and give to the poor. A liberal like me has to appreciate that." She's smiling.

"I—I—" I'm stuttering.

"Just tell me one thing."

"Yes?"

"How's the poor library's money doing?"

Oh yes! What an opportunity to…"Here's how it's worked out. I earmarked fifteen thousand for the library. I did the arithmetic and discovered that your haul at the end of the day is…forty-five thousand dollars."…show off.

Edie sits straight up. "Wow."

"Counting the ten, you're there."

"I don't want to be greedy, so maybe we should get that money out."

"It's too late. We'll have to wait until Monday."

"What if, God forbid, there's good news?"

"That's the gamble."

"How do you do this?" she asks, shaking her head slowly.

"I…don't really know."

"Whatever it is, don't stop." She places her elbow on the table and rests her chin in the heel of her hand. Damn, that looks great.

"Look, don't worry," I say. "I'll freeze your forty-five if the market goes against us on Monday. If not, you make even more money, you buy the bookmobile next week, and you'll be rolling in time for Santa Claus."

"Well, I'm Jewish," she says with a grin, "but that won't stop me from having a holly, jolly Christmas."

"It's the best time of the year."

We're quiet for several moments. Her chin remains in her hand and the grin remains on her face "I've always found you interesting," she whispers.

More spinning. "That's amazing, because I've always bumbled around you." I'm still not very good at this.

"Despite that, or perhaps because of that," she says, sitting erect. "I am interested. And, I'm afraid I have to go."

"Damn."

"A girlfriend in the city is taking me to dinner, then we're shopping until we're dropping all day tomorrow. I'll be back in AT after that. Want to get together Sunday?"

"Absolutely." Absolutely. Absolutely.

"Call me around noon Sunday?"

"No doubt."

Edie looks down and shuffles through her purse. She looks up and into my eyes. A smile grows. "You're cute."

"And, you…are beautiful." Go, man, go!

"Can't argue with that," she says.

Wow.

Thirty-Eight

8:00 AM
Saturday October 17, 1987

In the condo, lounging in the manly brown lounge chair, coffee number two, desiring a cigarette and a woman, in that order, listening to the second ring of the doorbell. Dow Jones Industrial Average: I can't believe it. I just can't believe it.

Goddamnit, you'd think I'd chase them all away. For a budding curmudgeon I get a helluva lot of people who want to talk with me. I pull myself up from my comfort, walk to the door, grab the knob, open the door, and...

"Edie! Good morning!"

"Hi. Am I interrupting anything?"

"No." I'm wearing a Steelers ball cap to cover up my bed head. A black sweatshirt and old gold gym shorts are my PJs. Edie's standing on my doormat in a knee-length tight navy skirt and a gray turtleneck sweater, holding her purse and a paper shopping bag. Her white hosiery is in flats. I'm barefoot. She's lovely, with a tasteful scent of Obsession. I haven't showered.

"Is there another woman here?" she asks.

"Are you joking?" I reply.

"Did she just leave?"

"No. You're the first since August."

"August?" she says as she reaches her hand to my unshaven face. "Poor baby." I'm stymied, until I realize— "Oh, fu—damn! Where are my manners? Come in!"

"Thank you, sir," she says.

"Anytime. And, I mean it."

She steps in, clears the threshold, and looks around. "Nice bachelor's digs you have here."

"I...I don't know what to say. No one ever comments on my place."

"It's awfully brown and white," she says.

"Someone from Cleveland owned it before and I never redecorated."

She glances at me and giggles. "You're funny."

There's enough lull in the conversation to think of something witty. "If you're here to shop," I say, motioning to the bag, "everything is fifty percent off."

"Gee, it has been since August, hasn't it," she says with a wink.

Uh...I'll try sincere. "I'm surprised to see you. I mean, you're always welcome, always, but I look like hell and you look so good."

"Well, aren't you a charmer! And, don't worry, you're still cute, in a sporto-just-out-of-bed sort of way."

I pause, deftly examining her with glances. I am a lucky man. Then, curiosity overcomes my tact. "Tell me. What's in the bag?"

"Well...I have some things I wanted to show you, so that's why I'm here."

"Okay," I say, wondering what I'm in for.

"First, does the condo owners' association let you smoke outside, that is, if it's not too cold for you in your...sleepwear?"

Smoke! I have to mask my glee. "No, I'm fine with it and so are those pretenders, just as long as we're quiet and not prancing around naked."

"No fun here, eh," she says.

I gather my old beat-up loafers and place them on my feet. We go out the front door and walk through the chill and the dew in the grass to my patio near the pool. There's a wooden bench there where we sit. Edie pulls a pack out of her purse. "You want one? Virginia Slims. You don't mind a girl's cigarette, do you?"

Be still, my beating heart. "I'd be happy."

"Cool," she says as she places two in her lips. She lights one and hands it to me, then lights the other. "I see you're comfortable with your manhood."

"Most of the time," I say, as my manhood is nearly making an appearance. "And, I haven't had a smoke for a while. A long while."

Our eyes meet. "One, two, three," we say in unison, "Since August!"

I laugh, sucking air and smoke at the same time. "I tried to quit, too," she says with a puff. "Started again recently."

I puff again, back to back. It's a wonderful thing, a cigarette. "Really? Recently?"

"Thursday," she says.

"Oh."

"Bad day. The cravings…"

"Tell me," I say.

"They rescued Jessica!" she exclaims. "How about that! See, you told me it would be okay, and you were right."

"The power of prayer."

"The power of prayer," she repeats. Edie rests her Slim on the bench with the ashes hanging over. "Now…for the bag."

"Okay. Finally, the bag," I say with a smile.

"First, let me explain…I was on national tour with *A Chorus Line*."

"Really! Damn!" I'm in love with an actress! A real, tactile actress! This is better than the crush I have on Mary Tyler Moore!

"Yep. We were actually like the minor leagues of national tours, though, you know, one night in Western Virginia, and stuff."

I bristle. "West Virginia."

"Yeah, that's it. Anyway, we did tour nationally."

"Wow."

"Overall, it was fun. Point Park College, BFA musical theatre, putzed around for a while doing bit parts for soaps and network TV like *M*A*S*H* when it was funny before it got maudlin. Then, I landed this for a few years, then hung 'em up to get married. The audiences were heavenly, but the road sucked. That's my show biz career in fifty words or less."

"I knew you were a star," I say, admiringly.

"Now, how did you know that?"

"Your posture, your presence, and I think I detect a special tonal quality in your speaking voice."

She jumps to her feet. "Get outta here!"

I jump to mine. "Yes!"

"You are so full of shit!"

"No!"

"Anyway, in here are photos of me and the cast. Here." She looks into my eyes and hands me a stack of a half-dozen or so. The first one is…it's her radiant face, complete with those soulful brown eyes, a young Edie in danceskins and straight leg faded denims, on stage…she's not skinny like an emaciated ballerina, thank God, and she's not slender because she's not tall enough…she's petite. It looks like Edie's head on Fenz body. I go to the next photo of Edie in the same outfit in the middle of a dance move. I see Edie and Fenz. I see today's Edie. I don't know what to say to her. "Well, I see you've always been stunning and beautiful," comes out.

"Aren't you something," she says. "Thank you." Edie blushes. "Have you seen the show?"

"Yes. Three times." I flip to a third photo…petite Edie with slender women. Edie is by far the best looking one.

"Did you like it?"

"Of course!"

"You want to guess—"

"Val."

"How—"

"I can just see you doing 'Dance Ten, Looks Three.'"

"How can you see that?" she says with a grin.

"You're spicy. Saucy. Sassy. I can hear you belting out 'Tits and ass.'"

"Presently, a lot of the latter." There's the pout face that always gets me.

"Don't worry, gorgeous," I say quickly. "You are doing…just fine." My hand touches hers. My gym shorts heat up.

"Oh, yeah?" she says, back to grinning, squeezing my hand. "Just how fine?"

"Oh, if I didn't have coffee breath, I'd sweep you into my arms."

She reaches to the bench for her Slim and takes a big draw. "Mason," she says seductively, "Kiss my ash tray."

And, I do just that.

The kiss is the most wonderfully exquisite thing that has ever happened to me. Trouble is, I'm in gym shorts…only. For two months, I've been able to will It, but right now, It has a mind of its own. I self-consciously back my hips away. She thrusts hers forward. Oh…hell.

"You're glad I'm here, aren't you," she says into my shoulder as we embrace.

"Sorry, it's so obvious."

"Very."

I clear my throat and raise my head. "Let's look at some more pictures."

"A man of restraint. I'm impressed," she says to my eyes.

"Patience is a virtue."

"Is that how you make money in the stock market? Patience?" She doesn't let go.

"Well…I guess, and luck."

"You're modest. And, you can look at more pictures only if we sit and you hold me with at least one of your arms."

I do just that, too. "Thanks. This is the program?"

"Yes."

The playbill flops open to her bio. "What a beautiful, beautiful head shot. Of course, that only makes sense."

"Thank you. I'm going to get there again."

"I thought you hated the road."

"No, there." She flips through a few more pages and shows me a photo of her without the denims. "There. Size four petite."

That's Fenz' dress size. "Oh—"

"I've started a diet. The Rotation Diet." She snuggles in. It's driving me wild.

"Is that where you eat every morsel of meat and fat around you until you smell like an organic chemistry lab?"

"That's the one."

"Doesn't sound like fun."

"Thirty pounds less sounds like fun. No, twenty-five. Okay, shoot the moon, thirty-five. I'm tired of looking like this."

I hold her more tightly. This moment will be looked upon as the pivotal point of our relationship. I'd better not screw it up. "Edie...you're a challenging woman in a sense that I'm running out of adjectives to describe just how gorgeous you are. You do what you have to do, do what is right for you, but...if it were up to me...well, you just don't know how I feel about you."

"Is it good?"

"It's great."

"How good?"

No, this moment will be looked upon as the pivotal point of our relationship. "Edie, I've fallen in love with you."

"That's pretty good," she says without missing a beat.

"I have. So, there." We savor it all. I sit, victorious. I sort of don't care if she says it back. No, that's bullshit. I don't care when she says it back. Actually, the sooner, the better. I do have that bargain with God.

"Love," she says. "So, you've just given me the perfect answer."

"What was the question?"

"How can I avoid snacking on pounds of pork rinds and beef jerky?"

That is truly funny. "See. I'm good for you," I say.

She puts her face *thisclose* to mine. "Of course you're good for me, Mr. Impress-Me-With-My-Research-Skills."

I don't move, except, well, you know..."I've always found the Dewey Decimal System a real turn-on."

"I've always wanted you on the research desk."

"Stop it before I think you're serious."

"Would you settle for half-serious?"

"Half-serious? That's the best offer I've had in a long while."

"Since August." The corners of her mouth turn up. Her eyes are laughing. She kisses me again. Sweet surrender.

"Now...what did happen in August?" I say. "Let's see...seems I've forgotten."

"What about your friend Cindy Claudia Crawford?"

"I told you. That's just business." My fingers softly find her cheeks. I bring her lips to mine and give her my best wet kiss. Edie moans.

"I'd better go before I stay," she says breathlessly.

"Can't your shopping wait a day?"

"A day? A day? You can do without me for a day?" She sits up in fake indignation. "I thought you said you love me!"

"Well...I do love you. So, let's start off again on Sunday evening and see what happens."

"I'll see you then. Call around noon?"

"You bet."

10:00 AM
Saturday October 17, 1987
In the condo, at the dining room table, writing in the journal, third Arn
Dow Jones Industrial Average: DOA

Journal entry: Saturday October 17, 1987

I'm drinking this morning because, after that encounter with Edie, I must keep everything down. I think it's going to happen with her. I think she's going to love me, and I must continue to save myself for her until she decides the time is right. Edie's the one for me, and I have to be a good man, except for the cigarettes. I've already smoked the one she so kindly left with me. I could lace up the Nikes and jog to the quick mart for a pack, but that would be ironic.

What I'd better do is act like a man whose financial assets totaling a million eight are in mercurial options. So, here's my take on things:

First, the numbers: The Dow fell ninety-one points last Tuesday, the day I was painting. With all that has happened to Wylie and my car and Christine and Claudia and Edie, that seems like forever ago. But, it's been only nine trading days. That was a record one-day slide. Since then, that record was broken twice, culminating with the one hundred eight point drop yesterday. More numbers: Sunday, I was talking with Edie at the library about last week's one hundred fifty eight point collapse. So, what do you call this week's two hundred thirty five point slam? Carnage? Come up with all the descriptive nouns you can, it's all bad. Or, good, if you're me.

The Dow's down eighteen percent since the time I proclaimed my intentions to John and the rest of the Fuller Busher douche bags in August, just a few days before I shorted. I subsequently covered, but with the puts I have found a way to make a hell of a lot more money. And, the risk was greatly reduced by the timing. The Dow's down some two hundred sixty points since I bought in. Four days. However, readers of these memoirs of my life, think not that I am a genius. Live by my second law of truth: I'd rather be lucky than good. Then, combine it with the first law – whatthefuck, I'd rather be lucky than good.

The volume of stocks involved in this collapse/carnage is astounding. Three hundred thirty eight million shares traded yesterday, by far a record. People with money? That's a lot of people in one day moving a hell of a lot of money. When you see volume of that magnitude swirling in a falling market, it's not a runaway truck, it's a convoy of runaway trucks piggybacked on a caravan of runaway freight trains. In other words, get the hell out of the way.

I caught Louis Rukeyser's *Wall $treet Week* on PBS last night. Each show he has three panelists and one guest. My main man Marty Zweig is a regular and last night was one of the panelists. I've been listening to The Zweig Forecast hotline for years. Marty has never been more on it. Dr. Zweig called it. He said last night he had been negative for some time but didn't want to call attention to himself. However, his newsletters record it: he's on it. All over it. I've used the words 'collapse' and 'carnage.' Marty's less literary and calls it a 'break,' meaning a significant decline in prices over a short term rather than a bear market that is spread over years. Last night, he said the action is reminiscent of 1946 and 1962, and in some ways (aghast!), 1929. These are times during which the meat of the decline took place in a matter of months. In 1962, the damage was done in two months; in 1929 (the horror!), ten weeks. Worse still, Marty thinks we are merely in the middle of the break.

Beer refill. I'll be back with my fourth Arn.

I'm back. Marty was not very encouraging for the other two panelists. Mary Farrell, a money manager and another regular, thinks this is not a 'crash.' 'Crash.' I didn't say it. She did. Anyway, Mary says it's a 'correction,' a financial term for an annoying extended drop in prices, after which the bull market is still on. Louis Holland, another money manager, took Mary a few steps further. He said the unpleasantness is ninety percent over, and that sometime between now and the end of first quarter 1988, we'll see substantially higher prices. So, you have an extreme negative, a reassuring words of wisdom, and a storms-be-damned-full-steam-ahead. Pick your poison. For me, a) two out of three of these folks are positive on higher prices, making the sentiment instrument flying indicators in my favor, b) interest rates spiked this week, so the monetary air is unsuitable for aircraft, again in my favor, and c) the momentum is the runaway trucks piggybacked on the runaway freight train, making all three essential components of market forecasting…in my favor. Besides, Marty says so.

Not to worry. I deserve a break. Maybe I'll start my sixth novel. Then again, maybe I'll enjoy the cloudy, ugly fall day and count the ways I'm going to improve my lifestyle with my winnings.

Thirty-Nine

4:30 PM
Sunday October 18, 1987 – the twenty-ninth Sunday in Roman Catholic ordinary time
In the condo, writing in the journal, no Arns
Dow Jones Industrial Average: render to Caesar that which is Caesar's

I called Edie at noon as I had promised. The conversation was on the sweet side of cursory, but I'll take it. It was so difficult all morning to avoid calling earlier. I stayed late after ten o'clock mass talking with anyone, just trying to kill time and keep myself away from the phone. It is a proven fact that all obsessive-compulsives are not stalkers, but all stalkers are obsessive-compulsive. I feel as if I live on that fine line, and the testimony of Joan's friend still freaks me out.

Anyway, Edie's coming over at five thirty. I have the beer. She'll call in the pizza. The condo is spotless, scented candles have been burning for a couple hours, and I'm not watching replacement NFL today so the action in the games doesn't fuel a hormonal fire that would be manifested in some sort of mating ritual. I'm extremely amorous, and I'm afraid of myself, afraid that I'll blow the evening by obsessing on sex with Edie. It's now hers to decide. She knows how I feel. She saw that yesterday morning. If I had some saltpeter, I'd take a dose right now.

Another fear I have: in our time together (a little over a month) the longest conversation we've had was about fifteen minutes in duration. Verbal stumbling was prevalent in others, while yesterday's visit was defined by the hard-on I carried in my gym shorts. In other words, she's been normal while I've had some sort of a blockish affliction through it all. Embarrassing, yet true.

What the hell will I talk about today? The market? That's dull as dirt. My PhD? There's something I haven't shared with her, although it may raise a few questions from her, like, 'You?' Previous marriages? Oh, that's really bright, just delve more deeply into past failures. Current events? What is this, high school civics? Football? Nope. Too much danger of boring her with that magical time of my life.

Face it, Mason, you just don't have a rap. Everyone knows you gotta have a rap to get the babes. This entire evening is going to suck, especially when I consider...love.

I'm sure that, as I re-examine it, I made a huge error in revealing my feelings of love so early. I mean, where the hell do you go from here? I love you...a lot...very much...immensely...enormously...with unbridled passion...in so many ways I can't possibly count them...like a rock? What does she think of me now? It's love already, look at the two of us, strangers in many ways? That may have worked for Karen Carpenter, but in reality after a few dozen days and a dozen encounters of the bland kind, only the...obsessed...profess love.

Joan may have given the money back to me, but as it turns out I indeed possess the traits of a stalker. All those visits to the library under the guise of a researcher...and you know Edie saw through it. It's simply amazing that she's coming over to the condo, for the second time, after being witness to my behavior. Maybe she's a big of a loser as I am. Two of the desperate joining forces, not the foundation for a healthy relationship, especially if you're among the co-dependent. Or, if not that, who of us will be the jerk and who will be the enabler? Okay, Dr. Bricker, back it off a couple notches. Look at the most probable reality: I'm pursuing Edie because Fenz turned me down flat and Edie's coming to me because she's a woman in her late thirties who thinks she has a wide ass and has therefore resigned herself to the fact that there are limited possibilities.

Thankfully, there are a few holes in that argument:

a) I'm a millionaire after taxes, and millionaires have more of a selection of women than non-millionaires. Case-in-point: I heard Ally's comment over the phone Friday. She had just counted my winnings; 'Call me.' I love her, but what a primo golddigger.

b) Edie is gorgeous, and I continue to raise the topic of the size of her fanny more often as my anxiety grows. So, if I simply calm down, I will realize again that in addition to her nice butt…there is the matter of those beautiful eyes staring into mine, as well as the juicy, full lips kissing me.

    c) Revisiting anxious…Edie has the ability to attract attention. Hypothesis: Greg was not back for money only. Edie said that to make me think just that, thereby making me second guess myself and raising her stock, then giving me two more things to think about: 1) handsome Greg in Edie's arms makes her so much more desirable, and 2) Greg came back for money from a low-salaried woman? Holy Hidden Assets, Batman! Just who is her money manager?

    d) All the above in c) worked like a charm on me.

    e) The fact that there is a d) makes me still more anxious.

    f) As I take a deep breath, I must get a grip on my emotions or this evening will be a fuckin' disaster.

    g) I need a beer.

Therefore, here's what I've come up with, something I call A Guide To The New Reality:

    a) You already told her you love her, so for God's sake don't say it again until she says it and means it.

    b) Act like you've been here before.

    c) Be yourself, but add a little debonair to the sauce, okay?

    d) If you go for sex with this woman, all you'll get is heartbreak.

    e) Pride plus Desire equals Champion works only on the gridiron. In this man/woman stuff, it's Pride plus Desire equals Dickhead. Keep your pride to yourself, let her desire roam, and you'll be a man of self respect.

    f) Most of e) doesn't make any goddamn sense.

    g) Make doubly sure you follow a).

    h) But, the most important one is b).

    i) Count your blessings that you don't have it as tough as Michael has it right now.

    My grandmother once told me that the most egregious sin a woman can commit is to tempt a priest. Apparently, one of Michael's friends has not conferred with my grandmother. He visited me not a minute after I got off the phone with Edie and told me of his plight in detail enough for me to get the general idea. The conversation went something like this:

Mason:	Has anything happened?
Father:	Well…
M:	Was it sex?
F:	No.
M:	Then, you're set. No worries.
F:	That's not the point. I was tempted. She looks like JoBeth

Williams from *The Big Chill.*

M:	Tempted. I can see why. Both ways.
F:	I've prayed a lot about this.
M:	That's good. Just don't overreact.
F:	I feel so…sick.
M:	Michael, you are so handsome and nice that you don't know how

many women you tempt. It's going to happen. And, it's not your fault.

F: I feel so bad for making her feel that way.
M: You want to know something ironic?
F: What.
M: God made her feel that way.
F: I guess—
M: God made you look like a black Roman god. God gave her the appreciation for good-looking men. Throw in that nice thing and a cupful of unattainable and you have to wonder why it doesn't happen more often.
F: How—
M: And, God stopped it in its tracks. He kept sex from happening. Thank God.
F: This isn't right.
M: Take a cue from Counseling 101. There is a big difference between feelings and actions. It's okay to feel.
F: I'm afraid of what could have happened.
M: But, it didn't.
F: What am I going to do?
M: Do you want to remain a priest?
F: Of course. No doubt.
M: Then, if you feel it again, don't do it, just like you didn't do it this time. Then, go to confession. Confession is the greatest thing. And, whatever happens, Michael?
F: Yes?
M: You'll always be my hero.
Michael broke down in tears.
I wish I could straighten out my life as well as I did his.

Forty

6:01 PM
Sunday October 18, 1987
At the condo
Dow Jones Industrial Average: I...forgot.

Edie is thirty-one minutes late. Am I freaked out more by that, or just merely by her? Just the general her. This...this...love I have been consumed by for over a month is rolling pretty damned hard down the tracks, and it scares me. So, I know what to do. If she stands me up, I have no other choice but to call Fenz and commiserate. She will see my blatant need for TLC and – one woman at a time, Brick, and truly, and you damned well know this to be true, Edie is that one woman. I know. Positive indicator: I've never scrubbed my bathrooms so hard, and never except for Edie would I have scrubbed them twice. Not for Christine or Joan. Within an hour. While wearing my herringbone blazer.

My hands smell like Lysol. Maybe I should do something about that. Too late. There's the bell. Fuck. I'm going to be sick. I walk to the door and open it.

Edie stands there holding a pizza box and a big purse. I'm not abandoned after all. My stomach feels better.

"Hello!" I say cheerily.

"Good evening!"

"How is it?"

"It's…for God's sake, let me in!" she says, "The pizza's getting cold!"

"For God's sake, come in!" I'm slightly embarrassed, stymied by her presence.

She enters, walking by me to lay the pizza box on my coffee table. Bending over is required to do that, and does she ever. If you think about it, the traditional fashion-fearing woman would frown on placing that butt, as nice as it is, into black leather pants. However, since Edie's picture is in the dictionary beside the word 'panache,' you have to go along. Besides, I like it.

"You know?" Edie asks, turning to me, catching me looking.

"What?"

"This is our fourth date."

"Four?"

"Thursday, Friday, Saturday, and today."

"That means you threw a beer in my face on our first date."

"But, we were in a bar together, and you could say we shared a couple."

"Okay, you win."

"Get used to it. You'll be saying that a lot." She reaches up on her toes to kiss my lips. That's sweet.

"I hate the word 'date,'" I say for no apparent reason.

"Me, too."

I finally notice her tight black long-sleeve cotton sweater. Heavenly Father, give me a break. "I prefer 'dah-tey,'" I say, trying to be witty and reel myself back to the matter at hand. It's not working.

"Dah-tey! I love that!" she exclaims.

"Dah-tey."

"So, how's this dah-tey going so far?"

"Great," I say, boldly, finally succumbing to my desires, conquering my fears, and taking her into my arms.

"It's the beginning of a wonderful relationship," she says to my face.

"You bet." We kiss softly. Ahhh…yes.

"You know it," she says.

"Monosyllabic, but, hey," I say. We kiss softly again. I gaze into her eyes.

"A wonderful relationship."

"How nice!"

Edie and I take the love seat. I lean toward her. She folds her legs under her fanny. "May I suggest a beer at this point of the dah-tey?" she says.

"Oh, of course. Sorry for my lack of manners. You're…you look…will I ever be able to…be cool around you…he asks."

"I hope not."

My heart flutters. "Beer." I stand to walk to the fridge to get two Arns. I return. "Is Iron City okay?"

"Is there any other?"

"No." We toast.

"Here's to breaking the rules," she says.

"Cheers," we say.

"Have some pizza."

I pull the coffee table to us and open the box. "No sweat," she says, "Let's just eat it from here. I'm starved." Edie scoops a slice from the pie and in one fell swoop places the tip in her mouth. I can't describe how erotic that is. "Here, Mason, you get one, too." I wake up and reach for a slice.

In mid-chew, I look into her deep brown eyes. I've been known to lose all reasoning at these junctures. Now, it's worse. I'll tell you how much worse. I have this overwhelming need to know more about Greg. This is one of those times that are indigenous to a guy, after which is the sound of a gun going off in his foot. Why, Mason? Why must you ruin things, putting them at jeopardy to feed your insecurity?

"Interestingly, E—uh, yeah, whew!" After that delayed reaction to the eyes… "Wow, this is a bad time to bring this up, but what about Greg?"

"Oh, he's just Greg," she says with nonchalance.

"He's really handsome."

"But, you're terminally cute, and that puts you way ahead," she says, right before she places her fingers on my chin and her full lips on my pizza mouth.

"Thank you," I squeak out. I hope that answers that question, you idiot.

"Now, before I flip head-over-heels for you," she says, "is there any reason why I shouldn't?"

"Reason?" Flip?

"Married. Gay."

"Divorced and straight, but there is one thing you should know."

"And, what's that?" she asks.

I'm going to sneak this in. "You're Point Park? I am Duquesne," I say proudly.

"Nifty! What did you study?"

"Writing."

"Oooo…doctorate, by chance?"

"How did you know?"

"Why else would you mention it…honey?"

I laugh at myself. "Damn, I thought it would have been my persona."

She giggles. "How did you get in the writing business?"

"Long story, so I'll keep it short. I have so much to say that no one can possibly listen to me."

She looks at me with suspicion. "I don't believe that. I'd listen." She smiles. I smile. "Anyway, with the PhD, why be a money manager?"

"Chasing the mean green."

"I do hope you're over that."

"Let me unwind these contracts and we'll see."

"Yeah," she says, pumping her fist. "Good luck with that. Gooo…library!"

"I'll take care of you. Yea, bookmobile!"

"Yes! Are you going to teach then?"

"I hope to."

"The coeds will love you. So much competition they will be," she says.

"Oh, really? Have you had a conversation with a coed recently?"

"Hmm...yeah. Everyday at the research desk."

"And?"

"They're not terribly bright, but there is the matter of those tight bodies," she says.

"Well, I like your body." I normally do not say things like that on a fourth date, but I've rarely been on a fourth date.

"Do you want to make out for a few minutes?"

I'm sure my jaw just hit the floor. "Uhh..." I emit, caught by surprise.

"A simple yes or no will suffice," she says, like she's negotiating a deal. Wherever this is going..."Well...then...yes."

A few minutes later.
Sunday October 18, 1987.
Making out on my love seat.
Dow Jones Industrial Average: Leave it.

Edie has wrapped her leg around mine as her bare foot caresses my knee. Talk about double trouble.

The pizza sits alone, nearly uneaten. Feeling the need to speak, I offer, "Sorry. I smell like Ly—"

"Shhh..." she kisses me big.

6:30 PM
Sunday October 18, 1987
Outside, in the dusk, sharing Arns and Virginia Slims
Dow Jones Industrial Average: If I unwind the puts early, maybe I can get Edie to take the afternoon off with me.

In a matter of a half-hour, I have determined that this Edie woman is more difficult to keep up with than I would have imagined. I don't know if I'm up to it. Good thing I started smoking again.

She takes a draw, then rests the cig on the bench. After digging in her purse, she produces two..."What the hell are those?" I ask.

"Breathalyzers," she says. "Like the cops use."

"Oh."

"I want to monitor how drunk we're going to get. Blow."

Under orders, I take the fist-size instrument and blow into the mouthpiece.

"Five seconds," she says. "Here, I'll do it, too." What I'd give to be her breathalyzer. We finish, one after the other.

"Point oh two," I say.

"Point oh four...let's see what the accompanying chart says...mild loss of inhibitions...yeah, that's me."

"Good," I say with a wink

"What are you 'gooding' for?" she asks with a shove. "I still have to wait, young man. Remember the cramps, the bloat? Anyway, there's something more important to talk about."

I'm amazed at how earthy Edie is with me on the subject of her menstruation. "Okay…"

She closes in on my face. "'Every audition," she says in familiar prose, "I mean, I'd dance rings around the other girls and find myself in the alley with the other rejects…'"

This is going to be wonderful! "Oh…yeah! It's *A Chorus Line*! Right in my backyard!"

"That's right, Dr. Bricker. You're getting a private performance from a national tour star. Stand back and enjoy it!"

"Go, baby!"

"As I was saying…'But after a while, I caught on. I mean, I had eyes. I saw what they were hiring. I also swiped my dance card once after an audition. And, on a scale of ten, they gave me for dance: ten. For looks: three.' Well…"

"Well?"

"Well…"

"Okay?"

"'Dance ten, looks three,'" she sings…and dances. "'And, I'm still on unemployment, dancing for my own enjoyment. That ain't it, kid. That ain't it, kid. Dance ten, looks three, is like to die. Left the theatre and called the doctor for my appointment to buy…tits and ass! Bought myself a fancy pair, tightened up the derriere. Did the nose with it, all that goes with it. Tits and ass…had the bingo-bongos done, suddenly, I'm on nash'nal tours! Tits and ass won't get you jobs, unless they're yours!'"

"You're hired! You're hired!"

"I accept employment," she says to me, squeezing in still closer than before.

"That was…completely out of this world."

"Thank you. That's just part of it," she says.

"Stupendous." I hold my open arms out.

"Tits and ass, my baby." Edie places them and the body attached to them in my arms.

"You are a remarkable singer," I barely say.

"Keep it coming…"

"A remarkable performer."

"You can stop now, but, don't."

"You are one fine woman."

"Now, that's what I wanted to hear," she says right after a kiss.

"No doubt," I say. We kiss again. The lip lock lasts a couple of days. She takes a breath. "You are so good for me."

"I'm good for you? Darling, the things you have done for me."

"Less than an hour into this dah-tey and it's…"

"Barry Manilow? Looks like we've made it?"

Her face twists. "That was gross, Mason."

"It's all I could think of. Manilow? Man, I've lost it."

We pause, holding on to the embrace. "Still, I hate the word 'date,'" she says.

"Yep, 'date' sounds like a point in time."

"Maybe most dates are just like that."

"Some are like this one, part of a continuum."

"Holy shit, Doc, we're too deep! Let's wait until, say, eight thirty before we delve into that."

"Agreed." We kiss.

"Deal." And another. What a happy day I'm having. I get so trite when I'm fulfilled…and it's getting worse. The cynicism is dissipating, at least until tomorrow. One cannot own a million eight in puts and be nice.

7:15 PM
Sunday October 18, 1987
In the condo, back on the love seat, turned to each other, holding hands.
Dow Jones Industrial Average: Could not care less.

Edie reaches to the coffee table where the breathalyzers are resting beside the pizza box. She grabs them, handing mine to me.

"Here," she says. "Blow."

I blow, hold, then release. "Point oh six."

"Point oh eight," she says.

"We're almost there."

"I am losing motor functions, it says here on the chart." She giggles a cute one.

"I want you to keep a few motor functions." I give her my best sly look.

"I am a child of the sixties," she says.

What? "Congratulations."

Edie slaps the back of my head. "No, assbutt, I'm making a point."

"Assbutt?"

"As a child of the sixties, I distrust corporations."

Don't argue. "I can see your point."

She unloads her fist into my shoulder. "No, listen—wha—you can?"

"The profit motive left unchecked is dangerous to everyone," I proclaim.

She smiles. "I want to say I'm surprised, but I know what's going on here. You're a drunk Republican trying to pick up a beautiful liberal."

"Transparent, I am always, but I'm only point oh six. And, darling, you are beautiful."

"You…are a sweetheart, and you obviously have a lot of money, you drunk Republican."

"Why is it so obvious, and I'm going to keep my promise to switch."

"It is obvious because you gave the library twenty-five smackers and you're damn straight you'll switch."

"Smackers?"

"What kind of car do you drive, rich boy?"

"I don't own a car."

"Everyone owns a car."

"I don't own a car."

"Why?"

"It's a long story."

"With you, everything is a long story," she says, smiling.

"You're ravishing," I say.

She jumps to her feet and juts her hands to her hips. "What happened to gorgeous?"

"I don't want you to think I'm easy."

"Well, do you know what I think?"

"Go ahead."

Our faces get close again. "I think...I am a child of the sixties," she says.

"And, I am a child of the seventies."

Closer..."I am socially responsible."

"I dig disco."

"I—you what?"

"No. I really, truly hate disco."

"I am really, truly socially responsible."

"I believe you."

"I have a little money that's invested with a socially-responsible investment company," she says with a smirk.

I knew it! A well-to-do liberal. "I thought you said you didn't know anything about money."

"That's why I have the company...sweetmeat."

"Okay. I can go with that."

"I thought you would," she says, leaping into my lap and kissing me.

Taking a deep breath, I want to speak. "I know something about socially-responsible investing. What are your issues, my darling?"

"Commitment to justice and a clean environment," she says proudly, remaining on my lap..

"So you avoid companies who pollute and/or fuck over people?"

"Oooo...I sense a non-believer."

"Answer this: who are the good guys?"

"What?"

"The companies you're invested in. The good guys. "

"Maytag, for one," she says.

"Socially-responsible washing machines?"

"Affirmative action programs."

"Oh."

"Doctor Doubt."

"Okay."

"Others: Knight-Ridder, the publisher, for women's opportunities; Fannie Mae helps out with housing for all; Sigma-Aldrich, the specialty chemical company—"

"Whoa right there! Chemicals! A polluter in our midst!"

"Not Sigma-Aldrich," she says, "Two more, assbutt: both because of equal opportunity, Apple Computer and Ryder Systems."

"Ryder rents trucks?"

"The one and only."

I'm most impressed. "Sounds like you have thought this through."

"Yes, I have. As I said: I...am...socially-responsible."

"You most certainly are. Who's the company?"

"Socially Responsible Investment Group."

"Hugh Kelley," I say.

"You know him?"

"No, I don't know him, but he was on *Wall $treet Week* last week. Socially Responsible Investment Group? What an ostentatious name, by the way."

"What's a Wall Street Week?" she asks, leaving my lap and wrapping her leg around mine. She smiles.

"Investment show on PBS," I barely get out, overcoming all odds. "Informative and entertaining. Another question."

"Yes?"

"Who are the bad guys?"

"IBM," she says definitively.

"Wow! Big Blue! What did they do?"

"They make too much money in South Africa. And defense."

"Hmm...One could say that, in addition to supporting an oppressive government, they are employing South Africans with good jobs."

"You have to draw the line somewhere," she says, squeezing my leg with hers. She is going to have to stop that.

"What are some other lines?"

"Tobacco."

"That's interesting," I say, in reference to her habit.

"I'm trying to quit," she whines.

"The last time you tried to quit, you threw a beer in my face."

Edie taps my cheek with a love slap. "Big chemicals are lines in the sand, too. DuPont and Union Carbide."

"The harder they fall."

"You get the picture?" she asks.

"I do. Now, allow me to raise some concerns."

The leg is pulled away. She sits up on the love seat and lounges back in the corner. "I'm ready," she says.

"About tobacco. You know that, among all stocks, tobacco was the top money-making sector last year."

"As I said, you have to draw the line somewhere."

"At the sacrifice of performance?"

"Don't sell out," she says.

"Even though RJ Reynolds and Philip Morris contribute significantly to their communities in the South?" I ask.

She crosses her arms under the boobs. "Hugh Kelley wrote in his annual report that he doesn't want to wake up one morning to discover one of his stocks is from a corporation that is paying for something really bad they did. No tobacco and no polluters and no companies who fuck over people."

I'm unfazed. "Okay, what if one of your socially-responsible companies has a big retirement plan that has an investment in RJ Reynolds? How would you feel about that?"

"I don't know," she says.

"I've stumped you."

"Then, kiss me." And, I do. Big and wet.

"I made a nice amount of money in tobacco stocks," I say after laying another on her.

"And, I still like you."

"That's good to know."

"Kiss me again."

"Yes, ma'am." And, I do. Soft and heartfelt.

"That was good."

"It will get better."

"I'm yours," she says.

"And, I'm yours."

We pause, looking at one another for the longest time. "You look like a man with a question about some topic concerning money," she says.

I nod, following her lead. "Well…back to socially-responsible investing—"

"Beating the dead horse…"

"What's so noble about not investing in the defense of our nation?"

"Well, Doctor I-Voted-For-Iran-Contra…"

"I'll never live that one down, will I."

"You still going to become a Democrat?"

"I've told you – yes."

"Then, I'll stay," she says.

"God bless you. And God bless the USA. Now, what's the deal with defense?"

Edie sits back slowly. "It's part of the dialogue. There are plenty of people like you standing up for defense. I'm taking the other side, saying 'Wait, now, let's think this through.' If more people would have done that, maybe illegal arms sales to one of our biggest adversaries wouldn't have happened."

I'm most impressed. "Good answer."

"It's the only one I have."

8:15 PM

Sunday October 18, 1987

Back outside the condo, burning two Virginia Slims and draining two beers in the dark, but only after blowing into our breathalyzers.

Dow Jones Industrial Average: Isn't Edie just gorgeous?

We're sitting on the bench on my patio near where we first kissed. I'll preserve the wood. What a romantic sucker I am.

"Point one for me," she slurs. "You?"

"Point oh eight."

"You're sandbagging to get me drunk and take advantage of me, aren't you."

"Uh…no." Uh…maybe.

"Bullshit."

"No, I want you to ask for it."

"Never," she says, "Until point one two. By the way, at point one five, I start begging."

"Have another," I urge.

She laughs. "I have the Woman's Curse, remember?"

"Th—oh. I forgot."

"First I bitch, then I cry, then I bitch more—"

"Then you throw a beer in a man's face."

"Will you ever get over that?" she asks, punching my arm "And, not just any man, but only you." She squeezes my tricep.

"I'm special?"

"Yes. Now, Special Man, tell me about your first marriage." She draws from her Slim.

"First? Try 'only.'" Do I really want to do this?

"Oh, no. Men always remarry, or become gay."

"Not me. Either way."

"So, tell me about your only marriage." She draws from my Slim. Well, that was nice...

Okay. "Okay, what do you want to know?"

"The basics. What's her name?"

"Joan."

"Joan d'Arc?"

"She had the balls of Joan d'Arc."

"Did that threaten you?"

"Ohhh, no. Quite the opposite. I love big brass stones in a woman," I say.

"Oh, yeah?" Edie smiles big.

"And seeing as how you are the definition of big brass stones, it only follows that..."

"That?" She smiles even bigger.

Don't tell her you love her. "That...we are together right now."

"About the ending...did she tell you or did you discover them in the shower?" She asks the most difficult questions. "No, she had the class to tell me."

"Well..." Edie's voice trails off.

Instantly, I hurt for her. "No, please don't tell me—"

"Yep."

"I am so sorry!" The pain! The lout!

"That's okay. It stung. But when I get stung, I sting back harder."

"And?" I ask, smiling.

"I had fair warning, so I took an instant photo of them glistening naked. I threatened to make copies and put them up at their law office."

"They were—"

"Ohhh, yeah. So, Greg, the staunch Republican, the epitome of corporate greed...Greg's ex-money, a lot of money, is invested like any good Democrat would invest money. It's socially responsible."

What a woman. "Uh-oh, Greg!"

"Cool, isn't it?" The smile is broad.

"Very. Question."

"Yes?"

"Why did you marry a staunch Republican?"

"I thought I could reform him," she says, "I like to hear the other side. Besides, he is very handsome and dashing."

Oh, yeah? "So handsome and dashing that..."

She slaps my chest. "I know. Three weeks ago, I sold out. Again. Even I compromise my—"

"Common sense?"

"I deserve that," she says.

I touch her hand and grin. "No, you don't. You don't deserve anything bad. You deserve good. By the way, I'm pretty good."

"At what?"

"Being a significant other."

She nods. "I've been thinking about that."

"And, your conclusion?" I ask, chin up.

"We shall see," she says.

"If you need to examine more evidence..."

"Yuck. That was so predictable...so..."

"Banal."

A smile. "Finally, there's a PhD word. Now, about this Joan d'Arc..."

"What about her?"

"What does she look like?"

"Victoria Principal."

Her face falls a bit. "Oooo...talk about a sell-out."

"Yep. You're right. A sell-out."

"August, perhaps?"

"It's all over my face, I guess."

"All over your face? Now, there's your kinky."

I smile big as I remember. Sometimes..."She was creative."

"That stings," Edie says.

Uh, oh. "You have no worries." I reach to her cheek and kiss her.

Edie acts disinterested. "Oh, yeah? Well, it takes two Victoria Principal asses to make one of mine."

Trying to get back to the place we were before I made the 'creative' remark, I decide to say, "We really haven't discussed the subject of your ass, now have we." On second thought, how in the hell is that going to help the cause, Brick?

"That's a topic to avoid." She gives it another draw, still upset.

"Oh, no. To the contrary. Recall yesterday morning?"

"Okay..." she says, on her way back.

"Your ass...awakened the sleeping giant...uh...sorry...I don't mean to imply..."

She laughs. "You guys are all alike. It's the motion of your ocean, Dr. Bricker."

I lean into her to kiss her. "I'd like to know where you got the notion."

"Fantasyland."

Hmmm..."Oh...really? Who's the fantasy man?" This is interesting.

"You, of course. What about you? How did you survive since August?"

Wow! I'm the 'it' guy! "I was okay until September."

"What happened then?"

"I met you."

"Ohhh…"

"However, I struck a deal with God."

"What was the deal?" she asks.

"No hanky-panky until you and I were together."

"None?"

"None whatsoever. All for you."

"A man, committed to his principles. Well, do me Tuesday," she says, planting a kiss on my cheek. "Mark it on your calendar."

"Okay!" I'm actually kind of scared, but I'll be there.

She snuggles in closely. "Looks like we will indeed fulfill each other's fantasies."

"Looks that way."

There is a long pause. The world is quiet. "I've never had a conversation like this," she says.

"First for me."

"It was nice."

"There's only one thing left to do," she says.

"What's that?"

"Blow."

We blow into our respective breathalyzers as we look into each other's eyes.

"Point one one," she says.

"Point oh nine."

"Two more Arns and I'm trashed."

"I'll take care of you." I gently place my arm around her shoulders.

"Give me two days," she says with the high beams on, "and I'll take care of you like you've never been taken care of before."

Uh…"You keep saying that."

Edie and I sit in contentment, holding hands. The past few moments have been most surreal. I don't know how I would have guessed the mid-game would have taken place, but it surely would not have been this. No arguments here. I'm flattered that she thought of me as she did, or even that she thought of me at all. All those lonely days and nights of doubt…wasted time.

9:00 PM

Sunday October 18, 1987

Back in the condo, lying on the sofa, Edie's head on my chest.

Dow Jones Industrial Average: Just over twelve hours and a million eight from opening, but miles away from my conscious mind.

"So, I'm point one one flat," she says.

"Point oh nine here. And counting."

"You're bigger. Not fair!"

"What's not fair? You're winning."

"Tits and ass," she says suddenly.

Someday I'll get used to her capricious nature. "I've noticed."

"You are a charmer." She kisses my lips.

"It's easy to be a charmer around you."

She bolts upright. "I say, tits…and ass."

Things stir. "I'm beginning to have the same reaction I did yesterday morning."

"Yeah," she says, "I have never been so flattered. Seriously."

"Happy to help."

"Tell me…" she says, remaining up on one elbow. We pause to drink. Gotta keep this buzz alive.

"Yes?"

"What's your 'tits and ass' story?"

I squint. "What are you talking about?"

She lays her head back down on my chest. "You know, mine being the national tour. That's my 'tits and ass' story. My big story. Everyone has a 'tits and ass' story. It's just that some are more interesting than others. A lot more interesting."

"I'm afraid—oh, I get it. My 'tits and ass' story. Yeah."

"I bet yours is a doozy."

"Maybe."

"Let's hear it," she says, settling in to listen.

"Well, it's like this: I played football for The University of West Virginia."

"Big fuckin' deal," she barks.

"By itself, that's no big deal, but one year the coach, our head coach, accepted a bribe to play a white guy quarterback instead of a black quarterback, who was a much better player. The coach was paid off by a rich racist. Well, a friend of my late father approached me with the evidence and asked me to leak it to the press. I did that, and—"

"You're him," Edie says, quickly interrupting.

"I'm who."

"You're the guy!"

"What guy?"

"You're the renegade!"

Ohh…ooo…"Oh…yeah, I guess I am."

"Oh…my God! I was back here then in between TV shows doing the weather for KDKA-TV. We heard about that and rushed down south that Sunday to find your ass."

"Who're 'we?'"

"Some girlfriends and I. Remember telling you I spent a night in Montani? We couldn't find you, so we just checked into a hotel room and got drunk."

"I'll be damned. I was in Vegas, a newlywed with Joan d'Arc."

"Well, too bad for you, because you could have had four attractive women."

"I don't know whether to count my blessings or be extremely frightened."

"I'd lean toward frightened," she says.

"Yeah, I guess."

"Man, that was such a hot thing to do. Talk about tugging at my liberal heartstrings." Edie runs the tips of her fingers down my sternum.

"It got better," I say, proudly.

"How is that possible?"

"After my new wife and I returned, Jesse Jackson visited me."

"Get outta here!"

"You like Jesse?" I ask.

"I—I like you. Yeah." Edie kisses my entire mouth.

"Oh, yeah?" I say, voice scratchy. "Well, I like you."

"I thought you said you love me," she says with a smile.

"Not only do I love you, but I like you. And, to finish the story, Joan liked Jesse and Jesse liked Joan."

"And, I want you."

"We—I—I—so—"

"I just love it, Mason! You always know when to stutter."

9:20 PM
Sunday October 18, 1987
In the condo, cuddled up on the manly brown love seat.
Dow Jones Industrial Average: collapsing under the weight of its self-importance

In my arms, Edie's drunk on my lap, sitting directly on—

"Did you go to mass today?" she asks.

Another interesting question. "Well…uh…yes."

"How was it?"

"Good. A good one."

"You ever been to a bad mass?"

"If I have, I wouldn't admit to it."

A pause. "I'm Jewish, you know," she says pointedly.

"Yes, you mentioned that."

"Does that present a problem?"

"No."

"Are you sure?" she asks.

"Absolutely sure."

"You don't sound sure."

"How can I get more sure than absolutely?"

"Just checking."

The fog I am in…"What I'm not sure of is why you are concerned if I am sure."

"Because…I'm…" she pulls out her breathalyzer, blows, and reads, "point one two. Blow yours."

I do. "Point one," I say.

"All right! Neither of us can regally—I mean legally drive!" She laughs so hard she rolls into the floor.

"That takes the pressure off."

"You don't own a car, anyway," she says, looking up to me.

"Nope."

"You going to tell me your long story?"

"It's totaled. My car rolled off the downtown levee into the Ohio."

"What was it doing on the levee, if I may ask?"

"I was taking photos." It makes more sense than 'I was paying a bookie.'

"You're a photographer?" she asks, still on the floor.

"I was. Now, all my equipment's at the bottom of the river."

We pause. Edie pulls herself back up to the love seat and gazes at me lovingly. "I don't want you to get hurt."

"Thank you. I don't want to get hurt, either."

"Into the river…no wonder you go to mass."

"That's one of the reasons. To keep from getting hurt."

"I want you to go to mass," she says.

"Okay." And…

"Sometimes, we Jewish people have a difficult time with you Catholics."

Oh…"That's understandable."

"Joke," she says.

"Shoot."

"How can you tell when a Jewish-American princess has an orgasm?"

I'll let Edie tell orgasm jokes all evening. "I…don't know."

"She drops her nail file."

I laugh hard, yet appropriately. "Good one!"

"God, I still cackle at that. You don't think it's funny, do you."

"It's hilarious."

"You didn't guffaw."

"Hell, yes, I did, but we Catholics sometimes don't know when to laugh at Jewish jokes."

"You know, Reagan really pisses me off," Edie suddenly says.

Keeping me guessing…"I know the feeling."

"Especially as a Jewish-American…princess."

"You're not a princess—I mean—"

Edie bolts upright and crosses her arms in the classic aggressive stance. "Oh…thanks. You don't think I'm a princess."

"Not with the bad connotation you gave it, no."

"I'm just busting your ass. However…what do you think of me?"

"I've told you. I love you."

"I know that. What do you think of me?"

I pause to consider. Taking her hand, and looking into her eyes, I have decided I should speak from my heart, because I don't know what the hell else to say. "I think…in the short time I've known you…and in our limited conversations, conversations with substance…and after tonight—"

"Get on with it," she slurs, "I'm drunk."

"I think you are a remarkable woman, a remarkable woman with whom I want to spend more and more time with and get to know even more and more so I can find out that you are more remarkable than I had ever dreamed."

"Thank you." She begins to weep.

"It's okay, Edie." I softly pull her to me and hold her in an embrace, a long, loving embrace.

"God," she says, padding the tears from her eyes and cheeks with the back of her hand. "I thought you just wanted to get in my pants."

"I do want to get in your pants. But, I maintain, you are remarkable."

"That's why I wore leather."

"Okay." Okay?

"Leather makes you want to get in my pants even more."

"That is correct."

"Damned period. Promise you'll wait for me." She almost pleads.

"Of course, darling! I'll wait for you."

"I don't want any other man." The crying continues. She *is* drunk.

"And I don't want any other woman." I'm trying to cry, but it's not working.

"Especially Claudia and Ally Fence?"

"Especially them."

"Blow." Edie juts the breathalyzer in my face. I comply.

"Hovering at point one," I say.

She blows hers. "Point one two. Drunken confessions."

"A truth serum for me."

"Me, too."

"You don't know how much this makes me happy," I say.

"Yes, I do."

We embrace again, holding on like the new lovers we are…or at least half of us.

"I hate Reagan," she says into my shoulder.

"Yeah." Right now, I'll say and listen to anything.

"Do you know who Yaroslav Stetsko is?"

"No."

"He's a big shot with the World Anti-Communist League. He's from The Ukraine."

"I know what the League is. This doesn't sound good."

"Reagan knows Stetsko," she says.

"That stands to reason."

"Reagan and Stetsko are friends."

"Anti-Communists. Makes sense."

"Stetsko was a Ukrainian officer early in the war who turned Nazi and presided over the slaughter of seven thousand Jews at Lvov."

I'm mortified. "Jesus, that's horrible!"

"My grandfather had a friend there."

In all my years, I've never been this close…to…I don't know what to say. "I'm sorry. I don't…know what to say."

"I'm sorry I brought it up. I'm a real party-pooper. I just wanted you to understand the kind of people Reagan has aligned himself with."

"That's a side many, too many, don't know," I say, still not knowing what to say.

"Motherfucker," she says.

We sit in reverence and reflection of the gravity of the events of that time. Edie's family was directly involved, and I could never be so far removed. The Roman Catholic guilt is powerful. I—

"Let's take the wet blanket off this party," she says, "I'm sorry. We don't have to talk about that any more. Can we still have fun?"

"Whatever you think is appropriate."

"I think it is appropriate to move on," she says.

"Then, I'll begin. So…your family…" Your segue ability sucks, Mason.

"France," she says, "Aix les Bains, in the French Alps."

"Ohhh…" Oooo…yeah….

"My grandparents are French. My parents are French. I was born in France. We moved to Pittsburgh when I was four."

"To the ethnically-diverse Pittsburgh." Edie is now officially *white* hot.

"How did you end up here?" she asks.

"Ashton Township is a place chosen randomly after the divorce. Except for most of college and the last few years, I was a lifelong West Virginian."

"So, you're from a foreign country, too."

"Ha, ha."

"How ya making it?" she asks. "The divorce, I mean."

"Great," I say with a huge grin. "I'm holding a woman who's wearing leather pants."

"'Pant' being the operative word." She kisses my face.

"Tell me about it." I wet-kiss her in return.

"It's been a long time since I've just made out with a guy."

"You're so beautiful, I'm sure you've missed some great opportunities."

"With a guy, that is." Edie turns to me, straight-faced. It is times as these that I am completely speechless.

"Oh," I emit.

"I'm just kidding," she says. "You ought to see the look on your face right now!" She laughs hard. I'm glad I made her happy.

"Edie, I don't care, really." Perhaps I'd like to watch it, but otherwise I don't care.

"You ever made out with a guy?" she asks.

For God's sake, man! Don't act indignant! "No, I can't say I have."

"You ever wanted to?"

"No."

"Then, I've never wanted to make out with a girl."

"That makes us sexually compatible."

Edie gives it the loudest laugh I've heard from her. "What did the priest talk about in mass today?" she asks, quickly calming.

Interesting question. "Render to God that which is God's."

"In a lesser sense, render to Caesar that which is Caesar's," she says.

"That's the parallel."

"Celibacy in the priesthood is so fuckin' asinine," she announces. "You do realize that priests did not have the vow of celibacy until the tenth century. Jesus did not decree it."

"I know." I know, and I know, and for Chrissake, I hear this once a week if I hear only one thing at all.

"Why are you so agreeable?"

Back to reality. "Because I want to get in your pants."

"And, you will."

"And, that will make 1987 the best year ever."

"What about your years with Victoria Principal? And, Claudia? And, Ally Fence? You've had so many good lookin' women. Do I have to worry about Victoria Principal?"

224

"No."
"I'm not buying it."

10:00 PM
Sunday October 18, 1987
Outside the condo, both of us smoking yet another Virginia Slim
Dow Jones Industrial Average: Tokyo has opened. We shall soon see.

"Do you think that now is the time for you and me to have a discussion on the subject of my butt?" she asks. I think she's serious.
"Uh…I'm up for that." Shock! Fear!
"If I weren't so flattered by that remark, I'd say 'Keep your powder dry, bud.'"
"Okay. With powder dry as dust, I'm up for that." And, just where is this one going?
"My butt has never been bigger."
"Well—"
"Really. This is the most I have ever weighed."
"Edie, you're—"
"And, half of it is in my ass."
"You—"
"I've got a lot of junk in my trunk, Mister Doctor."
"May I—"
"Do you really want a woman with a crankcase the size of mine?"
"Yes!"
"Give me one good reason."
"Uh…yesterday morning."
"Give me another good reason."
"Right now."
"Boo-tay, Mason."
"Exactly! Call it what it is."
"Boooo-tay!" she shouts.
"Your ass is so fine, I've been afraid to touch it."
"Touch it," she says with the burners up.
"Are you sure?" I ask meekly.
"Do it," she commands.
"Once I touch it, there will be no turning back."
"There already is no turning back for us, Bricker. We're on our way to the stars. We're going so fast, we've escaped our escape velocity."
"Wow!"
"I was president of the Rocket Club in junior high school."
"Well, you're not burning out your fuse up here alone."
"I'll give you a nine point five for timing," she says, "and a three for originality."
"Thank you. Now, where were we?"
"Mason."
"Yes?"
"Hold my butt."

"Gladly." I place a hand on the round leather. This is nice.

"Oooo…" she coos.

"Yes." This is fun.

"Caress my butt."

"Okay." I caress, yet another dream come true.

"That's nice."

"I love your butt," I say, right about the time I achieve full arousal.

"There is a lot to love."

"I love you."

"Don't stop," she says.

"I won't stop as long as you want me not to stop."

"Please hold on…until Tuesday. Will you do that for your Edie?"

"Of course."

"Hold on," she pleads.

"Yes."

"No one else."

"For as long as you want me."

"Not just a piece of ass, my lover, but the entire ass, and that's saying a lot."

I crack up laughing. "And, you—"

"Let's see…on the subject of men I want as my lover, there are a) you, and b) no one else on this planet."

This moment is fulfillment. "And…"

"Yes?" she asks.

"You, my dear, will get a belated birthday present."

"You remembered!" she squeals.

"Tomorrow, baby! October 19."

"And I'll be…"

"A day away."

"Oooo…I like that. There's only one thing better than being a day away," she says.

"What's that?"

Edie rolls on to me on the cold grass and straddles my hips. "Being on it."

I feel that familiar feeling. "Uhhh…we'd better talk about something else."

"Just don't stop stroking the fanny."

"Oooo-kay. I think I can handle that." I have my doubts.

"Seen any bad movies lately?" she asks.

"Oh, yes…*Baby Boom*."

"Oh, why did I sit through that?"

"I thought Diane Keaton and Sam Shepherd would eventually turn it into something."

"They did. They turned it into yuppie trash."

"Yuppie ad executive."

"Almost worse than a yuppie stockbroker," she says. Uh, oh.

"Or, a yuppie money manager," I counter.

"Not the money managers. Not you, sweetie. Any others?"

Note: steer away from yups. "*The Color Purple*," I say.

"You hate a critically-acclaimed movie? I'm impressed!"

"In that movie, in my opinion, no black man has one redeeming quality. They're portrayed as violent and sexually amoral."

"Goes against everything you fought for, right?"

"Yeah, but—"

"No 'buts.' You were brave. Brave excites me."

"Well…"

"You are something else indeed, Dr. Mason."

Just say it, Edie. Three little words. "What movie did you like?" I ask.

Broadcast News."

"Oh, nice."

"I felt so sorry for Albert Brooks' character. Holly Hunter sold out. I know. I sold out, too."

"I did, too."

"Now, I get handsome as well as kindness and talent."

"Same here…sweet thing."

"I'm handsome?" she asks with a smile.

"Yours are the most beautiful angel eyes I have ever seen."

"Mason! Will you listen to us? Lovestruck, we are."

"Yes. We'd better calm this down before Karen Carpenter comes back and…"

"Nahhh…nah, nah, nah…close to you," she sings.

"We can't get any closer than this."

"Ohhh, yes we can," she says, nuzzling my neck.

"Oh, yeah. Now, that's close."

"'Til Tuesday, my love?"

"Love?"

She pauses. "I want to tell you something, but to keep in its proper perspective, you must keep caressing my butt."

"Gladly." I do as she says.

"Here goes."

"Okay."

She looks hard into my eyes. "I think…I think…I love you."

In spite of the skyrockets going off in my head, I remain calm. "So, you think."

"That's right," she says, maintaining the same stare, "I think."

"You think, therefore you are," I say, looking for substance.

"That's not what that means."

"It made sense, though."

"What? Why?" she asks.

"It made sense. I'm point one one, and you're…"

"Point one three. Therefore, I am."

"Am what?"

"I am pretty goddamned drunk." Edie laughs and laughs.

I finally find room to speak. "How did you get here?" I ask.

"Mason, I drank at least seven beers in four hours. What do you mean how did I get here?"

"No, sweetie, how did you get to my condo?"

"I live just over the hill. On Bowhunter." This…could get to be a lot of fun.

"Oh, yeah? How long you been there?"

"A year."

"Why haven't I seen you at the pool?"

"Do you want to see this in a swimsuit?" she says, sweeping her hand down her body.

"Yes."

"Whoa. I like that, too." Her legs squeeze my hips.

That almost did it. "It is again time to change the subject."

"A little giddy, are we?" she asks with an evil grin.

"Yeah. Let's take this party inside," I say. And, we do.

On the sofa, Edie is on me, and my hand is on her butt. My back is damp from the nighttime moisture on the lawn. I look at her, lost in my love. "You've heard of the Dow Jones Industrial Average, have you?" I ask, rallying back with something innocuous.

She smiles. "I'm not as excited about it as you are, but, yes, I have heard of it."

"Now, how about – ah, good one, Edie – how about the Chinese philosophy Tao t-a-o Jones?"

"Dow? T-a-o? Pronounced 'dow?'" she asks.

"Yes. Tao. Like Lao Tsu. T-a-o."

"How now, Lao Tao," she says, giggling.

"Cut her off!" I say, laughing.

"Okay, what's the significance of the T-a-o Tao philosophy to Wall Street?" she asks, the skeptic.

"Taoism encourages intuitive thinking. On The Street, you have to use both sides of your brain, the logical left side and the intuitive right side. In this way, you have the best chance to make the best decisions."

"Compelling, yet reminiscent of bullshit."

"Works for me. The numbers find the opportunities and the intuition tells you whether or not it is so much garbage."

"Okay. How did the Tao t-a-o Jones help me buy the bookmobile?"

"In this case, it was purely intuitive. My investment partner—" Oh, shit, Mason, what an idiot you are!

"Just great!" Edie bolts upright and off my hips, immediately moving my hand from her fanny. Not that!

I'll try to explain the pragmatism of the whole deal. "Sorry, but she's in and I have to get her out just like I'm getting the library out and then she's out. Out of my life."

"I have a funny, intuitive feeling about her."

I scramble. "It's moot. I love you and only you. I said I'll wait until Tuesday…and…look, Edie, I've told my investment partner about you and—"

"She gave me her seal of approval."

"Well, yes."

"I'm so fucking honored."

Now, I'm in a panic. "There's…there's nothing more I can tell you except I love you. And, that's everything."

"You jerkass. Jerkass consorting with a woman like that."

"Like what? We didn't…"

"Didn't what?"

"We did not."

"Bought herself a fancy pair, tightened up her derriere. You jerkass." She's steaming.

"She's history, Edie."

"Does she have a name? Oh, wait, I know…her name is Claudia."

"Claudia is a page in my book of historical occurrences."

There is an excruciatingly long pause in our conversation. Mason, you *are* a total jerkass, whatever that is.

"You primo jerkass," she spits.

"I have to get her out."

"Yes," Edie interrupts quickly, "I would prefer that. I would prefer Claudia to be out of your life, like, last month. And I prefer you unwinding or whatever without seeing her."

I sigh, realizing that I have greatly overestimated the positive nature of my current position. Might as well tell a palatable version of the truth. "That's not possible." And, that's all I have to say before I say something inane.

This pause is longer than the previous pauses combined. "Rub my butt, you jerkass," she finally says.

"Gladly." Looks like I escaped this one…

"And don't for one minute think you have escaped this one."

"I love you."

"Jerkass."

I take a few silent and deep cleansing breaths. Edie sits near me to my left. "Is this a good time for your jerkass to ask you a question?"

Her arms are crossed and her face is pinched. "Go ahead, jerk."

"Were you really a Navy nurse in 1942?"

She relaxes. "I had a very vivid dream about that the night before I saw you at Green Boy's that next day."

"Was I in it?"

"Ohhh, you were in it."

"Sounds interesting."

"You were my patient."

"Ooo-kay!"

"If you're still giddy, I can't tell you what I did."

This woman does not stop. "Let's save it for later."

"Now, I have a question," she says.

"Go right ahead."

"Maybe in your overly heightened state I shouldn't ask it."

"Try me."

Edie reclaims her position on my hips. "What's the sexiest thing you've seen, besides me?"

"So, the second sexiest thing I've seen? I can answer that."

"Now, be original. Don't say, 'Claudia's tits,' or anything normal like that. In fact, if you mention Claudia, I will kick your ass. Or Fence. Or Joan d'Arc. Ass-kicking, I promise you." Edie has me by the neck. I think she's serious.

"They're not anywhere near what I'm thinking," I barely get out.

The squeeze remains. "So, what are you thinking?"

"I'm thinking since you asked the Q first, you give the first A."

"Fair enough."

"Be my guest."

"When some men are in their early to mid-twenties, their Levis hug their butts and are gloriously loose around the waist, with the fly button hanging a couple of inches below the navel. If that jeans-wearing young man is with no t-shirt and a buttondown oxford or something like that, and the young man leaves it unbuttoned, that is the sexiest thing I've ever seen, besides you."

I pause to think about how that would work in my favor at this stage of my life. "Wow. I can see it."

"Did you do it?"

"Yep."

"Now, I'm giddy," she says, pressing her…against…me.

"Excellent."

"Your turn," she says, still bringing the pressure.

"Women cellists."

"That…is original."

"Let me explain."

"No explanation necessary," she says.

I smirk.

"I still have my cello from high school," she says.

"I thought you were president of the Rocket Club?"

"When I play the strings for you, your rocket will glare red," she says into my neck.

"That almost did it."

Her lips are on my clavicle. "We'd better find some way to calm you down."

"Name it."

"I see a VCR. Do you have any movies?"

"A few."

"Something funny."

"*Trading Places*. Dan Ackroyd, Eddie Murphy…"

"Jamie Lee Curtis, jerkass."

"Anyway, let's watch it."

1:00 AM
Monday October 19, 1987
Standing arm-in-arm at the front door of Edie's condo.
Dow Jones Industrial Average: Tokyo's in the middle of it. London opens in a couple of hours. The wheels are in motion.

"That's always a funny movie," I say.

"Oh, hell, admit it, Mason. You just watch it to get to the part where Jamie Lee Curtis drops the blanket and displays her superb bingo-bongos."

"No, I don't."

"Yes, you do."

We fall silent, two drunks, leaning on each other in a loving embrace.

"What's going to happen tomorrow?" she asks.

"Well, tomorrow is today, birthday girl, and I'll buy you lunch, okay?'

"That's lovely, but I'm thinking about my bookmobile."

"Oh, I'm out early."

"So, how do you think the day will start?" she asks.

"Down, I hope."

"You hope? Hope? Tens of thousands are at stake, and you merely hope"?

"Chances are there will be an overreaction down."

"Chances?"

"Chances. Don't worry. That's the best I have to offer."

"Not from what I see." She caresses me through my Levis.

I sigh. I laugh. "Anyway, girlfriend, your money is as safe as where it stood on Friday after the close."

"So, I'm your girlfriend," she says.

"Absolutely. And, I'm your man?"

"Without a question."

"Superb!"

"I'm holding you to that lunch," she says.

"Okay, if you say."

"I say."

"Good night, Edie, my love."

"Good night, Mason, sweet Mason."

"Love ya!"

"That's nice." We laugh, which of course involves loss of balance.

"Call me," she says, recovering.

"Guaranteed."

"8-6-7-5-3-0-9."

"I know."

"Can you believe I have that number?" She cackles, surely waking the neighbors two streets over.

"Yes, I can."

"You're okay," she says.

"I love you, too."

"Call me first thing in the morning.'

"I will."

"Before your first cup of coffee," she says.

"You bet."

"But, after you gargle."

"You're nagging."

She giggles. "Good night." And with that, Edie spins, staggers, giggles again, inserts the key and turns it, opens the door, and makes her exit from the night by tripping into her living room. Beautiful.

Well, she said it once. She really has to be ripped.

Forty One

8:30 AM
Monday October 19, 1987
Leather-tongued in the dining room of the condo, writing in the journal
Dow Jones Industrial Average: 2,246 – 18.4 percent off all-time high

Entry: Hungover in Ashton Township

Water, coffee, more water, and stronger coffee…and aspirin. Joan and I used to get Coke slurpees from 7-11. That seemed to work, but my car remains at the bottom of the Ohio. No food. Food is bad. Need sleep, but there is the matter of the million eight. That's important now. The attractive brunette on CNN says that both the Tokyo and Hong Kong markets were hammered last night in response to our bad (or good if you're me) day on Friday. London and Paris and wherever they trade in West Germany are also hurting badly, and the day is not done in Europe.

Treasury secretary/executive cowboy James Baker met with his West German counterpart yesterday and told him that we would no longer support the dollar against the D-mark, hoping that would give us a short-term band-aid for our out-of-control trade deficit. However, this makes West German assets in the US, as well as any other foreigners' assets in the US, suck methane. They'll sell. They'll all sell. Good job, Baker. You think you did well, but you choked on a big one right when the markets are extremely frightened. I'll write my thank you note tomorrow.

Rawhide bombed an Iranian oil platform just an hour and a half ago in retaliation. Now, I'm happy with my Republican vote in '84. Thank you to you, too, Mr. President.

What a sweet day. And, today's Edie's birthday. Her…thirty-eighth? I've never asked, I've just done the algebra from that afternoon in the library. Oh my, I haven't gotten her a present. Maybe the boss bookmobile will be it, but that's too cold. What should I get her? It's just another thing to worry about today on a sweet day with a lot of worries. Should I get out at the opening and enjoy my life, or should I submit myself to blood-spitting stress and play it for all I can and exit later today, or should I just bury my head in the sand and the sun will come out tomorrow? I don't know about you, but if I mix metaphors like that again, I ought to have my degree disconferred. That's not even a word, but it still sounds more refined than 'discombobulated,' which, by the way, is a word and is, in a word, what the markets are right now.

There's the doorbell. I'd better answer it.

Walking to the door, I check the smell of my sweat shirt…uhhh, acceptable. Maybe it's Edie. I grab the knob, twist it, and open.

It is Edie. She stands before me wearing a Pirates ball cap on her bedhead and bunny slippers on her feet. She's draped in a comforter and carrying an overnight bag.

"Whatever you want, you've got it," I say with open arms.

"Don't kiss me," she says. "I have buffalo breath."

"I don't care if you had French fried garlic for breakfast, get in here."

She pads in, dropping her bag beside the television. I close the door and sweep her into my arms. We kiss passionately. She is right about the breath.

"There," she says into my eyes. "That will have to do, because I'm going back to bed. Your bed…if it's okay with you."

"Well, birthday babe, you're welcome to anything that's mine. Now, walk down the hallway, I'll tuck you in, and you get how much ever sleep you need." We do just that.

"What about you?" she asks with allure.

"I have to work."

"Well, no work for me. I called in for a vacation day. Sick would have been more accurate." Edie falls into my bed and curls up. I still haven't seen what's under that comforter.

"What time should I awaken you?"

"An hour. Give me another hour."

"Do you need anything else?"

"Yes, but the latest indications say that it's still Tuesday."

Damn. "I'll get you up," I say, reaching down to softly kiss her cheek. I turn to walk.

"Oh, Mason?" she says with her face in the pillow.

"Yes?"

"It's true."

"What."

"I love you. I love you when I'm drunk. I love you when I'm sober."

The market could jump five hundred points today and I now officially do not care. "That's good, Edie, because I love you, too."

"Now, get the hell out and let me sleep this one off," she says. I'm smiling.

9:00 AM
Monday October 19, 1987
In the condo, glued to CNN, with the journal.
Dow Jones Industrial Average: today…will be the revenge of the counterculture.

Entry: Market talk as my woman sleeps

The pride of Ted Turner is playing the market, The News of the Day. CNN has finally come around, lining up bears as the experts, with just enough bulls to keep them honest. One lady, Elaine Garzarelli, a sexy quantitative analyst from a major Wall Street investment house, said this morning she recently saw the bad market in a bad dream. I'm not making that up. It's difficult to believe, but at this point I'll hang on to anything. After her nocturnal admission, she said she made the recommendation to her firm's clients to be careful, which in Wall Street parlance means to head for the hills. Ms. Garzarelli then referred back to the August trade deficit announced two weeks ago as the beginning of the end. The Economists/Rocket Scientists of the Day were optimistically expecting a decline, but got a number that was worse than they wanted. Once again, my position has been confirmed by a good-looking woman. I'm locked and loaded.

9:30 AM
Monday October 19, 1987
Still with CNN and the journal
Dow Jones Industrial Average: showtime

Entry: More market talk

One pessimistic pundit after another looks back to the recent increase in West Germany's interest rates, and each one arrives at the same conclusion: James Baker has had enough, but he's making all the wrong moves. Secretary Baker, who for sport hunts rattlesnakes with a handgun, threatened a currency war this weekend by shaking his tail and making noise about driving the dollar down, in direct violation of the Louvre Accords. I think this is the same Louvre where earlier this year I saw Mona Lisa, but the agreement among the seven nations (including the US and West Germany) to keep their currencies stabilized is now so much smoke. As I've so eloquently written before only an hour ago, the lower dollar improves the trade deficit. Right now, short term, that is. The real problem with the trade deficit, in my humble opinion, is the fuckin' budget deficit and the inability of the GOP gung-ho-ists to get along with the Democratic doomsayers. However, today I am ecstatic that there is such a wrangle. Solve it later, but give me today. Give me today.

10:30 AM
Monday October 19, 1987
Still in the condo, still watching CNN
Dow Jones Industrial Average: 2,145 – down 99 today and 22.0 percent off the all-time high

There are thirty stocks in the Dow Jones Industrial Average. As of right now, eleven have not opened because of order imbalances, which means there are too many sellers and not enough buyers. If those silent eleven were to open immediately, the Dow would be lower than 2,145. Much lower. What that means is it sucks worse than it looks. I'd rather be lucky than good.

"What's going on?" Edie asks as she enters the living room. She's wearing my long West Virginia '88' jersey that used to belong to Joan, another part of the divorce settlement in my favor. Navy with silver trim, a rip in the shoulder, I wore it well. My new woman is doing better.

"It doesn't look good, except for you and your bookmobile," I say.

"Yeah. Claudia and I can get together and celebrate." She crosses her arms under her boobs and cocks her head back. Claudia…always right on the surface.

I've had it for her disdain for Claudia, but I think of what is under the jersey. "Edie, you need not concern yourself with Claudia. Claudia never meant anything to me, and you mean everything to me. Now, what does that mean to you?"

She ponders, or feigns pondering. "That means I want to meet this bitch and let her know where she stands."

I can't allow that to happen. "Edie, my love, have a seat here beside me." She does. We're on the sofa. I look to her. "You must realize the difference between you and Claudia." That…was a mistake to say that.

"Well, jerkass—"

"The difference between you and Claudia, or at least one of the differences, is you absolutely own my heart. The other difference is—"

"Is I'd better own your heart," she says with no spite at all. Edie crawls onto my lap. There is nothing on under the jersey except panties. I am aroused. You gotta love her.

11:45 AM
Monday October 19, 1987
In the condo, on the sofa, under Edie's comforter.
Dow Jones Industrial Average: 2,240 – up 95 points from thirty minutes ago, making it down six for the day. Yikes.

CNN is following no other news stories, devoting its airtime to the stock market. The latest rally has been quick and sharp…and hopefully fleeting. If I had any sense of risk, I'd close out. However, my sense of drama overrides. The rally won't get legs. Too many things are going against it. Besides, right now, I really don't care, because I'm completely naked under this comforter. Completely, along with Edie and her panties. There is no hanky panky, however. I'm just naked. I haven't had a look, just physical attachment, just two bodies together. Lots of laughter, lots of comments, lots of caress…

"Are you worried?" she asks.

"Oh, no, I figure I'm just as big as the next guy."

Edie giggles. "Okay, Mason, focus on my bookmobile. Can you?"

"I am able," I say, smiling.

"On the bookmobile. I'll repeat the question: are you worried?"

"No."

"Why not?"

"These turnarounds are so predictable," I say. "Momentum is decidedly down and down hard and has been for a few days, but there are actual people actually buying stocks right now thinking…no, not thinking…hoping that it's the right thing to do. It's like the sellers are giving the buyers enough rope to hang themselves."

"How do you know that's the wrong thing to do? Devil's advocate, of course."

"It's complicated, yet simple in its explanation in that you go with the odds. And right now, momentum has the odds."

"Well," Edie says to me…while almost completely naked, "there's only one thing to do."

"And, what's that?"

"Get dressed and go to lunch, my treat."

1:15 PM
Monday October 19, 1987
At Green Boy's. Edie's turning heads in her round gray V-neck and black slacks.
Dow Jones Industrial Average: 2,140 – 22.2 percent off all-time high and down over 100 points today.

Our tummies are more stable. Edie has a club and fries, I have a chicken sandwich and chips. Two draft Arms share our table. I've spilled a little on my Levis. Both of Green Boy's TVs have CNN on. And, all CNN keeps talking about is the stock market. My cellular telephone rings.

"Well, that's annoying," she says.

"I'll get it and get it over with," I say, as I grab the phone out of the bag and press the button. "Hello, this is Mason."

"Mason!" Fenz' voice says. "Where the hell have you been? The market's going crazy. I thought you'd call by now. Where are you? What are you doing? You've got a couple million—"

"Hello, Fenz," I say, not wanting her name to grace Edie's ears, but it could not be avoided. In one slash, Edie deftly grabs the phone from my hand and places it to her lovely face.

"Hello, Ally? This is Edie Marie, Mason's girlfriend?" There is silence. Her face is intent. Then, a grin, then, a smile. "Well, yes, I have acquiesced to my suitor. That means he is mine." More silence, more smiles, then a laugh. "We're at Green Boy's now, right across the street. I'd love to meet you, too." A pause. "Oh, I understand why they won't turn you loose. It's wild, isn't it." Another pause. "Let me check with the man." Edie pulls the phone away from her lips. "Ally has invited us over."

I can't take that right now. "Edie, honey, it's not like we're going over for cocktails. It's an office." I lean in and lower my voice. "It's an office which the last time I 'visited' I was fired and kicked out of. We can't just waltz—"

"We'll be there soon," Edie says into the phone. There is another pause. "Here, hon," she says to me as she hands me the phone. "Ally wants to talk with you."

Had I thought a couple of weeks ago that I'd be in the middle of a conversation between these two women… "Yes, Fenz."

"She is so sweet! Mason, what a catch!"

"Thank you."

"You'd better get over here. There's a rumor they are going to close the Exchange. The Dow's dropping as we speak. I don't know where you stand right now. I haven't had a chance to add it up. It's been way too crazy over here. I don't know what else to tell you except you are winning."

"I'm watching CNN, so I'll stay away for now. Anyway, closing the Exchange would be suicide. You think there is panic now…no one's going to close the Exchange. I can tell you this, I'm out today, sometime today. Wild shit is happening, and hogs get slaughtered. I'll figure out what to do and call you by three."

"Well, you may want to call Wylie. He's here."

"What?"

"And, guess who else is here?"

"Who?"

"Ronnie Miller."

"Corncob! No lie!"

"Yep," Fenz says, "The company plane back to Philly was diverted here. Mechanical problems. He needed some place to camp out for the day, so we are honored."

I know I'm smiling the biggest since under I was underneath the comforter. "Then, Edie and I will definitely be there."

"When?"

"Have Wylie call me. See you soon."

"Bye, honey," she says.

I press the button and place the phone back in the bag. "I agree. We'll visit. I want to show you off, anyway."

"Show me off? Little ol' me?" Edie leans her beautiful head across the table to me. I fall in love again.

"Yes. The black slacks will make them forget all about the fact that their stock market is collapsing."

She smiles and touches my hand. "Then, drink up."

2:15 PM
Monday October 19, 1987
At Green Boy's with Edie, Arn number three for each
Dow Jones Industrial Average: 1,948 – 29.2 percent off all-time high and down almost 300 points today.

We haven't moved, mesmerized by the beer. The image on the TV screen is also surreal. A pretty blonde CNN reporter in a gold dress and overcoat is interviewing an aging hippie in denim, who along with other aging hippies in denim has formed a protest line outside the New York Stock Exchange.

"What are you chanting?" Ms. Gold Dress asks.

"We are protesting Reaganism," says the hippie. "This market crash today is evident of what's wrong with the unbridled consumerism and capitalism that marks the decade of the eighties. Down with Reagan! Down with MBAs! Down with yuppies! The Eighties are over! The Eighties are over! The Eighties are over!"

My attention turns from the overly fervent graying longhair to where it should be. "Edie," I say, "what do you think of all this?"

"Were you at Woodstock?" she asks.

"No, I couldn't get a note from my parents, so I went to Boy Scout camp instead."

"A half million went to Woodstock, but millions say they were there," she says. "That's what I think of aging hippies. As for the market, you'd better get us out today."

"Why?"

"Lao Tsu, you Taoist, you."

The bag phone rings. Before I can move, Edie has answered it.

"Mason's office, Edie speaking." Silence. Who…is she talking to? Edie looks at me. "It's Claudia. I'll take it. Claudia! I'm Edie, Mason's woman." A pause. "I've heard a lot about you, too. Listen, I understand you and I are in the same watercraft here." Silence. "You're where?" Edie looks at me with an evil grin. She covers the phone with her hand. "Claudia is at Fuller Busher."

Holy fuck!

"Yes," Edie says into the telephone. "We'll be there shortly."

"Edie, I have to speak with Claudia."

"I'll allow you," she says. "Here." She hands me the phone.

I place it on my chin. "Claudia," I say.

"Hi, darling!"

"Hi."

"We're making a lot of money, Wylie says."

"You're with Wylie?"

"Yep, and he is so cute. This whole office is cute. They've been taking care of me all afternoon, even those grumps Ronnie and John."

"May I please speak with Wylie? And then I'll want to talk with you more."

"Heeeer's Wylie!" Claudia giggles.

"Mason!"

"Wylie?"

"I'm out. AMA, but after Friday's disaster, I had to work."

"Look, Wylie, I don't know about that, but—"

"Claudia used to be Christine, right?"

"I do remember that."

"Anyway," he says, "she is a beaut. It explains everything. Good job."

"Can I speak with her again?"

"No, she just stepped out. To The Café, I think."

Just not here. "It looks like I'll see you this afternoon," I say.

"And, I'm looking forward to it. And, it looks like I'll have to call you the winner on this one, Mason."

I pause, looking for the words. "I feel…not vindicated…lucky. I feel very fortunate."

"Want me to count it real fast?" Wylie offers.

"No. The Kenny Rogers factor weighs heavily."

"Then, I'll see you when you get here."

"It's nice to talk with you, Mac."

"You, too, Brick."

I hang up the bag phone, looking up to discover that Edie is looking at me. Lovingly. "CNN says the Dow's down three hundred thirty and sliding," she says.

I nod to the affirmative.

"Listen, Mason, I don't know how much money is involved here. It sounds like more than I have, and possibly much more than you had, just gathering from the motherfuck of the move. My point is," Edie takes this time to reach across the table and grab my hand. "My point is a lot of good can be done with a lot of money."

"I know. There's a lot of responsibility associated with this. Just to let you know…I can tell you this, since we're close and have sat around with no clothes on and stuff…I began today with a million eight hundred thousand. But, the strategy I used is so risky, I should not have stuck with it. In other words, I'm lucky."

"Well, you did stick, and the library's better off because of you, and Claudia's better off because of you, and ask her yourself, because here she is." She releases my hand.

Edie is peering over my shoulder at Claudia behind me. I turn to see her. She is…well, classic Claudia. Navy clinging sweater, tight denims, and slings. I've discovered Edie to be volatile, and I like that, but Claudia's always been cool, hopefully just enough to defuse any potential for a…you guessed it…cat fight.

"Hi, Edie, I'm Claudia Brown," she says as she takes a chair from another table and sits with us. "I can't believe I'm finally meeting you. I've heard so much about you."

"The pleasure is mine," Edie says, glancing at me, maintaining her greeting grin.

"So…you're in this, too," Claudia says to Edie. "I've always known Mason to share the wealth."

Edie looks at me again, this time with a relaxed face. "Yeah, he's some guy," Edie says, reaching for my hand again.

"This is so sweet!" Claudia exclaims. "Now, you take good care of my friend Mason Bricker," she says to Edie. "And, Mason," she says, turning to me, "you take care of Edie and the bundle. Do what you have to do, call me, and we'll arrange a way to get me the money. Do you think it will be today?"

"Almost guaranteed," I say. "I'll call."

"Or, I'll call," says Edie.

"Well, have to get my daughter from school." Claudia stands. "Bye, folks. I hope to see you again, Edie."

"Same here, Claudia."

Claudia turns and walks. I do not watch the event.

"How can a woman look like that after childbirth?" Edie asks. She's fishing around in her purse, then produces a pack of Virginia Slims and a lighter. She lights two and hands mine to me. I'm glad she's fiddling with all this because it gives me an opportunity to think of something to say that's not insensate.

"I've never really thought about it."

"Oh, fuck you, Bricker, sure you've thought about it." Edie pulls on the Slim like a vacuum hose.

"Claudia is – was – a long time client."

"It's going to be difficult to get a long time client out of your life."

"No, it's not. I'm going to call her with the results, give her the money, then I think we'll mutually call it a game."

Edie takes another puff. "Good."

I want to extract the same from her concerning Greg, but that's an incredibly foolish and petty idea.

3:15 PM
Monday October 19, 1987
On the elevator with Edie headed for the seventh floor of The H.
Dow Jones Industrial Average: around 1,900 – about 30 percent off all-time high and down around 350 points today.

The bell dings, the doors open, and there's the familiar logo of Fuller Busher with the gold foot-tall Times New Roman font letters against the gray walls.

"And, we're underway," I say.

"You're funny," Edie says.

We step out and turn left toward the open double doors. My gut is churning. I reach inside my herringbone blazer to rub it. Why am I upset? I am winning, after all.

The first person we see as we walk in is, thankfully, Fenz. She's in a navy suit with white hose, looking fine.

"Good afternoon!" she says. Fenz glances at me, but immediately turns her attention to Edie. "Edie," she says, "I'm Ally," and they embrace. "Congratulations on getting together, you two! I'm so happy for you!"

"Thank you, Ally." Edie fakes exasperation. "I guess it will be okay." Fenz laughs appropriately.

Wylie steps out of his office and walks up to me briskly. I haven't seen him since our cryfest Friday, but it all seems the same as before. Same affable Wylie. Same charcoal gray suit, white shirt, and red paisley tie. Same ol' stuff, different week, just like last week didn't happen. Nominal. Nominal Wylie working in a nominal office with nominal people, so nominal that they all probably think that today is just another bad dream that will just go away. I know these guys. They know this market crash is but a blip on their commission screens, like how do we make money off this. You know? I don't care how they act, just as long as my man repays me the fifty.

"Here," Wylie whispers, slipping me an envelope behind my back. It's probably the fifty. Where the fuck did he get it? "Hi. I'm Wylie McInally," he says to Edie, "You must be…"

"Edie Marie. Nice to meet you, Wylie.'

"Just had Claudia up here," he says. "She was a real diversion from this totally awful market. A real, live diversion. Can I get you two coffee?"

Only, 'Gee, Mason, just how was it to screw Claudia every Monday for five years?' could have been worse. "No coffee here. Edie?"

"Oh, Mason, you know me and liquids in containers. I think I'll pass."

Wylie laughs. Fenz looks confused."

"Brick, what are you going to do, buddy?" Wylie asks suddenly.

"I'm out today." I say.

"Well, we have about forty minutes left in today," he says. "Let's get to work writing tickets. Ally? Will you join us?"

"Why, certainly," she says.

The four of us head for the conference room. I open the door to discover Corncob standing, dressed in a power suit, in the middle of an intense conversation on the telephone. I thought I heard, 'It's going to stop right here, turn around, and not be that bad.' I'm sure I heard that. Corncob never surprises me. In fact, the only thing about Corncob that surprises me is the enormity of his head and the ears that are attached to it.

"Let's go somewhere else," Wylie whispers. "My office, perhaps?" We turn and walk that way.

Edie is staying near my side. I hope she's not uncomfortable here, but I can't worry about that. She and I have been playing around all day, but now it is time to do some serious work. There are forty minutes remaining, but I have only a half-hour to map out this strategy and execute it. And, I don't really know how to do it.

We enter Wylie's office. "Here, Dr. Bricker," he says, motioning me behind his desk. "You've got the pilot's seat." I take it, not thinking too much about the pomp with which it was offered to me. There is no time for that extraneous stuff. What the hell am I going to do?

"Mason," Wylie says, taking the seat beside his desk, "what do you want to do?"

Fenz is looking at me. She's got a stack of yellow 'SELL' tickets that she is already flipping through, entering my account number on each one. "Sorry, Mason, I don't mean to rush you, but there are twenty-one tickets to write and the time is three twenty five."

"In fact, it's too late to enter tickets by wire," Wylie says. "We're going to have to phone it in directly to the trading desk in Philly."

Fenz grabs Wylie's phone and punches in a four-digit number from memory. I check Edie just when she's checking me. We smile. She winks. My stress is reduced.

"C'mon, Mason. I have trading on the line," Fenz says. "What do I do?"

The stress is back. I still don't know. Now, I don't know about today. How will we close today? What's going to happen tomorrow? Do I want to sleep with all this again tonight after the chaos we witnessed? If I sell now and I continue to be right, how much money will I leave on the table? If I don't sell now and Corncob's right, will I choke and hold on to my losses to the bitter end?

"They have better things to do than to be put on hold, my man," says Wylie.

"Put them on speaker," I say. Fenz hits the button and rests the phone in the cradle.

"Okay," Wylie says, "You're on speaker and I have my client with me. And, Timmy, he's not just any client."

"Okay," the voice on the phone says. It is Timmy. Timmy the Trader, I used to call him. Gee, I hope he's not pissed off about that right now.

"Timmy," I say. "It's Mason. Mason Bricker."

"Holy hell! I thought John had you run out of town. How ya been, partner?"

"I—" I want to say 'I'm ready,' but...

"Mason, sweetness," Edie says as she reaches for my hand. We look directly into one another's eyes. "The new bookmobile already has a hot tub, a DJ, a wet bar, a crystal chandelier, and one of those disco balls hanging from the ceiling. I think that's enough." She air kisses me. I get the message.

"Okay, Timmy, let's do it."

"Man, I have your account right here with the positions you want to unwind. You're a legend with a big swinging dick. It will be an honor to sell these puts for you."

"Thanks, man. Do what's best. Just close me out before the end of the day."

"You got it, brother," he says. The light on the phone goes dead.

We take deep breaths. I look to Edie. She raises her elbow, dangles her arm, and swings it.

"It's metaphorical," I say. Fenz covers her face as Wylie flips through papers.

We sit in silence as an occasional person walks by. Some wave in a friendly fashion, others barely acknowledge me. I wasn't a favorite around here, especially with the brokers. Todd walks up and peers his head in the door. "Hey, Wylie, who was the supermodel?"

"A friend of—a friend of a friend. A client," he says.

"Nice…real nice," Todd says, and strolls on.

There's a break in the action. I think of last week and I still don't know what to say to him. "How's Geri?" I ask. That seems calm enough.

"She's doing well, thank you. She sends her best. Geri is my wife, Edie, and she's very successful in real estate. She plans on closing on five houses this week alone, and did seven last week. And, this is the slow season." Wylie's proud, and in denial.

"Well, I'm sure you're proud," Edie says. "Real estate is pretty lucrative around here in AT. I thought about it once, you know, becoming an agent. I just don't have the drive your wife does. I'd spend too much time taking the afternoon off." We laugh. Since I haven't told her about last week, she doesn't make any connection. Wylie and his ordeal was such a bummer, I just didn't want to spoil the moments with her. Hell, Fenz and I haven't talked about it.

More conversational lull. "Is the football strike over? What are the odds that would have happened?" Edie asks. Uh-oh. "How have the Steelers done during the strike? They're either one and two or two and one. My man here used to play football." She pats me on the knee.

"Not with the Steelers," I say. "They would have broken me in half." Fenz giggles. The phone buzzes. Ally hits the speaker hands-free button.

"Yes?" Wylie says.

"Trading on two," a voice says.

Fenz hits line two. "Wylie's office."

"Is Mason nearby?" It's Timmy.

"Gotcha, Timmy," I say. My gut tightens.

"The market's dropping five points a minute. The Dow's near eighteen hundred. It looks like mutual funds are bailing out," Timmy says.

"Suggestion?" I ask.

"Just to double check: do I have the discretion to get as much as I can and get you out today?"

"You got it," I say. "May the force be with you, Timmy." The line two light goes off.

It's funny that during this nice conversation, we've ignored the collapsing market. As we're silent, I watch the 'DJIA' on Wylie's Quotron green screen to see the numbers change at an alarming rate, and they're going deeper into the minus territory.

Jason walks up. "Hi, Mason. Hi," he says to Edie. "I'm Jason."

"Nice to meet you, Jason. I'm Edie."

"You know, Jason, Mason, it was pretty confusing while he was here," Jason says.

"'Confusing' is the most accurate word you can use to describe it," I say. Wylie laughs.

"This market sucks," Jason says. "My clients are losing their ass."

"Don't you think you should do something about it?" Edie asks.

"Nah. Ronnie Miller says it will stop and be back to this summer's levels sometime soon," he says.

"Who's Ronnie Miller?" she asks.

"He was the guy in the conference room frantically on the telephone," I say.

"Ohhh," Edie says. "He needs to calm down. Maybe some aroma therapy." I laugh. Fenz laughs, too. Jason and Wylie draw a blank.

Wylie's phone buzzes again. Fenz picks it up. "Thanks," she says, and she punches the flashing line three button.

"Yes?" Wylie says.

"Mason, it's Timmy. We've got ten minutes left and the executions are dribbling in. We're busy here, so if you don't mind, I'm going to wait for all of them and shout them down over the squawk box."

I laugh. "The squawk box, eh? For everyone to hear?"

"It'll be like your victory lap," Timmy says.

"Well, that's appealing," I say.

"I thought you'd like it," he says.

"Yeah, nice touch," Wylie says. I look at him in shock. He looks back and shrugs his shoulders, like 'what can I say?'

4:30PM
Monday October 19, 1987
Still in Wylie's office, with Edie returning from Green Boy's with the beer
Dow Jones Industrial Average: 1,738 – off 36.8 percent from all-time high achieved just two short months ago, and down 508 points for the day

Wylie, Fenz, Edie, and I have cracked open our first ones of what could be several. Timmy hasn't squawked yet.

"I'm getting nervous," I say.

"C'mon, Mason, what's the worst thing that could happen right now?" Fenz asks.

"The worst thing that could happen right now is if key executions of mine didn't go through before the close. That means I'd have to sleep on it another night, and after this black hole of a market, and with the distinct possibility that Corncob could be right from here on, I wouldn't sleep much."

Edie looks at me and smiles. I know what she wants to say, but Fenz and Wylie are here, and here come Jason and Todd.

Jason and Todd and Wylie are dressed alike, if not the same. Six of us are now in Wylie's office, with the three of them standing, all with hands in their pockets like used car salesmen awaiting their quarry.

"You made a lot of money, didn't you, Mason?" Jason asks.

"I don't know. Timmy hasn't gotten back to us yet."

"Well," Todd says. "so you did it this time. But, your strategies won't work again."

"Todd—" and Edie stops me by laying her arm out over my chest.

"Who's your babe?" Todd says to me.

"Todd, this is Edie. Edie, Todd."

"It's a pleasure, Todd," Edie says.

"Edie, if you ever get tired of Bricker here," Todd says, "call me."

"Call you what?" Edie asks.

"Call it what you like."

I try to jump up again, and Edie does the arm thing again. "I can take care of myself, baby," she says to me.

"Baby," Todd says to me, "if it was up to me, you'd be out of this office, again."

"It's not up to you," John voice says from the doorway to Wylie's digs. "It's up to me. And, I say he stays as long as he needs us."

I rise to see John. Corncob is with him. "Well, John, thank you for the welcome mat. And, it's getting crowded here in Wylie's office, so let's go to Green Boy's. I'm buying." Why not?

"I don't drink," says Corncob, the cold-shower son-of-a-bitch. "And, I have to deliver my market summary address to the firm in one minute. It will be the most important speech I've ever given." A real son-of-a-bitch.

We all look at the floor and nod accordingly to the affirmative. "So, you're going to use our squawk box phone to squawk – I mean, address everyone?" I ask.

"Yes, the Ashton Township office of Fuller Busher will originate my call."

What? What does that mean, and who the fuck are you, Corncob? "But Co—Ronnie, I'm expecting a call."

"After mine," he says. "All brokers and analysts and traders need to hear my remarks."

I motion toward the conference room. "Mr. Miller, be my guest." Your subjects await, you geek.

4:45 PM
Monday October 19, 1987
In the conference room, witnessing history – how will Corncob dance out of this one? Dow Jones Industrial Average: 1,738 – off 36.8 percent of all-time high…kind of rolls off your tongue, doesn't it?

The squawk box has been moved from its altar to the middle of the conference room table, skewed some toward Corncob. The men sit on Corncob's left. The ladies and I sit to his right. Edie is to my right. We're playing footsie.

Corncob tightens his red paisley tie around his white shirt collar. He tugs at the lapels of his charcoal gray suit, then nods to Fenz, whose job it is to dial the telephone for him. Jeez Louise!

Edie turns to me. "Is this our finest hour, or what?" I can barely contain myself.

Claudia walks in. Just out of the blue, still in the navy boob sweater and denims. Her timing is exceeded only by her theater. She's also not one for protocol, but I guess she doesn't have to be. On cue, the men's eyes go bugged. I'm used to her. Edie grabs my wrist. "I just thought to mention," she whispers, "today is now officially Tuesday."

"No, it's Mon—ohhhh…" Oooo… "Well, darling, how about in Wylie's office?"

Edie snickers. "Don't you think we're attracting enough attention already?"

"Claudia, have a seat with us," Edie says, smiling at me. Fenz stands up and moves a chair for Claudia between her and Edie.

"Testing," Corncob predictably says. "Testing."

"Had I known there was going to be a test," I whisper to Edie, "I would have studied."

"Shh," she says, smiling.

The Cobster clears his throat. "Good afternoon. This is Ronnie Miller. Our markets took a blow today, but it was far from fatal. Far, and far away from fatal. From this day and forever more, we will live and prosper. In fact, I am proud of each and every associate of mine with Fuller Busher for the way they professionally comported themselves in very trying circumstances. I spent the day at our Ashton Township offices near Pittsburgh. John Findlay is the resident manager and captain of this tight ship, Wylie McInally is the top producer here and among the top five in our firm, and Todd O'Reilly and Jason Beckham are the up-and-coming rookies, and who can forget the contributions of the lovely Ally Fenz. Ladies and gentlemen, these people and all you people out there are the reasons why we will indeed live and prosper. I have confidence in the financial markets of the world, but especially in the markets and the economy of our great nation founded two hundred eleven years ago. Now is the time when it is critical that common sense prevails, and America's economic system is the strongest in the world and remains fundamentally sound. Now, go out there and tell your clients that the equities of the strongest economic system in the world are bargains. Go for it."

He's finished. It was all there. Patriotism, optimism, love for country, respect for the flag…everything platitudes, skillfully omitting market and economic analysis. That's my Corncob.

Fenz clicks the phone light off. I quickly scan the room, gauging everyone's faces. John has no choice but to be with the program. Nor does Wylie, since he needs fifty thousand PDQ. Todd is nodding and has thrown his hat into the ring. Jason is interesting…he looks slightly puzzled, almost bewildered.

I turn to our side of the table. Fenz is the good company woman. She knows who feeds her fashion budget. Claudia has by far the best poker face I've seen, but I bet she is thinking Corncob has just unloaded a scow full of beach litter. And, Edie? She looks the same, like a gorgeous woman who has something to say.

"Well, Mr. Miller," she says to Corncob, "I want to party with you, big man!"

My head reflexively flops onto the table. I twitch a couple of times in silent laughter, gaining control only after feeling Edie's hand on my back. Looking up, I see that Jason is still puzzled, Todd is still cocky, and John and Wylie still run the show, while Corncob still has the glow from his magnificent performance.

Now, I'm pissed.

"Ronnie," I say to him, "first, it's 'live long and prosper.' Second, you and I agree on this market, that is, the market as it stands right now. There are yard sale bargains out there, and some good companies, too. Two months ago, IBM was selling for twenty-four times earnings. Now, you can pick up a buck of Big Blue profits for twelve dollars, half the price it was when the weather was hot. Problem is, you were buying all the way up there and all the way down to down here. Presently, you're making the right call, in my opinion, but you've lost your credibility. How can anyone who bought your General Motors recommendation on August twenty-fifth follow your advice tomorrow? 'If you liked it at seventy-five, you'll love it at sixty!' That's the way you think. And, you're right about one thing. The blow is not fatal. The economy will survive, with the FDIC and a wise Federal Reserve and a hot, deficit-driven engine running things. But, Ronnie, the markets will suck for a while, months, a year maybe, until all those who were told to hold on through the worst single day in financial history get the courage to go back in there, where, and you and I agree once again, where they belong right now. It's going to take some time, but I don't know if you have the time for three reasons: a) this is a transaction-based business and the transactions are not going to be there anywhere near the levels of August, b) you guys are going to starve waiting, and c) you, Mr. Corncob, don't have the capacity to understand how you got here."

Corncob leaps from his chair, flinging himself prostrate on the conference room table. With teeth clenched and bare, he slithers like a snake toward me, jabbing his hand at my throat, for Chrissake! I rock back reflexively, wide-eyed, I am sure, just like everyone else who is witnessing this spectacle, except Edie, who jumps on Corncob's head like she's protecting us from the explosion of a hand grenade.

"Wylie," says a voice in the squawk box. We freeze. It has to be Timmy. Please, let it be Timmy.

"Yes?" says Wylie.

"Tell your client he's the six million dollar man."

Claudia and Edie turn to each other. Edie extracts herself from Corncob's face and jumps into Claudia's arms. The ladies vault up and hug, and jump, and scream, and squeal, and hug more. That alone is worth waking up this morning.

The ladies calm down. I know Fenz wanted to be in there, but we men couldn't have taken that without some serious wear on our cardiovascular system. Edie sits in her chair, and Claudia follows, in her chair, of course. We're all silent. Silence. I've discovered that's when my new woman and love of my life always opens her mouth.

"What can you say?" Edie asks Corncob, "Nothing succeeds like success!"

Forty Two

1:00 PM
Friday October 23, 1987, the fifth Tuesday of the week
With Edie at Jim Morrison's tomb, Cimetriere du Pere les Chaise, Paris, France
Dow Jones Industrial Average: it'll wait

Dead people are buried all over each other here. Shoulder to shoulder, knee to knee. There is barely room for the proper placement of the bust of The Lizard King, but here it is on his tomb, with the perquisite cigarette hanging from its mouth.

The day is cloudy and blustery. An occasional sprinkle fans through the air. What a perfect day, and a perfect place, for yet another victory picnic, one of nearly a half-dozen we've had since we arrived in France Wednesday.

"What wine was that?" Edie asks, pointing to the drained bottle.

"It's our third, the pinot noir we bought at the wine market down the *rue* from the fruit market beside where you got the croissants we had mid-morning in the hotel lobby when that cute French couple had a domestic quarrel."

"Quarrel, my ass, that was a fight," she says, "and no, I thought it was the pinot noir you picked up on the boulevard two blocks away from Champs d'Elysses where you nearly walked into a tree gawking at the woman, until we got close enough to discover she hadn't bathed nor shaved recently."

"I did not gawk."

"But, I'm right. She hadn't gotten anywhere near soap for awhile. Imagine—"

"That's stereotypical bullshit, but I really could never be French."

"Great place to visit and forget about it all for a while, though," she says. Edie then takes this opportunity to weave around Jim and kiss me. That's a nearly a dozen kisses a picnic over a nearly a half-dozen picnics. I'm on a streak.

"Yeah," is all I can say.

There is a pause in the conversation. Edie takes a breath in anticipation of saying something. "Can we talk business for a minute?" she asks.

"If you insist."

"I know you've been trying to avoid the topic since—"

"Since Monday suddenly became Tuesday—"

"And the calendar has not advanced…and why should it?" she asks with a flame.

"I like Tuesday," I say. "I could do Tuesday all month."

"Ohhh, yes," she says, snuggling in. There is a pause in conversation for a few moments. "Now, answer this," Edie says. "are you really going to do that with all that money?"

"Yes," I say definitively.

She reaches for my hand as only Edie can. "I'm not shocked, I'm just…I'm not even surprised. I don't know what I am. It's what I would have expected. You are a beautiful man, and I love you like I've never loved a man before, and that's saying a lot because I'm a national tour star and I've been through a few…several…too many men, and I can still say I've never loved any man like I love you. Does that make sense?"

"I can tell the third bottle of wine is almost gone, but…I can't believe it…oh, fuck it, I can believe it." My emotions are getting the best of me. "Finally, I can turn it loose and let it happen. Just let it happen." Tears happen. Goddamnit.

"Oh, Mason, don't worry. Don't cry," she says, stroking my cheeks. "Don't worry, baby. The wine is not almost gone. You have another bottle."

I laugh. "I just wonder how long the gendarmes will stay away and let us picnic in peace with Jimbo," I say. "I pulled out all the francs I had in my pocket. It was neat how he turned his back to me and wagged his fingers. Classic. I love Europe. Graft and lust rule."

Edie moves to my side of the tomb and snuggles with me. "My lust really kicks up when I think of what you're going to do with that money…but, it's so confusing after the third bottle…again, just what are you going to do with that money?"

"We're keeping a half million to get us started, and the rest, around five million, goes into a charitable foundation we'll establish as soon as someone tells me how to establish a charitable foundation. The charitable foundation will be invested in stocks as I have done since I was a perpetually aroused teenager. We will pay out to meaningful causes five percent per year, which I hope will be equal to the gross national product plus inflation. The rest of the year's growth will be invested the following year, so we can grow and give away more and more money."

"Gross national product? Inflation? You're the only man I know who can turn philanthropy into a dismal science."

"We have a responsibility," I say, "You said it yourself. A responsibility to grow and contribute."

"Well," she says, "I love ya. You're so dull, no one else will."

"I'm a lucky guy. Hey, are those sparks I feel or are our wool sweaters just liking each other?"

"That is one sad pick-up line, but it proves my point. You are dull."

I smile, "That I am."

She smiles back and kisses me on the cheek. "What are you going to name the charitable foundation?"

"Well, Morning in America is taken. So's The Shining City on a Hill."

"How about something Democrat, damnit."

"The Tax and Spend Charitable Foundation."

"Oh, hell," she says, "we'll name it later. It could be like what that aging hippie said on Monday in front of the New York Stock Exchange."

"The Eighties Are Over Charitable Foundation?" I say.

Another cackle from Edie. She locks her lips on mine, then to my chagrin, releases me. "Well, my darling Mason," she says, "when you think about it, you know, me and you, together…what a way to end a decade."

www.ingramcontent.com/pod-product-compliance
Lightning Source LLC
Chambersburg PA
CBHW030409020726
47493CB00003B/992